ECHOES OF
FATE

ALSO BY CHERYL CAMPBELL

SCIENCE FICTION

Echoes Trilogy:
Echoes of War
Echoes of Darkness
Echoes of Fate

FANTASY

Burnt Mountain: The Monster Within
Burnt Mountain: One in the Chamber
Burnt Mountain: Do and Die
Burnt Mountain: Rhyllia
Burnt Mountain: When Heroes Fall

ECHOES OF FATE

BOOK THREE
IN THE ECHOES TRILOGY

CHERYL CAMPBELL

SONAR
PRESS

Published by Sonar Press,
South Portland, Maine, USA, 04106

Published 2021
Printed in the United States of America

ISBN: 978-0-9897608-8-1 (pbk)
ISBN: 978-0-9897608-9-8 (e-bk)
Library of Congress Control Number: 2021907964

Formatting by Katherine Lloyd, The Desk

CHAPTER 1

A figure next to a tree stood with hunched shoulders and lowered head against the wind-driven rain. Lightning cracked and lit up the night sky, briefly illuminating a woman and the forest around her. She pulled her hood lower and shifted her stance, favoring one leg. Moments later, the thunder boomed loud enough to make her flinch.

Dani watched Mary for another moment before approaching. Like Mary, she was dressed in military skins that allowed her to blend in with almost any environment, but Dani had no trouble recognizing Mary's shape among the shadows. The rain stung Dani's cheek, so she turned her head to avoid the needle-like punishment coming around the side of her hood.

Lightning flashed again, and Mary gasped, startled to realize someone was next to her. She placed her hand against her chest. "Jesus, Dani, you're going to kill me doing that sneaking-around shit."

They wore the camouflage skins so they could break into one of the Commonwealth of North America's buildings in Bangor in the middle of the nor'easter. They were both guilty of sneaking around and hadn't even broken the law yet—if Dani didn't count the original theft of the skins from a few years ago. That thought made her smile.

Mary took a few deep breaths before speaking. "Where's Aunt Hattie?"

"She left before I did. I think she was making her rounds through town to make sure folks saw her."

"Giving herself an alibi."

Dani nodded.

"What about ours?"

"We can head back into town after we're done to create ours. Show up at the brothel, have some ale in the pub, that kind of thing."

"Think Colonel Houston will care about alibis when she learns someone broke into her base?"

"Probably not." Dani didn't want to be here tonight, standing in the middle of a storm doing some cloak-and-dagger shit for Hattie. She'd been back in Bangor for almost two weeks after being mostly gone for the last three years. She had only another week left before she, Mary, Miles, and Oliver were due to meet up with General Ramos for another diplomacy trip to wherever the fuck he was taking them next.

She didn't want to think about leaving again and being back on the ship. She liked her feet on solid ground, not on *Splendor*'s deck as it pitched to sometimes terrifying angles, depending on how angry the ocean felt on a particular day. Dani forced her thoughts away from dread of going back on the destroyer.

"You're still limping," Dani said. She turned to Mary, and their faces were illuminated for a second when another bolt of lightning flashed overhead.

Mary shuddered. "That shit is just *too* close! My leg is fine."

"You fell off a roof. Your femur was sticking out of your skin."

"Yeah, yeah." Mary waved her hand. "That was last week. It's fine now."

"The healing patches are still on, which means your leg isn't healed yet."

"Relax. I'm fine."

Dani grumbled and crossed her arms. The thunder clapped so loud, it hurt her ears, and she felt the vibration in her body.

Mary snorted a laugh. "Watch us die out here while waiting for Aunt Hattie."

"That's not funny."

"Don't be so serious."

Dani grabbed Mary's arm. "That fall could've killed you. You don't get a regen. Hattie asked you to fix the comm, and you rushed right up there without waiting for me."

"So you could fall off instead?"

"I can at least regen if I die."

"And forget everything when you do."

Dani released her arm and frowned. "Most of it comes back. Eventually."

They waited in silence for a few minutes before Mary spoke. "Next time you die, do you think you'll remember everything?"

"I don't know," Dani said.

Hattie's voice came from close behind them. "Let's shoot her and find out." She erupted with her usual cackling laughter.

"Took you long enough," Mary said. "Did you get lost?"

"With you two yapping your heads off? No. I just followed the noise." Hattie passed a small pack to Dani, then pulled the hood of her skin lower over her head. "Ready?"

"What? No," Dani said. "What are we doing tonight? Why are we here?"

"You didn't have those questions when I asked you earlier to put on skins and meet me out here in this wretched weather," Hattie said.

Dani didn't have a good response for the older woman, so she remained silent.

"Fine," Hattie said. "Houston's doing some sketchy shit. I'm not sure exactly what, but my source is worried about it enough that I was contacted to have a look for myself and decide if it needs to be destroyed."

"Destroyed?" Mary asked and rubbed her hands together, smiling. "We're blowing something up?"

"Really?" Dani asked, turning to Mary. "You should *not* be this excited. Hattie, we can't blow a CNA building. It's no longer Brigands against the Commonwealth and hasn't been for years. We can't blow something of theirs just because you have a burr up your ass with Houston."

"Calm down, Mary," Hattie said, ignoring Dani. "We can still destroy things without explosives."

"Where's the fun in that?" Mary asked. "You strapped a bomb to Houston's chair before."

"A technicality," Hattie said before turning to Dani. "This is more than my personal fight with Catherine."

"How do you know about whatever Houston is doing? Who is this source?" Dani asked.

"I can't say."

Dani shook her head and grumbled. "You and your secrets."

"If we're going to do this, we have a limited time frame in which to do it," Hattie said. "We will have help on the inside, but tonight is our best window."

"Why tonight?" Mary asked.

"Because I'm pulling a page out of Dani's playbook and attacking in the middle of a storm."

Mary snorted. "Perfect. I love it. I'm in."

"What?" Dani asked her. "How? You don't even know what we're doing."

"Doesn't matter," Mary said, and shrugged. "Houston is up to shady shit. No shock there. I want to know what it is and ruin her day."

Dani sighed and lowered her face into her palm.

"Make up your mind, Dani. Mary and I need to get cracking if we're doing this."

She shook her head, sighed, then dropped her hand. "Fine. I'm in."

"Good," Hattie said. "Because we weren't going to be able to do this with just the two of us. You know the best ways to get in."

"Fuck me," Dani groaned.

Mary hooked her arm through Dani's. "You love this. Admit it."

"No. No, I don't." Dani shook her head. Mary tugged on her arm, and she started walking with them.

Dani led them to an area just outside the base perimeter fence that was still within the forest. The storm had driven most of the security staff indoors and out of the wind. Hattie used her hand to shield the light emitted by the comm device while Dani opened the hole in the fence that she'd used many times to slip inside the base to steal food and other supplies before the Brigand-CNA treaty.

Mary slipped through first, followed by Hattie. Dani passed through last and pulled the portion of fencing back into place.

"Next big crack of lightning, expect a bit of a boom," Hattie said. "The transformer linked with the lab will blow. We're going into *that* building," she said, and pointed.

"Their R&D complex? Why?" Dani asked. It had been used for storage before, and she'd breached it many times. Its use since then had changed. She had no idea what they were walking into.

"The building will come back up with secondary power, but the security system will be offline long enough for us to get in," Hattie said.

Hattie had avoided answering her question. Dani asked, "How much time will that give us? When does the security system come back up?"

"My contact will keep that under control while we're in," Hattie said. She pointed at the building. "We enter through that side door, which is an emergency exit. We'll take the stairs up to the third level."

Lightning flickered in the distance, trailed by a rumble of thunder, and Dani looked up. They were still concealed by trees, but there was a strip through the wooded area where trees had been cleared. She realized the clearing was created for the row of poles and power lines leading to this part of the Commonwealth base. Her gaze followed the lines from the building to the trees. She spotted the transformer on the top of a pole ten yards away.

"Shit." Dani grabbed Hattie and Mary and shoved them away from the transformer. "Go!"

A bolt of lightning flashed, and a second later the transformer erupted into a blinding explosion of light and sparks. Dani covered her head with her arms until the sparks diminished. Her ears rang, and Hattie lay on the ground with Mary on top of her. Dani touched Mary's shoulder.

"Hey. You okay?"

Mary nodded and lifted herself from Hattie. Hattie rolled to her feet.

"That wasn't supposed to happen," Hattie said. "I didn't know we were so close to that thing."

"Give me your comm and head back to town if you want," Dani said.

Hattie swatted her hand away. "I'm old. Not dead."

"Any other fun surprises we should know about?" Dani asked Hattie.

"Guess we'll find out soon enough." Hattie led them toward the R&D building.

CHAPTER 2

They made it up one flight inside the building with Hattie leading, followed by Mary. Dani stayed at the rear to make sure no one came up behind them. They were headed up the second flight when Mary tripped. Her injured leg struck the edge of a step, and she stifled a yelp with the impact, clutching her leg.

"Shit!" Dani scrambled to reach Mary. "Did you rebreak it?"

Mary bit her lip and shook her head. She took a few slow breaths and winced when she shifted her position.

"We don't have time for this," Hattie said. "Get up. Both of you."

"Give her a second, Hattie." She said to Mary, "Can you stand or do I need to drag you out of here?"

"I can stand," Mary said.

Dani hooked her arm around Mary's waist to help her up.

"Today, people," Hattie said.

"I say we blow Hattie up with whatever we're toasting in here," Dani said to Mary.

Mary chuckled and leaned against her. "You were really worried about me."

"Nah. Just assessing if you were dead weight best left behind."

"Why do you still try to lie your way out of things? You know you suck at it."

"Because maybe one day I'll be able to lie and you won't know it," Dani said, grinning, and they resumed their way up the remaining two flights.

"Good thing you're an Echo and will have lots of lifetimes to practice," Hattie said. "Maybe in a few thousand years you'll figure it out, if you ever stop forgetting everything with a regen."

Dani nodded and said to Mary, "Yeah, we're totally blowing her up."

"What if we don't need to blow whatever it is we're going after?" Mary asked as she limped up the stairs.

"We'll blast it anyway just to kill her."

"That's one way to take out an Echo," Mary said.

Hattie stopped and turned, glaring at Dani.

"Oh!" Mary said. "You're in trouble now."

"What did I do? I was only joking about blowing you up, Hattie."

Hattie growled. "You told her I was an Echo."

Dani's eyes widened. "I didn't!"

Mary chuckled. "Hattie, I've known for years that you are an Echo. There are history buffs, and then there are people who've lived it. You're the latter. Get over it. I haven't told anyone else what you are." Mary shifted to face Dani. "And you? What the *fuck*? You knew she was an Echo and never said anything?"

"Wait. Why am I getting yelled at? *You* knew and didn't say anything to *me*."

"You told Miles she was an Echo, though, right?" Mary asked.

Dani hesitated a half second too long.

"Goddammit," Hattie said.

"It was an accident," Dani said. "I swear."

"Oliver?" Hattie asked.

Dani shook her head. "He doesn't know. Just Miles."

Mary laughed, which earned her a sharp shushing from Hattie. "I don't know why I bother with you two. Mary, tell anyone and I'll kill you. Dani, tell anyone *else* and I'll kill you too. Now, can we get on with the lab?"

"A lab?" Dani asked. "We're breaking into a lab? Wh—"

Hattie's snarl silenced Dani's next question before she could ask it.

"You're not just an Echo," Mary said to Hattie. "You're one of the Ancients, aren't you?"

"For fuck's sake, stop talking!" Hattie spun and resumed going up the stairs, and Dani and Mary followed in silence. Mary winked at Dani, and Dani tried to keep her expression neutral. She had already known Hattie was an Ancient—one of the original Ekkohrians who settled on Earth hundreds of years ago. The Wardens would scorch Maine to capture an Ancient.

Hattie was normally cantankerous, but she was in an exceptionally foul mood now. Mary's steps became steadier as she worked some of the soreness out of her leg and no longer needed Dani's help.

They stopped at a door on the third level. The security panel next to the door was a blank screen, so Hattie eased the door open and led them into a corridor. They passed several other doors as they moved through darkened hallways while the wind continued to howl outside.

Hattie stopped again. "This is it." She led them into a room glowing with green light everywhere. The door clicked shut behind them and locked.

Dani didn't like being locked in. "Was that supposed to happen?"

"Yes. My insider is controlling everything. Secondary power is semi-on and the security system is rebooted now. He can get us back out and past the locks and cameras once we're done."

Dani noticed Hattie had referred to her contact as a male. Hattie always had more people working for her than Dani would ever know, but she was certain she knew the identity of their mysterious helper tonight.

Dim lighting activated inside the room, and Dani could only stare at the sight before her. Multiple rows of fluid-filled tanks stood in the center of the lab, a mass of blinking green lights encircling them. Floor-to-ceiling computer banks were between the tanks and linked to them with a series of tubing. A few bubbles slowly made their way up through the viscous liquid within the tanks and tubes. Fog flowed down the tanks to the floor. She glanced at the others, and Hattie—but not Mary—was frozen with unblinking eyes.

Dani approached the fog and bent to pass her hand through it. "Coolant." She righted. "What's in here?"

Hattie pointed to one of the panels on a tower. "Open the pack I gave you. In it you'll find a small panel with wiring and everything you need to tap into a computer."

Mary walked around a tower to the access ports. Dani noticed Mary's lack of shock with the place and her ease of finding the ports. Dani removed the items from her pack and passed one of the cables to Mary, who plugged it in. Dani turned the panel on; she watched Mary while the panel booted up.

Hattie was off wandering around the lab, and Dani continued to observe Mary.

"*What?*" Mary asked, keeping her voice low.

"You've been in here before," Dani whispered. "You know what this is."

"I didn't know this is where Aunt Hattie wanted us to come."

"What is this place?"

"It's—"

The panel in Dani's hands beeped.

"What do you do once you're in?" Mary asked.

"I'm not sure. Maybe *you* should be the one doing this."

Mary scowled at her. "Don't be an ass."

The screen blinked a few times, and then a sub-screen on the device opened and a script started running. Text quickly scrolled down the screen, but it wasn't so fast that Dani couldn't read some of it. Mary stood close at Dani's shoulder and gazed down at the panel.

"Shit," Dani said. "This program is decrypting data that is localized to this room. These files aren't shared with the rest of the CNA."

"Houston doesn't want anyone knowing what she's doing," Mary said.

"Is that an assumption or statement of fact because you already know what she's doing?"

Hattie arrived at Mary's shoulder. "Care to elaborate?" she asked.

Dani wasn't sure when the woman had finished her wanderings, but it didn't matter. Dani wanted Mary to answer the question too.

Mary finally relented. "The Echoes look just like humans because they frigged around with their DNA to mimic human physiology and anatomy. Houston has a group of researchers monkeying around with Echo DNA samples to try to give humans the ability to regen."

"To turn humans into Echoes," Hattie said.

"Well, no. Yes. In a way. She's not cloning people, but she's trying to keep her troop numbers up."

"And the Wardens recondition Echoes into Wardens to keep their troop numbers up," Hattie said. "Exactly how is what Catherine doing different from the Wardens?"

"The Wardens get their subjects by capturing them. Houston's are volunteers," Mary said.

Dani stared at Mary as seconds ticked by in silence. When the information sank in, Dani realized a bigger truth. "Goddammit, Mary. *You* volunteered?"

"Why not? I'm human. I die, I'm gone. The fall off the roof almost killed me. Houston offered me the chance to test-drive her Echo experiment, and I took it. So what if I gambled to get some regens out of the deal?"

"This experiment works?" Hattie asked.

Mary shrugged. "Don't know yet."

Dani shook her head, frustrated. "The Echo DNA—is that coming from volunteers too?"

Mary's face paled. "Oh, um, I'm not sure."

"Do you at least know who she put in you?"

Mary nodded and took another moment before answering. "You."

Hattie's cackling laughter startled them both. "That's just perfect. You want to become an Echo so you get Dani's faulty DNA put in you. Remember the part where Dani regens and forgets everything? She's not a normal Echo! Mary, you're such an idiot." Hattie continued laughing.

Dani ignored Hattie. "This is fucked up, Mary. I never consented to Houston or anyone else collecting pieces of me."

"Okay, yes, that part is fucked up. I agree. I didn't know how she got her Echo samples, and, um … I didn't ask."

Dani's screen blinked that the data transfer was complete, and another screen popped up asking if she wanted to terminate the lab. She turned the screen toward Mary. Hattie sobered and moved closer to read the screen's message.

"Hattie, what happens if we move forward with this?" Dani asked.

"Another program will run to activate a worm that was installed as soon as the script started pulling down data from the servers in the towers. The lab won't blow up—sorry, Mary, no fireworks. But the data will corrupt, as will the cooling systems. Everything will be lost. It won't stop Catherine from trying again, but it will slow her down."

"The Echo DNA she is using, do we have a way to know if any of them consented to this?" Dani asked.

"Does it matter?" Hattie asked.

"Mary wants to be a guinea pig, that's her choice. I wasn't given a choice, so, at minimum, my sample gets trashed."

Hattie activated her comm, then glanced up at Dani. "Tell him what you want."

"Search the data you just pulled. Are there any documented consents for any of the Echo DNA being used in this experiment?" Dani asked.

The panel in her hand blinked a few times before the screen changed to show one word: *No.*

"Scrub any mention of my name and Mary's from the records," Dani said, certain the person on the other end of the comm was someone she knew.

The screen blinked again: *Done.*

"Everything? You're sure?" Dani asked.

The entire screen filled with one word, *YES!* before blinking back to its other screen asking if she wanted to terminate the lab. Hattie closed the comm with her contact.

"What if the experiment works?" Mary asked.

"I don't have a problem with the experiment, Mary," Dani said. "It's the ethical gray area that concerns me. Why is the data *only* in this room? Why is none of the data on any other CNA databases? Why is she not getting the consent from the Echoes she's using to be part of this? Why—"

Mary waved her hand. "I get it. I get it." She took a deep breath. "Destroy the data and lab. If the colonel is hiding this from everyone, she's too sneaky to not be up to something else. Or she's using this project as the foundation for something even worse. Hell, maybe she would go as far as to try cloning at some point."

"You're both good with me activating the worm?" Dani asked.

They nodded, and Dani pressed the prompt on the screen to destroy the lab's software, databases, and coolant tanks. Another screen popped up that she wasn't expecting. "Uh, it wants a password."

Hattie rolled her eyes and used her comm again for a moment, muttering with disgust the entire time. "I'm *so* killing this jackass."

"A lot of death threats going around tonight," Dani said with a smirk. "Who else is on the shit list, Hattie?"

Hattie sighed. "Password is *I am a god*—one word, all lowercase."

Dani barked a laugh as she typed it into the panel. "Anton. I figured he was your insider."

"How did you know?" Mary asked.

"He's smarter than anyone in New England," Dani said. "All the magic used to get us into this place by manipulating the power and security has Anton's name all over it. Password sealed it, though. He used that phrase on me once in the sim control room." She entered the password, and another program began running on the screen.

It blinked a few times and alerted her that in two hours the lab's destruction would be complete and she needed to disconnect the cable from the column. She unplugged the cable and threw it and the panel into the pack. The green color of the coolant in the tubes began changing to a reddish hue, and Dani didn't want to hang around to see what would happen next.

They left the building without any trouble, but the weather had somehow worsened. The wind and rain lashed them as they darted back across the base to the hole in the fence. They sprinted for the trees to get a little bit of a break from the storm.

When they stopped, Dani used her hand to block the wind-driven rain from coming around her hood and pelting her face. "Anton's program said we had two hours before the lab would be destroyed."

"Give me the pack," Hattie said. "I'll head to the brothel to make sure I'm seen. You two head back to town and show up a bit later. Make sure you're in the pub when that last hour is up."

"What happens to the lab at that time?" Mary asked while Dani passed her pack to Hattie.

"Not a damn clue, but you can bet Catherine will know it's gone to shit and come looking for heads to roll. Given how much she hates you, Dani, she'll come for you first. Make sure your alibi is solid," Hattie said before leaving them.

Dani sighed and led Mary through the forest and back to the brothel by a different route. To prevent being seen by anyone in their stolen gear, they changed out of the CNA camouflage, stashed the skins in one of Hattie's underground bunkers, then darted across the backyard through the rain and into the rear of the brothel. Dani was cold, wet, and not in the mood for reveling in the pub. She ran her hand through her hair and flung the extra water off her fingers.

"C'mon," Mary said.

Dani followed her to her room. Mary tossed Dani a towel, which she immediately passed over her hair. Mary started stripping out of her wet clothes, so Dani turned and continued to work on drying her hair.

"Here," Mary said.

Dani glanced back. "Huh?" She quickly shuffled the towel to one hand and caught the clothing that Mary threw to her.

"We can't go out there soaking wet. Change. Wait …" Mary said, grinning. "Are you staring at my body?"

Dani blinked. "Sorry. I— sorry." She turned to face the wall and busied herself with the trousers and shirt in her hands while her face felt like it might burst into flames.

"Do you still have a thing for me?"

"I'm with Miles."

"That's not answering my question."

"We need to get changed and be seen in public." Dani pulled her soaked shirt off and slipped the dry one on.

"Dani?"

She refused to turn around. She pulled her boots off, stepped out of her wet jeans, and pulled Mary's pair on. She knelt to put her boots back on. When she stood and turned back around, Mary still wasn't dressed and was watching her. "Christ," Dani muttered, and stared at the floor.

"Please look at me."

Why can't I just lie and get away with it for once? Just once! Dani winced. She sighed before looking up. "Okay. You are absolutely fucking gorgeous and I have a hard time thinking when you're standing there naked and wanting to have a conversation with me."

Mary smiled and her face flushed. "That's the sweetest thing ever." She turned to her closet and pulled her yellow dress from a hanger. She placed the garment in front of her body. "This better?"

"Oh, God." Dani groaned and turned around; Mary always looked stunning in that dress.

Mary put the dress on and walked over to her. She turned her back toward Dani. "Can you help me with this?"

Dani mumbled some semblance of an affirmative answer and zipped the back of the dress for her.

Mary faced her again and took her hand. "You *do* still have a thing for me," she said, and smiled. "I still have one for you too, but I know you're with Miles. As much as I love being your friend, sometimes I wish we were more." Mary shrugged. "Maybe in some parallel universe we get to be together," she said, releasing Dani's hand. She pulled a bottle and two glasses from a small cabinet. "And now we get shit-faced!"

"We need to be seen in public, not seen smashed in public," Dani said.

Mary poured the brownish liquid into the two glasses. "We need to look like we've been in the pub for a while. This will speed that process." Mary handed one of the glasses to Dani.

She sniffed the contents and frowned. "Courage. Mary, you know I can't drink this."

"You *can* drink it. You just can't handle it." Mary put her glass to her lips and drained it. She waved her hand at Dani, indicating it was her turn.

"Just one. That's it," Dani said. Mary refilled her own glass in reply. Dani sighed and drank her courage, recalling that the first time she'd consumed it, she'd made out with Mary instead of assembling Hattie's solar panel.

That time seemed like ages ago now, though it had been only a few years. Before the Brigand-CNA merger. Before Portland. Before Boston. Long before diplomatic trips and a ridiculous title of Ambassador Ireland that Dani still couldn't remember to answer to when formally addressed.

"You okay?" Mary asked.

"Um, yeah," Dani said, blinking. "Just thinking." She handed her glass back to Mary and placed her hand on the wall.

Mary laughed and drank two more shots. She put her glass down and took Dani's arm to lead her out of the room toward the pub. "Let's go, Cheap Date."

Dani's balance wavered as soon as she left the wall. "I'm not staying long. I'm going home to Miles tonight."

"Sure," Mary said, her voice full of sarcasm. "Once you're able to walk without assistance, you can go."

"Sometimes I hate you."

"But you still think I'm fucking hot."

"That will never change." Dani gasped when she realized what she'd said. "Wait. I didn't mean— Well, you are, but I didn't mean that like …" *Shit.* She didn't know what she was trying to say. "Why did you make me drink that crap?"

"Because this is the version of you that is the most entertaining."

CHAPTER

Miles finished cleaning up after dinner while Oliver sat at the table working on a drawing. He smiled and watched his son for moment while he drew with one hand and scratched Brody's head with the other. The lantern on the table cast enough light to continue working well after dark.

"You're watching me again," Oliver said without looking up.

"Yeah. So?"

Oliver set his pencil down and looked up. "I want to go into town tonight to see my friends."

"In this weather? Have you lost your mind?"

"You let Dani go."

Miles barked a laugh and sat at the table. "*Let* her go? We're talking about the same Dani, right?"

"You didn't try to stop her."

"Because that would've been pointless. Visit your friends tomorrow when this weather has passed."

"Is she coming home tonight?"

"Uh, maybe. I'm hoping she doesn't, since this storm just keeps getting worse."

"Why did she go to meet Mary?"

Miles sighed and got up from the table. "I don't know. They were helping Aunt Hattie with something."

"Something illegal?"

"I hope not." He walked to the door to open it. "Brody, let's go, buddy. Out."

The dog remained next to Oliver and lowered his head; Oliver snickered.

"It's not that bad out," Miles said to the dog. "C'mon."

"He's not dumb, Dad."

Miles sighed and took Brody by the collar to lead him out. He opened the door and was immediately battered by the wind and rain. Miles turned his head aside, went out with Brody, and took him to the side of the house to shelter from the wind. By the time Brody finished relieving himself and they made it back inside, they were both drenched.

Oliver knelt and welcomed Brody back in with a towel to dry him off.

"Where's my towel?"

"You have thumbs, so you can get your own."

Miles playfully shoved Oliver so he tipped over. Brody pounced on the teen and started licking him while Miles headed to the bedroom to dry off and change. He'd just finished dressing when Brody started barking in the other room. He picked up his plasma pistol and emerged from his room. Oliver was on his feet, and Miles gestured for him to back away. Bangor was a safe town, but it still had some crime. What concerned him the most was that someone was at his door in this storm.

He turned his body to conceal the pistol in his hand before easing the door open. When he recognized his visitor, his eyes widened, and he yanked the door open the rest of the way. "Oh, shit. Sorry, sir! Come in!"

General Ramos chuckled as he entered, and shook water from the duffel he carried.

Brody bounced around the new arrival, and Oliver smiled. "Santi!"

"Hey, Oliver."

Once he had the door closed, Miles glanced around for a place to stash the pistol. "Um, sir, I—"

"At ease, Miles."

"Yes, sir."

Ramos grinned and passed the duffel to Oliver so he could pet Brody. Ramos looked up. "Miles. Seriously. At ease. I'm in your home on a social call, more or less."

"Yes, sir. May I put this away?" Miles said, glancing at the pistol still in his hand.

"Of course."

Miles darted back to the bedroom and overheard Oliver and Ramos in the other room.

"Oliver, how have you enjoyed being home and off the ship?"

"It's been nice to have my own room instead of sharing a bunk area with the guys, but I miss joking around with them."

"I understand. It's easy to make friends, and perhaps a few enemies, when sharing tight quarters."

Miles reappeared minus the pistol and with a towel instead. Ramos took the offered towel to wipe the excess water off.

"Dani around?" Ramos asked.

"She's in town, sir."

"Hope she's staying the night. This nor'easter has turned into a Category One hurricane, possibly edging into a Cat Two before it's over."

"Why are you out, sir?"

"I'm heading to Portland tonight and wanted to stop by first to drop off Dani's new uniforms."

Oliver hefted the duffel. "In here? Can I see?"

"Sure."

Oliver placed the bag on the floor and unzipped it. He shoved Brody's nose out of the way so he could reach in. He pulled out the uniform top with "Ireland" on the upper left front of the shirt. It was a plain-looking bluish fabric without anything fancy or extra patches on the shoulders.

"We're closer than we've ever been before to winning this war," Ramos said. "Commonwealths all over the world have formed Brigand partnerships because of our efforts. The next cruise will be crucial to reinforcing those treaties for the final strikes against the Wardens. I figured before we started the new diplomacy summits I'd give Dani a break from the more formal uniform. She always walks around in it like she can't stand it touching her skin."

"Because she can't," Oliver said. "She hates that shit."

Miles couldn't hide his look of horror at his son's response to the general. "Ollie! I'm sorry, sir."

Ramos waved his hand. "It's fine. Tell me more, Oliver," he said, and took a seat at the table.

Oliver joined him, and Miles took the remaining chair.

"She hates CNA uniforms. Always has. You'll never see her in uniform one second longer than necessary after those meetings you make her attend."

Ramos nodded. "I've noticed that."

"Once she starts talking to the other Brigands, though, she forgets she's in uniform and is more herself."

"That's when the magic starts and the civilian forces flock to her," Ramos said. "It still amazes me how the Brigands of other countries respond to her. I need her more relaxed, though, and that's why I decided to put her in regular fatigues."

Oliver shook his head. "No, Santi. Let her be who she is and dress like a Brigand. Let her be the Brigand who broke into the Bangor barracks. That's who the people need to see."

Ramos leaned back in his chair and remained silent for a

moment. "Hmm. You're a smart young man, Oliver." He turned to Miles. "I need your opinion on something."

"Do I need to leave?" Oliver asked.

"Not at all," Ramos said. "We have other parts of North America the Wardens still hold, but I'm more concerned with the Northeast. They still hold three-quarters of Quebec City and are so entrenched in Toronto that we don't know how to get them out without suffering massive casualties—assuming we don't suffer an outright loss. I don't know if we need more diplomatic efforts in the region to bring more Brigands to the civilian army with the Commonwealth or if we need more recon."

"Both," Miles said.

Ramos shook his head. "I can't have my people doing both the summits and recon."

"Ah. You want Dani."

"I want the team that penetrated Boston and started the Warden demise in that city. You, Dani, and Mary."

"Sir, Rowan took my son and held him in Boston," Miles said. "We didn't go there to defeat the Wardens. We went to get Oliver back. That's all."

"But the chaos you caused paved the way for Colonel Houston to attack and win."

"Oliver was shot. Mary and I were almost killed, and Dani *was* killed and went through a regen. Her regens aren't normal, sir. They're difficult for everyone. We've been on a ship and in meetings for the last three years. In that time, we've done nothing in the field—recon, combat, or anything else."

Ramos fell silent for a few minutes, then stood. "So I'll keep you involved on the diplomacy side of things. Thank you, Miles."

Miles stood and saluted.

Ramos picked up the duffel. "Since Dani won't be needing these." He smiled and shook Miles's hand. "You really suck at being at ease."

Oliver snickered, which earned him a grin from Ramos.

The general left, and Miles stood at the window and watched the general drive away. He didn't envy his long ride to Portland in this weather on terrible roads.

"Dad, you don't like this summit crap any more than Dani and Mary do. Why do you stick with it?"

Miles faced his son. "Because it continues to help boost troop numbers. It has turned the war in our favor and kept it there."

"Dani and Mary have been Brigands their entire lives. A three-year break won't make them forget how to sneak around and do recon. It's all they know. Even when Dani forgets everything with a regen, she still remembers how to be a Brigand and survive."

"I know."

"We don't win until the Wardens are gone. They won't stop killing humans or taking Echoes until they're wiped out."

"I know."

"The war doesn't end if they keep parts of Quebec."

"I *know*!"

Oliver flinched and turned away.

Miles immediately regretted his outburst. "I'm sorry. I didn't mean—"

His son gathered his papers from the table and took them to his room. Brody followed him and hopped up on his bed. Ollie closed his door.

Miles grumbled with frustration. He left the lantern on in case Dani came home later and went to his room. He shut the door harder than he intended. Ollie turned sixteen in less than a week. At seventeen he would be required to enter the CNA forces. Miles was desperate for the war to end to save his son from the horrors of combat. He was equally desperate to keep those he loved alive, and that included Dani.

CHAPTER 4

The pub was full of people escaping the storm, and the noise within rose ever louder so the music and people could be heard over the wind. Conversation quieted only when a crack of lightning struck so close that it sounded like an explosion. Immediately afterward, people cheered the violent weather and went back to drinking and laughing.

Dani's head continued to spin from the shot of liquor, so she was careful to just sip her ale instead of guzzling it like she usually did. Mary was well ahead of her in pints, and Dani knew better than to try to keep up. She was determined to go home tonight. Though she and Miles shared a room on the ship, being back in Maine was different. They lived in the small, rustic home on the river a few miles from town that she'd shared with her brother, Jace, when he was alive. Oliver had taken Jace's old room, which was an extension off the main part of the house. Miles and Dani moved into her old room since it had a door and offered them some semblance of privacy.

She wanted to be back in her home and in her bed with Miles before General Ramos made them leave again. Instead of taking another sip of her ale, Dani left the mug on the counter and wondered how much longer she needed to stay in town for appearances before she could leave. She checked the time; she still had another twenty minutes before the lab and the data would be destroyed. *Can't go yet, dammit.*

Apparently, alcohol had numbed Mary's still-healing leg enough so she could dance. The song ended and Mary worked her way through the crowd back to Dani with Kelsey following, her hand in his.

"Look who I found," Mary shouted over the noise and nodded toward Kelsey. "It's hot in here!" Her words slurred, and she took Dani's mug and drank her ale.

Dani didn't mind losing her drink. "Hi, Kels."

"Hi," he said and kissed her cheek before leaving.

"That was quick," Dani said.

Mary shrugged. "He's gotta piss."

"Oh."

Mary said something Dani didn't catch with the noise. "Huh?"

Mary stepped closer. "I asked you if you were mad at me over the DNA thing."

"No, I'm not mad. It's your choice."

"What about me using your sample?"

"I'm mad Houston took it and used it without my knowledge. That's all."

"You are okay that I wanted you inside me?"

Dani was caught off guard with Mary's choice of words. "Um ... well ... we're still talking about DNA, right?"

Mary laughed and threw her arm around Dani's neck. She placed the mug on the bar and put her other arm around Dani's waist.

"What are you doing?" Dani could feel Mary smiling against her neck just before she placed her lips next to Dani's ear.

"I have a secret to tell you."

A sudden, pleasurable chill coursed through Dani when

Mary spoke, her breath against Dani's skin. "Mary, honey, you're drunk. *Very* drunk. Are you sure you want to start telling secrets now?"

"Uh huh. I know you're with Miles."

"And you're with Kels."

"Yeah, but it's not the same as what you have with Miles."

"I'm sorry. I thought you loved him."

"I do—in a way. Sometimes I wish you weren't with Miles, and that I was the one in your bed."

Dani wasn't sure what to say, and Mary continued. "I believe that in some parallel universe, you and I are together instead."

"Yeah, you've mentioned the parallel universe before. You believe in those?"

Mary laughed, which sent another shiver through Dani.

"No one used to believe in aliens, but we learned they existed when the Wardens started the war. Why not other universes?"

Dani drew in a sharp breath when Mary's tongue touched her skin as her mouth traveled up her neck to her jaw. "Mary, stop. You said you wouldn't do this again."

"You smell amazing."

Dani turned her head away, putting distance between herself and Mary. "Please don't do this." Her mind was at war with the physical sensations in her body, and the statement was meant for both herself and Mary. *Miles. I love him, and—oh, fuck,* she thought when Mary's hand began migrating up toward her breast.

Dani caught Mary's hand and pushed it back down. "You said you wouldn't flirt anymore."

Mary's mouth neared Dani's chin. "This isn't flirting," Mary said.

No. No, it's not.

Mary placed both palms on the sides of Dani's face and

leaned in. Dani pulled away. "No," she said and shook her head, her eyes downcast.

"Why not?" Mary asked.

"Because you—"

"If you don't want her, I'll have her," a man said just before he shoved Dani aside.

She stumbled and tripped over someone's foot. She twisted to try to catch herself as she fell, but she still landed with a grunt when her shoulder struck a stool before she finished her fall. She struggled back to her feet, jostled by the people standing all around her, and heard Mary's voice over the noise.

"Dani? Shit! Are you okay? Asshole! Let go of me."

Dani moved much faster when Mary's angry outburst was followed by an agonizing scream. She forced her way through the people. The man had one hand gripping Mary's shoulder with his other hand clamped on her thigh—the same leg she'd recently broken. He forced his hips between her thighs, though Mary clawed at his hand to remove it from her injured leg. She released his hand to reach for a mug just beyond her fingertips.

"She's one of Hattie's whores anyway," he said with a sneer to his friends. "She knows what comes next."

Dani stomped toward him. "Do you?"

"What?"

When he turned to look at her, Dani slammed her fist into his mouth. His head rocked with the impact, and he released Mary. Dani grabbed his shirt and pulled him away from her friend. She struck him again and followed him to the floor when he fell. She hit him several times, and blood spurted from his mouth. When he tried to speak, she hit him again.

"Jesus, Dani, stop!" Mary said. "That's enough."

"*Never* call her a whore." Dani had her fist ready to drive into his face one more time, but hands dragged her off.

A fist clipped Dani's cheek, and she stumbled. Powerful

arms held her upright, though her knees had buckled with the blow. Her vision blurred, but she heard the sound of a shattering mug. One of the men holding her loosened his grip. Dani's vision cleared enough to see Mary swinging a stool as the crowd moved away from the growing fight. The stool splintered across the back of one of the men holding Dani.

She swung her fist downward and struck the other man in the crotch. He released her and crumpled to the floor. The man struck by the stool charged toward Mary. Dani jumped on his back. She wrapped her arms around his neck and tightened her grip. He pulled one of her arms free before she could choke him into unconsciousness.

He turned and drove his back toward the bar. Dani wasn't able to release him quickly enough. He smashed her between his body and the bar. She winced with the impact and slid to the floor when he stepped away. He grabbed the front of her shirt and hauled her back up. He pulled one arm back, his fist ready to strike her, but then he froze.

Mary had the sharp end of one of the broken pieces of the stool pressed against his neck. "Let her go."

The man released Dani's shirt and kept his hands open as he backed away. Dani noticed Mary had a scrape on her chin she hadn't had before.

"Whore!" the man shouted at Mary.

Dani snatched the stick from Mary's hand and swung. The stick connected with the side of the man's head and broke. He collapsed to the floor and moaned. Dani dropped the piece still in her hand when Bangor's police entered the pub. That was also when she noticed Hattie standing a few paces away, glaring at her with her arms folded across her chest. Dani had seen the same disapproving look from Jace many times.

Others in the pub told the police the men had started the fight, so the police hauled the men out.

One of the officers approached Hattie. "Aunt Hattie, let us know if you will be pressing charges against them."

"I'll let you know what I decide in the morning. And you're taking these two with you," Hattie said.

The officer glanced at Dani and Mary. "But …"

"They go to jail just like the others," Hattie said.

Dani scowled at Hattie, indignant that she would be jailed for protecting Mary, until she realized Hattie was helping seal their alibis. Dani glanced at Mary as she wiped blood from the cut on her chin. Soreness from the fall and collision with the bar began to settle in as the adrenaline wore off, and Dani touched the lump forming on her cheek.

"You're not going to give me any trouble, are you?" the officer asked them.

"Nope," Dani said.

"Not me," Mary said.

The officer guided them out of the pub, and Dani noticed Mary's limp was worse than before. "You okay?"

Mary nodded with a goofy grin. "That was *so* much fun." She stumbled, and Dani took her arm to steady her.

"Great. You're still shit-faced."

CHAPTER

The foul weather had kept people indoors and out of trouble, with the exception of the pub brawl participants. The Bangor jail was empty except for the three men in the cell on the opposite end of the corridor from the cell occupied by Dani and Mary. Dani had managed to sleep a little, but once Mary started vomiting, she was awake again.

Mary groaned, her head hanging over the toilet bowl. She lifted her head and rolled from her knees to her rump. Dani kept her from tipping over.

Mary wiped her mouth with the back of her hand. "I think I'm done this time."

"You said that last time."

Mary half smiled.

Dani helped her up from the floor and to the lower bunk, and they sat.

"I am *so* sorry," Mary said.

"I've helped you through puking your guts up before."

"That's not what I mean."

"The jail?" Dani chuckled and passed her gaze over the cell. "I spent all my prior lives—from what I was told—avoiding capture by the CNA for stealing, but this is a new experience. Of course, Bangor didn't even have a local police department again until, what, a couple years ago? What they had before then wasn't—"

"*No!*" Mary winced and held her hand to the side of her head. She lowered her voice. "Just shut up and let me apologize."

Dani fell silent, and Mary continued.

"I can't believe I said those things to you. I should not have come on to you like that, and I'm sorry, Dani. I said I wouldn't flirt with you anymore. I drank too much, and I acted like an asshole. I'm never drinking again."

Tears welled in Mary's eyes, and Dani couldn't stay irritated with her, though the intimacy of the encounter with her in the pub had made her quite uncomfortable.

"We're still friends, Mary."

"I swear it won't happen again. I'm serious about not drinking another drop. And I'll apologize to Miles next time I see him. It wasn't fair to him either. I am *sorry*, Dani."

Dani helped her friend lie down on the bunk.

"I should have asked you before using your DNA," Mary said. "I just wanted to have a shot at a longer life. I mean, Echoes die, come back usually in their twenties, keep their memories, and don't have to make the same mistakes going through another life. Well, except you."

Dani shook her head. "I know it sounds like a fairy tale, but it's not. Wardens hunt Echoes, and when we're caught, we're reconditioned to be like them. Do you really want to be a genocidal shit-head? If you're lucky and don't get caught, you'll get to watch all the humans in your life die. Being an Echo is a curse."

"If this works, I won't die," Mary said, struggling to keep her eyes open.

"Get some sleep."

Mary nodded, and Dani climbed up to the top bunk. She

flopped to her back, then flinched. She rolled to her side to stay off her sore shoulder. The bunk reminded her of being on the ship again.

Her first four days on the British destroyer with General Ramos had had her stuck in her quarters, either in bed or lying on the deck next to the toilet. Seasickness had been a misery unlike anything she'd ever experienced before. Once it passed, her body had adjusted and she got queasy only when they were stuck crossing open seas in dreadful weather.

She'd learned to cherish her time on land and still couldn't believe that the rescue mission to retrieve Oliver from Rowan and the subsequent victory at Boston over the Wardens had been three years ago. Dani's intention to quit helping Colonel Houston and the Commonwealth turned into Ramos's worldwide diplomacy tour. She'd adamantly refused the title of ambassador that Ramos gave her, but he'd still changed her uniform and used the title every time they stopped in a port. She still inwardly cringed every time she heard it. She was a Brigand—a scavenger and survivor. None of this ambassador bullshit.

Dani sat up and passed her hands over her face. Her head came up when she heard someone enter the holding area, but she didn't bother leaving the bunk. From the sounds of approaching footfalls, a few people were headed her way.

Colonel Houston, a pair of MPs, and a Bangor officer arrived at the cell. Dani sneered at the colonel. Too much betrayal had caused Dani to despise the woman.

"Bring them to a room for questioning," Houston said. "Get up, Dani."

"Fuck off."

"Open the cell," Houston said to the officer.

"I'm a civilian and you can't do shit in this town, Catherine. The Commonwealth doesn't own Bangor."

"I can do what I must when someone attacks a CNA base."

"Someone? You mean *me*?" Dani waved her arms. "I've been here all night, you moron."

Houston turned to the officer and growled. "Bring them to an interrogation room now!" She turned and marched back down the corridor with her own military police.

The officer looked apologetically at Dani and opened the cell. "I'm sorry, Dani. There was some sort of mishap on the base, and Colonel Houston is on a rampage. We don't have all the jurisdictional crap sorted out between the CNA and Bangor's council yet."

Dani sighed and slid off the bunk. "Can you at least get word to General Ramos that this is happening?"

"I'm not sure. I can't interfere with a CNA investigation."

"Hattie, then?"

The officer's face brightened. "Yeah. I can do that."

"Thanks." Dani shook Mary's shoulder to wake her. Mary needed a few minutes to steady herself and drink some water before they followed the officer out. Dani grinned at the men still in their cell as they passed. They'd suffered more bruises and scrapes in the scuffle than she and Mary had.

When they arrived in the designated interrogation room, Dani thought it looked more like a room where officers might have their meals, except Houston and her MP bookends were there instead. Mary limped over to one of the chairs at the table and sat. She slouched in the chair and touched the side of her head. Dani stood behind Mary with her arms crossed.

"Where were you last night, Mary?" Houston asked.

"Here," Mary said.

"Before that?"

"Pub."

"Before that."

"My room."

"Before that."

"Oh, fuck off, Catherine," Mary said, lowering her hand.

"Why do you need to know?" Dani asked. "What's this crap about the base?"

"A project in one of our R&D labs suffered a data loss. I want to know where you were," Houston said.

"Because you think I did it? What was in this lab? What was lost?" Dani asked.

"That doesn't matter."

Oh, but it does. Dani shook her head. "You can't be straight with me, yet you expect me to cooperate?"

Houston turned to her MPs. "Leave us."

They glanced at each other for a second before leaving. Houston was about to do something where she didn't want witnesses. Dani's gut knotted with fear.

Houston drew her pistol and pointed it at Dani. "Back up."

Dani uncrossed her arms. "What the hell are you doing?"

The colonel gestured with the pistol for Dani to move. When she backed up a step, Houston moved in toward Mary and slammed the base of the pistol into Mary's injured thigh.

Mary screamed and doubled over, clutching her leg.

Dani's charge toward Houston stopped when the colonel aimed the pistol at her face.

"One shot and you're gone forever," Houston said to Dani. "No regen if you're headless."

"I'll fucking kill you."

"Tell me where you were or I'll hit her again."

Dani scowled at the colonel.

Houston used one arm to wrestle Mary back upright and raised the pistol again. Mary's eyes widened, and she struggled to get the woman away from her.

"Stop!" Dani said.

Houston held her strike. "Start talking."

Dani hesitated, and Houston swung her pistol down again. Dani dove toward them and caught the weapon before it met Mary's leg.

"Stop! Stop. I'll tell you everything," Dani said. She could've ripped the weapon from Houston's hand, but she didn't. She had another, far more insane idea, instead.

"No!" Mary said.

"I have to," Dani said, shaking her head.

Houston flashed a triumphant smile as she backed away and holstered her pistol. "Tell me what you know."

Dani began pacing.

Mary caught her hand. "Don't do this."

Dani withdrew her hand from Mary's, took a deep breath, and released it slowly. She looked up at Houston. "Hattie asked us to help her with something."

"What?" Houston asked, inching closer.

"Dani, *don't*," Mary pleaded.

Dani resisted the urge to grin. Houston was hungry for information, and that's exactly what Dani wanted. She shook her head. "That's what I told Miles. I told him Hattie needed me to help her and Mary with something."

Houston's brow furrowed. "So you're saying Hattie didn't need you?"

"Yes." Dani drew in a shaky breath.

"Why were you in town?"

Dani struggled to find the right words. She swallowed a few times, stalling. She *had* to make this lie work.

"Well?" Houston demanded.

"Before we went to the pub, we were in Mary's room as she said."

"Why?"

"What?" Dani asked, and laughed nervously. "Why do you think we were in her room? Sex, Catherine. It's called sex! I've been fucking Mary, and Miles has no clue. No one does." She refused to look at Mary and instead stared at the floor and crossed her arms as a hot flush moved from her neck into her face, praying Houston mistook her attempt at lying as embarrassment over an affair. "It started on the ship three months ago."

Houston snorted a laugh. "Took you long enough."

"That's not funny," Dani said, looking up at her with a frown.

"What time was this happening?" Houston asked.

"I don't know!" Dani said, waving her arms. "Wasn't like I put a timer on us."

"Nine," Mary said. "We started around nine, then had some drinks after." She caught Dani's eye. "I was watching the time to get you back home before it got too late—except we drank too much."

Dani sighed. "The fight started when that asshole hurt her."

Houston paced around them a few times, then went to the door. She walked out and left it open. Dani wasn't sure what to do, so she and Mary stayed in the room. The Bangor officer returned and told them they could leave, so they did.

CHAPTER

6

Once Dani and Mary were well away from the jail and headed back toward Hattie's, Mary shrieked. "I almost shit myself when I realized you were trying to lie to Houston. What's even crazier is she actually *believed* the story you made up. You fooled the human lie detector, and it was brilliant. I mean, you always suck at lying, but holy hell, you nailed it this time!"

Dani winced when Mary squealed again.

"How did you do that? Dani?" Mary said, touching her arm. "Talk to me."

She didn't slow her steps, though she didn't walk so fast as to leave her limping friend behind. "We'll talk when we're in your room."

Mary frowned and stopped trying to engage her in conversation.

They arrived at the brothel and went to the back of the building to Mary's room. Mary opened the door, and Kelsey rolled over in the bed.

He groaned and rubbed his eyes. "The jailbirds are out."

"Grab your med kit to check Mary's leg," Dani said.

He sat up. "Why? What's wrong?"

"She's gotten a little banged up is all. Make sure it's healing okay and replace the patches. If I see or hear about her climbing on roofs, dancing, or doing anything else stupid before she's completely healed, I'm coming after you. I'll cut your fucking bits off, Kels."

"Okay. Yeah, I get it," he said, rolling out of bed.

"You're overreacting," Mary said.

Dani led Mary back into the hall while Kelsey dressed.

"What the hell is wrong with you?" Mary asked.

Dani's hands were clenched into fists.

"Where's all this sudden anger coming from?" Mary touched her arm. "What's wrong? I've never seen you act like this before. You went off on that man last night like you were going to kill him. Would you have killed him had those guys not pulled you off?"

Maybe. "No," Dani said. She wasn't ready to admit to the uncontrolled rage she'd felt inside when teeing off on the man's face.

"And lying to Houston? Where did that come from?"

"I don't know. She's so arrogant, and when she hit you, I really did want to kill her. I don't know why I decided to lie to her instead."

"Well, it was fucking perfect. Scary, but perfect. So, why are you angry at me? Punishing me for last night? I'll apologize again if you want me to."

"No, Mary. No. I just … I don't know," she said, and finally opened her hands. "You're taking too many risks. I don't want you ending up dead."

"It's my life. My choices. I'm responsible for what happens as a result, not you."

Dani shook her head and sighed. "I'm going home." She was tired and well beyond irritable, so she left.

"Don't leave like this, Dani. Please."

She continued down the hall and left the brothel. The sun was out after the worst of the storm had passed, but the wind continued to lash the trees. She walked around a few downed limbs as she headed home and had another mile left in her walk when she spotted Oliver and Brody. The dog darted ahead to meet her. She couldn't help but smile when he arrived, tail wagging, and she petted him.

"Hey, oh," Oliver said. "What happened to you?"

She touched the swollen bruise on her cheek. "Got into a scuffle last night."

"Why?"

"Some guy in the pub was an ass to Mary."

"You spent the night with Aunt Hattie?"

"Not exactly."

Oliver waited for her to answer.

"I spent the night in jail," she said, and shrugged. "Hattie didn't like us being involved in the fight, so Mary and I spent the night in a cell."

He frowned with what Dani guessed was confusion, and then his expression dissolved into one of sadness. She hated the sudden guilt that welled inside her chest, knowing she'd disappointed him.

"Oliver, he hurt her, so I beat the shit out of him," she said, then wished she could take it back. It made her sound like an even worse person. She sighed, realizing that in the last twenty-four hours she'd behaved horribly. *Trespassing, breaking and entering, destruction of CNA property, more trespassing, brawling, destruction of Hattie's property, arrested, threatening a CNA colonel, lying—*

"Dani?"

"Huh?"

Oliver shook his head. "Did you hear what I said?"

"No. Sorry."

"I'm the teenager. I'm the one who's supposed to be the delinquent. Not you."

Dani grinned. "It's no secret that I'm a shit role model."

Oliver laughed. "You really are," he said, then sobered. "Santi came to the house last night."

"Why?"

"To talk to you and Dad. What would be the best way to end the war? Keep working to bring more Brigands into the fight with Commonwealths or recon on cities still held by the Wardens?"

"Both need to happen."

Oliver rolled his eyes. "Oh, you're just like Dad."

"What does that mean?"

"Dad said the same thing. Santi's interested in going after Toronto and Quebec City, but he doesn't have the best intel or recon on the ground for it. Well, he didn't say that, but that's what he implied."

"Okay, so he needs to get the right people in there."

"Exactly. He can't do that if you're in jail."

Dani's brow creased and she tilted her head.

"The war needs to end, Dani!"

"Yeah, I agree."

"In a year? Can you end it in a year?"

Her anger flared. "I don't need you to remind me of the deadline."

"You promised!"

"I'm doing my best. Christ, Oliver, I'm only one person. I've done everything I can to help turn the war around, even Santi's diplomatic shit. If it's not over by the time you turn seventeen, I'll get you out of here so the CNA can't reach you."

"And then what?"

"*I don't know!*" she roared at him. Dani grimaced and lowered her face into her palms. "I'm sorry. I haven't slept, and … I'm sorry."

When she lowered her hands, he was already walking away. *Fuck.* Dani trudged the rest of the way home with the third of the four closest people in her life annoyed with her. Maybe Oliver was right and it was time to change tactics. When he was twelve, she'd promised him the war would be over before he had to enter the CNA. That was four years ago. She wasn't sure why she thought a war that had been raging for over sixty years would end in a few years, much less within the next twelve months.

She heard the sounds of wood being chopped before she could see the small house by the river. Miles swung the ax much harder than necessary to split the logs. He was having a bad day too, but Dani's shit day improved a little upon seeing him shirtless and swinging the ax.

The two pieces of the former tree trunk fell from the base with his next swing. He leaned over to move the pieces aside and noticed her. He sank the blade of the ax into the base.

"You're finally back," he said, a little out of breath.

Dani greeted him with a kiss.

He eyed her bruised cheek. "Rough night?"

"Something like that. You?"

Miles grunted and headed inside. Dani followed, poured them both a mug of water, then sat at the table. He told her about his evening and morning events, and she told him everything that had happened to her between last night's trip to the base and lab, the pub brawl, and jail time, including her lie to Houston about the affair with Mary. When she finished, he refilled their mugs and leaned against the counter instead of sitting again.

"Are you angry?" she asked.

"At you? No, not at all. I just can't believe Houston struck

Mary and pointed a gun at your head. She was always such a good leader." Miles shook his head. "I don't get it; she's changed."

"Miles, are we really making a difference going around with Santi?"

"I know we are."

"Could we do more?"

"It's a war," he said, shrugging. "Who knows how long this damn thing will drag on?"

She went to his side. "That doesn't answer my question."

Miles sighed and set his mug down before pulling her close. "I feel like I don't have any ideas anymore."

She nodded, knowing exactly what he meant. Fighting against the Wardens was exhausting, especially when the enemy army could regenerate and fight some more.

"Actually, I lied. I do have one," he said. "How about we get past Ollie's birthday before we try to figure out what to do next."

Dani put her mug down before wrapping her arms around his waist. "I like it."

"Another thought." He nuzzled the side of her neck. "He's annoyed with us, so he won't be home for a while."

"I like this idea too." Dani grinned and buried her fingers in his hair while his lips moved over her skin. "Mary and Hattie are annoyed with me, so they won't be dropping by unannounced anytime soon."

"Perfect," he said, lifting his head to kiss her. He had her shirt off and tossed aside before they reached the bedroom door. They fumbled with their boots for a moment to remove them before their jeans came off. Dani moaned when his hands slid over her body and his mouth found her favorite places to be kissed before returning to her lips.

The bed was an old mattress on the floor, and Dani was ready to be on it with him.

His hand pressed into her mid-back. She flinched.

"What's wrong?" Miles looked over her shoulder. "That's quite the bruise. If you're that sore, we don't have to—"

She covered his mouth with hers, and he pulled her down to the mattress with him. She swung one leg over his body and settled on him. *This* was where she had wanted to be last night.

CHAPTER

7

Dani had stayed home with Miles for the last few days and hadn't gone into town until this morning. The roof comm that Mary had tried to fix wasn't broken at all; it just didn't have a charge. The solar panel was the problem. After being on the roof this morning with a pair of Hattie's other workers, Dani found the issue, dismantled the panel from the array, then worked with them to lower the panel to the ground with ropes.

Once they had it moved inside the brothel, Dani went to work. She wrestled the solar panel up to rest against the wall in the basement. Now that it was where she wanted it, she sat on the floor and removed the back cover. The solar cells all looked fine, so she started tracing the wires, inspecting them for breaks in the insulation or other damage.

She looked up when footsteps started down the stairs, and recognized Hattie by her shoes. The older woman descended the steps a bit more slowly than usual, but then, Hattie was in her late seventies—possibly already in her eighties, assuming she told the truth about the timing of her last regen.

"Hey, Hattie," Dani said from her spot on the floor.

Hattie reached the base of the stairs and moved through the

lower level of the brothel without answering. She retrieved a medium-sized box that she had to carry with both arms, then started back for the stairs. Dani hopped up.

"Hattie!"

The older woman stopped without looking at her. "What?"

Dani hadn't expected such a cold reception. "Uh, do you need help with that?"

"No."

"You seem angry. Have I done something wrong?"

Hattie turned to face her but remained silent.

"Look. I said I was sorry for telling Miles you were—" She lowered her voice and shrugged. "You know."

"That's not it."

"So I have to *guess* my crime?" Dani grumbled. "Christ, you don't make anything easy. The fight in the pub? It wasn't exactly planned, but going to jail was great. It was perfect for our alibis."

"The alibi part happened to work out in your favor. I let the cops take you to jail because of how you acted. I left you there because I didn't want to look at you."

Dani's face fell. She was ashamed and didn't even know why. All she knew was that she'd disappointed Hattie somehow and it made her feel terrible. "What? Why?"

"You beat the shit out of that man. I've seen rage many times before. You had lost control until the men pulled you off him."

"Okay, yeah," Dani said, nodding. "I was really angry, but—"

"*Rage*, Dani. It's different from anger."

"It was just anger, Hattie. I knew what I was doing."

"Which makes it even worse," Hattie said, and started back up the stairs.

Dani stared after Hattie until her feet disappeared. She jumped when the cellar door slammed closed. "Fuck." Dani passed her hand over her face and wondered if there was a way to fix this thing with Hattie. Nothing came to mind.

She checked the time, and she needed to leave anyway. Dani tidied up her work area, then left for the CNA base on the other side of Bangor for her meeting with General Ramos and Colonel Houston. She arrived a little early, so she studied the maps of New England and northeastern Canada on the wall and table. Dani fiddled with one of the panels and got the digital three-dimensional map of Canada up, but she couldn't figure out the controls for how to shift and zoom in on it. With a curse, she abandoned it for the paper maps.

Her thoughts wandered, and she kept losing her focus. Oliver's words haunted her. If the war didn't end before he turned seventeen, what *would* she do? Hiding him in the forest to keep him away from the CNA wasn't a great solution. Dani wondered if reentering the war was what she needed to do. Ramos was still focused on diplomatic missions, but maybe that time was over.

What more could they do to recruit additional Brigands to help the CNA? There was a good chance they'd already recruited whomever they were going to get and those resources were dried up. Maybe it was time to just throw everything and everyone at the Wardens in one big hit to end the war—just like the Wardens had done to start it. Except there wasn't a way to guarantee the CNA-Brigand forces would win using that tactic. The Wardens had attacked a bit prematurely decades ago, so they hadn't been able to complete their hostile takeover of Earth. Instead, they'd beat the shit out of Earth's residents and thrust everyone into a war without an end.

The door opened, and Dani glanced over her shoulder as Mary and Miles arrived with the CNA brass.

"Figured you'd be late instead of early," Houston said.

"I'm just full of surprises today," Dani said, her tone flat.

Miles moved to stand next to her and whispered, "You okay?"

Dani tightened her jaw. He nodded, knowing not to ask her anything else right then and they'd talk later.

"Let's get started," Ramos said.

Houston manipulated the digital map of Canada with a flawless precision that Dani envied a little. She returned her attention to the wall map while Houston spoke.

"We can't get the Wardens out of Toronto. CNA and Brigand forces in the region have tried everything. We can't even attack because they are so entrenched."

"Around Toronto?" Ramos asked.

"We have Buffalo and Rochester, New York, plus Ottawa, and many of the smaller towns under our control, but the Wardens still control the river. We haven't been able to hold anything of importance on the Saint Lawrence River."

"The southern portion of Quebec City is ours," Mary said.

Houston shook her head. "One quarter of Quebec City isn't enough."

Ramos frowned. "We have naval support from England helping us where the Atlantic and the Gulf of Saint Lawrence meet."

"Again," Houston said. "It's not enough."

Dani eyed the map. Toronto sat on the northern coastline of Lake Ontario. That lake's outflow was the starting point of the Saint Lawrence River, which ran for three hundred miles or so until reaching the gulf.

"You mean we have *nothing* around the lake?" Ramos asked.

Houston frowned and shook her head.

"Goddammit," Ramos said. "We need the river *and* Lake Ontario to take Toronto."

"Wardens control that entire area of the river, except for a spit of water around southern Quebec City," Houston said. "We have coastal areas of New Brunswick, including Fredericton and Moncton, but those are too far away to offer any leverage against Quebec City, and certainly not Toronto."

Dani leaned in closer to the map and used her finger to trace the river from Quebec City through Trois-Rivières, past Montreal to Cornwall to Lake Ontario. She eyed Toronto for a moment before turning her gaze back along the river.

"Colonel," Miles said. "You think we should start with Quebec City to take the rest of it first?"

Houston shook her head. "I want Toronto."

"No," Ramos said. "If we take Quebec City, everything else will fall. The northeastern part of North America is their last major stronghold on the continent. It's an embarrassment that we have not been able to secure that region."

"You think I've been sitting on my ass with this?" Houston barked, then said, "Sir."

Dani glanced at Houston and smirked. The last successful military battle credited as being led by the colonel had been Boston. Everything since then had required major reinforcements from other states. Houston had rank in the CNA, but she always needed help when it came to something big.

"I'm not implying that, Colonel," Ramos said. "In the last few years, all Commonwealths across every continent have made great strides in taking strategic points back from the Wardens. But the world is watching *us*. Maine was the catalyst with Portland. Then you did it again with Boston, and the rest of New England fell soon after. This is the final piece for the Commonwealth of North America. Everything else falls once we have Quebec City."

"Montreal," Dani said, eyes still on the wall map.

The others turned to face her.

"Nice of you to join the discussion," Houston said. "We're talking about Toronto and Quebec City, in case you missed that part."

"I heard you, Catherine," Dani said, refusing to use the woman's title. She'd lost all respect for Houston after the battle for Boston.

Houston shook her head and returned her attention to the general. "Toronto is the first city we need to take," she said.

Ramos kept his attention on Dani, which caused a deep frown to form on Houston's face.

"Montreal, Santi," Dani said. She respected the general but used his first name since that was how he'd originally introduced himself to her well before the battle in Boston had occurred. During her time working so closely with him over the last three years, she considered him a friend and someone who could be trusted, unlike Houston.

"Why?" Mary asked.

"Because it shuts down the back door to Quebec City and the front door to Toronto. You're arguing about which end of the candle to burn first." Dani tapped the map. "Start in the middle. Montreal."

"We'd need to get control of the locks on the South Shore Canal," Ramos said.

Dani shrugged. "Not the priority. You can't get through the Lachine Rapids safely, so you'd have to use the canal to pass through. That's a death trap that the Wardens hold. Skip the canal for now. There's a ton of maneuvering room in the larger part of the river. Attack Montreal and stay north of the rapids."

Miles joined her at the map and nodded. "The city is on an island, a *big* island, between two rivers—Prairies River to the north and the Saint Lawrence River to the south. Naval forces could blockade that area more easily once they move south of Quebec City. You're right," he said to Dani. "If we avoid the locks, we can go in with bigger ships."

"Once the city falls, it'll be a hell of a lot easier to go after the locks and control the Saint Lawrence Seaway," Mary said.

"It's an unimportant island," Houston said.

"And you're still an idiot, Catherine," Dani said, which

earned a horrified gasp from Miles and a snort of amusement from Mary. "Santi, Montreal is where we need recon."

"Does your focus on Montreal have anything to do with your boyfriend being based there?" Houston asked.

Dani's brow crinkled.

"Rowan, *idiot*. Your Warden boyfriend."

"Fuck," Dani said. Knowing Rowan was in Montreal made her gut tighten. She'd always been so far away from him when on Ramos's ship, pretending to be an ambassador.

Houston grinned.

"I know your history with him, Dani," Ramos said. "He wants you dead, and we want him dead, so his personal vendetta is irrelevant."

Not to me, Dani thought.

"Dani," Ramos continued, "you, Miles, and Mary will stay in Bangor. Get any data you can on the region and start analysis. I want the most accurate information we can get. In the interim I'll put together a team and go in."

Dani's eyes widened. "Wait. Sir. I didn't mean for *you* to do the recon."

Ramos shrugged and started for the door. "Not my first time in the field." He waved a finger at Dani and her friends. "Stay here and dig up data," he said, then turned to Houston. "Give them access to whatever files they need, Colonel."

Dani watched as Houston's jaw worked, tightening so hard, she thought the woman's teeth would shatter.

"Yes, sir," Houston said. She shot Dani a glare before following the general out.

Mary whistled. "Wow. She *really* hates you."

"What else is new?" Dani glanced at Miles. He was still rather pale-looking since her insult to Catherine. He'd get over it. She returned her attention to the maps.

CHAPTER

Rowan grumbled as he shuffled reports around on his desk. His quarters in Montreal were much smaller than what he'd had in Boston. Hell, he didn't even have enough space for a home office. Devon played in the area between the kitchen and the corner of the room where Rowan's desk resided. His nine-year-old son made rumbling noises as he pushed his trucks and airplanes along the floor. Rowan flinched when his three-year-old daughter, Katy, shrieked with excitement as she barreled out of the bathroom and headed for her father. That she could make such a high-pitched, loud noise from such a tiny body still baffled him. He scooped her up.

"I did it!" she said.

"You did?" Rowan asked, smiling. He caught Ella's eye as she emerged from the bathroom. She shook her head. Toilet training with Katy had been a nightmare and was taking forever. "Keep practicing, okay?" He kissed her forehead, and she wriggled to be put down.

"Okay, Daddy," Katy said. As soon as her feet were back on the floor, she was off to join her brother.

"Shouldn't she have this toileting figured out by now?" Rowan asked.

Ella passed her hand over her rounded belly. "She's making progress. She'll get there soon."

Rowan smiled and placed his hand on hers. Ella had been the nanny-turned-mother for his children, and she would birth his son in a few months' time. He couldn't love her, though—not the way he had loved Ana. Ella was young and had never held a plasma rifle, been in battle, or had a regen. Rowan had been through enough regens now that he'd lost count. In linear years, he was old enough to be Ella's great-great-great-grandfather. But his Echo regens kept him looking the same age as her.

Ana had been a Warden. She knew of battle and regens and the importance of taking Earth from the useless humans. She hated the humans as much as he did. But his world had been wrecked when Dani murdered her.

He returned to his desk as memories of the past washed over him. For everything that Ella lacked as a true battle-hardened Warden, she was still a pure Echo and would give birth to his child. She had also accepted that Rowan couldn't love her the same way he'd loved his wife. She enjoyed the higher social status of being with Rowan, and they both enjoyed the sex that came with their arrangement. She didn't require any declarations of love from him, and for that, Rowan was thankful.

Boston.

He scratched at the stubble on his chin while staring at nothing in particular on his desk. The Wardens' loss of Boston had been catastrophic, and Rowan had been put on a ship that deposited him in Toronto while his family sheltered in Montreal.

The trial for his slaying of the former vice regent of Boston had been short-lived. He hadn't had much difficulty proving Vice Regent Aubrey's many failings and that her inaction was a direct cause of the Commonwealth being able to launch an attack against the city. Add to that the video of Ana's head being splattered when CNA forces infiltrated Warden housing, and he didn't need to defend his actions much since Aubrey's failed leadership had essentially caused Ana's death. Sure, he had been sentenced to two years in jail, but he was released after one, thanks to Curtis's relentless appeals for Rowan to be reunited with his children in Montreal.

Maine continued to haunt him. Colonel Houston and Dani remained alive and well while the CNA entrenched themselves in Boston. He'd tried tracking Dani's movements, but that had become more difficult once she was brought into service under General Santi Ramos.

Rowan pulled one of his panels closer, the one that held all the data he had on Dani. He pulled up an image of her in the Commonwealth uniform declaring her to be Ambassador Ireland. *Ridiculous.* His breathing quickened as rage swelled from within. This was the woman who had played a role in several of his last regens. This was the woman who had sprayed Ana's head all over a stairwell wall. "You will fucking *burn.*"

The alert to his quarters chimed, and his head came up. Rowan glanced at the time and left his desk.

"Daddy, who is it?" Devon asked, pausing his play.

"Work," Rowan said. If he let Curtis in, Devon and Katy would want to visit with their uncle, and Rowan wanted to get away from the noise of the children playing. There was work to do. Earth still hadn't been secured for the Wardens, and this war wasn't over yet.

Rowan slipped through the door to leave, and Curtis stepped aside to make room for his hasty departure.

"Sir?" Curtis said. "Everything okay?"

"Yes. What have you got?" Rowan asked as he started down the corridor, not bothering to explain why he needed to leave his home in a rush.

Curtis increased his pace to keep up and passed Rowan a

panel. "Maine's CNA is actively working with Boston officials. Both Quebec City and Toronto are likely targets."

Rowan's eyes skimmed the information. "This isn't exactly revelatory."

"No, sir, but the CNA is showing increased activity in both Maine and New Brunswick. Ship movements in and out of Boston have increased too."

"They're moving their chess pieces."

"Yes, sir."

Rowan nodded. "Any chance the vice regent will transfer me back to Toronto or to Quebec City?"

"No, sir. Your early release was contingent on you remaining in Montreal."

"They're still not bending on that?" Rowan asked, and Curtis frowned. "Ugh. Fucking morons, the whole lot."

"They granted you a position back with R&D, sir, when you were supposed to be confined to barracks, but—"

"It's not enough!" Rowan's anger continued to simmer. He cast a sideways glance at Curtis. Curtis had been his friend and most loyal staffer until Boston. They'd carefully planned to manipulate the chancellors into electing Rowan as vice regent, but the chancellors had instead ousted Aubrey and voted in a new VR in his absence. Everything had backfired on Rowan while he was in the city fighting the CNA and trying to capture Dani. He missed the election, and upon returning to headquarters in Boston, he encountered the newly elected Vice Regent Curtis. Rowan still wasn't sure he believed Curtis's claims that the election was out of his control. The title hadn't lasted long once the city fell and they were forced to retreat to ships.

"Sir, please let me finish."

Rowan flicked his hand as permission.

"General Ramos arrived in Burlington two days ago."

That stopped Rowan in an instant.

"I only just got the information today, sir. He has a small team with him, but his purpose there isn't known." Curtis held his hand up before Rowan could speak. "Ambassador Ireland isn't with him."

Rowan growled. "Don't call her that. She's a fucking Brigand."

"Yes, sir. *Dani* isn't with him."

"So he's not there for his diplomatic charade," Rowan said. "A CNA general this close to Montreal? No, this isn't diplomatic. I want a team to scout the border."

Curtis smiled. "Vice Regent Keran is aware and has already sent three teams in. I put in a request for a special research team to deploy as well so we can field-test some of the new gear. It's been approved and we leave in the morning."

"Now! We leave now."

Curtis's brow creased.

Rowan rolled his eyes. Curtis was expecting a bit of praise for that last part. *Fine. Needy bastard.* "Good work, Curtis, but I want to expedite our departure to today. We need to find and capture Ramos while he is here."

"Yes, sir."

"Go. I'll meet you in the department after I grab a few things from home." Rowan didn't wait for an answer before leaving; he sure as hell wasn't about to physically pat Curtis on the back. Granted, Curtis *had* provided him with some wonderful news and pulled off an approval for Rowan to leave the base, but Rowan had a score to settle with the CNA.

He had been careful to avoid mentioning that he intended to pursue Ramos all the way back to Burlington if he had to. He didn't give a shit about borders or which side owned which piece of territory. The Wardens had loosened Rowan's leash, and he would show them the damage he could do to the Commonwealth. The Wardens were too slow to make the CNA pay for retaking both Maine and Boston. He would wreak his own havoc.

He was a goddamn immortal. He would exterminate every human from the planet one at a time if that's what it took to claim Earth for his people.

CHAPTER

9

Just as Dani stepped off the ladder after fixing the solar panel on the brothel roof, a man in his early twenties came out the back entrance. He headed for Mary, who was gathering up the harness Dani had used. "Hey, Mary, a courier dropped off that package you were waiting on. Small, thin envelope. It's on the table in the kitchen."

"Thanks, Andy." She set the harness aside, and Dani and Mary headed inside.

Dani asked, "What's the package?"

"It's probably the one for you—well, for Oliver."

"*Really?*" Dani asked, surprised by her own level of sudden excitement. She quickened her pace, and Mary chuckled at her. Dani took the back steps two at a time and threw open the kitchen door. She rushed to the table and picked up the envelope. She glanced back as Mary caught up.

"Open it," Mary said.

Dani pulled the knife from her belt and sliced the end of the envelope open. She smiled broadly as she pulled the papers from it and read the letterhead and first few lines of the letter. "He got in. Holy fuck, Mary, he got *in!*" She threw her arms around her friend. "Oliver's going to shit himself when he sees this."

Mary laughed. "I think you're already doing that for him."

Dani reread the acceptance letter for Oliver's participation in an artist community event in Portland in a few weeks. "They weren't accepting many participants, but I really wanted Oliver to get in on this. He's been talking about this for months but wouldn't send a portfolio in—said he wasn't good enough, the little shit."

"His portraits are unreal; he's earned this."

"He's been in a rotten mood since I spent the night in jail. I hope he won't be pissed at us for copying his drawings and sending them in." Dani winced. "He didn't exactly give Miles or me his permission."

"I think he'll forgive you once he reads the letter." Mary held out her hand and took it and placed it back in the envelope. "I'll put it with the art materials I got him for his birthday. If you take this home, he may find it. It'll be safe in my room here until the party tomorrow."

Dani jogged the few miles home. She didn't have a need to rush, but she wanted to tell Miles the news. Instead, when she got home and went inside, Miles wasn't there and Oliver was. She had to switch her excitement off if she was going to keep Oliver's letter a secret. He looked up from the table and his drawing.

"Hey," she said, and wiped sweat from her brow. Brody bounced around her feet, so she leaned over to pet him.

"You've been running." Alarm crept into Oliver's voice. "Something's wrong."

"No! Nothing is wrong," Dani said, happy to not have to try to lie to him. "I finished up with the panel and wanted to come home early." Another true statement. She slid into one of the empty chairs at the table, and Oliver put his pencil down.

"Something *is* wrong," he said.

"No. Well, a little, but not like you're thinking." She leaned on the table. "Things in this house have been way too tense lately. I'm sorry I got in the fight at Hattie's. Going to jail wasn't actually part of the plan."

"What plan?"

Shit. Dani winced; she hadn't meant to make that slip, but it was too late now. "There was an event on the base that same night."

"An event?" Oliver snorted. "A lab and every server in it melted down."

Dani's mouth hung open.

"Anton told me. You did that?"

She nodded.

Oliver grinned. "I figured. Dad said you wouldn't do something like that, but he thinks you walk on water. I know you better."

"Oh, that hurts, Oliver." Dani's pride was stung a little. "Besides, Miles already knew I was involved, so joke's on you," she said with a smirk.

"That's not fair!"

Dani laughed. "Mary and I went to the pub to be seen by others—alibi and all that. But then this jerk grabbed her, and I kinda clobbered him," she said, and frowned. "Hattie thinks I lost control, but I didn't. I was just *so* angry that he'd hurt Mary. Then Catherine was an ass, and it was just a giant, rotten night and day. I'm sorry I yelled at you."

"I wasn't exactly being fair to you with my questions," he said, and lowered his gaze to the table.

"You're scared. I get it. You turn sixteen tomorrow, enlistment starts when you hit seventeen, and this war is just not showing any signs of wrapping up anytime soon." She reached across the table and took his hand. "Look at me, please."

He lifted his eyes.

"I have been doing—and will continue to do—everything I

can to keep you out of this fucking war. Santi is gone to do his own recon, and I think that's where the next phase of whatever his plan is will lead. The diplomatic mission crap is done. We have all the Brigands we're going to get; our numbers are way up now. If I need to reenter recon, I can in a heartbeat and be fine."

"I don't want you and Dad in on the fighting."

Dani released his hand and leaned back in her chair. "Can't say I want to be in on that part either, but I'll go where Santi needs me."

"If you're doing recon, I can't go with you like I could on the ship."

"No."

"I'll be stuck waiting here—waiting for you and Dad to come home."

Dani nodded.

"I hate that part."

"I hate it too. I've gotten where I kinda like having you around every day." Dani lightly kicked his leg under the table, which made him smile. "Since we don't have to deal with that crap right now, we can just hang out and annoy each other, and I can be a bad influence on you," Dani said. "Do you have homework?"

"Yeah."

"Want to go fishing instead?"

Oliver grinned and nodded.

"Where's your father?"

"Oh, we, uh, argued again. He went out for a walk."

Dani left her chair. "I know where we can find him. We'll bring an extra rod so he can help us catch dinner. Birthday party is tomorrow!" She walked past Oliver and rumpled his hair. He pushed her hand away but still smiled. "Let's go, street urchin. Dinner won't catch itself."

CHAPTER
'10

ani's excitement for Oliver's birthday party increased as the day progressed. Everything for his party was ready, but Oliver was missing. Dani made a quick sweep through the brothel and spotted him lurking in the hallway outside Hattie's kitchen. She touched his shoulder and he startled.

"I hate when you sneak up on me like that," he said.

"Sorry," Dani said, recalling the many times her brother's silent movements had startled her when he'd showed up unexpectedly next to her. He'd also always chided her for not learning how to move with stealth, but she'd obviously learned *something* from him.

"I don't want to go in."

"What do you mean? This is your party, Oliver."

He grimaced and wrung his hands.

"Oh. Is this your first birthday party?"

He nodded. "We moved so much, I didn't have many friends. Birthdays were always just me, Mom, and Dad. What do I do? How does this work?"

Dani snickered. "You're asking *me*? I've never had a party either—well, not that I can remember. I don't even know my birth date. Just follow Mary's lead; she's the social butterfly. Pretty sure you just need to have fun."

"Okay." He took a deep breath. "I can do this."

He entered the kitchen, and Dani followed, smiling. Brody bounded over to Oliver and bounced around him. Hattie, Mary, and Miles looked up from the table where his cake sat between two boxes. The envelope wasn't on the table with the other gifts. She and Miles had decided to leave that one until after the main party was done.

"Where have you been?" Miles asked his son.

"Oh, we just took a few minutes to talk," Dani said. "I was giving him pointers on how to be a responsible adult now that he's sixteen."

"Responsible adult?" Mary snorted. "*You? Never.*"

"Yeah. It was a long shot." Dani shrugged. "I mostly just babbled and didn't have any real advice for him." She squeezed Oliver's shoulder. He smiled at her, and then his eyes widened when the back door opened and other people filed in. Two of Oliver's friends from school entered, followed by Dresden, Kelsey, and Cameron. They greeted him and remarked on the cake and gifts.

Dani went to Miles and hooked her arm through his.

"You weren't really giving him advice," Miles said so only she could hear. "He okay?"

"Yep. Just nerves. Cam!" Dani said when Major Cameron approached.

He kissed her on the cheek and shook Miles's hand. "Nice to see you both."

"Wasn't sure you'd make it," Miles said.

Cameron rolled his eyes. "I know. I only just got off the ship a few days ago in Boston. Happy to be on solid ground, though it may not last long. General Ramos—"

"Later," Miles said.

Cameron nodded and left to sidle up next to Hattie and put his arm around her. The move almost earned him a stab wound with the knife she held.

"This is for the cake, but I'm happy to run you through with it instead," Hattie said, feigning anger.

He kissed her on the cheek but still backed away. Dani laughed, though she could see that Hattie enjoyed the Brit's flirting. A forty-year age gap didn't bother Hattie. Didn't seem to bother Cam, either.

The party went well, and Dani thought Oliver had a good time. He was excited about the new sketchbooks and other art supplies his friends and Mary had given him. The cake was reduced to crumbs in record time. Dani couldn't remember ever having had cake before, and she marveled at its sweetness. His friends and the others left an hour later.

Oliver sat at the table, smiling, and rubbing his palm over his cake-distended belly. "The cake was wonderful, Aunt Hattie."

"I'm glad you liked it, honey," she said.

Dani glanced at Miles and Mary. Miles nodded, and Mary removed a fancy envelope with a green ribbon on it from a kitchen drawer. Dani made a mental note to thank Mary for putting the letter in a nicer envelope with the decorative touches; green was Oliver's favorite color.

"Oliver, I know you wanted to go to the art event in Portland but were afraid to send them a portfolio. I hope you're not angry, but your father and I sent an application in for you," Dani said.

Oliver sat up in his chair with a frown. "I can't join that community, Dani. I'm not good enough. I didn't want to be embarrassed!"

"You won't be," Miles said. He took the envelope from Mary and passed it to Oliver.

The teen stared at them for a moment, then picked at the end of the ribbon to pull it loose. He worked the letter free from the envelope. As he read, tears spilled from his eyes. He placed the letter on the table and buried his face in his palms.

Dani's eyes widened; this was not the reaction she'd expected. She glanced at Mary, who shrugged. Miles, however, smiled and knelt next to his son's chair.

"It's exciting, isn't it? Kinda overwhelming right now, yeah?" Miles said.

Oliver nodded.

Dani sighed with relief. Tears of joy—something she'd never been too familiar with.

Oliver put his arms around his father, and Miles hugged him tightly.

"I'm proud of you. Mom would be proud of you, too."

"All right," Hattie said gruffly. "Enough waterworks, kid. You have another gift."

Oliver released his father and wiped at his face. "I do?"

"He does?" Dani asked.

"Yep. I've got your transport lined up to take you down to Portland. You have lodging and meals taken care of too," Hattie said.

Miles winced.

"*Not* a brothel," Hattie said to Miles.

"Oh, good," Miles said. "Well, I mean—"

"Just shut up," Hattie said.

Miles nodded. "Yes, ma'am."

Oliver left his chair and made his rounds hugging every-one. He neared Dani to hug her last but stopped when the door opened.

Colonel Houston and four MPs entered the kitchen. The MPs

were armed and had their weapons raised. Three had plasma pistols; one had a tranquilizer pistol ready.

Brody growled, and one of the MPs immediately fired a tranq bolt into the dog's shoulder. He stumbled a few steps before collapsing to the floor, asleep.

"Hey!" Oliver moved to go to Brody, but Dani kept him with her. Brody would be fine.

"What the fuck is this?" Hattie said.

Dani turned to place herself between the MPs and Oliver. She noticed that as she moved, Hattie had shifted closer to the table and slid the knife off, tucking her hand out of view.

"Because of the ongoing crisis with the war, I have no choice but to invoke the age law," Houston said. "It's time for Oliver to enter the service with the CNA."

"You can't!" Dani said.

Miles shook his head. "He's only sixteen, Colonel."

"Seventeen, Major. I researched his birth records. They were tampered with to change his birth year to make him younger. Given what happened to your sister, I can understand your attempt to keep him out of the ground troops a bit longer."

Dani was stunned for a moment; Miles had never mentioned that he had a sister.

"No! He's *sixteen*," Miles said, trembling.

Houston gave him a condescending smile. "I know when you're lying, Miles."

"You're not taking him, Catherine," Hattie said.

"As the commanding officer of the Bangor barracks, I can and will."

Miles shook his head. "Colonel Houston, *please.*"

"The Commonwealth needs fine young men like Oliver, Major Jackman. You understand."

Oliver gasped and recoiled from the MP reaching around Dani to take him. Dani grabbed the officer's wrist, twisted it, and placed him in a shoulder lock. The officer yelped with pain, and a second MP swung the butt of his rifle at her head. Dani ducked, and Miles slammed his body into the officer who had tried to strike her. The remaining two MPs shifted their aim, unsure who to point their weapons at. The confusion was going to get someone killed, and Dani didn't want anyone in the room dead except for Catherine.

Mary moved to rush Oliver out of the room through the other door, but two more MPs arrived and blocked them. It took three MPs to restrain Miles while a pair had Dani pinned with her chest against the wall. Hattie was in motion after Houston. An MP fired on her, and she stumbled with a plasma shot to her side, dropping the knife. A second shot caught her in the chest, and she collapsed.

Mary snatched a towel off the counter and slid to her knees next to Hattie while Dani watched in horror. Oliver joined Mary and could only stare at Hattie with wide eyes.

"Not really necessary, Sergeant," Houston said to the MP who had shot Hattie. "Cuff these two," she added, waving her hand at Dani and Miles.

"Colonel, please don't do this," Miles said.

The MPs placed the I-cuff on him, and once it was activated, he could move only his lower limbs.

Mary futilely held the towel against Hattie's chest wound. The towel was soaked, and blood pooled around the older woman's body.

"Take the boy," Houston said.

An MP grabbed Oliver by the upper arm and hauled him up from the floor. Mary kept one hand on the towel and reached for Oliver with her other one. The MP smacked his rifle stock into her wrist. She cried out and pulled her hand back, tucking her injured wrist against her body to splint it.

Dani twisted free from her captors and lunged at Houston.

She winced when the tranq dart pierced her back. Dani swung her fist at Catherine's head, but her strike fell short as she stumbled. The tranquilizer prevented her muscles from doing what she wanted, and Dani sank to the floor on her hands and knees.

Houston knelt to face her.

"I'll fucking kill you," Dani said, though her arms and legs quivered with spreading weakness.

"Heard that one before," Houston said.

Dani's limbs crumpled, and her cheek struck the cold floor. Houston rose. "Take her."

Hands grasped Dani's arms to drag her out of the room. The last thing she saw was Hattie's final breath and Mary's helplessness to do anything for her friends.

CHAPTER
11

The agonizing throb in Mary's wrist blurred her vision. She'd felt the *pop* when at least one of the bones in her wrist cracked during its collision with the MP's rifle. Additional shouts outside and around the brothel erupted. Something crashed to floor in the pub, and there was more shouting and a scream.

Mary stared at the blood-soaked towel in her hand and realized how ridiculous it had been for her to grab it in the first place. Hattie would regen, and Mary had delayed that by slowing the bleeding and prolonging her life in her damaged body. She needed Hattie's help *now* to stop Houston.

The pub's barkeep, Jakob, entered. He had a cut on his forehead and a lump under his left eye. "Where's Aunt Hattie?"

Mary stood and strode over to the man, blocking him from entering the kitchen another inch. "Out!" She pointed back to where he'd entered. She realized she still had the towel and threw it down. Her bloodied hands looked rather macabre, even to her, but she still used her good hand for gesturing. "Get the fuck out!" Mary said, grabbing his shirt at the shoulder and turning him to shove him out of the room. Hattie would not want anyone gawking at her during regen, especially since only a handful of people in the state knew she'd lied about being human.

"What's happening? Why is the CNA taking people?" Jakob stumbled with Mary's shove. "Are you hurt? Whose blood is that?"

Mary followed him out, and once she had the door closed, she stopped and leaned against the frame a little for extra support. With everything that had happened and the pounding in her wrist, her legs weren't as strong as they could be.

She took a deep breath to refocus her thoughts. "Jakob, who else did they take?"

"Andy, Elise, and Janelle."

Mary nodded, though she thought, *Fuck!* Elise was eighteen, Janelle was twenty, and Andy was twenty-two—Houston had targeted Bangor's youth. Andy was a general maintenance helper at the pub and brothel, doing minor repairs. Elise was a math wizard and Hattie's bookkeeper-in-training for both businesses, and Janelle was one of the pub cooks and an occasional brothel worker when she wanted some extra cash. And they'd all just been stolen, Oliver included.

The CNA in Bangor had never taken civilians, even those seventeen or older, to be forced into service as ground troops. The age law was really only enforced on existing CNA troops' children. Other cities, including Portland when Houston ran it back when Miles was a lieutenant, were infamous for "recruiting" civilians into the CNA by means of capture and hauling them off. The Commonwealth-Brigand partnership that began in Bangor a few years ago had ended the practice.

Today, everything had changed. Houston had crossed a line. The colonel's personal war with Dani had made her an instant enemy against all Mainers. Mary wondered if Houston actually realized the magnitude of her fuck-up. *Probably not.*

Rowan had made the mistake of kidnapping Oliver to

provoke Dani into coming to Boston, which she had, and the Wardens had lost Boston soon after.

"She did this on purpose," Mary muttered, rubbing her forehead.

"What?"

Mary looked up, realizing Jakob was still there. She lowered her hand, gave Jakob his orders, sent him away, then returned to Hattie's side. Her body had just begun its blue glow, and Mary knelt next to her.

The blue light luminesced from Hattie's skin, and the holes in her chest and side sealed themselves. The older woman's features smoothed as wrinkles vanished, leaving her with soft, brown skin. Her gray hair turned black, and she drew in her first breath. Mary had seen only one regen up close, Dani's, and when Dani woke, she was terrified and didn't know anyone.

Hattie blinked a few times before fully opening her eyes. She glanced at Mary, then raised her hand, examining the youth now present in her fingers and skin. "Goddammit," she said, and sat up. "Catherine." Hattie shook her head. "Fucking Catherine."

"Do you need anything? Or can I do anything? Do you need to rest?"

Hattie shot her a glare that made Mary back away a little.

"I don't turn into a basket case when I regen, Mary. I'm *not* Dani."

"I know."

"You and that damn towel. I couldn't get enough air to tell you to stop trying to save me. Such a human thing to do."

"Fuck you! I *am* human." Mary stood. She went to the sink to wash the blood off her hands. "I was trying to help in the only way I knew how." She heard Hattie's movement as she rose from the floor. "Houston also took Andy, Janelle, and Elise. I don't know how many others. I sent Jakob to retrieve the council members."

"Good."

Mary felt a hand on her back while she continued to rinse her hands, careful to not jar her injured wrist. Hattie's gesture was the only kind of apology she was going to get from her, and she was fine with that. "Houston will lock down the base. She knows we'll come after our people, so she'll shut it down to Brigands."

"What else?" Hattie asked.

Mary glanced at her. Blood covered Hattie's shirt and the side of her trousers. She also had blood on her arms from lying in the pool of it on the floor. "She arrested Miles and Dani, though they tranqed Dani first. Why didn't Houston arrest you? You went after her with a knife. She had to know you were an Echo."

Hattie nodded and folded her arms across her chest as if wearing her own blood all over her and plasma holes in her clothing was as natural as her own skin attached to her frame. "She knew what I was. She's taunting me—she's taunting us all. Catherine's action was a deliberate move to take Oliver from us." She shook her head. "We can't go against her alone. We need the council, and I'll handle them. Contact Santi." She glanced at Mary's wrist. "You gonna deal with that?"

"Yeah. I'll take care of this soon." Mary headed for the door. She paused. "Oliver doesn't know you're an Echo. I saw his face. As far as he knows, you're dead."

"Can't fix that now," Hattie said, and started out the back door.

"You're not going to change?"

"Nah. It'll add to the shock value for the council. They need to see what Catherine has done."

Mary had to agree with the shock value part. Hattie walking down the street as a resurrected corpse drenched in blood would create a massive stir, and that's exactly what they needed to go after Houston. She kept her wrist close to her body as she started down the cellar stairs. Mary accessed the hidden room behind the wall that held the best communication equipment.

She keyed in the codes to activate the comm to General Ramos. He hadn't sent any messages since the day he'd left for Canada, and there still weren't any new ones. Mary entered the pass phrase to let him know there was an emergency. While she waited, she grabbed a med kit from one of the shelves. She placed the kit on the table and opened it with one hand. She checked for a response. Nothing.

Mary removed the larger healing pen from the kit, turned it on, and passed it over the lump on her wrist. The bone's accelerated healing caused her to gasp. The healing process was easier to bear when drugged up. Beads of sweat formed on her face, and then the nausea started. She'd pass out if she wasn't careful. Mary slid to the floor to finish repairing her wrist. Once it was complete, she wiped her face.

She flexed her wrist a few times, noting residual stiffness. "Good enough," she said, and stood. "C'mon, Santi. Talk to me." Mary repackaged the kit and left it on the table. Still nothing. "Shit."

She kept the link to Ramos open and created a new one. Kelsey responded immediately, so she put him on audio.

"Mary! What the hell is happening?"

Cameron's voice joined in. "We saw MPs unload Miles out of a transport. Dani too, but she was unconscious. I couldn't tell if she was wounded."

"We tried to get to them, but we were ordered back at gunpoint," Kelsey said.

Mary nodded, though they couldn't see her. "Dani was tranqed; she'll be fine—well, until she wakes up. Oliver. Have you seen him?"

"No, but a second transport that came in with the first one

kept going—straight to the airfield where a helo was waiting," Kelsey said. "Two MPs herded four people into the helo. We couldn't see who they had."

"Four? You're sure it was four?" Mary glanced back at the message to Ramos. Still no reply.

"Yeah," Cameron said.

"Cam, at the party, you tried to say something to Miles about Santi, but he told you to wait. What was it?" Mary asked.

"Colonel Houston issued an internal statement this morning. General Ramos is listed as MIA."

"Fuck," Mary said.

"Anton is pulling together everything he can find for where Ramos was going and last pings off his comm," Cameron said. "He thinks he can use topographic maps to create a decent guess of which way his team would've hiked in."

"Oh, I love that kid. You guys think you can slip off the base?"

"Not a chance," Kelsey said.

"I'll come to you as soon as I can. Aunt Hattie's convening the council now. Use this comm, not my personal one, if you get anything new." She ended the link and headed for the base, but guards turned her around a hundred yards from the entrance. She considered sneaking in, but if caught, she wouldn't be able to help anyone from a cell.

Mary returned to town and raced up the steps to the old courthouse. This was the same place where the Brigand council had met with Houston and other CNA leaders to create the original partnership. They had spent days working out the details, and Houston had unraveled everything in minutes.

"You're not part of the council," a man standing next to the door to the meeting room said.

Mary brushed past him and entered anyway. All eyes turned to her.

"What have you got?" Hattie asked.

CHAPTER
12

Oliver forced himself to take deep breaths as the transport truck continued past the one that had stopped. His two friends at the party were a little older than him, and they weren't in the truck. Oliver recognized Andy, Elise, and Janelle from Aunt Hattie's. *Aunt Hattie.* His eyes burned with tears to remember her dying in her own home. He took another deep breath to keep himself from unraveling. *Dani says panicking is death. Don't panic.*

The other three people in the transport were older than him, and they were all—Oliver included—connected to Aunt Hattie. He was only sixteen. Colonel Houston had lied, which meant the colonel had made this a deliberate attack on Aunt Hattie. *Why?*

He heard the unmistakable thump of helicopter blades and hoped his truck wasn't headed toward it. As the sound grew louder, his hopes sank. Not only was the colonel taking him away from his father, but she was *flying* him away. *Dad will come for me. Dani will too—if they can find me.* The truck came to a stop, and the MPs ordered them out. Once on the ground, Oliver put his hands up to shield his face from the wind whipped by the helicopter, but the MP grabbed his arm, pulling him along.

The noise was deafening, and he opened his eyes when he bumped into someone else. He looked up and recognized his father's friend Javi. The older man, who had fought with the CNA and Brigands at both Portland and Boston, looked down at him.

"I'll put him in," Javi said to the MP. The MP nodded and stepped aside. "In you go, son."

Oliver climbed in, followed by Javi. He thought Javi might go with them, but instead he strapped Oliver into his seat between Elise and Janelle. Andy sat on the other side of Janelle.

"Why is this happening?" Oliver asked.

"Keep your head down, do as you're told, and don't create a fuss," Javi said. He continued when Oliver tried to speak again. "Anton and I will do everything we can to help you, your father, and Dani from this side, but you must *not* draw attention to yourself. Understand?"

Oliver nodded, though he didn't really understand anything that was happening.

Javi finished adjusting Oliver's straps and left the helo. Oliver couldn't prevent the tears that spilled from his eyes to see the man leave. The hatch slid closed, and the helicopter blades spun faster. As the helo lifted from the ground, he rocked a little to the side. Elise gasped and wept silently. Oliver took her hand and glanced at Janelle and Andy. Both were visibly shaken.

Inside the helo, it was too loud for them to talk without yelling, and Oliver wasn't really sure what they should discuss anyway. *Hello, nice to see you're having a shit day too.*

The sarcastic dialogue inside his head didn't help his mood, so he tried to see where they were going. He twisted in his seat a little, earning a concerned look from Elise. Oliver had enough of a view through the glass to see the coastline—land on the left, ocean on the right. They were headed north.

He tried to see more, but Elise squeezed his hand. When he

turned, she was already leaning in close enough to him to have her mouth near his ear.

"What can you see?" she asked. She turned her head so he could speak directly into her ear.

"We're going north. New Brunswick, I guess. Maybe Nova Scotia."

"What?" Janelle asked, leaning toward him.

Oliver repeated his message, and she relayed it to Andy. *Okay. Not the most efficient way to talk, but having something to do besides crap myself makes me feel a little better.* He half smiled at his own joke. He'd spent enough time with Anton in the computer labs, digitally enhancing maps and working on the combat simulations, to know about the northeast Canadian Commonwealth ground-troop camps.

Oliver went through a mental checklist of each person with him in the helo. Andy did maintenance and light carpentry work for Aunt Hattie—*Oh. Aunt Hattie. I wonder if I should tell them the CNA killed her?* His eyes began to burn again. *Maybe not.* He went back to his list. Elise helped keep the business books in order and was rumored to be scary good with numbers. Janelle worked in the pub as a cook and sometimes on her back in the brothel.

There had to be a way for them to stay together and not have to do any real fighting. He just needed to figure out how to make it happen. He stayed lost in his thoughts and trying to not be swallowed by fear. Elise released his hand to wipe at a few new tears, then placed her hand back in his. He didn't mind.

He kept a watch on the scenery, too. The helicopter banked left to swing inland and eventually landed.

"New Brunswick," Oliver said once the blades slowed and the noise lessened enough for him to speak almost normally.

"How do you know?" Andy asked.

"We went inland instead of out to sea."

"Oh."

The helo door slid open and they were ordered out. They unfastened their seat straps and filed out to be ushered toward a group of single-level buildings with metal roofs lined in a row. Oliver's head swiveled, and he tried to absorb as many details as he could.

A group of twenty or so recruits marched by. Their faces were hardened as they carried their rifles and never looked at the new arrivals. Oliver suppressed the desire to shudder. He didn't want to be like them. He wasn't supposed to be here. This was all a mistake.

He took a long, slow breath.

They moved together in a clump instead of a line, and Oliver noticed Andy's rising panic, his hand movements nervous and a wide-eyed gaze at everything and nothing. Oliver touched his arm. "Take big, deep breaths, Andy. If you try to run, they will just tranq you."

Andy stared at him for a moment, then nodded.

They were brought to one of the buildings and given training fatigues, helmet, boots, and toiletries. Oliver struggled to balance everything in his arms when they were herded back out. They arrived at one of the buildings with an *F* on it. F *for fucking nightmare*, he thought.

Inside, twelve recruits in their late teens and early-twenties watched them enter.

"Change into your uniforms and put your other things away," their escort said, and then left.

Oliver stared at the four empty bunks and couldn't suppress a shudder this time.

"These four didn't sign up," an older girl said. She strode forward, frowned, and eyed Oliver and the others. "Where you from?"

No one else offered an answer, so Oliver spoke up. "Bangor."

"Bangor? They stopped stealing civilians decades ago. You're lying."

"Colonel Houston changed the rules."

"Bullshit."

"Believe what you want," Oliver said, disgusted. He moved around the girl to place his things on one of the bunks. "Where are we supposed to change?"

"Heads are in the back," the girl said, and jerked her thumb over her shoulder.

Oliver took one of his uniforms and the boots and carried them in the direction the girl had indicated. The toilet stalls had no doors. There wasn't a private place for him to change, and this only irritated him more. Angered by everything today, he stripped out of his clothes and changed into the CNA-issue fatigues. After he had his boots laced, he straightened and looked at his civilian clothes on the floor.

He was actually *in* the CNA now—a place both his father and Dani had promised he'd never end up. And Aunt Hattie was dead, covered with her own blood. Oliver pinched his eyes closed, buried his face in his palms, and wept as silently as he could.

His shoulders shook with sobs that he fought to keep quiet. He wasn't sure how much time passed, but he heard the others arrive to change also. He grabbed some tissue near a toilet and blew his nose. He avoided any kind of eye contact and went to a sink while the others changed. He splashed water on his face and ran his fingers through his hair, realizing he'd seen Dani do this same thing before when she struggled to wake up. Right now, he just needed to think. He tried to remember everything his dad had told him about his time in boot camp. Oliver had never liked the stories, but now he wished he'd paid closer attention.

He noticed Andy, standing motionless, gazing down at the

fatigues hanging from his lean frame. Andy's last name wasn't on his shirt, but Oliver's uniform already had his last name on it. "She planned this," he whispered. "Oh, shit, she *planned* this!"

"What?" Andy asked.

"Oh. Nothing," Oliver said. Colonel Houston had already known in advance that she was going to take him from his father—long enough to get his name patches made in New Brunswick. But she had taken the others too. *Why?*

Neither Elise nor Janelle's uniform had name patches. *Shit. Shit. Shit.* He needed to get a message back to his father, but to do that he needed access to comm equipment. He already had training with Anton on many of the advanced CNA electronics, and *that* was going to be his ticket out of combat. Oliver smiled for the first time.

"You're smiling?" Elise asked. "Our lives are fucked, and you're smiling." She frowned and shook her head.

"I know how we can stay together and avoid the front lines," Oliver said.

CHAPTER

13

Miles paused his pacing long enough to glance at Dani when she stirred. They'd been in the cell for over twenty-four hours, and she'd woken only long enough to stagger to the toilet and back to the bunk, where she collapsed again. It had been Dani's idea to adjust the tranquilizer serum to maximize the impacts on the Wardens, but Wardens were Echoes, so the sedative also flattened her. She rolled to her side and slid her feet to the floor. She leaned forward, resting her elbows on her knees, and dropped her head into her hands.

"How are you feeling?" he asked, his pacing resumed.

"Shitty."

She groaned when she stood. She used the tiny sink next to the toilet to splash water on her face and rinse her mouth. She ran her wet fingers through her hair and sighed.

"Oliver is actually sixteen, right?" Dani asked.

Miles spun to face her. "Of course he is!"

"Okay," Dani said, raising her hands in surrender to his angry outburst. "Just making sure."

He stalked closer to her, brow furrowed. "I'm not the one in this relationship who breaks the law."

"Bullshit. You defied orders to go after Oliver when he was

in Boston. Don't act like you've never done anything wrong before."

"Oh, I've made mistakes," he said, giving her a lingering glare before turning his back to her.

"Christ, Miles, what the hell is that supposed to mean?"

Everything had turned into an absolute nightmare. Ollie was supposed to have an amazing birthday, and he had until Houston showed up. Cameron had tried to tell him something about Ramos at the party, but Miles had told him to wait until later. He now wished he knew whatever that piece of information was.

Neither Aunt Hattie nor Mary had been by yet. Hattie would have regened after the fatal shot to her chest, but Miles had seen his son's face. He was the only one in the room who believed Hattie was a human and dead forever. Aunt Hattie had a soft spot for Ollie, and he would be crushed, thinking she had died. His son's birthday would be forever marred by this.

"Miles? Miles!"

He closed his eyes, desperate to remain in control of his anger, but every second without any information on his son made it more difficult. He didn't want to lash out at Dani, but Christ, she was pushing him.

"Please talk to me."

He opened his eyes and turned to face her. "What?"

"Do you have any information on Oliver? Has Catherine been by?"

"*Why* did you have to provoke her?"

"*Me?*" Dani touched her chest. "You're blaming this on me?"

Everyone seemed at fault. Miles had agreed to go with Ramos and leave his service under Colonel Houston. Sure, the general outranked her, but Ramos had given Miles the choice, and he had taken it. Houston had lied about Ollie's birth records being altered. But Aunt Hattie and Dani had a thing for agitating Houston every chance they got. He couldn't understand why the colonel had gone after his son, though.

The only goal Miles had ever had in his life was to keep his son out of the war, and yesterday his former friend and commanding officer had taken Ollie from him. Houston had changed. She'd put a rifle in Ollie's hands and throw him into the fighting, and Miles was helpless to do anything about it. His nerves were beyond frayed, and he was stuck in a cell with Dani, who wouldn't shut up now that she was awake.

"This is one of her manipulation games, Miles."

"Game? You think this is a fucking game?"

"In her mind it is."

"My son is gone!"

"I'm well aware. Stop taking this out on me." She took a deep breath and lowered her volume. "Catherine manipulates everyone. We're all pawns to her in one way or another, and that includes Oliver. She wants something; we just have to figure out what it is."

"Shut up."

"What?"

The last of his patience evaporated. "*Shut up!* Stop fucking talking, Dani. Shut the fuck up!"

She winced at his outburst and turned away from him.

At the moment, he didn't care that he'd hurt her. He needed to think, and she was making him nuts.

Minutes passed in silence until the door at the end of the corridor opened. Six armed MPs approached the cell and opened it. One held out a pair of small silver bars—inactive immobilization cuffs. "Major Jackman, will you or Dani need to wear these?" one of the officers asked.

"No." Miles glanced at Dani. "Correct?"

"Oh. I can speak now?"

"Just answer the goddamn question."

"No," she said to the MP.

He and Dani entered the corridor, flanked by a pair of MPs and followed by the remaining four. Six armed officers to escort two unarmed prisoners was absurd, but Miles couldn't say anything since he was one of the prisoners. The MPs placed them in an empty room and sealed the door. Four walls, no windows, and no seating. Miles noticed a camera in the corner where the walls met the ceiling.

Dani spotted the camera too. She raised her arm and extended her middle finger.

"Still trying to piss her off, as if you haven't done enough already," Miles said.

"Fuck you, too, Miles." Dani lowered her arm.

They paced the room without speaking or getting too close to each other. He figured at least an hour had passed by the time the door's lock released and Houston entered with the same six MPs who had brought them to the room.

Miles half expected Dani to lunge at Houston despite the guards—hell, Miles even considered doing it himself—but the guards were ready to shoot them, and not with tranq pistols.

"Colonel, I swear on my life I didn't alter Ollie's birth records. Please tell me where he is."

"New Brunswick. He and the others started basic training this morning," Houston said.

The news shook Miles to his core. He suddenly couldn't breathe, and his mind refused to accept that his son was part of the CNA. He leaned forward to place his hands on his knees.

"You know Oliver isn't army material," Dani said. "You don't want him and never have. That means you want something else."

Miles forced himself upright when the colonel approached, the MPs keeping their weapons on him.

"General Ramos is MIA," Houston said. "We lost contact with his team after he left Burlington."

"You want us to find him?" Miles said. "Let Ollie come back home." He glanced at Dani. "We'll find the general."

"Pick your team wisely, Major. You may not want her with you on this."

"Why not?"

"She's been lying to you for a while now."

His brow furrowed with confusion.

"She's been cheating on you."

Miles froze. Dani had already told him that she'd lied to Houston about having an affair with Mary. What caught him off guard was Houston deliberately using what she thought was the truth to influence him. Dani was right; Houston wanted something and was happy to manipulate anyone to get it. *We're just pawns.* He needed to figure out how to handle this, and fast, but he sucked at lying.

Dani groaned. "Oh, God. Not now, Catherine."

Thank you, Miles thought, directing his gratitude toward Dani. She was playing the liar-caught-in-the-act role, which meant he needed to play the lover-just-finding-out-she's-cheating role. He figured looking shocked and angry shouldn't be too hard to pull off since he'd been bouncing between the two emotions for more than a day—except he and Dani had been at each other's throats and now they needed to be a team against Houston.

Dani turned to him. "Miles—"

"I don't want to hear one goddamn word out of you," Miles said. He gave his full attention to Houston for fear that if he kept looking at Dani, he'd lose his resolve to try to shift the manipulation game against the colonel. "You want me to go in to retrieve General Ramos, and you'll remove my son from the CNA ground troops?"

"Once you've returned with the general, yes."

Can't be that easy.

"Another thing," Houston began.

Ah, here it is.

"Request a transfer from Ramos back to my command. I need you on *this* side of the war, Miles. Not the diplomacy crap."

"Done." He was digging his own grave by agreeing, but if it meant Ollie's safety, so be it.

"Let me know who you want on your team. No Brigands."

Christ. I can't leave Dani behind. Houston might kill her. "I need Brigands, Colonel. Dani and Mary are the two best saboteurs I've ever seen."

"Rethink that request, Major. Mary is the one Dani's been fucking behind your back."

Miles winced and rubbed his palms over his face. It was the shock of seeing Houston's manipulative tactics in action. He felt a sudden surge of hatred for the woman, and he couldn't keep the expression off his face. The colonel misinterpreted it though.

"Dani will get you killed in the field," Houston said.

He paced while he tried to figure out what to do. *Shit. Dani and Mary are both in danger if they stay here.* Miles stopped pacing. He shook his head and faced Houston. "I need them both with me, Colonel. They can sneak into places in ways Commonwealth troops can't."

Houston shrugged. "You're making a mistake, but it's your life."

He decided to push his luck. "I need Kels, Cam, and Dresden too."

"Major Cameron can go, because if he dies, he's not one of my CNA soldiers that's gone. He'll be England's loss."

"Kelsey and Dresden too."

"Kelsey only. Dresden stays. That gives you a five-person team. Take it or leave it."

"I'll submit the transfer request today, and Ollie doesn't progress out of basic training."

Houston nodded. "I'll keep him where he is. Once you're back with Ramos, Oliver is out of the CNA and shipped back to Bangor."

"Thank you," Miles said, furious to have to thank this woman who was holding his son hostage in exchange for a mission that would probably get him and his team killed.

"I'll send you every piece of intel we gave to General Ramos before he left," Houston said. She turned to leave and paused to address one of the MPs. "They're free to go. Escort them out, and continue to escort Dani off the base entirely."

"Yes, Colonel," the MP said.

Miles finally turned to Dani. "Find Mary and pack your gear. I'll pick you up from Aunt Hattie's," he said, and left the room without waiting for her response. He was still angry with her from before, and he also needed to keep up the act of a betrayed lover in front of the MPs.

CHAPTER
14

n Hattie's hidden bunker below her brothel, Dani examined the gear laid out on the table in front of her one last time before she started placing items into her pack. Mary had already finished packing, and waited for her by examining the maps and other data sent over from Houston. Hattie reviewed the data with Mary while Brody napped on a blanket on the floor. Dani's prep and organization of her gear was hindered by her inability to concentrate.

Once she had the last of her gear packed, Dani joined the women at the map on the wall.

"Don't bother studying that intel," Dani said. "It's a trap."

"How do you know?" Mary asked.

"Because Houston willingly coughed it up. I think she sent Santi into a hornet's nest of Wardens on purpose."

"To kill him? You're not serious."

"From the woman who just lied and kidnapped Oliver to fuck with us? She's completely capable of murdering a general who's interfering with her plans."

"Dani's right," Hattie said. "You'll need to be extra careful in the field—more so than usual."

Dani stared at Hattie for a moment. Her new, younger

appearance still caught her off guard; it would take her time to get used to it since Dani had known only the older-looking, grumpy version. Now she had to adjust to the younger-looking, grumpy version.

"The council can't go after Houston head-on," Hattie said. "Sure, we have enough explosives and weapons to obliterate the Bangor base, but we don't want to be the ones retaliating with violence. Instead, I've reached out to the CNA leadership in Boston. I leave tonight to go down there. I'm taking the lab data and some other dirt I have on Catherine with me."

"Wait," Dani said. "We destroyed the lab and the data, did we not?"

"All names and data on participants and donors were scrubbed. I kept enough evidence about the experiments in case I needed it later. It's later. I want to take her down from within the CNA and not by blowing her up."

Mary shrugged. "Blowing her up sounds great to me."

"Me too," Dani said.

"Which is exactly why the two of you will never be on the council for this town."

"You have to take Brody with you," Dani said, and the dog's head came up at the mention of his name.

Hattie shook her head. "Not a chance."

"Mary and I will be gone. Miles will be with us, and Oliver is wherever Catherine is hiding him. You've lost other staff here with her stunt. Take him with you."

"Damn mutt," Hattie said, and rolled her eyes. "Fine."

"Thank you, Hattie," Dani said. She sighed and returned to the map area between Burlington and Montreal. "Miles was foolish to agree to Catherine's terms so quickly. She's lying; I know she is. She won't let Oliver go now that she knows what kind of leverage she has against Miles."

"No, she won't," Hattie said.

"We have no choice but to hurry and find General Ramos," Mary said. "And hope this doesn't get us all killed."

"If he's still alive, and—" One of Hattie's panels beeped. When she looked at it, she smiled. "Anton is one sneaky little bastard." She looked up at Dani and Mary. "Turns out he hates Catherine as much as we do."

"What did he send you?" Dani asked.

"Oliver's exact location and the non-altered data from Ramos and his team's last known location," Hattie said. "The data pings she sent us weren't completely accurate. She's got some bullshit report about his exact location requiring top-level clearance because of his rank."

"So a bottom feeder like Anton can get around that clearance?" Dani said, and snorted a laugh. "He may wear a CNA uniform, but he's a Brigand at heart."

Hattie transferred the data from her panel to a palm-sized one, then tossed the smaller unit to Dani. She caught it and scanned the information.

The switch to the fake wall activated, and the women turned to see Miles opening the entry to the hidden room. Brody hopped up from his bed to greet Miles.

He glanced at the table with the two packs. When his gaze fell on Hattie, he paused while rubbing the top of Brody's head.

"Yeah, get the staring over now," Hattie said.

"I'm sorry, Aunt Hattie, it's just—well, I know it's you, but, it's not …"

"You'll get used to it probably before I will," she said, and laughed.

Dani noticed that Hattie's cackling laughter still sounded the same, as did her often harsh tone. A younger body hadn't changed those traits. She almost smiled, except Miles's gaze had turned to her, and the tension and anger she'd felt when in the cell with him returned. She hadn't forgotten his bitter words to her.

"We need to go," Miles said. "Cam and Kels are upstairs."

Dani grabbed her pack and slung it over her shoulder. Brody raced ahead of her up the stairs, and she followed him up. From behind her she heard Mary grumbling. "God, I hope the entire trip won't be like this."

Dani didn't hear a response from Miles. *Yep. Probably going to be a shitty trip.* Another thought struck her, so when she reached the top of the stairs from the cellar, she stepped aside to let Miles pass.

"I'll catch up in a sec," she said.

He continued walking without responding.

"Hattie," Dani said, "since there's a good chance we're getting screwed on this, you know you'll need to look out for yourself, right?"

"What? You mean Catherine's MP shooting two fucking holes through my body wasn't enough of an indicator that my life is at risk?" Hattie asked.

Dani marveled at the heaps of sarcasm only Hattie could produce. "Okay," Dani said, waving her hand dismissively. "Just making sure."

They arrived in the kitchen and Miles was already outside, pacing.

"Oh, this is gonna be fun," Dani said with a glance out the window.

"You two need to work this shit out now," Mary said.

"Yeah. I'll talk to him." *If he'll talk to me.*

"Sounds like a blast," Hattie said. "I won't tell you to be safe because you won't, but I would like you both to come back in one piece. Or mostly one piece. That's fine too."

That was Hattie's version of "I love you." Dani grinned. "We'll do our best." She knelt, and Brody went to her. She scratched his ears and kissed the top of his broad head. "See ya, big guy," she said. When she and Mary stepped outside, Miles looked at them briefly before leading the way to the transport truck.

Mary quickened her pace. "I'll drive. Kels, you ride shotgun. Cam, take the roof."

Mary was arranging everyone to force Dani and Miles to be in the rear seat together. This was not going to work. Dani caught up to Miles and touched his arm before he climbed into the truck. He stopped but didn't turn to face her.

"I know we're both on edge about Oliver and what Catherine has done," Dani said, careful to keep her tone soft. "I'm sorry I yelled at you earlier, Miles. This mission has red flags all over it, but I don't care. I'll do whatever is needed for Oliver's sake. Please, can we just agree to work together for the sake of getting him back?"

He nodded and climbed into the truck.

Her anger flared again. *At least he could fucking speak to me!* She was *not* riding in the back with him. "Here," she said. When Miles looked at her, she tossed him the palm-sized panel Hattie had given her. "That has the info with Oliver's location and the accurate coordinates from Santi's last pings. Whatever Catherine gave you is inaccurate." She was on the same side as him, but he was too angry to see it.

He caught the device, and she thought his face softened just a little.

"Thanks," he said.

"You're welcome," she managed to say without biting his head off. Cameron arrived, and Dani stopped him before he entered the truck. "Cam, hold up. I'll take the gun on the roof. Ride with Miles and make sure he gets some sleep. Drug him if you must. I don't think he's slept since the night before the party."

"Sure. Anything else?"

"Are you aware that Catherine doesn't give a shit about you? If you die, you're England's loss, not hers."

"Oh, sure," he said with a shrug. "She just likes having me around for my wit and British ties."

"Your wit?" Dani said, and chuckled, glad to have a little tension leave her.

"Hey, that was Hattie in her new body I spotted through the window, yeah?"

Dani nodded.

Cameron whistled appreciatively. "I know she was married to Jace and was—is—your sister-in-law, but would you mind if I, you know …"

This made Dani laugh outright. "If you think you can handle Hattie, go for it. It's been nice knowing you, pal." She climbed into the truck and up into the hatch to access the roof and the gun mounted on it. The jarring ride to Vermont would leave her battered and bruised within the first hour of the trip, but she was determined to keep her distance from Miles until they both cooled off.

CHAPTER 15

Rowan had forgotten how much he loved and missed field work. Curtis's plan to be in the field under the guise of testing new weapons had worked brilliantly. Rowan was given a team of eleven people, including Curtis. He immediately split the teams and sent Curtis with one half while he kept the other half.

Curtis, of course, protested, but Rowan didn't care. Technically, his status was now below Curtis, but Curtis still respected Rowan's prior position as director of research and development. That had all been stripped as part of his sentence for killing Aubrey. By the time they reached the field, one of the three other teams the vice regent had already dispatched had been eliminated during a battle with CNA forces.

As soon as this was reported to Vice Regent Keran, the VR dispatched more reinforcements. Rowan appreciated Keran's swift, decisive actions—something Vice Regent Aubrey never had. No one missed her incompetence; they just couldn't openly thank Rowan for purging her from the ranks of Warden leadership. They did thank him by reducing his sentence, and then releasing him early to return to his family. Turning him loose in the field was Keran's way of putting one of his most effective weapons—Rowan—into direct play against the CNA.

Although the loss of the Wardens was terrible, they had solid proof that the Commonwealth was indeed lurking in the region. They had bodies in CNA fatigues to prove it; however, none of the corpses was General Ramos. Rowan communicated with the other Warden teams and organized a search grid so they could coordinate their efforts. Mines had been placed in several locations, so he was careful to note those for the other teams.

"Maintain your assigned search areas and report in only if you confirm contact," Rowan said. "Otherwise it's radio silence."

The teams acknowledged their orders, and Rowan silenced his comm.

"This isn't a mere field-testing assignment for our equipment," Yura said. "We're hunting Commonwealth." She was the only woman on his team, and she was smart, had seen lots of battle, and had been through four regens. He wished she'd been part of R&D when he was in Boston.

Rowan grinned and slipped his comm into his pocket. He liked Yura.

She grinned back at him. "Perfect."

"There's a CNA general out here somewhere. I want to find him first."

"Good luck beating me to him," she said, smirking, then left to join the rest of the team.

Oh, he liked her *a lot.*

The days they spent searching were slowed because his team needed to stop and make adjustments to some of their equipment. Curtis's team carried the newer weapons, and Rowan's team was more responsible for testing new tactical gear and armor. Rowan and his crew were armed, but they still operated under the R&D angle.

On the second day of hiking, Rowan took his knife to his boots to carve out an offending area pressing against his lower leg. Delgado hacked a seam apart on his armored vest to give him more maneuverability for his arms. Rowan didn't mind Delgado making his modification to his armor on the fly. The original vest design hadn't accounted for someone with Delgado's impressive musculature.

Orson played with heat signature sensors. He tinkered with the devices in the evenings when they stopped to rest. Orson was content to keep manipulating them, but Rowan's patience was gone.

"Is it not working properly?" Rowan asked one night.

"No, sir, but I think I can fix it."

"You've wasted enough time on it. Throw it in your pack and leave it there. Deal with it once you're back in the lab."

"I—" He caught Rowan's glare and changed his response. "Yes, sir."

Rowan didn't sleep much at night. His mind was a mix of thoughts, but the one that plagued him the most was wondering where Dani was in all this. Ramos was in the area, so Rowan figured Dani would turn up soon. Her ability to change tactics during attacks was something Rowan could have admired in anyone else but her. He just wanted her dead, and her talents be damned.

The next day, everything changed. Days of moving through the wooded areas around the border of Canada and the United States finally yielded them something solid. Webb and Ceci discovered an area with blood mixed in with leaf litter on the forest floor.

"Could just be where a deer that was injured fell," Webb said.

Rowan circled the area, examining the ground.

When Ceci tried to move closer, Yura held him back.

Rowan squatted and continued to just look at the ground. Yura joined him. She tilted her head and pointed.

"An animal wouldn't leave that path of disturbed leaves," Yura said. "They tried to cover their tracks but missed a few places."

Rowan picked a few leaves up and turned them in his hand. He tossed them aside and picked up a few more. "One of them is injured, for sure. There's too much blood here for a minor injury. The injured person has someone helping him, maybe more than one helper. It's hard to tell."

"Can't be more than three people involved, sir," Yura said. "There just isn't enough disturbance for there to be more … unless the others were a distance away from whatever happened here."

Rowan nodded.

"Should we notify the other teams?" Delgado asked.

Rowan stood. "Search the area first. See if we can determine anything else about how many people we're dealing with. One of them has a serious injury, so they can't be moving quickly or going very far on any given day. Once we have more intel, I'll contact Curtis and the other teams. I don't want to risk a signal intercept by the CNA without knowing more."

"Yes, sir," his team said.

"Yura," Rowan said, "coordinate the men for a detailed search of this immediate area."

"Yes, sir," she said.

Rowan squatted again and gazed back at the ground, wishing he knew for certain if the blood belonged to Ramos or not.

By the time his team had scoured the area, Rowan didn't

have any new information. He decided to hold off on contacting the other teams. He'd rather the Wardens continue to work a little blind than use the comm and be detected by the CNA.

"We'll stay here for the night," Rowan said.

His team began their prep to make camp, but Yura approached him.

"We're close," she said.

"I know."

"When I find him before you do, you buy me dinner when we're back."

Rowan turned to stare at her for a moment. "Deal. But you buy after I find him first."

She gave him a quick smile, then left to take the first watch.

He continued to watch her departure until he heard Delgado's heavy footsteps on the leaves. Rowan growled. "Delgado, learn how to move more quietly or I'll kill you myself."

The big man turned to him and sheepishly lowered his gaze. "Yes, sir."

Brigands. Rowan shook his head, irritated he hadn't thought of it before. The injured person they were hunting had at least one Brigand helping to conceal their tracks. That was the only explanation for why they hadn't found the remaining CNA troops yet. They'd lost the day, but tomorrow morning, they would change gears.

"Orson, get those sensors out and have them working by morning."

"Yes, sir."

CHAPTER 16

The ride to Vermont was as annoying as Dani had expected, and she was deliberate in her shift rotations on the roof-mounted gun, driving, or rest periods to avoid Miles. When they did finally arrive in Burlington, they took an extra day to rest and get more local intel from the CNA and Brigand forces in town. She and Miles didn't speak of anything outside of mission-related topics. The tension between them gnawed at her insides and didn't make mission planning any easier.

Miles stood with the group, a map spread on a table before them. "We leave at first light tomorrow, and the guide will take us to the same point where she parted ways with General Ramos's team. We'll hike the rest of the way to Warden territory, which will take us another four to five days, depending on the weather. I haven't told anyone here about the additional data we got from Anton."

"Why not?" Mary asked. "Other teams going up there could be in danger with Houston's deliberate misinformation."

Miles shook his head. "We can't confirm it's deliberate."

"Christ, Miles," Dani said, resisting the urge to physically shake some sense into him. "You've seen the discrepancies. We know it's rigged."

"There are discrepancies, but that's not unusual."

"He's right," Cameron said. "Commonwealths get their intel from different sources. Sometimes that data doesn't perfectly align."

"We didn't have issues with our Portland and Boston intel," Dani said.

Cameron shrugged. "Because you went down there and got it yourself."

Dani shook her head, disgusted. "She's lying. She sent Santi out to die with her altered data."

Cameron didn't need to, but he lowered his voice anyway. "You're accusing Colonel Houston of deliberately sending tampered intel to General Ramos?"

"Yes, Cam. That's exactly what I'm saying."

"Murder?"

"*Yes!*" Dani said, then brought her anger back under control.

"Dani ..." Miles said.

"She's stooped to kidnapping, right?" Dani said. "She came into Hattie's with armed MPs—only one of whom was decent enough to use a tranq pistol. Regen or not, Catherine didn't care that one of them shot Hattie. She's a goddamn monster, and Santi threatens her command in Maine. Catherine is crazy enough to resort to murder—even if it's a CNA general."

Mary spoke up. "Miles, I'm sorry Oliver is part of this mess, but Houston set you up, too. Santi specifically said he wanted you, Dani, and me to recon Montreal instead of using Houston's people. Did you see how pissed off that made her?"

Miles nodded, and Mary continued. "Santi is MIA, and she conveniently wants you to find him, knowing you'd take us with you. Now she has you, Dani, and me—sorry you're dragged into this too, Cam and Kels—out here to retrieve Santi with the same shit intel."

Dani appreciated Mary's input and agreement. "We threaten

her control of Bangor because we challenge her bullshit," Dani said. "She can just about do whatever she wants with us out of the way … especially if we're permanently out of the way."

Miles began pacing, and Dani watched him. *Use your head, man. You know this is the truth.*

"Hattie wants to take her down from within the CNA," Mary said. "We're still going after Santi, but we need to be careful and return with the *right* intel."

Miles stopped pacing and nodded. "Yes. We need the intel that proves she's guilty of treason, if we can get it. But she can manipulate records like she did with Ollie's birth records. She can weasel out of it."

"We still have Anton on our side," Mary said.

"So," Kelsey said, gesturing to himself and Cameron, "what are our roles in this?"

"Collateral damage," Dani said. They both scowled at her, and she shrugged. "It's true."

"I'm sorry, guys," Miles said. "I was trying to get a team together that I could trust. I tried to get Dres too, but Houston wouldn't let me have him. At the time, I didn't know how fucked up this was. I was desperate to get my son back. I'm sorry."

Cameron shrugged. "I'm not backing out, Miles."

"I'm not either," Kelsey said.

Miles nodded and sighed. "Thank you. We'll need—" His panel lying on the table blinked with an alert. He switched screens and read for a few seconds. He cursed under his breath and turned the panel around for the others to view it.

Dani leaned in first and scanned the message from Anton. It was an intercepted Warden transmission that included names and photos of Dani, Mary, Miles, and Ramos. "Goddammit." Dani walked away from the table and growled with frustration.

"Dani," Miles said. "You and Mary are going—"

She spun to face him. "What? Going back?"

"Yes."

She snorted. "Fuck you."

"Mary—" Miles said.

"Fuck you, Miles," she replied.

"*Please* just stay here then. Wait until we're back."

Dani ignored him and returned her attention to the maps. She used her finger to trace the route from the guide's drop-off point at the Canadian border up to Montreal. "This is the area we need to check first. It's where Catherine sent Santi and where Anton says there's a Warden-patrolled area."

"So right into the thick of the shit," Kelsey said.

Mary nodded. "Yeah."

"Sounds good," Cameron said.

Miles waved his arms to get their attention. "Is anyone listening to me? I *am* still the ranking officer here."

"Are you?" Dani asked. "Best fucking act like it and stop trying to break up your team before we even get started."

Miles glowered at her, but Dani didn't care. He was being an ass.

"Pack up and get some rest," Dani said to the others. "We leave early."

The others dispersed and Miles caught her arm when she tried to leave. She winced, given his tight grip. He released her and held his hands up to her in surrender.

"Sorry," he said. "I didn't mean to grab you that hard. Why are you fighting me on this?"

"You are *not* the only person who loves Oliver. You'll give everything to save him, and so will I. So will Mary. Don't you dare try to stop us again."

"This broadcast from the Wardens changes things. They're actively looking for us—not just humans and Echoes—*us*."

"And when has Rowan not been looking for us?"

"This is different, Dani."

"It doesn't change a goddamn thing. Santi for Oliver. Period."

"It's not that simple."

"*How* is it not that simple?"

Miles stared at the floor. Dani waited. He finally looked at her. "Telling you 'I'm sorry' isn't enough to fix the hurt I've caused you, but I am sorry."

Dani remained quiet. He wrung his hands, so he wasn't finished with whatever he wanted to say.

"My sister, Brianna, was four years younger than me," he said. "Our parents were CNA, and my father was killed in combat when she was an infant. Our mother was an MP but mostly served guard detail for warehouses. She didn't go into battle like my father had.

"When I turned seventeen, I enlisted—not that I had a choice, but I wanted to pretend it was my choice. My sister was devastated when I left, but she insisted that we'd be back together as soon as she turned seventeen too. I begged her to become a Brigand and avoid the war, but she wouldn't listen.

"She enlisted the day of her seventeenth birthday and breezed through basic training. It didn't matter that we were still getting our asses kicked by the Wardens; she *believed* the war would end in her lifetime. One week after completing basic, she was shipped to some outpost in California, where she was killed in a Warden ambush."

"Shit," Dani whispered.

"Bri's death broke my mother, and she killed herself."

Dani took his hand.

"If I lose Ollie, it will break me," he said, tears in his eyes. "Do you understand what I'm saying?"

She nodded.

"I panicked when Houston took him. I couldn't breathe or

think. All I could see in my mind was that stupid fucking CNA letter notifying me that Bri was dead." His voice cracked, and he wiped at the tears sliding down his face.

Dani's chest ached for Miles, and she didn't know what to say.

He cleared his throat and sniffled. "When I could finally think a little with Ollie gone, the anger took over. I uncorked decades of hatred for the Commonwealth on you. I realized what I was doing and had to stop speaking to you because I knew I would just lose it again, and that wasn't fair to you."

He released her hand and placed his palms on the sides of her head. "I am *so* sorry, Dani. I love you, and I'm apologizing for everything." He kissed her, then pulled her close.

Dani clung to him, torn between sadness for him, grief for Oliver, and happiness to have Miles back again. "Thank you for telling me about your sister. I've been an asshole. I didn't know you'd been through those horrible things." Dani released him and leaned back. "You need to understand that Oliver means the world to me too."

"I know. He and I weren't the only victims in this. I used to believe in Colonel Houston, and now …"

"This war has changed us all, Miles. The longer it goes on, the worse it gets."

"What do you mean?"

Dani's mouth went dry, and she released him. It was her turn to stall. "There's a rage inside me that is growing. Sometimes it's not so bad. Other times I'm afraid it will consume me. The incessant fighting has taken so many lives, and the Wardens won't stop. We can't keep fighting like this and expect to survive much longer. I'm terrified at the thought of losing you or Mary. That would break *me*."

"I won't stop, Dani, especially now that Ollie is in this living hell."

She shook her head and sighed. "I thought we had more time to end this war before …"

"We could not have known Houston would do this to him. If we had, I would've put a bullet through the colonel's head before she'd had time to create the lie that I'd changed his records."

"Santi for Oliver. We'll deal with Catherine later."

He nodded and turned his eyes to the panel still displaying the Warden notification. "At least Ollie is stuck in basic training for now."

Dani didn't respond to his remark; she didn't trust Catherine's word on anything. But she didn't want to take that shred of hope away from Miles. The situation they were in was terrible, but she and Miles had at least made peace after so much anger and bitterness spewed at each other. She turned her attention to the maps to learn the terrain where they were headed so she wouldn't need a physical map to get in or out.

CHAPTER

17

Oliver's plan to keep his group together was working well. The rumor that Elise was a numbers wizard was an understatement. She tutored him, Andy, and Janelle on all things mathematical.

"Why do we need this?" Andy asked during one of their after-hours sessions.

"They'll eventually train us on all sorts of things, including an academic portion," Oliver said. "When it's time to show that we can do more than just basic math—Elise excluded since she's a master—we'll have top marks for academic training. We'll still have to go through advanced infantry training, but after that, when it's time for Military Occupation Specialty school, we may have a chance to land a role where we aren't having to shoot or be shot at."

His task was to train the other three on technical equipment and computer systems. They didn't have actual machines to work with, but they would stay up at night huddled over pages where Oliver drew diagrams. They were forced to work on the floor in the toilet and shower area while the other recruits slept, but that didn't bother him if it meant keeping his friends away from the fighting.

"Learn the lingo so when we get a chance to actually touch one, it will be clear you know your way around the devices," Oliver said. "We have to show the CNA that we can offer them more than just being targets for the Wardens to shoot."

"Your friend Anton," Elise said. "That's how he's stayed away from the front lines?"

"Yeah. He hasn't held a gun since advanced infantry. He's never been in battle," Oliver said. He looked at Janelle and Andy. "Practice the math problems Elise gives you."

"You think knowledge is how we'll get out of shooting at other people?" Janelle asked.

Oliver shrugged. "It's worth trying."

"What about the rest of them?" Andy asked, nodding in the direction of the bunks where everyone else was sleeping. "We've made more friends."

"They willingly entered the CNA. We didn't. I don't know of a way to keep everyone out of the war," Oliver said.

They still had rigorous daily training, and Oliver continued to fail anything dealing with pistols or rifles. His general aversion to the weapons had him ranked at the bottom of his platoon for marksmanship, but he'd inadvertently caught the attention of one of his drill instructors while drawing during a little downtime when he could have been sleeping.

"Private Jackman!" Sotillo said.

Startled, Oliver sprang up from his chair and banged his knee on the small table, sending it toppling over. His papers fluttered to the ground, and his pencil rolled to a stop between his feet. Before he could respond, his DI spoke again.

"With me."

"Yes, Staff Sergeant!" Oliver said, but halted when Sotillo turned and barked at him again.

"Right the table first and bring your papers and pencil."

"Yes. Yes, sir, I mean, Staff Sergeant," Oliver babbled as he snatched his papers up. He shoved the pencil between his teeth and clutched the papers to his chest. Oliver used his foot to move the table back to an upright position, then scurried after his DI.

He didn't know where they were going; he just followed and noticed he was being led to a part of the training camp he'd never visited before. A knot formed in his gut the instant he read the sign over the door they approached: "Commanding Officer of the Weapons Training Battalion."

Oh! Oh, shit. Oliver's marksmanship scores had remained awful. There was no other reason for his DI to take him to the weapons training CO. His terror diminished a little when he spotted Elise already in the room. His fear was replaced with a bit of confusion until Captain Lundquist stood from behind his desk. Oliver figured vomiting on the CO's floor would be a bad thing. He tried to salute, but he'd drop his papers if he did. Instead, he contorted his upper body to manage some semblance of a salute that he knew made him look ridiculous.

The captain was a tall, lean man with piercing eyes. His command presence reminded Oliver of Colonel Houston—minus the treachery and lying.

"Private Jackman, I understand you and Private Torrent here," Lundquist said, nodding at Elise, "have been training your friends after hours."

Oliver figured trying to explain anything would just make matters worse. He scrunched his shoulders to reach the pencil with his fingers and pull it from his mouth. "Yes, sir."

"Although their technical and academic scores have been better than most, it's clear they do not possess the aptitude for technology that you do or the aptitude for mathematics that Private Torrent does."

Oliver wasn't sure what to say, so he remained silent.

"Show him the papers, Private," Sotillo said.

"Yes, sir." Oliver stepped forward and placed the pages on the captain's desk. He tried to smooth the worst of the wrinkles out, but Lundquist waved his hand away. Oliver stepped back and glanced at Elise, who only shrugged. *Great. She doesn't know what's going on either.*

Lundquist shifted the papers before picking one up. "Ambassador Ireland."

Oliver hadn't written her name on the page, which meant that Lundquist already knew what Dani looked like.

The captain lowered the page and picked up a few more. He paused at one and stared at it for a while before turning it toward Oliver. It was a drawing of the landscape along one of the paths the drill instructors ran them on every day.

"Shouldn't you be spending more time at the firing range instead of drawing pretty hills, Private?"

Oliver hesitated, considering his answer. He opted for honesty. "No, sir."

"No?" Lundquist asked with a raised eyebrow. "Explain."

"There isn't any amount of time at the range that can improve my terrible marksmanship, sir. Elise—Private Torrent— sir, is the next worst in scores. We would best serve the Commonwealth performing duties that match our natural gifts since we suck at weaponry. Sir."

"You're saying my weapons trainers suck, Private?"

Oliver's eyes widened. "No, sir! That's not what I meant. My failures are my own."

The captain put the drawing back down on his desk and watched him.

The silence that lingered made Oliver nuts. He somehow managed to avoid fidgeting.

Lundquist turned his attention to Sotillo. "How are their fitness scores?"

"Passing, sir, but that is all."

"Academics?"

"They are both at the top of the platoon, sir. Private Torrent is off the charts in mathematics, and Private Jackman is far above his counterparts in tech … and apparently art," Sotillo added, smirking.

The captain eyed Oliver again. "How are you with topos, Private?"

"Do you mean topographic maps or the topology of geometric objects?" Oliver asked.

Lundquist barked a laugh that made Oliver flinch. "I'm impressed you know the difference, Private. Staff Sergeant, continue routine weapons training with these two. They will continue all fitness tests and training per usual, but they are to move over to cartographic tech immediately to begin training there."

"Yes, sir," Sotillo said.

"After Basic, they will continue through artillery, supply, and advanced infantry training." He turned to Oliver. "Normally, your Military Occupation Specialty training comes *after* all that, but I want you and Torrent starting MOS early. You will have extra work every day." Lundquist returned his attention to Sotillo. "I want them to get a jump on their specialties now."

Sotillo nodded. "Yes, sir."

"Jackman," Lundquist said, "you will put those art and tech skills together with Torrent's mathematics. You may not have Miles's combat prowess, but I see Emily's artistic side made its way to you."

Oliver's eyes bulged.

Lundquist smiled. "Yes, I knew your mother. As kids, if Emily entered an art contest, the rest of us could only hope to take second prize."

"I didn't know," Oliver said. "She never drew or painted or anything that I remember. Sir," he added, remembering whose office he was standing in.

The captain sighed and straightened Oliver's papers. "The war takes those little things away from each of us, bit by fucking bit." He passed the papers to Oliver. "You're both dismissed."

Oliver didn't want to leave; he had many questions for the captain, but Sotillo's grunt snapped him out of it. "Yes, sir," Oliver said, saluting.

He left with Elise and trotted away from the building. Oliver feared getting called back at the last moment because the captain had changed his mind about their reassignment. Once he figured they were far enough away, he slowed.

"Did you have *any* idea that was coming?" Oliver asked.

"No," Elise said, shaking her head and smiling.

"This is *great*! I mean, it's what we wanted, but Andy and Janelle …"

Elise's shoulders slumped. "What do we do about them?"

"I don't know. We can keep tutoring them, maybe, try to help them test into the higher academic ranges."

"What if we can't?"

"I don't know." Oliver shook his head. He didn't know how rigorous the added training would be. They might not have time to work with the others anymore. The one thing he did know, though, was that this reassignment would put him working much more closely with tech, including comm tech. He was desperate to get a message to his father.

CHAPTER 18

Four days into their hike after the guide left them, Miles's team detected and avoided two Warden patrols. Things got worse when they discovered an area with signs of plasma rifle, quake rifle, and plasma pistol activity, complete with rotting, animal-chewed corpses. Ramos wasn't among them. Miles and Dani confirmed that none of the headless corpses could have been him since the bodies didn't have tattoos matching the ones on Ramos's arms.

He may have been taken prisoner, but they hoped he hadn't. They spent the next three days performing a grid search of the area beyond the battle zone and found another patrol and a few Warden land mines that Dani and Mary disarmed, but no Ramos.

Fatigue weighed on the entire team. Sleep was composed of short, broken periods because they needed to stay alert and on watch around the clock. Nothing about the mines were in Houston's reports, but Anton's at least had some data on them. His data wasn't perfect, but Dani could trust that he'd done his best to give them the most accurate information. Still, the mission was to find the general and bring him back to Maine.

Dani rolled her head to stretch her neck. The cramp in it

had been getting worse each night after sleeping on the ground, against a boulder, or inside a hollowed-out tree trunk.

Mary's gaze remained on the ground before them as they led the team. She gave Dani a quick glance. "You good?"

"Yeah. Neck's stiff is all."

Dani and Mary both froze when they heard a *click*—the unmistakable sound of a trap being activated.

Mary winced. "Fuck."

"Where is it?"

"Right side."

Dani didn't need to tell her not to move; she and Mary had both planted similar traps as saboteurs for the Commonwealth. They were well aware of the destruction and death that mines could cause. Dani gestured for Miles and the others to halt.

"I'm sorry. I didn't see it," Mary said.

Dani circled around Mary. She knelt and inspected the almost invisible wire touching Mary's right boot.

"Christ, this thing is hidden well. No one could've seen this one."

"Not making me feel any better."

Dani traced the wire to the right, picking leaves out of the way, and found the mine it was attached to. She dug around the device and found another wire. She followed that one to another mine and another for three more devices. Dani returned to Mary and traced the wire in the other direction.

No one spoke while she worked.

When she was back at Mary's side, she sighed.

"How many?" Mary asked.

"Nine."

"Goddammit."

"I'll talk to Miles. I can take care of this."

"Stop bullshitting me. There will be a web of these things— more than nine of them. One goes off, they all go off."

"I'll talk to Miles," Dani said while she began shrugging out of her pack. "They can keep going. We'll catch up."

"He won't agree to that."

"He doesn't have a choice."

Mary sighed. "Get the book from him. Just in case."

"Yep." She placed her pack on the ground and left to join Miles.

"How bad is it?" Miles asked.

"Horrible. Where's your map?"

His brow creased, but he removed his map and opened it for her. "We're here," he said, and pointed.

Dani glanced over the map and pointed to a different spot. "This is where you'll camp tonight. We'll meet you there."

"No."

"The general is the mission, Miles. Santi for Oliver. Mary's standing in a mine web, which means there are several subterranean ones all over this area. One wrong move, we all go up."

"There are too many Wardens in the area, Dani. You can't stay here by yourself."

"I'm not by myself. Mary's with me," she said, and smiled.

He scowled at her feeble joke. "I don't like this."

"I know. Mary wants Jace's journal … just in case."

He stared at her.

"Miles? The book with Oliver's portraits and notes to help me remember my friends in case I reboot," she said, tapping the side of her head.

"I know what you're talking about, Dani. I … it's just … I don't have it."

It was her turn to stare at him.

"It's in Bangor," he said. "I forgot to grab it when I left. I know that's been our little insurance policy in case you suffer a regen, but …"

Dani waved him off. "We won't need it. It'll be fine. Keep searching for Santi, and Mary and I will meet you tonight."

Miles sighed and looked at Mary. He turned and gazed at Kelsey and Cameron. He faced her again and gave her shoulder a squeeze before kissing her. "Come back to me."

"I will. Be *careful*, Miles. This trip wire Mary is on was hidden well. There are probably more."

He nodded and returned to the others.

Dani returned to Mary's side. "See? Piece of cake."

"Where's the journal?"

"Bangor."

"Jesus, Miles. You had *one* job, man."

Dani chuckled. "We'll be fine and meet them later tonight." She knelt to remove her disarming kit from her pack and glanced up. "How are you doing?"

Mary glared down at her.

"You're quite the captive audience right now. I can say all sorts of shit to piss you off, and you can't do a damn thing."

Mary grumbled, and Dani grinned. She needed to keep things light to prevent her nerves from taking over. Neither of them needed her rattled and with shaky hands. Her friend was standing on a literal death trap, and Dani was the only one in the group who could help her—provided she didn't screw up and blow them all to bits. Even if Mary's Echo DNA merger was successful, no Echo could survive being shredded by a mine.

Dani waited while Miles, Kels, and Cam left. They circled well around Mary's location, and once they were out of sight, Dani mentally counted to a thousand to give them more time to be out of range while she placed her tools near the mine to the right of Mary's boot. She needed to disable the mines on both sides but leave them connected before Mary would be safe—well, safe-*ish*. Disconnecting a mine would release the tension on the wire and activate the network. Without knowing where the rest of the network lay underground, they could still get caught in the mayhem if it went off. She could dig to figure out where the other mines were hidden, but they didn't have that kind of time.

Mary continued to hold her rifle and didn't move. Dani realized how statuesque she looked. *A beautiful statue, too.* Dani cleared her throat. *Focus.* She picked up her tools and scooted closer to the first mine. "Ready?"

"Just get this over with quickly, please. Legs are already starting to cramp."

Shit. They'd been hiking for hours, and now Mary was forced to remain motionless. With the stress of almost setting off a bomb with her boot on the trigger plus the fatigue from the hike, Mary was in much bigger trouble. Dani really did need to hurry.

She went to work on the mine and had it disabled in thirty minutes. It was way too long for them to be somewhat exposed. The forest wasn't as dense here, so they didn't have much cover.

She moved to the next mine, but stopped when she heard a voice somewhere in the forest. Mary was armed but still couldn't move. Dani kept working and tried not to worry too much about Wardens lurking nearby. After all, she had a much bigger concern—keeping herself and Mary in one piece.

There was no time to deactivate the second mine with the Wardens so close. Leaving Mary wasn't an option, so she'd have to rig the system with the right amount of tension to buy them time to run and hope they ran away from the mines. Dani wiped sweat away from her eyes. It was too cold for her to be sweating like this; she was stressed out of her mind.

She took a deep breath and dug through her kit. Dani found the tools she hoped would work. She stripped the covering off a piece of thin wiring, then snipped it. She worked the wire into a spiral and tested the tension on it. Dani's hand shook a little when she reached to touch the wire on Mary's boot. The wire's tension was higher than her spring, so she wound the spring a little tighter with her tools and trimmed it again. She checked the tension a few more times, adjusting her rigged spring.

"I see them," Mary whispered.

"They see us?"

"Not yet."

Dani eased the spring into the side of the mine, winding it over the trip wire. She had to lie on the ground and use her smallest set of pliers to push the spring into position beneath the mine's cover. *Hope this works.* "You can move back. Do it slowly so your legs can adjust and you don't fall."

Mary hesitated, and Dani could understand why. If this didn't work …

Mary removed her boot from the wire, and Dani kept her pliers in place on the spring to hold it between the two parts of the top of the mine where she'd wedged it. She looked up and made an educated guess about the subterranean mine network's location. After tromping around in a forest, a cleared area was a great place to lay a web. There was brush to hide the wires but not enough to deter anyone from opting to go through this place. That's where she would lay it too.

"Start moving to my seven o'clock into the thicker brush," Dani whispered.

"I can snipe them."

Dani considered that option. It would be a great idea if she wasn't physically connected to a couple dozen mines by a thin wire and pair of pliers. "No."

"I'm not leaving you."

"I'm not staying. Can you still see them?"

"No, but they're moving to our right. Once they hit the clearing, they'll see us."

Dani felt a tremor in her upper arm, the same arm that still held the pliers attached to the spring. "This rig won't last long. Once the spring slips out, everything goes up."

Mary reached for Dani's pack.

"Leave it. I release the spring and we have to get as far away as we can."

"How much time will we have?"

"No clue. Start moving back." Dani waited until Mary backed away a few paces. She took a deep breath, pulled the pliers free, and scrambled to her feet. Nothing exploded right away, so she and Mary fled. One of the Wardens shouted upon spotting them, but it didn't matter—the mine net erupted with a series of deafening blasts. Dani kept Mary in front of her and forced her own feet to continue moving despite pieces of shrapnel striking her back. A closer blast shook the ground, and Dani realized she'd misjudged the web's location a little. They were showered in a spray of dirt and bits of the forest. A shard of something hit her back like she'd been struck with a bat, and she tumbled forward. Her vision blurred, and pain in her leg kept it from working right.

Mary pulled Dani to her feet and half dragged her through the brush.

CHAPTER 19

Rowan's hunt resumed the next morning. They had to be getting close to finding the Commonwealth troops. The only area they hadn't scoured was full of mines. He stopped his team and pulled up an image of the map on his panel. He marked off the grids they'd just completed checking and frowned as he looked at the map.

"Here," he said, and pointed. "This is where we're going next. Notice the mine markers. You blow yourself up, that's on you."

"Sir, if they go into that area, we'll hear it," Delgado said.

"I'm certain they have Brigands with them. It's the only way they could manage to go undetected for this long."

"They're getting sloppy, though," Yura said.

Rowan nodded. "Fatigued. They're starting to make mistakes. We saw that yesterday in the area we found where they didn't spend much time covering their tracks. We're close. I know it."

"We'll find them, sir," Yura said.

Orson had stayed up most of the night working on the heat-detecting sensors, and Rowan didn't care that the man was tired. The devices were finally working.

"Orson, take point with your gear," Rowan said.

"Daytime temperatures will make them a bit less accurate, but I'll make some adjustments as we go to compensate for temperature changes," Orson said.

"Good." Rowan gave his team the rest of their orders for how he wanted them to search around the mine web, and then they moved on.

A few hours later, he halted his team again and gestured for complete silence. He thought he'd heard a voice, but wasn't sure. He signaled Orson to scan in the direction where the noise had originated.

Orson tweaked his scanner and then the sensors while Rowan's patience thinned. When the man's head came up, Rowan noticed his grin. Orson turned to follow his readings, and the rest of the team followed. When Orson stopped, they all stopped except Rowan, who continued until he was at Orson's side.

"What's wrong?" Rowan asked barely above a whisper.

"I'm picking up one, possibly two, signatures at eleven o'clock."

Rowan nodded. He would assume two people until he confirmed otherwise. He signaled to the rest of the team, gesturing for who he wanted positioned where—while keeping in mind the location of the mine web. As they resumed their pursuit and closed in, Rowan kept his rifle ready. He glanced at the others, and they, too, were ready to fire on anything that moved.

Two figures in CNA gear bolted, and Rowan only glimpsed them through the trees. One looked like a woman with blond hair, but he wasn't certain. He never got a good look at the other person.

His team immediately pursued, each of them eager to capture the enemy. When Rowan realized their proximity to the mine web, it was too late. He grabbed Yura's arm to stop her, but Orson and Delgado were inside the blast radius when the first mine went off. The ground ruptured up, tearing the forest floor apart along with Delgado and Orson. Ceci and Webb changed their course, but the mine web continued to explode. The blast closest to Rowan and Yura threw them aside, and Rowan blacked out when he slammed into the ground.

CHAPTER
20

ouston stood in the tactical planning room with her arms folded across her chest. She'd played the simulations from Anton for the Commonwealth's senior naval staff and now waited while they murmured among themselves and replayed portions of the sim of how the CNA could get past Montreal and take the larger target of Toronto.

Colonel Houston would serve as the commander, landing force, or CLF. Naval Vice Admiral Boseman would act as the commander, amphibious task force, or CATF, and Admiral Asllani was the JFC, joint force commander. She was the overseer of the mission that would be designed and carried out by the CLF and CATF. Houston smiled to herself as she thought of her new title and being called a *cliff* and Boseman becoming a *cat-if*.

Houston marveled briefly at the military's love of acronyms. Boseman and Asllani studied the simulations again, and Houston looked out over Boston's harbor. The planning room had an amazing view, and she had an excellent view of *Splendor*. General Ramos didn't deserve to have such a fine destroyer.

"Colonel," Asllani said.

Houston pulled her gaze from the window and uncrossed her arms. "Yes, Admiral?"

"I have concerns about using these canals," she said, pointing to the projection of the Saint Lawrence Seaway near Montreal.

"We'll use the canals and secure the locks. We will control anything the Wardens try to send at us from Quebec City or Toronto. By holding the locks, they will have limited accessibility to move either up or downstream. The canals and locks will become a death trap for them, not us."

Asllani nodded. Houston was more concerned with Boseman, who frowned.

Houston knew she didn't have him convinced yet. "With the expeditionary brigade, we'll have six thousand troops on the ground. I have my own spies inside Toronto sending me intel daily." She didn't have spies anywhere near Montreal or Toronto, but she needed to persuade the CATF to let the mission proceed. She was *certain* she could take Toronto if given the chance. With this kind of victory for the CNA, she'd get at least one statue in her honor. She'd be the kind of hero who lived forever in the history books.

She continued. "The brigade will give us enough firepower to grab the locks in Montreal and also take Toronto. With our volume of troops, we can control the tempo of the battle better than the Wardens can. What ships can you put in motion to make this happen?"

Boseman turned to another screen showing markers where all ships within the Commonwealth's fleet on the Eastern Seaboard were located. "I can assign two landing platform docks and three landing helicopter assault vessels. LPDs can hold up to eight hundred troops each, and I can put sixteen hundred troops on each LHA."

Houston nodded. She'd already factored this data into the simulations she had had Anton create. She knew which ships were where. The aircraft and armored vehicles these ships could deploy would provide both land and air support on top of the ships' armaments. "That will suffice." She glanced at Anton, who was busy staring at his shoes and wiping sweat from his brow. He might be CNA, but he behaved like a civilian.

"I have smaller ships," Boseman said. "Destroyers and littoral combat ships are faster and carry plenty enough firepower of their own."

"How quickly can you mobilize them?"

Boseman passed his hand over the gray stubble on his head. "I have five on hand, but it'll take a few days to get the rest of them this far north."

"And another couple of days to catch up, correct?" Houston asked. An LCS could move at four times the speed of an LHA and penetrate farther inland by using narrower waterways the larger ships couldn't navigate, but Houston didn't want to wait for the fast and deadly smaller vessels.

"Yes."

"Send the five. The others would be nice, but we don't need them. We'll go in with the larger ships—the whole shock-and-awe factor on top of landing thousands of troops. With the plan I've proposed, we can achieve full striking power at both the locks in Montreal and on the shores of Toronto in a short amount of time. I've proposed how we'll phase our troops ashore, and the sims confirm it. We'll still rehearse the plan while we're underway, of course."

Boseman nodded.

"My plan is only that, Vice Admiral ... an idea. As CATF, you'll prepare the ship-to-shore movement plan, but based on what I've proposed for the landing plan, I think you'll see the two match up well. I've proposed scheduled waves of both waterborne and airborne launches. You'll need to prepare the naval surface fire support on our approaches and landing, but I've outlined the target areas for both Montreal at the locks and Toronto."

Boseman's face twitched, and Houston recognized his doubt. She changed topics. "Vice Admiral," Houston said, "while we're on the water, the mission is yours. You will remain in command of the operation until I'm ashore in Toronto. I will be on the ground with the initial wave of forward-deployed ground troops."

Asllani replayed the simulation again, and Houston resisted the urge to roll her eyes. Boseman and Asllani watched the sim. When it finished, Houston interrupted Asllani before she could hit Play one more time. "Admiral or Vice Admiral, do you have additional questions on the mission for myself or my analyst?" she asked, nodding toward Anton and hoping neither officer would ask Anton anything. The young man was pale, sweaty, and looked like he might faint at any moment.

"Colonel Houston, amphibious landings are expensive in both firepower and lives," Asllani said. "They come with heavy casualties. They're risky."

"I am aware that they are not desirable operations to conduct, Admiral. But for us to take Toronto by the quickest means possible, we must control them from the waterway. Land control isn't enough. Troops will be moving on the ground to attack them from land, but this sea-to-land attack will be the most effective for keeping the battle in our favor."

"Are you sure you want to go ashore as early as you intend?" Boseman asked.

"Yes, Vice Admiral. You cannot dissuade me from that objective."

Boseman nodded.

"This plan will work," Houston said. "We have artillery, armored vehicles, amphibious assault vehicles, tanks, and aviation support."

"We don't have many of the newer Ancient fixed-wing jets. Any chance you can get more through your contacts?" Boseman asked.

"I'm sure I can," Houston lied. She refused to ask Hattie for anything. "They've already developed a newer-model helo that has capabilities similar to those of their jets." That part was true, but Houston didn't have any at her disposal.

"Good." Asllani stared at a map of Toronto for a moment before looking up. "You're confident this is the way to take Toronto?"

"It is the only way."

Asllani turned to Boseman. "Thoughts?"

"Based on the data and the sim, it's doable," the vice admiral said.

"Okay," Asllani said. "Let's make it happen."

Houston refused to show the feral grin she felt on the inside. She had taken a risk to push them into the embarkation phase of the plan. "Move the fleet to Yarmouth, Nova Scotia, Vice Admiral. I'm leaving today to take *Splendor* to port in St. John, New Brunswick. I have an asset to pick up in Fredericton, and then I'll meet you in Yarmouth. *Splendor* will stay there, and I'll transfer to the LHA of your choosing." She paused to see if the CATF would take the bait.

"You'll be with me on the *Karl*, Colonel," Boseman said. "I'll leave Boston tomorrow, but we should have the fleet together in Yarmouth in two days. A weather system is in the Atlantic, so it may slow things down a little. But we'll have the ships together soon."

She had them. Again, Houston suppressed showing her pleasure. "Time frame post-Yarmouth?"

"About five days to Montreal. We'll take what time is needed to take the locks, then move on from there. We should make Toronto two days later."

Houston nodded. In a little over a week, she might be attacking Toronto. She didn't bother hiding her grin this time. "Wonderful."

CHAPTER
21

Hattie's spoon clinked against the side of her cup as she stirred her tea. The Boston brothel and pub were both active and noisy, so she'd retreated to the kitchen to make a cup before heading to her private quarters. The tea had already gone cold during her absentminded stirring, but she wasn't interested in the drink. She was thinking.

Houston had gotten to Boston before she'd arrived, so Hattie was already playing catch-up to try to undo the damage Houston had caused in Bangor. Word of Houston's actions had spread quickly, so it made sense that she'd get the hell out of Maine.

Hattie had the Bangor and Portland councils' support, but the councils were made up of Brigands. She needed Commonwealth support, and her best ally, Ramos, was MIA.

She ticked through the list of other ranking officers in Boston. There were a couple of other colonels, but Houston's status, because of her successes in battle against the Wardens, made her the senior officer there.

Hattie removed her spoon and looked down at her tea. She took a sip and frowned. She dumped it out, then turned the burner on the stove on to reheat her kettle. "What does she want?" she muttered.

Brody's head came up, and his tail thumped against the floor when she spoke.

"I'm not talking to you," she said grumpily.

The dog's tail moved faster and he went to her. She rolled her eyes but rubbed his head anyway. When she knelt, he nuzzled her cheek with his snout before leaning into her for more rubs while his tail shook his body. "If you tell Dani I actually like having you around, I'll turn you into a rug." She gave him a final pat on his side, then stood. Brody returned to his spot on the floor to lie back down.

She knew Oliver was missing the dog and his family; hell, she missed the kid too. Hattie recentered her thoughts. *Houston.*

The colonel didn't crave power, though she had enjoyed her promotion from lieutenant colonel to full colonel after the Portland victory. Hattie knew the woman well enough that she *was* disappointed by not making brigadier general after Boston despite Houston's claim that she wasn't interested in another promotion.

Once Ramos pulled Dani out of Houston's forces to be with him, Houston's success rate in battle had stalled. She'd managed to take only smaller Warden outposts, and her ability to retain Brigand volunteers in her ranks decreased with Dani's absence. The only reason the CNA had been able to take a piece of Quebec City was the volume of Canadian forces involved. Houston and her Maine troops had played a role, but Canada's leadership got the credit for the battle's partial success.

She's pissed. Houston's fight has shifted from a focus on the Wardens to something more personal against Dani. Hattie nodded with realization. *Houston knows she can't have another major victory without Dani's tactics and the increase in Brigand forces that will come automatically with her presence. So Houston can't kill her ... Well, she shouldn't want to kill her. But Houston has become erratic. Unstable, even.*

Dani's charisma brought a greater level of energy to Maine's troops that Houston couldn't maintain or create on her own. Ramos had seen Dani's natural abilities and had taken her on his diplomatic trips for that very reason.

Hattie looked at the dog. "Take out Ramos, and that makes Houston the highest-ranking officer, more or less, in Boston and the entire Northeast, unless some other general comes up this way. She can do what she wants. The other colonels won't challenge her for taking a few civilians—spineless fuckers—because under Commonwealth law, it's still technically permissible to do so."

Brody tilted his head while she spoke.

She couldn't fight the law now; it would take too long, and Oliver didn't have time to wait out a legal battle.

Hattie hadn't bothered showing them the data from Houston's lab experiment. If they weren't troubled by Houston stealing teenagers, then they'd also turn their heads to lab participants where the recipients were volunteers and the donors might not know they'd actually donated part of themselves to a test tube and petri dish. *Goddammit.*

The kettle whistled. Hattie poured the steaming liquid into her cup and began the task of making another cup of tea. This time she headed to the portion of her Boston brothel that served as her private home. Brody hopped up to follow her.

When she arrived in her living area, she closed and locked the door after Brody came through. "There has to be a way to stop her without starting an all-out war between the CNA and Brigands." She placed her tea on her desk and sighed.

The comm in her pocket chirped, and Hattie pulled it out. She didn't bother to read the rest of the message and instead opened the link on her panel on her desk, where Anton's face appeared.

"Oh, uh, I was expecting Aunt Hattie," Anton said.

"Who else would answer this message?" she barked.

Anton leaned in closer to his screen, which distorted his features. "Oh, wow. Regen did a number on you."

Hattie narrowed her eyes at him. "Be glad I can't reach through this panel and grab you, Anton."

He leaned back from his panel. "Youth looks good on you. It was a compliment."

"Shut the fuck up."

"Yes, ma'am." He clamped his lips closed.

"Without Ramos, I can't make a move on Houston. The so-called leadership here thinks she shits gold, so they're not going against her on anything. Tell me you have something."

"Colonel Houston is making her move against Toronto," Anton said. "She's provided simulated models to the naval forces on how to attack the city and win. Problem is, the models are false. What she's proposing will never work."

"How do you know?"

"Because she made me fake them for her. Several thousand CNA troops will die, Aunt Hattie."

"Won't the naval officers see that her plan is bullshit? They have more experience fighting on the water than she will ever have."

"The water-to-land attack is mostly ship-to-land rockets and such. It's attacking from a distance, so that part is doable, and they know that. It's the shore landings that will get the CNA slaughtered. But because she's regarded as the boots-on-the-ground expert, they're not questioning her tactics. She's telling them she has troops on the ground already planting bombs and stuff, but she doesn't. Her recon data is a lie."

"She's making them believe she's got Dani and others in play as if she coordinated all the sabotage in Boston when she didn't. That was all Dani."

"Yeah. She's planning to lead the ground troops herself—be the hero and all."

That's it. Houston didn't want the promotions; she wanted the popularity that Dani had. Houston reveled in the attention she got for Boston even if she hadn't earned it; she happily took the credit for retaking the city from the Wardens. But if Houston got all those troops killed, she would never be the hero she wanted to be. "Anton, is she stable? Is she sane?"

"She's in complete denial about the loss of life with this plan. She believes it is solid even though the data is inaccurate and falsified."

Hattie nodded. *Unstable and delusional.* She leaned her hands against the desk and growled. She considered a good old-fashioned assassination of the colonel. *Tempting.* "Everyone I need to stop her is somewhere in the fucking woods between Burlington and Montreal."

"I have no news on them either. I'm sorry."

Hattie straightened and passed her hand over her face. Her younger body could handle the longer days that her aged body couldn't, but staying up till three or four in the morning every day as she'd been doing was wearing her down.

"Uh, Aunt Hattie, please don't kill me, but there's more."

She dropped her hand and sighed. "What?"

"Houston leaves Boston tomorrow with part of the fleet and will make a stop in New Brunswick to pick up Oliver."

"Why?"

"She's been tracking reports on his progress. She had me send word to his CO that she is pulling him out of training to be in the field with her for more direct grooming."

"He's out of basic training early as a result?"

"Yeah."

Hattie frowned. "She's keeping him close to continue to use him as leverage against Miles and Dani. She's going to get him killed."

Anton nodded.

"Who will be with Houston on the ship?"

"Javi will be there; he'll look after Oliver as best he can."

"You?"

"She's shipping me from Boston to Portland tomorrow."

"No."

"No?"

"Get your ass on that ship with her."

"But—"

"Anton, I don't care who you have to kill, what lies you must tell, or who you have to fuck. Get. On. That. Ship."

His mouth hung open for several seconds before he finally nodded. "I think I have a way in."

"Good. Keep a close watch on Oliver for me."

"I'll let him know you're alive."

"*No!*" Hattie paused before speaking again with a quieter tone. "That kid can't lie for shit. You tell him I'm alive, and he'll be too excited to keep it quiet. Houston will know we fed him the information. He needs to still believe I'm dead. As much as I hate doing that to him, it's for his own good."

Anton nodded. "I understand."

"Thank you."

"I'll send you updates when I can."

"Please do."

She ended the link and sank into the chair at her desk. Hattie dropped her head into her palm with a weary sigh. "Dani, wherever you are, honey, I hope you are headed back with Ramos soon."

CHAPTER

22

Every step that carried him farther away from Dani only made Miles more anxious for her well-being. If anyone could handle a Warden mine web, it was her, but that didn't make him feel any better about leaving her and Mary behind. He scanned the ground for additional Warden traps, but his head came up when he heard something rustle in the brush. He raised his hand to halt Kelsey and Cameron, and they froze.

Miles inched forward, using trees as cover. Careful to keep an eye out for traps, he scanned the ground before taking a step. That's when he spotted smeared blood on the leaves of the brush. The noise had come from someone who was injured and had passed through this same area just minutes before.

He kept his body behind a tree trunk as he pivoted with his rifle raised. He had his sights on a man seated on the ground and leaning against a tree. His pistol was pointed at Miles. The injured man's hand trembled. Miles focused on his target's face, and then, recognizing the general, he shifted his rifle to point it at the ground. "General Ramos! Kels, Cam, stand down." He waved his hand for them to lower their weapons.

Ramos lowered his pistol and sighed as he sagged against his tree. "Miles, it's good to see you."

Two other men with Ramos emerged and lowered their guns. The general slumped more against his tree, and that's when Miles noticed the extensive injuries to Ramos's left leg and his right side. Kelsey and Cameron were already in motion toward the general, with Kelsey shrugging out of his pack to access his med kit.

One of Ramos's men approached and held out his hand to Miles. "I'm Larsson. One of your guys a medic, Major?"

Miles gripped his hand, noting no insignia on his fatigues. Larsson was a Brigand. "Yeah. Kels is our official field medic. Cam is unofficial but has training."

"Good. That's Beckett," Larsson said, gesturing to the other man.

Both Beckett and Larsson had injuries too, but they were more minor than the general's. Miles intended to have Kelsey check them as soon as he was done with Ramos.

"We've done nothing but run from Wardens," Larsson said. "I can't tell you how many times they've almost caught us."

"You've done a damn fine job avoiding us, too. We've been out here for days looking for you," Miles said. He observed as Kelsey went to work but listened while Larsson provided updates with Beckett standing watch.

"We never got close to Montreal. Ran right into a fucking patrol we didn't expect would be as far south as they were. Blew us to shit, but we managed to take them out. They must have gotten word to their people before the fight was over, because we've been running from patrols since. We haven't been able to beat a hasty path south back to Vermont because we've done nothing but evasive maneuvers and backtracking to try to lose them."

Miles noted Larsson's remark about being caught unexpectedly in a fight with a Warden patrol. Maybe Dani was right and Houston really had sent Ramos into the area to be killed.

"How are you on supplies?" Miles asked.

"Out of food for three, maybe four days now. Med supplies have been depleted since yesterday. Water ran out this morning. We just haven't had time to forage."

Miles shrugged out of his pack and gave a few food wafers to Larsson. "Still have water treatment tablets in your gear?"

Larsson nodded and shoved the wafers into his mouth all at once.

While the man chewed, Miles pulled out his map and showed him where to find a nearby stream. "Refill all your canteens. We'll stay with the general."

Larsson nodded again and left to gather canteens. Miles brought food to Beckett, then went to the general.

Ramos groaned as Kelsey worked to remove debris from one of the wounds on his leg while Cameron passed a healing pen over part of the long gash on his side.

"Report," Miles said.

Kelsey kept his eyes on his work. "Lots of damage to his leg. I can fix the more superficial stuff, but the deeper shrapnel will need to come out in surgery. I can treat the infection for now, but we have to get him back to Burlington."

"Christ, sir," Miles said. "And you've been walking on that leg?"

"No choice," Ramos said. "We haven't had the luxury of stopping to make a litter or have much of a rest. We thought our luck had run out when we knew we were being tracked. Lucky for us, it was you this time. Not that I'm disappointed to see you, but what the hell are you doing out here anyway?"

Miles sighed and knelt next to the general. "Colonel Houston sent us." He considered mentioning the idea that she'd deliberately given Ramos bad intel, but without proof, Miles opted to keep that information to himself. "You were declared MIA, and I offered to come find you and bring you back in exchange for my son."

Ramos eyed him for a moment. "An exchange? What happened?"

Miles told him everything about the events at the birthday party, Houston taking workers from only Hattie's business, and the arrangement to trade the general for his son.

Ramos remained quiet for a few minutes. "Where are Dani and Mary now?"

"Mary activated a mine web, and Dani is with her, disarming it."

"You left them?"

"I … Dani, um … yes, sir. We have a rendezvous point established to meet them tonight."

"Have you run into any Wardens?"

"Several, but we've managed to avoid them each time."

"Good. They're getting close, Major."

"I know. Now that we have you, we can get the hell out of here. There's—" Miles gasped when the first explosion erupted in the distance. He winced and shook his head when it was followed by several more blasts. He stood and started to head in the direction of the blasts but stopped. "Fuck."

He couldn't leave the general to go to Dani. Ramos was already in danger from his wounds and the Warden patrols. Any Wardens who heard the mine web go off would head in that direction, which meant that if Dani and Mary survived, they'd have to avoid several Wardens at once. "Fuck!"

Dani would want him to stick to the plan to trade Ramos for Ollie, but Miles was desperate to go to her. If she had a regen, she would be confused when she woke. Mary would be able to help her, but that was assuming Mary wasn't injured or killed herself.

"Cam, Kels, keep doing what you can for the general," Miles said. "I'll work with Larsson to build a litter to carry the general out while Beckett keeps watch for us."

"Major Jackman," Ramos said.

Miles turned to face him. "Sir, we'll get you out of here."

"I know you will, Major. Build the litter as planned, but we'll find Mary and Dani before we leave."

"Sir, my orders are to bring you back to Maine."

"Fuck Houston. You have new orders."

Ramos was putting himself in more danger by not allowing Miles and his team to evacuate him to a safer area. Miles opened his mouth to argue, but the words that came out were "Yes, sir."

CHAPTER

23

Pieces of trees and chunks of dirt continued to pelt them, but Mary ignored minor cuts to her face and arms as she blindly tore through the brush, hauling Dani along beside her. She lost her footing and realized too late that she'd barreled through the brush and off the top of a steep slope. She wrapped her arms around Dani, and they slid and tumbled together to the bottom, where they stopped on an embankment near a stream.

Mary fought the dizziness plaguing her head to roll to her hands and knees while the final few mines exploded at the top of the hill. Dani lay a few feet away from her, on her side, unmoving, and there was a long tear through the right rear side of her armored jacket among numerous smaller tears. A shard of mine shrapnel protruded from the back of Dani's left thigh. Mary still had her rifle and a med kit in her pack, but she feared Dani's injuries were beyond what her kit could repair. She crawled to her friend and touched her shoulder. "Dani?"

Mary winced when she looked over Dani's shoulder. Dani's face was a mess of scrapes, cuts, and blood. She slid her fingers to the side of her neck and felt her pulse—thready and weak. Mary removed her knife and cut what was left of Dani's jacket off. She tore a wider hole in the shirt to inspect the worst wound on her back.

When she probed the edges of the wound with her fingertips, Dani moaned.

"Sorry." Mary worked her fingers around the wound and felt a few broken ribs. It didn't seem so bad until Dani coughed. The movement of her body caused her skin to shift and expose the much deeper slice through muscle tissue. Warm blood poured out of the wound and over Mary's fingers, and she could see down into Dani's chest cavity. She gasped at the sight. "Fuck me."

"That bad?" Dani asked.

"Oh, shit, you're awake. No, no. I just wasn't expecting … I mean. It's not that bad. I can use my med kit." *No. No. No! This is fucking horrible! I can't fix this without Cam or Kels.*

Dani shook her head. "Put me on my back."

"What? No, I need to keep you on your side to work on it."

"Roll me to my back."

Mary wasn't sure why Dani insisted on turning over, but she helped reposition her despite the additional pain it caused. Dani's hand fumbled at her hip for a moment until she withdrew her pistol. Mary's eyes widened. "What are you doing?"

Dani turned the weapon to place the muzzle on her own chest.

Mary trapped Dani's hands with her own. "No."

"Regen is faster."

"No!" Mary shook her head, though it was true. An Echo regen would heal Dani's extensive injuries much quicker than Mary ever could with a med kit that had only the right supplies to treat the shrapnel in Dani's leg and not her chest wound.

"If one Warden survived the blasts, we're fucked if we're found. I'm useless in this state."

"But you'll forget everything. You're about useless in that state too."

Dani managed a smile. "I know, but it's better than half a corpse. I can feel some of the metal inside me that will kill me anyway; it'll just take longer and hurt more."

"I won't shoot you."

"I'm not asking you to. Let me do this, Mary."

"We don't have the journal!" Their one backup plan to help Dani's memories after her wonky regens was in another state. Mary closed her eyes and shook her head. She opened her eyes again when Dani's fingers touched her face.

"I'll try to remember more than usual. Promise," Dani said.

Mary sighed. "Just don't come back as a child. I swear, Dani, do *not* do that or you'll be stuck with Hattie and me as maternal figures."

Dani started to laugh but stopped when it caused more pain. Mary winced when Dani's smile contorted into a grimace. She couldn't stand seeing her friend like this. Once the torment eased a little, Dani tried to position the gun over her heart, but she couldn't hold the weapon steady.

"I'll do it," Mary said, mortified by the words. She placed her hand on the pistol grip and steadied the muzzle over Dani's chest. Her finger touched the trigger, and she paused. "Okay." She took a deep breath. "Okay." Mary's finger wouldn't move. She adjusted her grip on the weapon and placed her finger on the trigger again.

Mary used her other hand to wipe at blood running down her face from a cut somewhere under her eye. She still couldn't pull the trigger.

Dani put her hand on Mary's and used her thumb to push Mary's trigger finger out of the way. She placed her thumb on the trigger.

Mary groaned. "Are you *sure* this is how this has to go?"

"Can you break my neck?"

Mary shuddered with the wave of nausea that struck. "Warden, yes. You, no."

"Knife in the heart?"

"Oh, God. You want me to stab you? I can't do that."

"Then this is how it has to happen."

Mary nodded, though inside her mind she was pleading for some other intervention like Miles's magical arrival to save the day or something. Anything would be better than helping her friend kill herself—even if Dani would regen. "This is so fucked up."

Dani smiled and nodded.

Mary continued to stall. "The Wardens might hear the shot."

"Which is another reason to get this over with now."

Mary grumbled, frustrated with having no other options. "I'm still going to help you, but I don't have to like it."

"I know, but I'm glad it's you who is here with me for this."

Mary shook her head. She took the remark as the compliment Dani had intended, but she still couldn't believe she was going to help her friend force a regen.

"After Jace died, I wasn't in a good place. Oliver made me promise to never do anything to hurt myself. We can't tell him about this."

"You won't remember it anyway."

Dani tried to laugh again and was wracked by new waves of pain.

"Shit. Sorry. Sorry! I get what you're saying, but the circumstances are a bit different now."

Dani's breathing slowed as the pain eased a little. "He may not see it that way."

"I won't say anything. Don't come back as a kid."

"I'll do my best."

"What is it with you and dying of friendly fire?"

"Bad luck, I guess. Mary?"

"Yeah?"

"Stop stalling."

Mary held the weapon steady. She nodded, and Dani's hand tightened over hers until the weapon discharged.

The shot went through Dani's upper body, and she immediately fell limp, her hands sliding off Mary's and falling to the ground.

Mary had still flinched with the shot but kept the weapon steady. She groaned and released the pistol, refusing to look at the hole in Dani's chest. She drew in a shaky breath. "Make this quick, please. Remember that I'm your friend. Remember that I love you. Miles and Oliver love you too. And—"

Mary's head came up when she heard rustling in the brush near the top of the hill.

"That shot came from this direction," a man said.

"There's more blood over here," a second man said.

They were voices Mary didn't recognize, so it wasn't Miles or one of the others looking for them. *Fuck.*

"Lots of broken stems on the plants. They had to come this way," the second man said.

Mary looked at Dani, who hadn't started to regen yet; it was too soon. She scanned the area and decided what she needed to do. She placed Dani's pistol into her lifeless hand, then stood. She slipped into her pack and picked up her rifle. Before Mary left, she knelt one more time and leaned down next to Dani's ear.

"When you come back, remember me, please." She kissed Dani's cheek, then left her, careful to cover any prints or other signs of her presence.

CHAPTER
24

Dani's chest heaved when she drew in her first, deep breath. It rattled inside her lungs, and she coughed. She wasn't sure where she was or what had happened; she just knew she felt like shit. Something pressed against her right wrist, and she couldn't move her hand. She moved her other hand to the insanely sore spot on her chest and frowned.

"You gonna wake up today?" a man asked.

She opened her eyes to two men in black body armor pointing their plasma rifles at her head. It took her another moment to register that she had absolutely *no* idea what had happened or was happening. Her breathing quickened as she fought the desire to panic. She tried to remember something—anything—from today, the previous day, *any* day. Nothing.

"Ireland," the man to her left said while looking down at her. He glanced at his partner. "Think this is the one Rowan is looking for?"

She had no idea what they were talking about or what her lying on the ground had to do with Ireland.

"Could be. She's filthy, so it's hard to tell," the second man said, then looked down at Dani. "Who are you?"

"Uh," was all she could manage to say.

The second man lowered his rifle and bent over to remove the pistol from her hand. Once he had her weapon, he removed his boot from her wrist. "She shot herself to force a regen. There's blood and shrapnel everywhere."

"I don't care how she died. I want to know who the hell she is. She must be—" His body twitched when a rifle round tore through his chest, and then his body collapsed.

Dani recoiled away from the man, unsure where the shot originated and if she was next.

The remaining Warden brought his rifle up, but a hole opened his neck before he crumpled. Dani rolled to avoid him falling on her. She scrambled to her feet but went only a few steps before she stumbled and fell. Her body wouldn't cooperate, but she managed to crawl over to a tree and use it to pull herself up.

A woman in combat armor carrying a Warden rifle emerged from the trees and headed straight toward her. Dani's knees wobbled when she released the tree to try to run. She wanted to flee, but her legs wouldn't hold her. The woman carried the rifle with the muzzle pointed at the ground and not at her, which gave her a sliver of hope that this woman wouldn't put a round through her too.

"Dani, darling," the woman said, and smiled. "Please tell me you remember more than just your name."

Dani's mind raced, but she could remember only images of a city being bombed. Today she was in a forest near a stream with two dead men on the ground. She turned and vomited.

"Guess not. Listen, my name is Mary. You and I are friends, and our day has gone to shit. You regenned, but your memories are fried. They'll come back, but it takes some time. Okay?"

Dani wiped her mouth with the back of her hand and shook her head. "*What?!*"

"Shh! Keep your voice down. Could be more Wardens near us."

Dani gazed down at her battered shirt and the hole in the fabric on the left upper side of her chest. "Did you shoot me too?"

"Not exactly."

Dani sensed she was in danger, but she didn't know how or why. If her legs would work, she could run away. "I've never seen you before."

"Oh, this is so much fun." Mary sighed and slipped the rifle strap over her shoulder. She pulled her knife.

Dani pressed her back into the tree.

"We're friends, Dani. Relax. Miles Jackman. Name ring any bells?"

Dani shook her head.

The first gunshot victim's body began to glow blue.

"Finally," Mary said, and knelt next to the Echo. She drove her knife into the side of his neck, and the glowing ceased.

Dani flinched with the violent action and would have vomited again if she'd had anything left inside her. Mary rolled the second victim around as she removed his armored jacket. Once he started glowing, she slammed her knife into his heart. She wiped the blade off on her trousers and resheathed it before pawing the bodies and removing weapons, food, and anything else of use.

Mary tossed the jacket to Dani and she caught it.

"Put that on," Mary said. "It'll be too big, but Brigands can't be choosy."

"Brigands," Dani muttered while staring at the jacket in her hands. "How do I know you are a friend when they might have been my friends that you just killed?"

Mary finished stuffing her pockets with everything she'd taken off the Wardens, then returned to her. "You woke up and they had guns pointed at your head. Friends don't do that." Mary placed the plasma pistol into Dani's empty holster. "They took your gun, and I'm giving it back to you." Mary then helped Dani put the replacement jacket on. "I know your name. They didn't."

Dani realized her question had been stupid. "Oh."

"Your mind's a bit fogged now, darling. It'll clear up. We have to go." Mary placed her hand on Dani's shoulder and moved her away from the tree.

"Darling?" Dani asked. "Are we—"

Mary gave her a light shove in the back. "Just go."

She took a few tentative steps and was pleased to find her legs working better. "Where are we going?"

"To grab my pack and meet back up with Miles and the others."

"Miles Jackson," Dani said.

"Jack*man*. Remember him now?"

Dani shook her head.

"Fine. Not important—well, it is, but not right this second. You are a Brigand, and what you *do* remember is that you know how to sneak around in a forest like a goddamn ghost. No more questions for a while so we can get the hell out of this area."

Dani nodded.

Mary was right; sneaking around in the forest without making a sound was easy. Dani still couldn't recall why she was with Mary or why they were out in the middle of nowhere. They hiked for a few hours, circling away from the destruction left by the mine web. When they stopped, Mary handed Dani food wafers and a canteen, then pulled out her map.

Dani chewed the wafers and gulped the water down while looking over Mary's shoulder at the map. She reached around her and pointed with a finger to an area on the map. Dani wasn't exactly sure why she wanted to go to that particular spot, but she did.

"Is that where you told Miles to go?" Mary asked.

Dani shrugged.

"We're not far from there. We can make it before nightfall."

"Your name is Marella, not Mary."

Mary stared at her for a moment. "God, the crazy shit you store in that brain of yours."

Dani shrugged again, feeling like she was doing that a lot lately.

"You and Aunt Hattie are the only two people who know my real first name. Everyone calls me Mary. It's easier that way."

"You keep your first name a secret?"

"Yes. File that away in your head somewhere. Don't advertise my name to anyone else."

"Are you in trouble?"

"Dani, this is not the conversation we need to have right now."

"Okay," Dani said. She guessed they'd get back to that topic later. "Who is Aunt Hattie?"

Mary sighed. "It'll come back eventually."

Dani shook the canteen and realized she'd drunk the last of the water. "Shit. I'm sorry. There's a stream a few hundred yards that way." She nodded in the direction of the stream. "I'll get more water."

"You can't remember your last name, but you remember where the streams are," Mary said.

"I have a last name?"

Mary groaned and took the canteen from Dani's hand. "I want you to rest. I'll get the water."

"Okay," Dani said, but nothing felt okay.

Mary left, and Dani absentmindedly ran her hand through her hair while she turned in a circle among the trees. She didn't want to rest, though her body declared otherwise. Her chest still ached, and she placed her hand on the area, though it was now protected by Warden armor. She'd been wearing a different jacket that had actually fit her. It was torn and tattered and had been lying on the ground next to her when she woke with the Wardens standing over her. Dani flinched when a memory of explosions erupting all around her flashed through her mind.

Mines. Mary had tripped a mine network, and Dani had managed to rig the system to buy them time to escape. Except it wasn't quite enough time, and she'd been injured. *Pain.* She shuddered. *Fuck. Lots of pain, and I forced a regen.* She shivered and rubbed her hands over her arms despite the jacket.

Dani hadn't realized she'd been pacing and had wandered away from where Mary had left her until she heard rustling. Her head snapped up. She drew her pistol and slipped into a thicket and waited.

A man in combat armor and carrying a rifle walked ahead of one pair of men, followed by a second pair of men carrying a litter with an injured man on it. Dani pulled her pistol and silently moved around the trees to arrive ahead of them. By the time the lead man spotted her, it was too late for him to do anything. She already had her pistol aimed at his head.

"Toss your rifle and pistol aside and get on your knees. Hands behind your head, fingers laced," Dani said.

"Christ, D—"

"Shut up! You three," she said, gesturing with her pistol at the lead man and the two men not involved with the stretcher. "Down. Now!" She waited while they complied. The man on the stretcher tried to turn, and he winced when he moved. As long as the other two men continued to hold the stretcher, they couldn't draw their weapons. She just needed the wounded man to be unarmed.

"No one moves," Dani said.

"What is this?" the man on the stretcher said.

The lead man on his knees groaned. "She's had a regen."

Dani stalked closer to the man. "Shut up!"

"Major, get this under control," the man on the stretcher said.

The man on his knees turned a little. "Regens make her—"

Dani swung her pistol and struck him. His head rocked to the side and he toppled. She pulled an I-cuff from his belt and applied it to his waist. She activated the device to fully immobilize him. He watched her with widened eyes and was unable to move or speak. She backed away from him and kept her weapon on the others.

"Dani!" Mary called to her while jogging to close the gap between them. "Dani, stop."

She glanced back as Mary approached through the trees. As soon as Mary arrived, she knelt to inactivate the immobilization cuff.

"Wait," Dani said.

"Jesus, Dani, *this* is Miles." Mary took his arm to help him up. "Miles, I'm sorry. I left her to get more water and she wandered off."

Dani finally noticed the name on his jacket. Jackman. *Well, shit.*

He touched the bleeding cut over the lump on the side of his head and frowned. "Disarming the mines apparently went well."

"I know them?" Dani asked, waving her gun at the others.

Mary placed her hand on Dani's forearm, lowering the weapon. "Yes. They're our friends."

They were friends Dani didn't know, but she holstered her weapon anyway.

Miles wobbled a little. Dani noticed his eyes remained on her, though he addressed Mary. "We heard the mines going off. What the hell happened? She get caught in the blast?"

"Something like that," Mary said.

"That's not her jacket."

"Got her a new one from one of the Wardens I sniped."

Hot anger rose inside Dani when they spoke like she wasn't there.

"Any left?" Miles asked.

"Not sure. We bailed after I took out two of them."

Dani was tired of this man staring at her. He seemed familiar, but she couldn't figure out why. "Mary says I know you. How?"

Miles looked at the blood on his fingers from his new wound. He dropped his hand. "We've been sleeping together for the last three and a half years."

She had no words, so her mouth just hung open. She glanced at Mary, who nodded.

Fucking hell.

CHAPTER

25

When Rowan opened his eyes, he was lying on his back and Yura was on her knees leaning over him. Her lips moved, but his ears rang so much that he couldn't hear her. She was wounded. Her right shoulder was a bleeding mess beneath the torn, armored jacket. She helped him sit up, and Rowan groaned with the movement. He had shrapnel in the side of his chest, arm, and thigh. Streams of blood ran down his face.

His vision cleared, and he recognized Webb and Ceci standing near him. Their armor was battered and bloodied, but they stood as if uninjured. *Regen*, Rowan thought. He'd been unconscious long enough for the two men to regen. He didn't need to ask about Orson or Delgado; he'd seen the mines tear them apart. The ringing in his ears lessened somewhat.

"Why are you still standing here? Go after the targets," Rowan said. "Bring them here alive."

"Yes, sir," the men said, then left.

Rowan looked around but didn't see his rifle anywhere. When he turned to Yura, she was using her good hand to unfasten the front of her jacket, and he understood what she was doing.

"Knife or pistol?" Rowan asked. "Or something else?"

"Knife works. Not as messy as a pistol." She grunted when she jarred her injured shoulder to open the front of the jacket more.

"Neck is cleanest if you're looking to keep this tidy," Rowan said, smirking. They were covered in blood, dirt, and bits of the forest. It would be a long time before they were clean.

She snorted a laugh.

Rowan removed his blade as she shifted to sit on the ground at the base of a tree trunk. She leaned back against the tree and watched him as he approached.

"Ready?" he asked.

"Yep. Make it quick. The clock is ticking on our bet."

Rowan smiled and nodded. He admired her courage to do what was needed; she had no fear of dying and he respected that. Yura was a true Warden.

She gasped when he slammed the blade into her chest up to its hilt. Life faded from her eyes, and her head slumped forward. Rowan pulled his blade free and gently lowered her to the ground to lie on her side. He adjusted the position of her head to something that looked more comfortable. He stayed next to her to protect her while she was vulnerable and unable to defend herself. Minutes passed, and as her body began to glow, he heard the sound of a rifle shot.

He knew the weapon based on the noise it made. It was one of the models of advanced sniper rifles his team in Boston had created. During the CNA attack on Boston, Dani's friend Mary Smith had gotten her hands on one of the rifles and put a round through his heart. For the power of the weapon, the noise it made when fired wasn't all that loud. Rowan knew the weapon well. He'd been directly involved in its development and sound-suppression systems. The rifles were magnificent. They didn't have the destructive power of a plasma pistol or plasma rifle to completely take a head off, but they could drop a Warden to be permanently killed during regen.

A second shot was fired, and Rowan shook his head. Webb and Ceci were down, and Rowan was unable to help them.

Yura's chest heaved with her first deep breath, and it took her another minute before she shifted to sit up. She worked her healed shoulder and nodded with approval. She looked at Rowan as he watched her.

He considered his options. He could send Yura after his other two team members, but the CNA had a sniper who would just kill her too. Or she could force his regen, and they could go together once he was healed.

"Sir?" she asked.

"CNA has a sniper out here with one of our advanced rifles."

She moved to stand.

"No. Snap my neck to get my regen started, and we'll go together."

She nodded and knelt behind him, using her leg to brace against his back. He liked the feel of her hands as she positioned them on his head.

"Ready?" she asked.

"Go."

She twisted his head in one quick motion. The sharp pain in his neck was over in an instant, and when he opened his eyes again, he was lying with his back against her chest, his head resting against hers, and her arms were around him. "Thanks," he said.

The shrapnel in his body lay among the leaves, forced out of his body as it healed. The ringing in his ears and pounding in his head were gone too. Yura stood and helped him up.

When they found the bodies of Webb and Ceci, Rowan pulled the comm from his pocket. Too much time had passed for him and Yura to go after the CNA. He didn't know how many of them they were chasing, and at least one was a sniper.

"Sir?" Yura said. She held a shredded CNA armored jacket out to him. She turned it so he could see what was left of the name badge: "—land."

"Goddammit."

"Think it's her?"

"Has to be." The blond-haired woman he'd seen before had to be Smith. Everything inside him wanted to go after his prey. Dani was close, and Jackman couldn't be too far off either. The three of them always operated as a trio. He gazed back down at the bodies of Ceci and Webb.

Ceci's armored jacket was gone, likely the replacement for Dani's torn one. Given the blood on Dani's jacket and on the ground, she had been through a regen. Smith was acting as sniper, and both women had food, water, and weapons they'd taken off his dead Wardens.

The last time he'd gone after Dani and her friends, he had gone through four regens in one day. For just him and Yura to go after two heavily armed Brigands who were the absolute best saboteurs the Commonwealth had in the region—possibly the continent—was suicide.

As much as he didn't want to do it, he activated the comm to contact Curtis and the other teams.

CHAPTER
26

The first night after her regen, once the others were resting or gathering water, Dani finally allowed herself to relax. More memories of Miles had returned, but not enough that she felt comfortable being alone with him. Her sleep was restless, filled with confusing dreams. She couldn't tell if they were memories or not. A hand touched her shoulder, and she startled awake with a gasp.

"Sorry." Miles raised his hands as he leaned away from the knife she held in front of him.

Dani resheathed the knife. "Shit. Sorry." She rubbed her palms over her face, and when she looked back at him, he was standing with his hand extended for her to take.

Her gaze moved from his hand to his face, then back to his hand. She grasped it, and he pulled her up. Despite the filth from being in the field for so long, she recognized his scent. New memories came in a rush, and she squeezed her eyes closed and groaned from the sudden headache and dizziness. She would have fallen, but he kept her up. He was saying something to her, but she couldn't listen to him right now. When the flashing images in her mind slowed, the pressure inside her head eased, as did the spinning sensation. She opened her eyes and blinked. Mary and Cam (at least, that's what Miles and Mary called him—Dani still didn't remember him) had arrived at her side.

Cam tried to shine a light in her eyes, and she frowned and swatted him away.

"She seems normal to me," Cameron said, which earned him a snicker from Mary and a scowl from Miles.

"I'm fine," Dani said.

"Lots of images and memories just come back at once?" Mary asked, and Dani nodded. "Yep, that's your norm."

"How many regens have you done with me?"

"Miles and I were with you for one a few years ago. And I had the one with you yesterday."

"Things come back to you in waves," Miles said.

"Oh." Dani passed her hand through her hair.

"Mannerisms stick, though," Mary said, and then she turned to Miles. "You must have picked that one up from her."

Miles shrugged. He said something to Mary, but Dani had stopped listening. Some of the images started sorting themselves, and things began making more sense.

"'Christ, Mary, what's wrong? It's how Brigands survive, Miles. If I don't scavenge, I don't eat,'" she muttered, her eyes on the ground, unfocused. "'The next time I tell you to leave, it will be with my foot up your ass.'" Dani shook her head.

"What?" Miles asked.

"No, that one wasn't me," Dani said. She wanted to pace, but the others still hovered around her. "Street urchin. Brody. I'll fucking kill you."

"*What?*" Miles asked.

Dani's head came up, and she smiled. "Montreal." She threw her arms around him and kissed him.

"Finally!" Mary said.

"What just happened?" Cameron asked.

"Her mind finished rebooting—well, enough so that she's remembered a good chunk of things now."

Cameron shook his head. "That's *not* normal for an Echo."

Mary grinned and waved her hand in Dani's direction. "She's our defective little alien we keep around for entertainment."

Dani frowned at her. "That's just mean." She returned her attention to Miles. "I'm sorry things take a while to come back."

Miles nodded and smiled. "At least they came back." He kissed her forehead.

Dani released him, then embraced Mary. She moved to Cameron next.

"I'm happy to see you," she said to him. "Hattie said that part about putting her foot up your ass."

"She did," Cameron said, and smiled.

Dani turned to Miles. "Oliver is in Bangor. No. No, that's not right." She paused to think. "Oh, fuck. That's all messed up. Catherine took him."

Miles nodded.

"Santi! Shit. Montreal is wrong. Well, not wrong, but that whole thing needs tweaking," she said, waving her arms.

"What?" Mary asked. She looked at Miles. "What is she talking about?"

"No clue," Miles said.

Dani moved away from them and spotted Kelsey with a man lying on a field stretcher on the ground. She trotted over to them and knelt. "Santi!"

Ramos opened his eyes and gave her a wary look. He glanced at Miles and Mary as they neared, then looked back at Dani.

"Hey, Kels," Dani said. Two other men approached. She knew they were part of the general's team, but she couldn't quite find their names in her jumbled mind.

"Hey. You're back," Kels said.

"Eh," she said, and shrugged. "Mostly. Santi, the Montreal plan needs some changes."

"Dani," Ramos said, "we never made it to Montreal. We have no intel on the city other than what Colonel Houston already gave us."

"Oh. Well, fuck her anyway. She gave you shit intel and sent you out here to die." She wasn't sure why she had blurted that—or if it was even accurate—but the words had spilled out of her anyway.

"Oh, God." Miles groaned.

Ramos turned his gaze to Miles. "What's this about, Major? Is this part of her regen confusion?"

Mary shook her head. "Nope."

Miles winced but still managed a response. "Sir, we don't have proof that the colonel intended to kill you. We do know that the intel she gave you and us was flawed, but we don't know if the mistakes were intentional or just bad data."

Dani jumped back into the conversation. "She's also been tampering with human and Echo DNA to make more Echoes—keep her troop numbers up and all." Dani wondered what the hell she even meant. "The lab fuck-up in Bangor. I was in on that to stop Catherine's version of Warden tactics to boost troop numbers."

Despite his injuries, Ramos sat up. All eyes were on Dani.

"Jesus, Dani," Mary hissed. "Shut up."

She shrugged. "It's true," she said, and then paused. "Pretty sure it's true. Memories are still rendering." She wondered where she'd gotten that last word from. *Ant-something. Antrim? Antoine?* "Anton!"

"What about him?" Ramos asked.

"Uh." Dani wasn't sure. She'd said the name only because she'd remembered it.

Mary stepped forward. "He has the proof about the lab. He

also has the data showing the conflicts between what Houston gave you and what he pulled together."

Ramos nodded. "I see. Beckett, Larsson, pick me up. Time to move out."

Dani turned to the two men. She knew they were Brigands, based on their scavenging skills and ability to find food, but she never would've guessed their names. "How come I have no memory of you?" she asked, pointing at them.

"You just met them yesterday, darling," Mary said.

"Oh."

"Dani," Ramos said as the men lifted his stretcher. "What needs to change about Montreal?"

"Oh, right. We can't just hit Montreal. You need to work with the other Commonwealths to make that attack day a larger, coordinated, global attack. The Wardens can't help each other if they're swamped dealing with their own fires."

"Houston already used that tactic with Boston by feigning an attack on Portsmouth," Ramos said. "The Wardens won't fall for it again."

"Nah," Dani said. "She did a watered-down version of it with Portsmouth and got lucky. I'm talking a much larger scale here. End the war the way it began: one big fucking bang."

Ramos stared at her as seconds ticked by. "You're serious?"

Dani nodded.

"Huh. Major, how soon can we make Burlington?"

"Three days, sir."

"Two," Dani said. "Terrain's a little rougher, but we can take a shortcut back that the Wardens won't expect. It'll take us out to an old path that used to be a trade route. The path will be easier going, but we will be a bit more exposed on it. We'll have to be careful since it's still close to the Warden territory lines, per Anton's maps. Catherine's maps say it's firmly within CNA territory, but that's bullshit."

"How do you know about this path?" Ramos asked.

Dani shrugged. "I don't know. I just do."

"Impressive, Ireland."

Dani turned to Mary. "Why is Ireland coming up again?"

"Christ," Miles said, and lowered his head into his hand while Mary laughed.

"Some inside joke I'm missing here?" Ramos asked.

Miles dropped his hand. "No, sir. It's part of her regen. Dani never remembers having a last name. She used to regen back to a child who didn't recall or know she had a last name, so that's a detail that gets lost each time she resets." Miles turned to her. "Dani, *your* last name is Ireland. We're not talking about the country."

"Oh," Dani said, hoping the embarrassment she felt didn't show on her face.

"The path," Ramos said to Beckett and Larsson. "Either of you know it?"

The men shook their heads.

"I do," Mary said. "I lived in the area for a time, scavenging. This was before moving to Bangor. The path is a bit exposed, as Dani said, but once we're on it, we'll make good time. Should even be able to get a comm signal out for an early extract."

Dani recalled another memory from years ago in some kind of basement or bunker. She'd held a piece of a helo rotor in her hand that Mary had taken off a downed Warden helicopter near Montreal. *Huh.*

"Done. Let's go," Ramos said.

"Yes, sir," Miles said. "Dani, Mary, take point as usual to check for traps. I'll follow with Cam. Kels, fall in behind the general."

The group gathered their gear to leave. For the first time, Dani realized she didn't have a pack or a rifle. She stood there for a moment. *My pack was lost in the mine-web blasts, and I never carry a rifle because I'm better with a pistol.*

Mary touched her arm. "Hey. You okay?"

"Yeah. You cannibalized a Warden helo for parts near Montreal."

"Wow. The useless shit you can remember versus the important shit you can't is truly astounding, Dani."

"It's a gift. Tell me more about the time you lived in Montreal while we walk."

"That was a long time ago. Things have changed."

"Tell me anyway."

CHAPTER
27

The sun continued to sink behind the trees, and Dani wondered why they hadn't made camp yet. One full day of hiking with another remaining before they got to Burlington left the group fatigued. Hiking in the dark was a bad idea, though, regardless of how close they might be.

Mary adjusted her rifle to stretch her shoulders. "I'm so ready for a shower."

Dani nodded. "Me too. I've given up counting the number of ticks I pull off each day."

"Kels has no idea what I plan to do to him once we're back at camp. Too many days in the field and not enough sex."

Dani couldn't argue with her; she was ready for some alone time with Miles.

"You?" Mary flashed her a grin.

Dani smiled when she glanced at her. She flinched and closed her eyes when something wet spattered on her face. Mary grabbed her sleeve, and Dani opened her eyes. Blood poured from the side of Mary's neck, her eyes wide with fear, and her knees buckled. Dani threw her arms around her friend to catch her.

A flash of heat seared the outside of Dani's upper arm, and she realized someone was shooting at them and had shot Mary.

Before she could call to others to both take cover and help her with Mary, someone else screamed, "Sniper!"

She dragged Mary to an area behind a tree and covered her body with her own. Dani pressed her hand to the side of Mary's neck—her fingers and hand were immediately covered in blood. "Fuck." She glanced up for help. Kelsey rushed toward them, and then a spray of organic matter erupted from his head as a round tore through his helmet. His body collapsed like someone had ripped out his spine.

Dani looked down and was glad her arm had been in the way so Mary didn't see her lover killed. Mary stared up at her, terrified. Tears spilled from the sides of her eyes as she lay on her back, contorted by the pack still attached to her. Mary's jaw moved as she tried to speak, but she couldn't make much of a sound.

"I've got you," Dani said, not sure what she even meant. She kept her hand over the wound, but the blood continued to seep around her fingers. She pressed a little harder, and Mary winced. "I'm sorry."

Mary coughed, and bloody bubbles sputtered from her mouth. "Dan—"

"Don't talk." Dani passed her other hand to the back of Mary's neck. Her spine was still intact, but blood spilled from the wound from the other side of her neck where the bullet had entered from the rear and exited through the front, shredding blood vessels, muscle tissue, and anything else in its path.

Dani didn't know what to do. Kelsey's pack held the gear that might save her friend's life. She removed her hand from the back of Mary's neck, and it, too, was covered in blood. She looked up for help—any kind of help. She ducked back down when splinters erupted from the tree's trunk near her head.

Miles was huddled behind an area of dirt, and his trouser leg was dark and wet with blood. He had already removed his belt and was wrapping it around his thigh. Cam had dragged Santi to an area providing them with cover. Of Santi's two remaining members of his team, Beckett was on the ground in a pool of blood and not moving. Larsson was also on the ground. Dani couldn't tell if he was injured or not, but the man didn't move.

Her mind was a jumble of panicked thoughts, and she didn't have any options available other than trying to keep Mary from bleeding to death and hoping help arrived in the next few seconds. She looked at her friend's face.

Mary's eyelids drooped and Mary's hand released the grip she'd had on Dani's jacket.

"No, no, no, no. Please, Mary." Dani's tears fell on Mary's face.

Mary closed her eyes and her head rolled to the side. Dani clutched the wound on Mary's neck tighter, but her friend was already gone. She begged Mary to live, but it didn't make a difference. She used her other hand to check for a pulse and cursed when she couldn't feel it. "Regen," Dani whispered. "C'mon, Mary."

She placed her palms on the sides of Mary's head, smearing blood across her friend's face. She watched her friend's body for any movement or glimmer of blue to indicate the start of the regeneration process. "Please, Mary." Minutes passed, but nothing happened. "Regen, Mary. *Please* regen."

Tears flowed down Dani's cheeks. "Goddammit, you *can't* leave me." More minutes passed.

The bodily glow didn't come. Dani lowered her head, placed her cheek against Mary's, and wept.

Miles called for her, but she didn't move or answer. Mary was gone, and Dani was devastated.

Night came, and the darkness seeped into Dani's soul. Grief and hatred began to mix. She lifted her head a little and hated the coolness of Mary's skin beneath her fingertips. Her hand shook as she traced over the scars on Mary's cheek. "It wasn't supposed to be like this."

Dani shifted, and a bullet took more bark off the tree serving as her cover. A rage swelled inside her. Mary was not coming back, and Dani wanted the Warden sniper permanently dead.

She shifted her position off Mary, and another shot tore pieces of wood from the tree. The sniper had night-vision capability for him—or her—to see Dani's movements. She didn't care. Dani dropped to her belly and slithered the short distance down the slope at the base of the tree. The sniper didn't shoot at her again, so she figured her enemy hadn't seen her departure.

No one had seen her leave, not even Miles, or he would have called to her.

She crept along the edge where the base of the hill met the dirt road. A hundred yards later, she turned to start up the hill. Dani moved soundlessly as she picked her way upward. Revenge was the only thing on her mind as she neared the upper area of the hill.

She heard Miles's voice through the trees. "Dani? ... Shit. Dani!"

He was still at the base of the hill. She wanted him to be quiet because his outburst caused the sniper to fire another shot at him.

Dani spotted the muzzle flash; she now knew exactly where her prey was hiding. She pulled her pistol and stalked closer to the shadow that had killed her friend. The sniper was covered in an armored skin, concealing his presence among the trees and brush except when the moonlight reflected off his gear. His head moved, and she recognized the helmet as one that allowed near-perfect night vision. She couldn't shoot and take his head off to end him; she'd have to get in close.

Miles or someone else must have been moving, because the sniper fired more shots down at the area she'd left.

Dani held her pistol in one hand and pulled her knife from its sheath with the other, knowing she'd have to make this attack quick. She squeezed the trigger, and the plasma shot slammed into the side of the sniper's helmet. It wouldn't kill him, but it would stun him long enough for her to attack.

His head rocked to the side, and he lost his grip on his rifle. Dani dropped her pistol to free up her hand and pounced. She got one hand under the edge of his helmet and pulled his head aside, exposing the softness of his neck between the helmet and armored jacket. She had the knife ready to thrust downward, but he stabbed her first. She cried out when the sniper's blade sank into her thigh.

Dani managed to hang on to him long enough to tear his helmet off and fling it aside. He yanked his blade from her leg, and she screamed again but grabbed his wrist. In the darkness they tumbled on the ground, fighting to end the other with their knives. She twisted his wrist so he dropped his blade, but he jerked free of her grasp and struck her jaw.

Though stunned by the blow and with him almost on top of her, Dani swung her knife upward, slicing his face open. He spun away from her, clutching the wound. She went after him, but her leg failed to move with the strength she needed.

The sniper countered by tackling her and slamming her to the ground. Dani lost the knife in the fall, and her air was cut off when he put his hands around her neck. She flailed against him, but strikes to his arms and face didn't make him loosen his grip.

Dani groped along the ground with one hand, hoping to find a knife or her pistol, but what she found instead was a jagged stone that filled her palm. She swung it up and caught him in the face. He slumped off her and fell to the ground on his side. Dani rolled him to his back, and he groaned, blood pouring from the deep gash near his eye. She couldn't hear Miles or Mary calling her name. She couldn't see the face of a young man before her. Rage blinded her senses to everything else as she brought the stone down on him again and again.

CHAPTER
28

As soon as Mary's knees buckled for seemingly no reason, Miles knew his team was in trouble. He couldn't get "Sniper!" out of his mouth quickly enough.

Dani had managed to get herself and Mary to cover, but Kelsey was gone in an instant. His body lay in the middle of the path with a pool of blood around his helmet. Miles's frantic dive to get behind a boulder near the side of the road hadn't been fast enough.

The sniper's round had torn through the side of his thigh. Miles had his belt off and was strapping it around his leg above the wound when he glanced up. Dani's hands were covered in blood as she hovered over Mary. Dani appeared okay or at least mostly okay, but Mary could not survive that much blood loss in the field.

Cameron and Ramos seemed unhurt, except for the general's preexisting injuries. Beckett was already dead, and Miles couldn't tell if Larsson was dead or not. If he wasn't, he was smart enough to lie still, since his position was exposed.

Each time Miles moved to try to locate the sniper, a shot ricocheting off the boulder or whizzing by his ear made him tuck back into his spot. Everyone was pinned. Miles maneuvered out of his pack, careful to not expose his head or limbs while doing so. He paused when he realized Mary wasn't moving.

"Dani!"

She didn't answer. The way she clung to Mary, her shoulders shaking with sobs, told him Mary was dead.

"Fuck," he said, and closed his eyes, forcing the desire to mourn out of his mind. He'd lost many friends in this war, but Mary was different. She was family. His team was pinned by a sniper who had already killed two of his people and at least one from Ramos's team. Miles needed to do something other than huddle behind a boulder and weep.

He fished his long-range comm from his pack and turned it on. They were still too deep in the valley for a signal. He needed to be on a hill, get lucky enough to find a signal, and send a message out. But the sniper wasn't letting anyone move. He had no choice but to wait. He adjusted the belt on his thigh to make it a little tighter. The bleeding had slowed, but it needed to stop before it weakened him too much.

Miles pulled the small med kit from his pack and worked to patch his wound.

The forest had been quiet after the initial attack, but now birds began chirping again. It would have been a peaceful setting except for the Warden sniper just waiting to kill Miles and the others. As darkness fell, Miles hoped that this was their chance to escape. That hope was dashed when the sniper fired in Dani's direction, splintering bits off the tree she was behind.

Miles could just see her form but only when she moved. Another shot was fired at her.

"Stop moving," he said, but she didn't reply. She was going to get herself killed, and he couldn't have that. Losing her was not an option.

He adjusted the belt on his thigh to loosen it a little. He was pleased when the field dressing held and the wound didn't start pouring blood again. Wiggling his toes caused some discomfort in his thigh. He needed to make sure he could stand, though standing would be excruciating. Miles rolled to his side, considering his chances to make it to Dani without dying. He froze when he couldn't spot her outline anymore.

Mary's body was still on the ground where she'd been lying, but he didn't see Dani near her. He sat up a little. "Dani?"

She didn't respond.

"Shit. Dani!"

She still didn't answer, and the tightness in his chest worsened with increasing fear. He ducked when a shot struck his boulder, taking a bit of the rock with it. A subtle blue light caught his attention as it illuminated Mary's body. "What the hell?" He paused, mesmerized by the glow. *The DNA thing worked!*

He still couldn't see Dani anywhere near Mary, so he rolled to a crouch. His thigh protested every movement, but he had to leave his cover. He bolted and used his arm to try to protect his head. His limping gate slowed him, but he managed to not take a rifle round through another body part during his sprint. He lunged the last few steps and slid to a stop next to Mary.

Dani was not there. He realized, to his horror, that Dani had gone up the hill after the sniper. A plasma pistol shot fired up on the ridge drew his attention. He couldn't get up the hill quickly enough to reach Dani, but Mary could with a fully healed body.

Mary drew in her first breath and groaned.

"Hey," he said, patting her cheek to make her wake faster. "Christ, Mary, make this quick." Dani's pained scream caused him to shift his hands to Mary's shoulders and shake her. "Wake up!"

She opened her eyes and moistened her lips with her tongue. "Holy shit, that was weird."

Dani screamed again, and Mary's eyes widened. Miles fed her arms through her pack's straps to remove it, then pulled her up while still tucked behind their cover. He thrust her rifle into her hands and positioned her hands on the weapon. "You got it? You can shoot?"

"Yeah."

"Dani went after the sniper. Get your ass up there and take him out."

"On it." Mary's first few steps were unsteady, but she was still quicker than Miles could manage.

He couldn't ignore the searing pain in his leg with each step, but he still moved as best he could. Mary bounded up the hill, leaving him behind. He and Mary both called for Dani, but he never heard her reply.

Mary reached her first, so Miles could only hear her say, "Oh, God."

He couldn't see Dani yet and feared he'd find her dead. When he arrived, his mouth hung open.

The moonlight cast enough light on Dani. She stood over a body, her chest heaving with exertion. She held a stone in one hand, and both she and the stone were covered in dark, dripping matter that could only be blood and other bits of a former Warden.

"Dani, look at me," Miles said.

She slowly turned to face him, and there was a blankness in her stare. She wasn't at all herself.

He took a tentative, limping step toward her, and she gripped the stone tighter. He holstered his pistol and held his hands up, palms out. Mary shifted her rifle to move it to her back.

Dani turned her hand and gazed down at the stone in it. She looked at the body on the ground, then back at the stone.

"You're okay, Dani. It's safe now."

She shook her head.

"It is. It's safe."

Tears spilled from her eyes as she continued to shake her head. She opened her hand, and the stone rolled out of her palm. "No."

Miles limped to her, and she pushed him away when he tried to touch her.

"No," she said, shaking her head. She swatted his hand off her arm and stepped away from him, but she stopped when she spotted Mary. Dani's face contorted into a deep frown. "No. No, it's *not* okay. It's not!" Dani drew in a ragged sob, and Miles touched her shoulder.

She continued to babble, shaking her head, and Miles pulled her close to him despite her efforts to break free. "It'll be okay," he murmured into her hair, but she continued to unravel and struggle to escape his arms. A tranq pistol hissed, and Dani flinched when the dart struck the back of her thigh.

The sedative relaxed her body, and her muttering ceased as unconsciousness took over. Miles lowered her to the ground.

"Why the hell did you do that?" he asked, glaring at Mary.

She holstered her tranq pistol and knelt next to Dani. "She's lost her goddamn mind." Mary frowned as she wiped some of the gore off Dani's face. "We don't have time to sort this shit out on a hill in the middle of the fucking night."

"I can't carry her down." Miles waved his hand at his injured leg.

"Okay." Mary shrugged. "So maybe the plan to tranq her could've been done a bit better."

Miles sighed and ran his hand through his hair.

"She'll be out for a good twenty-four hours," Mary said. "Radio for help. I'll check on the others."

"Hey," he said before she started back down the hill. "Kels, um. He … I mean, unless he did the Echo experiment like you … The round he took didn't decapitate him, so maybe he'll have a chance to regen."

Mary drew in a sharp breath and didn't move. "There's no chance."

"I'm so sorry, Mary."

She wiped her hand across her nose as she sniffled, then started down.

Miles buried his face in his hands and sighed. Kelsey was dead. Mary was dead, then had had an abnormally delayed regen. And Dani had come undone and smashed a Warden's head into nothingness, which left him essentially decapitated. He couldn't regen from that. "What a fucking disaster." He dropped his hands, pulled out his comm, and sighed with relief to finally have enough of a signal to transmit coordinates.

CHAPTER

29

Oliver was starving, but he opted to skip going for food when the others in the tech lab left. He glanced around one more time to make sure he was alone before leaving his computer station for the comm equipment. He had never gotten a clear answer for why he'd been pulled out of weapons training today, but it wasn't his job to ask questions—unless he wanted to get screamed at by his DI. He'd learned that lesson the hard way.

His hands shook when he picked through the comm gear. He needed to do this quickly. This might be his only chance to get a message to his father that Colonel Houston had planned ahead to take him on his birthday and send him to New Brunswick.

Part of their lab assignments were to dismantle and put equipment back together. Unfortunately, one of the comm specialists had just torn apart the communication gear, then left to eat. Oliver now had to put the damn thing back together, send his message, then tear it apart again before she returned.

His need to do this quietly dissolved as the minutes ticked by. He tossed parts and tools aside when done with them and then pawed through other tools to find ones he needed. The unit was barely together, and Oliver gasped when the light on it blinked to indicate it was operational.

He attached a small diagnostic panel and programmed the device to sync with his father's comm. His hands shook uncontrollably, and his palms were damp with sweat. He keyed in his message as quickly as he could. Oliver's head snapped up when he heard someone move the door handle to the lab. He didn't wait to see who was coming in before he ducked down.

Oliver spotted boots walking toward him, and he tried to finish the message. Parts and gear from the table behind him crashed down over him and bounced off his back. He looked up to see Anton, the person in the boots, standing on one side of him. Javi, whom Oliver hadn't known was there, stood on the other side and had been the one to shove the equipment off the table and to the floor.

His eyes widened and he couldn't speak.

Anton snatched the panel from his hands and disconnected it from the comm unit. He snapped the comm in half and tossed it into the rest of the mess surrounding Oliver. The lab's door opened again, but Oliver was still stunned and crouched on the floor.

"What the hell is all that noise?"

Oliver swelled with anger to hear Colonel Houston's voice. He started to stand, but Javi put his hand on his shoulder and kept him down.

"Oh," Anton said. "I accidentally knocked over some of the equipment."

"Where is he?" Houston asked.

Javi leaned down and shoved broken equipment into Oliver's arms and picked up a piece himself. He shifted his hand from Oliver's shoulder to his back and grabbed a handful of his uniform.

Oliver clutched the parts in his arms and stood when Javi pulled him up. An anger unlike anything he'd ever felt before clouded his mind, and he wanted to throw everything in the room at the colonel. He wanted her to suffer for what she'd done to him and his friends and forcing them into the army. He wanted to scream at her, and when he took a breath to open his mouth, Javi kept his grip on the back of his shirt.

Javi tossed the part he had in his other hand back onto the table. "He's here. Just helping clean up Anton's mess."

Anton nodded and bent to pick up more equipment and put it back on the workstation.

"Good," Houston said, and turned to head back out the door. "Leave the mess. Let's go."

Oliver finally regained his senses. He flung the gear in his arms onto the table. "I'm *not* going anywhere with her!"

Javi dragged him around the tables toward the door. Oliver tried to stop, but his boots only squeaked and slid across the floor.

Anton trotted to catch up. "Oliver, listen. We're leaving, including you, but Javi and I will be on the ship too."

"*Ship?* Where's Dad? This isn't right. She—"

"Shut up," Javi said. He stopped and leaned close to Oliver's face. "Not one fucking word about what happened. Anton and I know what she did was wrong. We are here to help you and are the *only* people you can trust right now. Do what she says. I don't care how much you hate her. Keep your goddamn mouth shut."

Anton nodded. "We're working on it, Oliver. I swear, we are. But you have to cooperate and play the game a bit longer."

Oliver shook his head. He *hated* Houston. "She killed Aunt Hattie!"

"I know," Anton said. "We know. But your dad, Dani, and Mary are out searching for General Ramos—"

"Santi's gone?" Oliver asked, unwilling to believe another friend was in trouble.

Javi glared at Anton, who clamped his mouth closed and opted to stare at the floor. Javi then turned his gaze to Oliver. "Your dad's safety depends on you doing what you're told. That's all you need to know."

Oliver nodded.

"Good," Javi said. He tugged on Oliver's shirt, and this time Oliver walked without fighting him. By the time they reached the door, Javi had released him.

Oliver imagined pummeling Houston when he spotted her. His anger almost made him charge her until he realized she was talking with Captain Lundquist. He didn't want to embarrass the captain. He also didn't want to do anything that would cause his father harm. Oliver wasn't sure what Javi meant about his dad's safety, so he opted to follow his advice. He didn't have to be happy about it, but he could at least avoid doing something stupid.

"Jackman," Lundquist said. "You're leaving today with Colonel Houston to go with her for on-ship training."

Oliver watched his captain's face. Before and after he spoke, Lundquist's lips blanched because he'd pressed them together so hard. The captain wasn't pleased with this arrangement either. Something was very abnormal for Houston to pull him out of basic training like this. He didn't want to go with her. Never in a million years would Oliver have believed he would *want* to stay in basic training. But that was what passed through his mind. Fear fluttered in the middle of his chest. Houston had killed Aunt Hattie. Maybe he was next. *No. Javi and Anton will protect me. Won't they?*

He wasn't sure.

She killed Aunt Hattie in front of everyone. If she wanted me dead, she could have done it at my party. She's up to something. Oliver decided to play along as Anton had said. He realized he'd never responded to his captain. "Yes, sir," he said.

Lundquist said, "Go to your barracks and pack—"

Houston interrupted. "No need, Captain. We have everything he needs on *Splendor*. Come along, Private Jackman."

Oliver wasn't sure how long he could tolerate following her orders. And now she spoke to him as though he were a puppy. "Yes, ma'am," he said through clenched teeth. He gave a lingering look at Lundquist as he passed, but the captain only nodded to him. He walked with Javi and Anton to a helicopter and climbed in.

Houston didn't say anything else to him, and Oliver was glad. It would be fine to never speak to her again. Once he was strapped in and the helicopter pilot readied to lift off, that was when Oliver realized he was leaving his friends behind. The sinking feeling in his gut was nauseating. He was alone in this nightmare, had never gotten his message off to his father, and was stuck serving under a murderer. Life couldn't get any worse.

"Oliver," Houston said, "I've seen your progress reports during basic. Thankfully, what I need you for doesn't require your dreadful marksmanship scores." She smiled at him. "I'm leading the ground assault for an attack on Toronto, and you're coming with me. Your cartography skills will be quite handy as we prepare for our assault."

He was wrong. Life had just gotten worse. The murderer was taking him straight to the front lines. He managed to speak only two words. "Yes, ma'am."

CHAPTER

30

Miles had called in an extraction, and the CNA arrived a few hours later with helicopters and a couple of jets for added firepower as escorts. Miles had avoided mentioning Ramos as one of the team needing extraction, but the Commonwealth in Vermont assumed that the general had been found. Mary didn't complain. The extra troops were the only reason they were able to take the bodies of both Beckett and Kelsey out too. Had Miles and his team been forced to hike out, the bodies would've been left behind.

Larsson had been injured and smart enough to lie still to avoid having the sniper finish him off, so he was one less body to add to the death toll Houston had caused in her attempt to sabotage Ramos.

Mary sighed. The tent in the Burlington camp was much warmer than their nights in the field, but a heavy weight remained in her chest. She dipped a rag into the basin of clean water, then wrung the excess water out. She'd been through four basins already, but at least now she was doing the final cleanup of Dani's face and arms. She worked in silence as she cut Dani's tattered clothes off and threw them on the floor.

Sometimes she needed to stop cleaning and weep for Kels, but she eventually got all the blood off her friend.

Once she finished, she pulled the blanket up to Dani's shoulders and tucked it in. Dani's new clothes were folded and in a stack on the floor next to her cot. Mary busied herself with straightening other items in the tent. It kept her mind occupied with something other than Kelsey's death and Dani's complete unraveling. She looked up when Miles entered. He was in clean fatigues, and his limp was gone. He watched Dani for a moment, then picked up the shirt from the floor that Mary had cut off her.

"How are her arm and leg?" Miles asked.

"Both repaired by one of the medics here."

He poked three fingers through the hole in the center of the shirt. "Mine shrapnel didn't do this. Why does this have a plasma pistol hole burned through it?"

"I, uh … we … I helped her force a regen. Shot her in the chest."

"So she survived the blasts."

Mary winced. "Yes and no. She was in terrible pain, and the wounds would've killed her in time—time we didn't have with the Wardens so close."

"Killing her sooner was your idea?"

"Hers. I didn't want to be there when she shot herself, but she couldn't hold the gun steady, and … Jesus, Miles, that was the hardest thing I've ever had to do in my life."

Miles dropped the shirt and touched her shoulder. "I'm not blaming you for anything, Mary. I'm glad you were there to help her."

Her eyes burned yet again, so she closed them as the hot tears formed. "This is so fucked up."

"I'm sorry about Kels." He hugged her, and she settled against him and wept.

When she pulled herself together, Mary stepped away and wiped her face. "Thanks."

"Yeah."

"What's Ramos doing about Houston?"

Miles sighed, and Mary assumed it was terrible news. They stepped out of the tent and found a place to sit. One of the Burlington locals brought them bowls of Brigand stew. Mary wasn't hungry, but she ate a little anyway. They sat in silence for a while, eating and watching the boats on the bay. She glanced at her watch; they had a good six hours or so before Dani would wake from the tranq dart.

"Houston's gone and not answering any of the general's messages," Miles said, keeping his voice low. "She took *Splendor* from Boston."

Mary swallowed too quickly with this news and coughed. When she could speak, her eyes were wide with surprise. "She took his ship *too*? Holy shit, that woman has some balls."

"She's headed north with part of the fleet out of Boston. They can track the ships, but none are responding to hails. General Ramos figures she's ordered them to maintain radio silence."

"So no one can change her plans for her."

"Right. He's pissed, Mary."

"As he should be."

"He's given new orders to stop the fleet movements and for Houston to return to Boston immediately."

"Which she won't do if she never receives the orders."

Miles nodded.

"So we put Santi on a bird and fly him out to *Splendor*," Mary said. "Let him take over everything from there. Throw Houston into the drink. Shoot her. Whatever."

"It's not that easy. The general is still in surgery. His leg was really fucked up, and the infection has spread. He can only do so much from a healing pod."

"How long is it going to take before he's well enough to leave?"

"A few days," Miles said, and shrugged. "Maybe longer."

"Goddammit," Mary said, shoving her bowl aside. She remained silent for a few moments. "What about Oliver?"

Miles gave her a smile. "Ramos has already sent word for him and the others taken from Bangor to be sent home."

"Good. How soon will that happen?"

"I'm not sure, but it should be quick."

"Finally, some good news," Mary said, nodding. "Houston's headed to Toronto; that's where she wanted to attack. We need to intercept her before she gets there and fucks everything up."

Miles's brow creased as he considered this option. He began to nod. "Yes. Yes! That's how we get in and stop her. Ramos can't fly but we can." He put his bowl aside and stood.

Mary caught his arm. "What about Dani?"

"Oh, uh," he said, and sighed. "We'll have to wait and see how she is doing. She may not be able to leave Burlington."

Mary winced when he said the words, though she knew them to be true. Dani's time in the war might be over. "I'll stay with her until she wakes and see how she is. Go to Ramos, and once he's awake, tell him what we want to do. Get us some new orders."

"I will. Send for me if you need any help with Dani."

"I can handle her." *I hope.* "Go."

Mary headed back to the tent and finished tidying things while Dani slept. She discarded the torn, bloodied clothes and dumped the basin. She brought in food and water for when Dani did wake up. With nothing else left to straighten or organize, Mary settled on the floor next to Dani's cot to try to rest. She wasn't aware that she'd fallen asleep until she startled awake when someone touched her arm.

She sat up and rubbed her eyes. Dani sat on the cot and held the blanket around her bare body.

"Sorry," Dani said. "Didn't want to step on you. I need clothes."

"Yeah. Of course," Mary said, trying to clear the fog from her mind. She picked up the pile of folded clothing from the floor and placed it on the cot next to Dani. "Need any help getting dressed?"

"Don't think so."

Mary nodded, and turned to give Dani privacy. She poured water into a mug and straightened the food wafers to kill time while listening to Dani move around behind her. "How are you feeling?"

"Like I was tranqed. You can turn around. What happened? I'm in a tent, so we must be in Burlington. How did that happen? *When* did that happen?"

Mary turned, and Dani was seated on the edge of the cot. She had her tank top and fatigue bottoms on while she pulled her socks on.

"What's the last thing you remember?" Mary asked.

Dani paused, one sock still in her hand. "Uh, we were on that trading path, and I remember wondering why we hadn't made camp yet because it was getting late."

Mary remained silent while Dani's expression shifted to a furrowed brow. Dani tilted her head. When her eyes focused back on Mary, she took a deep, shuddering breath. She launched off the cot, dropping the sock, and consumed Mary in a crushing embrace.

"You're alive. Christ, I can't believe you're alive. You were dead and didn't regen." Dani released Mary and frowned. "You *died*."

"The regen took a while to start, but I don't know why. Santi saw me when I started glowing. Miles and I told him and the others that I was always an Echo lying about being human so they wouldn't know I was one of Houston's lab rats. They think it took me a long time to bleed out, and we let them continue to think that."

"Ah." Dani nodded. "Good idea. Who tranqed me?"

Mary's face burned with embarrassment. "Me."

"*Again?*"

"The first time was over three years ago, Dani. Of all the shit you forget with a regen, you can't lose that memory too?"

Dani grinned. "I deserved it that time." She retrieved her sock to put it on. "Why did you tranq me this time?"

"The sniper who shot me, you, and the others … You, uh, killed him."

"I did?"

Mary pinched the bridge of her nose. "Sit." Once Dani was seated on the cot, Mary continued. "You're missing some big pieces from yesterday. The short version is you lost your shit when I didn't regen, killed the sniper, and lost your shit even more."

"Why?"

"A combination of things, I'm guessing. You fought the Warden, but by the time Miles and I got to you, he was already dead."

"Okay. So a dead Warden. No big deal," she said, and shrugged.

"No."

Dani frowned.

Mary hesitated, wondering how to tell Dani the next bit of news. She opted for straightforward. "You beat him to death. Then when you saw me back from the dead, you *really* lost it. So I tranqed you."

"I'm missing all *that*? Did I regen too?"

"No."

"Huh. So now I have memory gaps without a regen," Dani said. "Is this another complication of being a faulty Echo?"

"I don't know."

"I beat him to death?"

Mary nodded.

"Fuck me. I've never done anything like that before."

"No, you haven't. Are you okay?"

Dani began pulling her boots on. "I don't know. I don't remember a damn thing." She laced her boots and stood. "I've slept enough. I'm going for a walk."

"I'll go with you. Here." Mary passed Dani the mug and dropped several wafers into her palm. "You must be hungry."

"Starved." Dani popped a wafer into her mouth, started to leave the tent, then stopped. "Shit. Kels."

Mary didn't want to talk about him again. "Yeah. It sucks. Let's go."

CHAPTER
31

B y the time Rowan, Yura, and other members of the team picked up the trail of their prey, it was too late. Rowan ground his teeth and watched from a distant hill as CNA helos arrived. His team couldn't attack the CNA extraction team without getting obliterated.

"I put a sniper in this area," Curtis said.

"Not one good enough," Rowan said. Staying to watch the Commonwealth retrieve their people would only make him angrier, so he started back down the hill.

A few days later, they were back in Montreal, and Rowan stood alone in his office. He had a multitude of reports to both review and submit. Instead, he stared out the window overlooking the Saint Lawrence River and crossed his arms.

The chime to his door activated, and he was tempted to ignore it. He didn't want to be bothered by Curtis. The chime rang again, and Rowan spun and slapped the comm on his desk. "What?"

"Open the fucking door."

Rowan grinned to hear Yura's voice. He released the lock on the door and she entered.

"Took you long enough," she said as she strode toward him.

"Didn't know it was you."

She raised an eyebrow. "So if you had known, you would've opened the door right away?"

"Maybe."

She walked to his desk and started sorting through the panels lying on it.

"What do you think you're doing?" Rowan asked.

"I want to know what our next move is."

He caught her hand. "You do not have clearance for that information."

"I don't give a shit what the VR wants to do. I want to know what *our* next move is, Rowan. What are you plotting with Curtis?"

He released her hand and frowned. "Nothing."

"You're not giving up."

"No, I'm not. I'm just not planning anything with Curtis."

"You don't trust him."

Rowan shook his head. "I question his loyalty since he made VR in Boston. Sure, it was a brief appointment, but he took the role in my place."

Yura nodded and moved toward the window. Rowan joined her.

"What are your thoughts on him?" Rowan asked.

She shrugged. "My opinion doesn't matter. You don't trust him, neither do I. What do we do next?"

"I have a few ideas."

"Good. The CNA will burn for the Wardens they killed in the field."

He appreciated her spirit and willingness to do whatever it took to wipe out the CNA and humans. He'd blurred the lines on security clearances before and considered showing her what intel he had thus far. Rowan knew others were watching him. Any hint of detected treason and he'd be executed in an instant. He'd gotten away with it before, though. He didn't think Yura was a spy for any chancellors or the vice regent. She was different.

"Colonel Houston is the Commonwealth commanding officer in Maine," he said.

"Yeah. Heard of her. She's not as good as the CNA thinks she is."

Rowan turned to face Yura. "For whatever insane reason, our leadership tiptoes around her like she's some goddamn mastermind."

Yura laughed, and Rowan liked the sound.

"Mastermind?" Yura laughed again. "She got lucky, real lucky in Portland. And Boston? Aubrey allowed them to get too close."

Rowan nodded, noting that she hadn't mentioned Aubrey's cause of death being his plasma pistol.

"Why the fuck do the Wardens even allow the CNA to exist in Maine?" she asked.

"Because some are less devoted to exterminating the humans than they should be."

Yura returned to the panels on Rowan's desk. "They've grown tired and complacent. This war should have ended decades ago, with us owning Earth."

Rowan nodded, but was still cautious of Yura's intentions.

"So," she said, turning to face him. "How do we wipe these mortal assholes off our planet and end the war for good at the same time?"

Those words were the key to unlocking his hesitation to trust her.

Rowan swept the panels on his desk aside and turned his desktop into a larger screen. He pulled up a map of North America's Northeast. It showed colorized regions with vast swaths of Warden-controlled territory, including the southern portion of Maine.

"This is how things looked in New England when I was in Portland," Rowan said. "I begged for orders to overtake the state and was refused." He changed the screen to a new map showing the reduction in Warden territories. "This is from six months ago." He pulled up another map. "This is a week old."

Yura leaned in closer. "The CNA is expanding. Slowly at first, but now they're really on the move." She circled around the desk, never taking her eyes from the map, until she stood so close to Rowan that their sides touched.

He had a hard time focusing on the map.

"Zoom out," she said, and he adjusted the image. "Can you overlay the locations of their naval forces?"

He paused. Technically that data was above her rank. But she was smart and seeing the same things he'd seen in Commonwealth movements over the last several weeks. He keyed in the code to upload pinpoints for known ship locations. "It's not exact, but it's relatively accurate for what ships are where. Sometimes we can only get size data." He pointed at one of the colored dots. "This blue one near Boston is a carrier, but we don't know exactly what these others are. Likely LHAs, if I had to guess. These green ones are their smaller and faster vessels like destroyers. The red dots are various dock ships."

Yura whistled, then straightened. "Lots of red and green dots with a mix of a few blues clustering together." She turned to face him. "Carriers are huge. With the smaller ships, they can get through the locks."

"Yes."

"Huh. Ballsy. They're going after Toronto."

Rowan nodded, neither of them taking a step back to allow for more space between them.

"What is leadership doing about it?" Yura asked.

"Monitoring the situation."

Yura rolled her eyes. "Fucking idiots."

He couldn't agree with her more.

She returned her gaze to the map. "We failed to capture Ramos in the field. Any news on him?"

"No. I'm assuming he survived, but these movements look more like Houston's work. See these erratic-looking expansions of their territory?" He pointed to areas around the Saint Lawrence Seaway.

"Yeah."

"Leadership is more focused on those areas. Houston's prior tactics have involved feints as a means of distraction. Our people fall for it every time. *This*, though … this is truly erratic, and these are useless territory grabs."

She turned toward him again. "How do you know?"

"Nothing about Boston went as Houston planned. She had help from Ancients and some of her own troops, plus a couple of Brigands went rogue and entered the city on their own. They created a lot of havoc while here."

"And killed your wife."

"She was one of many who died in that assault. Houston's problem is arrogance. I've studied her service record. She has been promoted right up the ladder through the years. Except Boston. She got credit for retaking the city, but she was never promoted for it. She needs to make up for that slight and is going to try to show everyone how great a leader she truly is."

"Except she's a shit tactician."

Rowan laughed and nodded.

Yura grinned. "She'll foolishly go after Toronto and lose."

"Yes," Rowan said. "And that's where we come in."

Yura returned her attention to the map and adjusted the image to zoom out more. "She'll have to do an amphibious assault from the water to attack Toronto."

"Yes." Rowan fell silent. He wanted to see just how smart Yura was and if she would figure out the rest.

"The CNA navy will come up the seaway, but they'll be limited in the size of the ships they can pass through because of the locks," Yura said. "They control enough of Quebec City to get around the city's waterway without too much harassment from Warden troops there."

Yura paused and Rowan waited.

"Houston will be with the amphibious task force," she said. She looked up and grinned. "She has to come right by us to get to Toronto. We'll slaughter them right here in Montreal. Meet them at the locks, wreck the navy, and kill all the ground troops on their vessels."

Rowan smiled. "Nicely done."

"How do we persuade the leadership to focus their efforts here?"

"That's the hard part."

"But you have ideas on that already, don't you?"

"Yes."

"Good. You can tell me about them after dinner."

She started to walk away from him, and he grabbed her arm. He pulled her close and kissed her. When their lips parted, she gave him a smirk.

"Took you long enough," she said.

He lifted her to sit on his desk and, while she unfastened his trousers, leaned across her to set his office comm that he was not to be disturbed.

CHAPTER

32

attie stood before a closed door attached to a weathered house north of Boston on the coast of Revere, Massachusetts. She'd already banged on the door once, and her irritation grew while she waited.

"Usman, I know you're in there," she said.

When answered with silence, she pounded her fist against the door again, threatening to beat it off its frame until it was jerked open. The middle-aged man standing inside the home scowled at her until his eyes widened.

"*N'Diyae?*"

"Hattie. I've told you before to call me Hattie. Call me by that other name again and I'll permanently end you."

He rolled his eyes. "Yeah, yeah. And I've heard *that* before."

Hattie pulled the plasma pistol from the holster behind her hip and pressed the muzzle against his forehead. His eyes turned upward to the weapon.

"*Don't* fuck with me," she said.

With the muzzle still touching his head, Usman shifted his gaze to his battered door. "I think you shook the hinges loose."

She holstered the pistol and pushed past him. His home was old, dark, and stank of filth. She wrinkled her nose, figuring there was likely a decomposing animal carcass or two some-where inside the house. It was the perfect cover for a Brigand and especially an Ancient. He closed the door and joined her.

He touched her arm. "A recent regen. You look good."

"We don't have time for that," Hattie said. "I need to use your bunker."

He sighed and headed deeper into the house. "All business just like last time. Still with that hybrid? Jake?"

Hattie bristled with the question and didn't bother to clarify Jace's name or mention that Jace was dead. She and Usman had become lovers after arriving on Earth centuries ago. He still had a thing for her; she'd moved on. But now she needed his help.

He activated a trigger that opened a fake wall, revealing a spotless, well-lit stairwell. Hattie had been here before, so she started down the stairs, leaving him to seal them inside and fol-low. More lights activated as she moved deeper into the bowels of his bunker, and she heard his echoing steps a moment later as he began his descent.

Once she reached the bottom, she waited for him to catch up.

"What is it this time?" he asked.

"I need to get a message out."

He shrugged. "Use your own equipment for that."

"Can't. I need *your* gear."

He grinned and rubbed his palms together. "Interesting. What's it worth to you?"

Everything. "We'll talk price later."

"Oh, N'Di—um. Hattie, you know that's not how this works."

The death threat about my name worked better than I expected. She considered using another one, but instead changed tactics. "How about entering this war as an active participant and help-ing us turn this thing around?"

His brow furrowed. "That's just an invitation to get myself

killed. Besides, I've helped you plenty. My jets helped you take Boston, and you already have the new helo designs. Now you want me to play messenger for free? That's a shit business model."

"I'll tell you what I want done, and you can name the price. We'll bargain from there."

"Wonderful," Usman said, and smiled. "You're desperate." He spun and led her toward his comm room.

Shit. Hattie frowned and followed him. She was indeed desperate.

He powered up his gear, and Hattie, as always, envied his rig. Usman was a genius and had designed and built everything he used in the bunker. He had been an Ekkohrian engineer centuries ago and had not lost his gift. What the Commonwealth lacked in sophistication because of the war's catastrophic effect on technological developments, Usman just created what he needed and made it work. He'd built his bunker long before the war started and stayed here, operating under the Wardens' noses without ever being discovered. Hattie couldn't deny his brilliance.

He turned to face her once everything was powered up. "Who am I contacting and why?"

"The CNA's basic training camp in New Brunswick. I need to reach Captain Lundquist there," Hattie said.

He put his hands on his hips, waiting for the rest of her answer.

Hattie wanted to strangle him. "Colonel Houston of the CNA took four young Bangor residents and threw them into the ranks. I need to reach Lundquist to tell him to send them back. Houston's gone off the rails and needs to be stopped for several other reasons, but I need to get those Bangor kids home before she gets them killed."

"By law, the CNA is still allowed to take civilians."

"Not in my fucking town."

Usman grinned. "I see. It's a personal jab on both sides."

"Yes," Hattie said.

"So that's why you're desperate. One or more of these youngsters *that* important to you?"

She hated that he figured everything out so quickly. Despite her scowl, she nodded.

"Revenge! I love it. Then what?"

"Then nothing. Just set up the damn link for me."

"That's it?"

"Yes."

He frowned and turned to the screen closest to him. "Well, that's boring as hell. No coup to overthrow her? No message to an assassin to take her out?" He glanced back at her. "Nothing?"

Hattie would overthrow Catherine; that was a given. She just didn't need Usman's help with that part.

His panel beeped and he stepped aside, waving her toward the device. "This is set up to go straight to his personal device. You'll look like an incoming message from the very top of the CNA."

Hattie really wanted to know how Usman could create that kind of link through his system and wished she had his gear.

"Cost?" she asked.

"First one is free," he said, and winked.

She resisted an urge to shoot him. Hattie pressed the button to open the link. Within a few seconds, Lundquist's face appeared on the screen.

"What the hell is this?" Lundquist asked. "You're not the admiral."

"Colonel Catherine Houston took four of my residents from Bangor and dropped them at your camp for training," Hattie said. "I know she's on her way to your camp to pick up Oliver Jackman. She took him illegally since he is underage. You need to send all four of my people back to Maine."

Lundquist's brow creased. "Private Jackman left with Colonel Houston already. The other three arrived in Bangor yesterday."

"Oh. Um, I've been away for a few days. Who ordered them to be sent back to Maine? Houston?"

Lundquist hesitated.

"Santi?"

The captain nodded slowly.

This was both great news and shit news. Catherine had Oliver, but Ramos had been found and had sent orders to Lundquist to release the Bangor residents. He'd just sent the orders too late to spare Oliver from Catherine's bullshit.

"Has Catherine already left New Brunswick to sail for Toronto?"

Lundquist leaned in closer to the screen and lowered his voice. "Who are you?"

"I'm an Ancient and a key reason why the CNA has Boston back. Answer my fucking question."

"Yes," he said. "She already left."

"Headed for Toronto, yes?"

Lundquist nodded.

"Fuck." Hattie took a deep breath. "Can you reach her to let her know of Santi's orders to send Oliver home?"

"I already tried. She's operating on radio silence."

"Have you contacted the general to let him know?"

"I haven't been able to reach him. I'm told he isn't well."

Hattie paused, thinking. She had an ally in Lundquist, who was clearly loyal to Ramos and not Houston or he would never have answered her questions. If Dani and the others were still alive, they might be able to intercept Houston.

"Do you have any information on Santi's team in Burlington?" Hattie asked.

"How is it you have details of such sensitive information?"

"I just do, and be glad I'm on your side. Does he have Captain Miles Jackman or the Brigands with him in Vermont?"

"I don't have those details, but I'll contact them to inquire." He paused. "What is going on?"

"Houston is persuading everyone that Toronto is a viable target. It isn't. The ships headed there will get stuck in Montreal and our people will be slaughtered. She's falsified intel reports and attack models. She doesn't have the troops in and around Montreal as she's implied."

"Shit," Lundquist said.

"Yep."

"I'll continue to try to reach General Ramos and get back to you, um … I don't know your name."

"Hattie. Tell anyone I'm an Ancient, and you're a dead man."

"Understood," he said, and nodded sharply.

She turned to Usman, removed a panel from her pocket, and handed it to him. "Transmit everything on this to him, including a link so he can send encrypted messages to me on it." She turned back to Lundquist. "You probably won't be able to do anything with this data, because if you send it up the chain of command, you'll have to explain how you got it. I can't see that going well. But you'll see that I'm not lying about the cluster fuck awaiting our troops if Catherine isn't stopped. Do what you can to reach Santi and stay in touch. I'll do the same."

"I will. I'm sorry I couldn't get Private Jackman to you sooner."

Hattie nodded; she was sorry she had been too late tracking down his commanding officer and getting him home. She ended the comm link and sighed.

Usman worked at another station to send the data to Lundquist. Hattie noticed his silence. His eyes were downcast when he returned the panel to her.

"They're all gonna die in Montreal," he said.

"Yes."

"Tens of thousands will be killed. This would likely turn the war against us for good. The CNA would retreat with that kind of ass-kicking."

"Yes."

He lifted his head and met her gaze. "Can't have that bull-shit," he said with a sudden airy tone. "What do we do?"

Hattie smiled. "You have a network of Brigands and CNA here in Mass. I know you do. Round up all ground troops that you can across New England and send them north to Montreal. The fleet will have to slow down there to pass through the locks, and we'll need to be there in time to secure the locks and prevent the slaughter."

"You're still going to let Houston pass through them to go to Toronto?"

"Hell no! If I have my way, she drowns in that river. Santi can decide what he wants to do, but I'm betting he sticks with Dani's original plan to take Montreal and leave Toronto alone for now."

"What are you going to do?"

"I'll let you know."

"I'm not doing this for free, Hattie."

"I know. Now let me out. I have shit to do."

Usman led her back up the stairs and opened the door. The rank odor of the rotten house filled her nose in an instant. She winced at the smell and slipped out. "I'll be in touch," she said, and hurried out.

She wanted to take a chance at persuading the CNA brass in Boston to intercept Houston first. Then she had a stop in Port-land to meet another Ancient and a stop in Bangor to gather the rest of the Brigands in Maine to head for Quebec. She could only hope that Dani, Mary, and Miles were still alive, and wished for a quick confirmation of that from Lundquist. For now, she needed to hurry to get resources lined up and en route to Canada.

CHAPTER

33

Dani's wake-sleep schedule was still messed up after the tranq, so when she woke in the middle of the night, she unwound herself from Miles's arms to get up. The confusing nightmare just before waking helped motivate her to leave. She needed time to think.

Once extracted from his arms, she pulled the blanket over his naked body and noticed that he'd barely stirred with her leaving.

As she dressed, her mind churned. General Ramos's recovery following surgery had taken several hours. But he had awakened long enough to give Miles his new orders. Burlington didn't have resources like Portland or Boston, so they had to wait until the next day for a helo to arrive to fly them out to Levis—the CNA-held city south of Quebec City. From there they would take another helo to fly over the river and intercept Houston either north or south of the city, depending on where she was. She could avoid receiving radio comms, but she couldn't sneak her fleet past Quebec City without being noticed. The CNA troops in the city had not seen the fleet yet, so she was still somewhere downstream from it.

The helo would deposit Miles and his team on *Splendor*, and

Miles would deliver the general's orders for Houston to stand down and halt the attempt to take the locks at Montreal before any fighting started.

If everything worked out that way, it was a good plan.

Dani finished pulling on her boots and grabbed her jacket before heading out. She still had no recollection of bashing a Warden to death, and Miles wasn't acting like himself around her. She wandered toward the bay and recognized Mary's long, blond hair and silhouette. She sat on a bench facing the water, and Dani headed toward her, deliberately scuffing her boots on the ground so she didn't startle her friend.

Mary glanced behind her as Dani approached.

"Hey," Dani said, sitting.

"Hey."

They sat in silence for a while, watching the water and the clouds as they moved across the night sky, creating shadows as they passed in front of the moon. The breeze was crisp but not cold enough to send them retreating to someplace warmer. Dani tilted her head up to look at the stars between the clouds. It almost felt like being back in Bangor, sitting near the river, and a pang of homesickness struck.

"You're not sleeping well or you wouldn't be out here," Mary said.

"Had a bad dream, I think. Not sure." Dani shrugged. "It was more confusing than scary. How are you?"

Mary grunted as an answer.

Her friend wasn't ready to talk about herself, so Dani didn't press her. Mary was grieving for Kelsey and doing the best she could. The war didn't take breaks when loved ones lost their lives. The war just kept going, causing more death, terror, and grief every second it continued to drag on. Her thoughts drifted to Oliver, and she wanted to know he was safe even if he was stuck in basic training.

"I considered quitting," Mary said.

Dani's mind snapped back to the present when Mary spoke. "Quitting the war?" Dani asked.

"Quitting everything."

Dani turned on the bench to face her. "*No*, Mary. No."

"I can see now how you were tempted by suicide when Jace died. You could at least forget the pain of his loss with your screwy regens."

"And forget him, you, Miles, Oliver, Hattie, and everyone else."

Mary nodded.

"You wanted the ability to regen, and you got it. Don't make your next death permanent. It sounds like a good fix when the grief is the worst, but it isn't."

"I know."

"Mary," Dani said, taking her friend's hand. "Please, don't."

Mary turned to her and managed a small smile, though tears ran down her cheeks. "I won't. I considered it, Dani. That is all. I miss him."

"I know." Dani pulled her close. "I'm sorry he's gone," she said, refusing to imagine what her life would be like if she lost Miles.

"Thank you," Mary said, giving Dani a tight squeeze before releasing her. She shifted to sit forward with her elbows on her knees and looked out at the water. "How is Miles?"

"Exhausted. He didn't move when I got up to leave …"

Mary shifted her gaze to Dani when her words trailed off. "But?"

Dani frowned and stared at her hands in her lap. "He's acting weird. I catch him watching me like he's waiting for me to do something. When I asked him about it, he changed the subject. Even the sex is off. It's as if he's afraid he might break me or whatever."

"And the dream?"

Dani sighed and glanced at Mary, who continued to watch the water. "I was somewhere dark, but I didn't know where. I was angry at first but didn't know why. There was a dark shape on the ground, I was wet but it wasn't raining, and there was a silvery ghost-like thing watching me. I was afraid in that moment, but it wasn't because of the ghost. I don't know why I was scared. Then I woke up." She shrugged and rubbed her palms together to warm her fingers. "Just a bizarre dream, I guess."

"No." Mary straightened and turned to Dani. "It's a memory trying to resurface, not a dream."

"The Warden I killed?"

Mary nodded.

"You said I lost my shit when I saw you back from the dead after killing him. The ghost is you?"

Mary nodded again.

"Huh. Okay. So why is Miles on eggshells around me?"

"Dani, you bludgeoned a man to death and became incoherent when we arrived. Something inside you broke in that moment. You don't remember it now, but ..."

"But what if I break again?" Dani said, nodding. She fell silent, wondering what could have gone so wrong inside her head to make her beat a Warden to a pulp. The more concerning question was what if it *did* happen again, and would she recognize it in time to stop herself from completely unraveling? Who else might be hurt by her actions? Could she lose her shit enough to attack someone she loved while in the throes of whatever threat her mind perceived as imminent or lethal? Was the only way to know to put herself in that kind of situation and hope for the best?

She leaned forward and dropped her head into her hands. "I hate this fucking war. I forget why I'm even fighting anymore. It's just habit to carry a gun and try to kill Wardens before they kill me."

"They're shipping Kels back to New Hampshire tomorrow."

Dani lifted her head and looked at her friend. "Not Bangor?"

"He has family in Lincoln. I was just the girlfriend."

"No, Mary, that's not—"

Mary held up her hand, stopping Dani's protest. "He's going to New Hampshire, and I'm fine with that."

"I'm not! You should get a say."

"I did, and I told them to send him home."

Dani's brow crinkled. "Why?"

"Kels is one of the few people on this planet who has actual blood relatives still alive. I won't keep him from them."

"But—"

"He belongs with his family. He's dead and it's hard, but it's the right decision."

"Okay," Dani said, relenting. Mary had made her choice—a generous one, to Kelsey's family—but one that was final and not up for debate. "Are you taking a break?"

"From fighting? Hell, no. I want to—believe me, I do—but I won't. I'm sick of Houston's bullshit. As if the Wardens aren't enough of a headache, we now have her as an enemy too. She has to be stopped."

"I'm not sure I could be that stoic in the wake of … if … you know."

"You, more than anyone else, can accomplish whatever you set out to do."

Dani shook her head. "That's not true. I'm tired, Mary. I'm *really* fucking tired."

"Oliver," Mary said, standing.

"What?"

"You fight for Oliver. Always have, always will," Mary said, then left.

CHAPTER

34

D ani didn't like Mary's hasty departure, but she understood her friend's desire to be alone. She remained on the bench for a few minutes, squirmed, shifted her position several times, then left too. Unlike Mary, she didn't want to be alone, and returned to the tent where Miles continued to sleep. She pulled her headlamp from her pack and turned it on to see what had been left behind by other CNA soldiers who had passed through the camp's tent. A battered book with the cover and first few pages missing piqued her interest. The spine was too wrinkled to read, and most of the back cover was gone. She flipped through the book, pleased to find the pages readable though dog-eared in many places.

Dani adjusted her headlamp to dim the light and carried her new book with her to sit on the floor. She leaned her back against the bed frame. Miles stirred slightly but didn't wake. Satisfied she could read without disturbing him, Dani settled down with her find and enjoyed the small escape it gave her from the war, Oliver being in the CNA, Mary's traumatic death, and Dani's own horrific attack on a Warden. She lost all track of time.

A hand touched her shoulder, and she gasped, snapping her head up.

"Sorry," Miles said. "Are you okay? Why are you on the floor?"

"Oh." Dani blinked. It was still mostly dark out, but judging by the weak light filtering into the tent, the sun would be up soon. She hadn't planned to read so long. "I'm reading." She held up the book for him to see.

He slid closer to her. "What is it about?"

She liked the way his hand played over her shoulder and down her arm. "A princess and a pirate."

"A princess?" Miles half laughed. "I didn't know you liked fairy tales."

"It's a good story. You should read it."

"I don't know."

"There's a giant in it too."

"Any sex in it?"

Dani laughed. "That sounds like something Mary would ask. No. No sex."

"Pass."

They chuckled, and Miles touched her face.

"It's nice to see you smiling," he said.

"Yeah." Dani sighed. She removed her headlamp and turned the light off. She could still see Miles's features in the predawn light. "A lot of crazy shit happening lately." She paused, then decided she needed to ask the question burning in the back of her mind. She placed the book on the floor and turned to fully face him. "Miles, would you and Oliver do the experiment like Mary?"

He shifted to prop up on one elbow. "You mean to turn us into Echoes?"

Dani nodded.

"No."

She'd hoped for a different answer. "What? Why not?"

"Let's back up a sec. You said you, Mary, and Aunt Hattie destroyed the lab and all the data. You're telling me you didn't?"

"We did destroy everything as far as I know. But Anton can be sneaky. He may have kept some of the research."

"Why? Aunt Hattie told him to destroy it all."

"Yes, but maybe he didn't."

"Anton defying a direct order from Aunt Hattie? You really think he would risk the bodily harm that would come when—not if—but *when* Aunt Hattie found out?"

"Well, no."

Miles shrugged. "Then there's no point speculating about it."

"But what if you *could* become an Echo?"

"No."

Dani's shoulders drooped even more. "Why not?"

"Let's say I become an Echo. If I'm captured by the Wardens, I get turned into one of them. I become like Gavin. The man who used to be your and Mary's friend tried to kill you both once he was a Warden. I'd rather just die a human than risk turning into someone who murders my friends because my mind has been wiped and I can't stop myself from killing."

Gavin had indeed tried to kill Mary and Miles, but he'd hesitated, for *just* a moment, when he could have killed Dani during the attack on Boston. She'd seen a glimmer of the real Gavin in his eyes for a few seconds before the Warden reconditioning reclaimed him.

"Dani."

She looked up, not realizing she'd cast her gaze downward with her thoughts.

"Don't think for one second that I don't want to spend the rest of my life with you. Every day with you is amazing. But we can't mess with turning humans into Echoes. You know this or you wouldn't have destroyed the lab."

"But it's different now. We know whatever they did worked. Mary isn't human anymore."

Miles shook his head. "She's still human, Dani. She just happens to be able to regen now."

"Which is what makes her an Echo … or a hybrid. Okay, probably a hybrid. What if the war was over and won with no more Wardens? We could have a long time together."

"No, Dani. Wardens turn Echoes into Wardens. Now you, an Echo, want to turn humans into Echoes. What's the difference?"

"It's a huge difference! It wouldn't be for malicious purposes."

"But should it be done at all? It doesn't matter if it works or not if you're turning people into different things in a lab."

Dani opened her mouth to counter him, then paused. He had a good point. Dani's brother, Jace, had been a hybrid mix with their Echo father and his human mother. Jace hadn't inherited his father's ability to regen, though. Mary had been created with petri dishes, test tubes, and Dani's non-consent-ed-but-collected-anyway DNA. She still wanted to persuade Miles, even though she knew it was entirely for her own selfish reasons. "It would be your choice. Not forced like the Wardens."

Miles flashed a gentle smile. "And I choose not to do it."

Dani shook her head and groaned.

He leaned in and kissed her. "Dani, as an Echo you will outlive me. Please don't let that fear of losing me cause you to make poor decisions. Fucking around with DNA in a lab to *make* a human an Echo is wrong."

Mary had waded into murky ethical waters when she had agreed to the experiment. It was up to Mary to determine if she'd made the right decision or not. Dani figured Mary hadn't lost any sleep over it all and clearly had sentiments about mon-keying with DNA that Miles didn't share.

Dani ran her fingers through his hair and tried to give him

a smile. It only made her feel worse. "I fear losing everyone," she whispered.

"I do too." He touched his forehead against hers.

She pulled him close and held him for a while. Enjoying the feeling of him against her. When she relaxed her embrace, he kissed her with a fervor he hadn't displayed in far too long. It caught her off guard for only a moment, and her surprised gasp was quickly replaced with matching intensity.

They released each other to take a breath, and they both smiled. Dani moved away and stood. She stripped before him, dropping her clothes on the floor. He watched her every move. She neared the bed, and he lifted the blanket for her to join him.

He was aroused and so was she. Dani slid under the blanket next to him, but he didn't take her. He nuzzled her neck with the lightest of kisses while his hands moved over her body. This was the same gentle approach he'd taken with her before, and she didn't want that again.

"Miles?"

"Hmm?" he muttered against her neck.

"Miles, look at me."

He lifted his head. "Is everything okay? Do I need to slow down?"

"No! Fuck, no."

His brow creased. "Uh."

"Christ, Miles. I'm not fragile."

"Oh. But I—"

"You won't break me."

Realization dawned on his face. and his look of concern morphed into one of hunger. She grinned. "Yes," she said, the word sounding more like a hiss. He wanted her as much as she wanted him. "Now you get it."

Miles covered her mouth with his and rolled her to her

back. She pulled her lips from his to gasp when he entered her. *This* was the sex she wanted with him. She hooked one leg around him, lifting her hips to be closer to him. He used one hand to grip the bed frame for leverage, and Dani moaned, enjoying *everything* that followed.

CHAPTER
35

ani finished placing the last of her gear in her pack, which included the book she'd started reading, and checked around the small table to make sure she hadn't dropped anything in the grass. Satisfied that she had everything, she sealed the pack. Miles and Mary had their packs on and waited for her. They were due to be at the helo pad now so they'd already be present when their ride arrived. Dani hoped the helo was early, because the thick, dark clouds passing overhead made her dread a ride in the middle of a storm.

"We've got all day," Mary said. "Take your time."

Dani caught the snark in her tone and snorted. She slung the pack onto her back.

"Oh, shit," Mary said.

Dani looked up and turned, following Mary's gaze. General Ramos approached with a significant limp and leaning heavily against Cameron. Miles rushed to Santi's side to help support him. Dani grabbed a chair from beside the table, and they eased the general into it. Sweat poured down his ashen face. Santi drew in deep breaths, exhaustion etched into his features.

Miles sighed. "Cam, I know the medical team didn't clear him for a mission."

Cameron shook his head and frowned.

Ramos managed to lift his arm and waved dismissively at Miles. "I'm going, Major."

"The fuck you are," Dani said. "You look like shit."

Miles cleared his throat. Dani knew this was his signal that he wanted her to shut up, but she didn't care. Miles had to follow Commonwealth chain of command rules; she didn't.

"Sir—" Miles said.

Ramos pointed his finger at Miles. "Not another word, Major. I'm going."

"This is bullshit." Dani pulled her tranq pistol and pressed it against the general's neck.

"Christ," Miles muttered.

"The tranq is ramped up for Echoes, but it'll still flatten you for a few hours," Dani said. "Don't make me pull this trigger."

Mary chuckled and nodded. "She's crazy enough to do it, Santi. You need to sit this one out."

"I can—"

Dani interrupted him. "You're a goddamn corpse on legs. When your ass leaves this chair, it will be to go back to the field hospital. You can either walk there or go back on a stretcher with a tranq dart in your neck. Choose now."

Ramos wiped sweat from his face. He glared at her for a moment before his face softened. "It's Brigands like you who make me wonder why we partnered with Brigands in the first place," he said.

Dani reholstered her tranq pistol. "It's Brigands like me who will keep you alive a little longer so you can continue to pout about it."

Ramos chuckled and wiped at his face again. His demeanor turned serious when he focused his attention on Miles. "You'll still fly out today. You are to act in my place, Major."

"Yes, sir," Miles said.

Ramos pulled a panel from his pocket and typed while he spoke. "You're to reach the fleet at Quebec City, relay my orders to abort the attack on Toronto, and stop Houston. This will give you the clearance and my approval of those orders if anyone questions them. Arrest Houston and hold her in the brig until I can get there."

"Yes, sir."

"Once Houston is secured, I want you, Dani, and Mary back on the helo and proceeding to this rendezvous point for insertion into Montreal." Ramos passed the panel to Miles.

Dani leaned in for a closer look at a map on the screen.

Ramos continued, "Start recon ASAP and plant explosives where you decide it will give us the best tactical advantage. I'll work with the naval officers to develop a new assault plan. Montreal remains the target, and I'll send you new coordinates when we're ready to extract your team."

"Yes, sir."

Dani shared a glance with Mary. Their missions were beyond difficult. They had absolutely no idea what they would encounter when confronting Houston for treason. Santi didn't call the colonel's actions that, but that's exactly what they were. She'd tried to kill him. Catherine had no rules anymore. Assuming they did manage to get her in the brig without an incident, their second mission was akin to the stunt they had pulled in Boston. But that was different. They had been gathering intel on Boston for months. They didn't have much on Montreal, and they'd had no sim practice sessions. The odds of coming out of this mission alive were minuscule.

"Miles," Ramos said.

The general's voice pulled Dani from her gloomy thoughts. He always called Miles by his CNA rank and rarely his first name. Her insides twisted.

"I received word from Captain Lundquist, the commanding

officer in New Brunswick," Ramos said. "My orders to ship the four people from Bangor back home did not reach the CO in time. Colonel Houston had already removed Oliver from the base. He's with her."

"Fuck," Miles said.

Dani stepped forward. "Is he on the same ship as her?"

"I don't know," Ramos said. "Lundquist just said she took Oliver with her."

"She'll keep him close," Mary said.

Dani truly wanted to murder Catherine, and Mary was right. She knelt and placed her palm on the general's arm. "Who was with Catherine when she went to the camp?"

Ramos reached for the panel he'd given to Miles and began typing. "There will be a log of those who entered the base. Here." He passed the panel to Dani.

Mary and Dani both leaned in close to read the report. Dani recognized two names and grinned. She gave the panel to Miles.

"Javi and Anton," Dani said, beaming. "Of all the rotten news you've given us today, Santi, this is good."

His brow creased. "I don't understand."

"Javi is a longtime friend, and Anton is a computer guy who's with us."

Mary nodded. "Santi, use someone you trust to get a private message to Anton to let him know we're coming."

"Did the two of you miss the part where they're on radio silence?" Ramos asked. "All other means of communication coming in from outside the fleet will be blocked until the silence is lifted. Then they'll go through."

"Nah." Dani stood. "Anton is good. He will have a way to check for incoming messages and get around the fleet firewall. So that he knows what info you send him can be trusted, flag your message with these words: *You are a god*. All one word. He'll understand."

"Good, because I don't," Ramos said, shaking his head.

Miles turned to Cameron. "We'll meet up with you when you arrive with General Ramos. We need someone at his side that we can trust. Colonel Houston already tried ..."

Dani rolled her eyes. "You just can't bring yourself to say the words. Christ, Miles." She locked her gaze on the general. "Catherine tried to kill you once already. There is no reason to believe she won't try again. Cam, stay with him. Make sure the medical folks treating him don't fuck up, intentionally or otherwise."

"I'll keep him safe," Cameron said.

"Good," Miles said, then addressed the general. "Sir, do I have your permission to ship my son back to Maine once we secure Colonel Houston?"

"Of course, Major. *Splendor* is in Yarmouth, but Houston isn't there."

"She switched ships?"

"Looks like it. Probably got on one of the larger ones and left *Splendor* behind."

Dani grunted. "Santi, sounds like you need to take back what is yours and haul your sorry ass up to Montreal to meet us there."

Ramos chuckled in agreement.

"Hey," Dani said. "When you come, make sure you bring lots of those LC-whatevers with you."

Ramos's brow creased. "LCS? The littoral combat ships?"

She grinned and nodded. "Yeah, those quick little bastards. They'll be fantastic around Montreal. Bring them all plus some extra destroyers like *Splendor*."

"I'll see what I can do. We have some intel on Rowan. Review those files on the panel. He still has Curtis at his side, but he has a new ally helping him out. Yura. She's got a long and accomplished record with the Wardens."

"Yes, sir," Miles said.

Great, Dani thought. *Another Warden pal for Rowan*. Dani just hoped she wasn't as accomplished as Rowan's wife had been at kicking her ass when they'd run into each other.

"All right, the three of you, get out of here."

"Yes, sir." Miles looked at Dani, and she nodded.

Dani and Mary left with Miles. Dani noted the tightness in his jaw as his muscles flexed. He was on edge, so she remained quiet. Catherine had taken Oliver from him for a second time—from Dani again, too. She understood the anger boiling inside him.

The gentle thumping of a helicopter grew louder as it approached. Dani glanced behind her and smiled to see Cameron helping Santi back toward the field hospital.

They waited for the helo to land, and, once they were cleared to board, hopped in and stowed their gear. They strapped themselves into their seats, with Miles and Mary flanking Dani.

"What else is on that panel?" Dani asked Miles.

"It's the general's personal device, Dani. We can't just go digging around on it," he said.

"Catherine has your son. We have no idea what kind of shit show we'll be walking into when we reach her. Oh, and she's a goddamn lunatic who has no issues with slaughtering her own troops. We need any advantage we can get."

Mary nodded. "She's right. They may be on radio silence, but any info on which ships are headed deeper into Canada may help us figure out which one she and Oliver will be on."

Miles nodded and pulled the panel from his pocket. Dani couldn't hide her surprise that he'd caved so quickly. Mary grinned at her. Dani edged closer to him, eager to learn something to try to get the upper hand over Catherine. The colonel had stayed one step ahead of them the entire time. Dani was desperate to change that.

CHAPTER

36

Once they were in the air, Dani's gut clenched each time gusts from the approaching storm rocked the helo. Miles began to doze during the flight, so Dani took the panel. He fell into a deep sleep, and Dani envied his ability sleep anywhere.

Mary leaned forward to look at him. "How does he do that?"

Dani shrugged. "You do it too."

"Not like him. Not on this ride in these conditions."

"Are you gonna puke?"

"Nah. You?"

Dani didn't have Mary's confidence. "We'll know if I do."

Mary chuckled and placed her rifle across her lap. Dani returned her attention to Ramos's panel. She hoped she could do a little more research before any motion sickness kicked in.

Houston had the CNA's navy using mostly their larger ships with only a few of the smaller, faster ones. Dani couldn't figure out why the naval forces would allow such a formation. She dug deeper into the data on Santi's panel while Mary tinkered with her rifle. She pulled up the maps of Montreal and the river.

Files transmitted to CNA brass from Houston couldn't be trusted, so Dani searched for older maps with Warden troop markings. The old data wouldn't be reliable now, but she could at least assume it wasn't falsified like Houston's simulations. She needed something to go on that she could trust, even if just a little bit.

She flipped back and forth between Houston's files and the ones in the archive. She finally spotted the variance. "Fuck me. Shit. Shit. Shit. Oh, shit." The formation of the fleet was based off the river data for depth and width. Dani had to assume the depths were correct, but the numbers for the widths in some places had been altered. She patted Mary's leg to get her attention. "Look at this."

Mary shifted closer.

"I couldn't figure out how the navy could be so easily suckered into Catherine's lunatic plan, but now I know," Dani said.

"She faked the amphibious assault sims."

"No, this is way worse. She altered the fucking *maps*, Mary. The terrain *and* coastlines are different."

Dani flipped between the images for her.

Mary took the panel from her. After a moment of examining the images, she looked up. "Whoa."

"Yeah." Dani took the panel back. "If the Wardens put their troops in the right places, our ships might not even make it to the locks to get slaughtered. The fleet could get sunk long before that. Forget Toronto. Houston will get crushed in Montreal."

"Is the VR of Montreal that smart?"

"I don't know. But Rowan is there."

"Fucking hell."

"Right. I need to find other maps in the archives to compare them with the bullshit plan Catherine put together. We can at least start sending this stuff to Santi so he's aware." She gazed back down at the panel, and her vision blurred. Dani squeezed her eyes closed and rubbed them. The panel was snatched from her grasp, and Dani opened her eyes.

"Get some sleep," Mary said, holding the panel.

Dani reached for the device, and Mary gave her *that* look that told Dani there would be no negotiation or argument that would earn her the panel back.

"Sulk all you want, but go to sleep," Mary said. "I've got this."

Dani frowned but relented.

She knew she was dreaming, but that didn't ease the increasing tightness in Dani's chest or elevated heart rate. She stood among the rubble of buildings of what used to be a city. Ash continued to fall and turned her uniform and armor gray. It accumulated like snow on her shoulders and on the toes of her boots. She left a trail of boot prints as she walked through the thickening dust and ash.

She figured the city had been beautiful before it was destroyed. Dani stopped and turned. What she had assumed were boulders and chunks of the buildings turned out to be bodies. Hundreds of bodies. She took a step back from one and noticed a child-sized glove in the ash. Dani picked it up and shook the gray coating from it, revealing green fabric beneath.

"Huh. Oliver's favorite color," she muttered.

A hand emerged from the dust and grabbed her boot.

She yelped and jumped back, dropping the glove and stumbling over another body. She twisted to try to catch herself as she fell and landed face-to-face with a corpse that was bloated, its mouth gaping. Dani scrambled back to her feet and tried to catch her breath. The dead soldiers around her wore CNA uniforms. She calmed her mind enough to return to the one that had grabbed her foot. Maybe someone was still alive.

Dani crouched and touched the cold, lifeless hand. She shivered and resisted the urge to yank her hand back. Instead, she began clearing the dust away from the body. Her fear continued to escalate to the point of panic as she recognized the features of the boy she uncovered. Her hand trembled when she touched Oliver's cheek. He was the twelve-year-old boy from the first day she'd met him four years ago. *This isn't real. It's a dream. Just wake up*, she tried to tell herself.

He opened his eyes, and she gasped.

"Dani."

"Yeah. I'm here. You'll be okay." She glanced around for help, but everyone was dead.

"You promised you wouldn't let this happen."

She frowned, not knowing what he meant, until she realized that he, too, was in a CNA uniform. He had a hole through the center of his chest where the dust had caked over the blood and wound. There was no way he could be alive with that injury.

"You promised."

Tears fell down her face. "I'm sorry, Oliver."

He lunged for her, grabbing her chest armor. His soft features hardened. "You lied to me."

Dani tried to get away, but he remained attached to her. She pulled at his hands, but his grip held firm. More hands from other bodies grabbed her and began pulling her down. They dragged her beneath the dust, and Dani screamed and thrashed against her captors.

"Dani, stop!"

She opened her eyes and recoiled from Miles, which caused her to slam into Mary. She batted Mary's hands aside when she reached for her. Dani clawed at the straps holding her in her seat until she got them free. The wind rocked the helicopter, and she landed hard when she fell out of her seat.

"Mary, don't!" Miles said.

Dani spotted the tranq pistol in Mary's hand.

"I'm okay," Dani said. She was far from okay. "It was just a bad dream. I don't need that."

Mary holstered the tranq pistol, and Dani took an extra moment to try to calm herself. She was still trembling when she crawled back into her seat between them.

"What happened?" Miles asked.

"It was just a dream!" she barked. "It's not like you've never had them before." Her bitter words were out before she could stop them. Dani winced and shook her head. "I'm sorry. Just give me a minute." She struggled with the straps at first, but once she was secured back into her seat, her hands shook a bit less.

Mary leaned toward her. "I wasn't going to shoot you unless ..."

Dani nodded. Mary would have tranqed her if needed to keep her from doing something stupid in her panic.

"Here," Mary said, offering her the panel. "Catherine's original plan was best suited for Montreal, not Toronto. Miles and I put everything together, but we wanted you to review it before we sent it to Santi. We made some tweaks so the assault is on Montreal instead."

Dani was glad to have a distraction from the memory of the horrible dream. She talked through a few of the items with Mary and Miles, then nodded. "This is good. It's solid."

The panel blinked with an incoming message from an unknown sender. She glanced at Miles, and he nodded. Dani accepted the message.

Miles, honey, I've been in touch with Santi so I know this message is going to you and not him. I'll meet you in Montreal with reinforcements. Make sure you get yourself, Mary, and Dani there in one piece ... or mostly one piece. That works too.

The sudden rush of hope caught Dani's breath. She hadn't realized how much she missed Hattie until she'd read the message.

"Aunt Hattie," Miles said, smiling.

"She says she's meeting us in Montreal," Mary said. "Rein-forcements from where?"

Miles shrugged. "All CNA and Brigand troops from Maine are with Houston. Dani, do you know?"

She finished sending her reply on the panel and looked up. "Don't know. Don't care. She's on her way, and that's all that matters. I just sent everything to her and Santi."

"Major," the pilot said into their helmets. "We're coming up on the fleet."

CHAPTER

37

Rowan stood before the map projected onto the wall in one of the R&D labs. He'd spent hours looking at this map of Montreal and the waterways around the island. The Saint Lawrence River was the only way for CNA's fleet to get past the island. Of course, he never planned to let them get that far.

The lab door opened and Rowan glanced back. Yura raised an eyebrow and handed him a cup of coffee. "When I left, you were standing in that same spot. You plan to stare at that map until your eyes bleed, or what?"

Rowan took the cup and sipped the coffee. He liked how close she stood next to him. "I want more ways to secure Montreal. An island sounds like a good place to defend until your enemy has a navy."

"And it's a big island to try to defend."

He glanced at her; she was right. "Why the Wardens picked certain places to dig in over other, more easily defensible places, I guess I'll never know."

"Montreal has its tactical advantages, but for what we're trying to accomplish globally, there are better places to entrench and hold."

Rowan nodded. He turned to the table behind him and placed his cup on it. He shuffled through a few panels until he found the one with an inventory list of everything R&D had in the works and which phases of testing each weapon or device was in.

Curtis entered and looked at Yura first, then to Rowan.

Rowan noticed the flicker of uncertainty on Curtis's face. *Yes. You've been replaced.* "Curtis," Rowan said.

Curtis glanced at Yura again.

"What is it, Curtis?"

"Sir, perhaps we could go—"

"You can say whatever you need to say. She can be trusted."

Curtis continued to hesitate, and Rowan decided to wait him out.

Finally, Curtis relented. "I have confirmation that General Ramos is in Vermont, sir. Burlington. He's been in the field hospital since arriving, but I don't know the extent of his injuries."

Rowan knew there was more. "And?"

"Dani Ireland is there too." Curtis held out a panel for him.

That got Rowan's attention. He took the panel and scanned the images. There were several of Dani speaking with Jackman and Smith. "Can your contact who took these get to her?"

"No, sir. There is at least a twenty-four-hour delay with transmissions from my contact there."

Rowan growled. She could be somewhere else in twenty-four hours. Burlington wasn't far from Montreal and would've been dust long before now had he been in charge of Warden troop movements. The CNA should never have been allowed to fortify an area so close to Montreal. But that wasn't something he could fix today. Dani, however …

"Sir," Curtis said. "You can't go."

Rowan glared at Curtis, and the man took a step back. Rowan knew he couldn't leave Montreal, but he didn't need Curtis to remind him of that.

Curtis pointed at the panel in Rowan's hands. "There are additional reports there, sir. We're seeing CNA ship movements around Quebec City. With the data we have from naval operations in the north Atlantic, our leadership thinks the Commonwealth will make a move to try to take the rest of Quebec City."

Rowan laughed and shook his head. He and Yura had already worked through the scenarios.

"Sir?" Curtis asked, his brow furrowed.

Rowan trusted Curtis's data. His aide was a genius at data mining and gathering intel, but the day Curtis took the vice regent title from him in Boston was the day Rowan began doubting his loyalty. The data on the panel was likely accurate, but he wasn't sure about Curtis's motivations. He had an idea to test his former confidant.

"Is Houston part of this?" Rowan asked, waving the panel.

"Yes, sir. How did you know?"

"She wouldn't sit out an attack this close to her base of operations. You have the wrong target in mind."

"What? I mean, sir?"

"They already have a piece of Quebec City, Curtis. Taking the rest of the city won't really get them anywhere. They're going for Toronto, and I want a way to attack her directly when she goes by Quebec City." It was a big ask, but Rowan had asked Curtis for bigger things before, and the man had delivered. This time, however, Curtis behaved as Rowan had suspected.

"Sir, I can't get you out of Montreal. You're still under orders to remain here."

"We arranged field testing to get me involved in the hunt for Ramos. Why is this different?"

"Because they're watching everything we do, sir. I can't—"

Rowan waved his hand. All Rowan heard was how Curtis wouldn't help him, not that he couldn't help him. There was a difference. "Let me know when you have useful information. Dismissed."

Curtis opened his mouth to speak, then closed it. He nodded, then left. Once he was gone, Rowan flung the panel onto the desk and sighed. He'd almost forgotten Yura was there.

"He's afraid," she said.

Rowan nodded.

Yura snorted a laugh. "And our leadership thinks the target is Quebec City. They're too shortsighted."

"Now you see what I've been fighting for the last few decades." He took a sip of his coffee and picked up Curtis's panel. He had an idea.

"Did you know you get this weird look on your face when you come up with some new plan?"

"Hmm? I do?"

"Yes."

Rowan grinned.

"And?" she asked.

He loaded the naval data from Curtis's panel to merge it with his wall map. He adjusted the map to zoom out to see much of the north Atlantic, and the map populated with dots of CNA ships.

"We only had general information before. With this, we'll have a much better idea of how many and which ships are coming this way. The locks limit ship size, so we can estimate the size of their navy and ground troops aboard them." Rowan pointed at Quebec City. "They'll blow right by here without stopping, and they'll try to secure the locks in Montreal as quickly as possible to keep moving on toward Toronto."

"They will need to land troops to take the locks."

"And we'll let them have the locks."

Yura's brow furrowed.

"We'll put up a fight for the first lock, but not much. We'll instead have our troops lined up opposite the island from Longueuil to Sainte Catherine, all along the canal, and holding. We'll let them take the last lock, Sainte Catherine—rather, we'll let them *think* they have it."

"Attack and pin them in the canal."

"Yes, but *after* they get a ship into the Sainte Catherine Lock. That will be where the bottleneck starts. Their troops will be on the ground to hold the lock, but we'll swarm them to retake it."

Yura grinned. "They won't be able to turn around or retreat."

"We'll sink their fleet in the canal."

"That will block the canal for us to use later."

"We can handle the cleanup after. This defeat will cripple the CNA in the Northeast. They can't recover from losing most of their navy and a significant number of ground troops. What we gain will outweigh the temporary blockage of the canal."

"What about convincing leadership here? Still making headway on that?"

"Yes," Rowan said.

"And Curtis?"

"He's out of the equation. The people he's talking to are out of my loop."

"Ah. So you were testing him earlier."

Rowan nodded.

"You are a sneaky bastard, Rowan. I like it."

Rowan couldn't go after Houston to hit her in Quebec City, but he could wait for her to come to him. Dani still presented an issue, since he didn't know where she was. But his prior experiences with both women indicated that if Houston was making some sort of attack, with Dani back from her trips with Ramos, chances were good that Dani would turn up. He just needed to be ready for her arrival. *She* was the unpredictable factor in the equation. *She* was the one who tended to fuck up his plans.

"What's next?" Yura asked.

Rowan shut down the program and map on the wall. "We move the rest of this discussion to my office. The lab is too open for others to see what we're doing."

CHAPTER

38

The CNA wasn't inclined, as Hattie had feared, to stop Houston. She didn't have proof other than Anton's word about the faked sims. Anton was with Houston, so he wasn't available to testify before the CNA brass or show them the files. Hattie had his files, but couldn't use them since she wasn't supposed to have access to classified documents. She'd known it was a long shot to try to convince the brass based only on her word, so when her efforts with them crashed and burned, she wasn't all that surprised.

She'd heard back from Lundquist, who confirmed that Dani, Mary, and Miles were in Burlington briefly. Hattie finally got through to Santi, but his response times were slow, and he was still rather ill.

Her meeting in Portland took longer than expected, and Hattie was exhausted by the time she was on her way to Bangor, two days later than planned. She had at least been wise enough to hire a driver so she could rest on the ride up. The vehicle had barely stopped when she hopped out and headed into the pub.

"Hattie!" Jakob abandoned his post behind the bar and rushed to greet her. Brody barked and reached her first.

The place was empty. For business, at this time in the

evening, it was awful. But this also meant the Brigands who would normally be here were elsewhere. That was good.

"What's the latest?" she asked, slowing her stride enough to pet the dog.

Jakob gave her updates as they walked to the back of the building and to her personal living area. When he finished, she dismissed him and started packing. She threw her private stash of weapons and gear into her pack while Brody bounced around her. He yipped when she picked up his pack.

"Yeah, mutt, you're going on this trip with me."

Hattie scowled at the group of a few hundred gathered just north of Bangor. Usman emerged from the crowd.

"Jakob told me where to find you," Hattie said. She didn't like that Usman had beat her to Bangor.

"We emptied your weapons bunkers, so everyone here is at least armed with something, from a dinosaur revolver up to the latest and greatest." He smiled and handed her a pistol.

She glanced at the weapon, noting it was unlike anything she'd seen before. "I had more weapons in my bunkers than there are people here. Why so few? Where the hell are the rest of my Mainers?"

"Patience, Hattie. We have more." He gestured to the group, and they turned to head north.

She wished he would stop being cryptic but still walked with him. Hattie turned the weapon in her hand. Its design was sleek and likely deadly. "One of yours?"

"Oh, yes. This one keeps a charge and essentially never runs out of energized rounds of destruction."

"Essentially?"

"Your finger will fall off before it runs out. The recharge on this is exponentially faster than anything the Wardens or CNA have."

"Huh. Not bad. How many of these do we have?"

"Two."

Hattie frowned.

"I only made two for myself for fun. I wasn't expecting to go into battle with them."

Hattie tucked the weapon into the back of her trousers. "Let me shatter those expectations now. You're going into battle with only one."

He sighed but didn't argue. "Why the dog? Your pet can't come."

"He *is* going because he's a combat dog."

"What about Jake? He coming?"

"Jace. His name was Jace. He's dead, and you will not ever mention him to me again."

Usman held his hands up in surrender and fell silent.

"How many people do we have?" Hattie asked.

"Roughly fifteen thousand."

"Usman, you asshole. There aren't fifteen thousand Brigands left in Maine."

He dismissed her insult with a wave. "I can count, Hattie. I used contacts across New England to muster the larger numbers. We have five hundred here, mostly from Bangor. All other Mainers and New Englanders are already on their way to Montreal, if not already camped outside the city."

"How much of a head start do they have? It'll take forever to move that volume of people to Canada."

"Have faith, Hattie."

"Fuck faith. Stop playing these goddamn games. Tell me how you managed to get this number of Brigands together *and* headed north so quickly."

"Are you complaining about my success?"

"Bullshit me, Usman, and I'll permanently end you before we leave Bangor."

"Jeez. Always so violent."

Hattie growled.

"I played the Dani-in-distress card with the Brigands. I sent word to everyone that she was on a desperate mission into Canada to subvert the Wardens there like she did in Boston."

"But that's not how things happened in Boston. She went to Boston for Oliver."

"Turns out no one gives a shit about the truth. The Brigands all wanted a piece of the action to overthrow the Wardens with her. Ramos's political stunt of making her a Brigand ambassador was brilliant." He shrugged. "I used it."

"You lied to them."

"Eh. Sorta. Well, yes. I lied my ass off."

Hattie allowed herself a smile. She had played her own version of the Dani-in-distress story herself to rally the Brigands from Maine. It was easy. Dani was from Maine, and her fellow Mainers flocked to come to her aid. Usman took it a step further and rallied the rest of New England. Hattie knew he liked to think of himself as a hermit, but clearly he had a broad network of contacts well beyond just the Boston area.

Fifteen thousand Brigands. Fifteen thousand people born and raised to live by stealth and hardened by scavenging on a daily basis. Most would also already be comfortable using weapons. This was almost the equivalent of a fifteen-thousand-strong special ops army.

"I'm impressed, Usman."

"Impressed enough for us to take another shot at a relationship?"

"No."

"Hmm. It was worth a try."

Hattie laughed and shook her head. They still hadn't settled on her debt to him for him letting her use his gear to get a message to Lundquist. She hadn't forgotten and knew he hadn't either.

"Transport. What are you doing there?" Hattie asked. "We don't have the time to make a long march north."

"Oh, I may have made some CNA aircraft disappear from their inventory."

Hattie stopped and stared at him.

He tugged on her arm. "We don't want to keep the others waiting, Hattie. We're on the last flight out with this group."

"There isn't a runway around here that is functional enough to handle that large of a plane. The only runways capable of that are on the CNA base."

"It's not a plane."

"What?"

"You'll see."

Hattie sighed but continued alongside him. When they emerged from the woods into a clearing, she froze. Four large helicopters with dual tilt rotors waited in the field.

Usman flashed a beaming smile. "Vertical takeoff and landing aircraft and capable of so much more."

These weren't the usual CNA VTOLs, though. They were much larger and had a unique design with Usman's name all over it. "Yours?"

"Of course they're mine. They're magnificent!"

"How did you get them?"

His smile turned to a fiendish grin. "Vanishing inventory. It's both sad and astounding how easy it is to manipulate CNA databases."

"Easy for you."

"Yes. True. I gave them the new VTOL design a while back, and construction started immediately. They'd get a few done, orders were given to move them to new locations, then new orders to move them again would appear. The CNA and I shuffled them around to hide them from Warden spies and all, and a few got, well, misplaced."

"You stole them."

"I started keeping some for myself, yes. The CNA couldn't pay me what I was worth, so I paid myself. I figured they would be handy to have at some point. Some troops are en route by ground transport and other aircraft. But these birds, we've used them to shuttle troops north nonstop for the last few days while you were goofing off in Boston."

She allowed his remark to slide. "How did you get your hands on the fuel?"

"My personal addition to these birds is to not need fuel like the others, so I have space for more troops than the usual CNA VTOLs."

Hattie could never admit it to Usman, but she had utterly underestimated his engineering genius. "Not bad."

"That's it? 'Not bad' is all you have to say?"

"For now." Hattie strode toward one of the helos and climbed in. Brody jumped in behind her.

Usman sat next to her and strapped in while she clipped a strap to Brody's harness. Hattie pulled the panel from her pocket and smiled. She had a message back from Ramos. Usman wanted to continue talking to her, but she waved him off.

After a few messages with the general, Hattie sent one more, this time to Miles. She stared at the panel, waiting for a reply. She didn't expect him to respond right away, but she still hoped to hear from him soon. She had no idea where he and Dani were, and could only hope they were safe. Except Santi had said they were trying to intercept Catherine and stop the fleet. There was nothing safe about that kind of interaction.

When her panel flashed with a reply, Hattie opened it immediately. She scanned the report and embedded images and stopped at the ending text.

We sent this to Santi, too. Make sure you get your own ass here in mostly one piece. Dani.

Hattie burst into laughter. Her relief at knowing Dani was still alive thrilled her so much that she surprised herself when she wiped away a tear.

"What?" Usman asked. "What is it?"

She ignored him and started back at the top of the report, reading more slowly and taking everything in.

CHAPTER

39

Rowan looked up from the reports on his desk when Curtis entered. Yura had been examining the wall-sized map of Montreal and surrounding area. Rowan suppressed his grin as the two eyed each other for a moment. Curtis slowed his pace.

"Yura," Curtis said, scowling.

"Curtis," Yura said, then returned her attention to the map.

Rowan's emerging grin made the side of his mouth twitch. Curtis was finally beginning to understand that he truly had been replaced.

Curtis resumed his brisk walk to Rowan's desk. "Sir," he said, offering Rowan a panel. "I wanted you to see this instead of sending it through as a report to your queue."

Rowan took the panel and glanced over the information. "The CNA fleet has passed Quebec City and is headed this way. I already know this, Curtis."

"There's more."

Rowan continued reading. When he finished, he passed the panel back. He was not amused. "Houston was seen with a young-looking CNA soldier. Why is this important?"

"I had intel that Oliver Jackman had enlisted in the CNA."

Rowan barked a laugh. "*That* kid? No. He'd never enlist. Too soft even for a human."

"I agree, sir. There were rumors of an incident in Bangor where four people were taken into the CNA, not voluntary enlistments."

"Jackman was one of them?"

"Yes, sir. They were in New Brunswick for training. Houston's movements put her in New Brunswick before she and this lad joined the fleet." Curtis touched items on the panel's screen, then turned it toward Rowan. "It's not a great image, but that is Colonel Houston, and I'm certain that is Oliver Jackman."

Rowan leaned forward, examined the image, and nodded. "It could pass for him. Major Jackman?"

Curtis shook his head. "Current location is unknown. We know he, Mary Smith, and Dani have left Burlington. It's likely they will rendezvous with Houston on her way here."

Rowan frowned, unconvinced.

"My analysis indicates Houston is likely on the *Karl*," Curtis said.

"That is helpful. Anything else?"

"Another, smaller fleet has deployed from New England and is heading north. It's rumored to be General Ramos."

Rowan didn't like this news. Ramos remained alive and a problem. "You have the data points for the number and types of ships?"

"Yes, sir. I sent you those earlier today."

"Ah. I've been busy and haven't caught up on all my reading yet. What's your impression?"

Curtis shrugged. "I'm not sure what to make of this one, sir. It's composed of several of the small LCS-class ships. Nothing larger than a destroyer."

"Odd."

"Yes, sir."

"Anything else?"

"No, sir."

"Good work. Keep me posted."

Curtis nodded at his dismissal and left. Rowan joined Yura at the map.

She pointed to one of the dots marking the CNA fleet. "That's the *Karl*."

"It's not the lead ship." Rowan squinted at the map, thinking. "Create a program to track the larger ships and to notify us of formation changes. Houston is arrogant and will want to be in the lead. If any ship begins to push to the front of the fleet, that's the one she'll be on."

Yura was already tapping out commands on a smaller panel. "What about Curtis?" she asked.

"Can't trust him. He's too worried about getting caught doing something wrong now to be of much use."

"Do you think he'd turn on you? Report you up the chain of command?"

Rowan paused, then shook his head. "He's loyal to a fault. But he has lost a bit of his nerve. He hasn't been the same since Boston."

"That's unfortunate. He has an impressive service record."

Rowan nodded.

"Will you come by tonight?"

He shifted his focus from the map to her. "I can't. Family dinner with Katy and Devon."

"And Ella," Yura said.

"Yes."

"You don't have to avoid mentioning her for my sake, Rowan."

"It's complicated."

Yura laughed. "No, it's not. She takes care of your kids and is carrying another one for you. She's part of your life. I'm part of your life too, and we have sex in your office or at my place when the mood strikes. It's very simple, Rowan. She is a mother. I am a soldier. You just happen to be fucking us both. I have no issues with any of it. Ella might, but I don't."

Rowan was stunned into silence for a few minutes. Yura, unconcerned, had gone back to work.

She reminded him so much of Ana. He recovered his thoughts and returned to his desk. He sifted through the panels until he found the two he wanted. Rowan quickly read Curtis' report on the additional group of ships moving north. It still didn't make sense, so he left that panel on his desk. He returned to Yura's side and transferred a map overlay from the panel he'd kept to the wall map.

"We need to make some changes," Rowan said.

Yura's eyes narrowed at the overlay. "These are our troops your friends approved you to have for the plan to trap Houston."

"Yes."

"What needs to change?"

"When we trap the CNA in the canal and start sinking their ships, survivors will need to make it to land or drown."

A grin spread across Yura's face. "Burn them as soon as they set foot on solid ground."

"Yes. I want to determine the most likely beaches they may try to use to land an amphibious force once they're in that canal. It'll be an act of desperation, of course, which will make it even more fun to cut them down."

Yura pointed to the map. "These parts of Montreal's coastline are already reinforced. Analytics will easily pick up potential areas. I can write a program—"

Rowan produced another overlay from Curtis's report. The new dots were the additional CNA ships. "What do you make of these?"

"They're small and fast. They can easily catch the larger,

slower-moving fleet before they get to Montreal. They would have maneuverability around the island the larger ships can't manage. Some may even be able to get past the Lachine Rapids, but it won't do them any good to separate from the fleet when the ships are trapped in the canal between the locks." She glanced at him. "You're frowning. Why?"

"Ramos." Rowan began to pace.

"And?"

"Something isn't quite right about this, Yura. Ramos may have been wounded, but if he's coming north to join the fleet, it just doesn't seem right. Houston is the CNA's ranking officer with the fleet. Why does Ramos need to join too?"

"Maybe he's the one to lead the assault, but Houston was acting as stand-in until he was better."

"Then why rush everything instead of waiting for him? They had to have known he would survive his injuries if he's in motion now. Not like he'd get off a death bed to pull this stunt."

"You're afraid of Ramos."

He spun and glared at her. "I don't fear him."

Yura shrugged. "You have no respect for Houston. That is clear, Rowan. She's incompetent. She's never made you pace like you are now. What is it about Ramos that concerns you the most?"

Rowan took a deep breath, regaining control of his anger. "Dani."

"The Brigand? Your concern about Ramos is Dani? I don't understand this at all."

"Dani and Houston had some sort of disagreement a few years ago, after Boston. They parted ways, but Dani has been with Ramos since. Houston might have Oliver Jackman with her. Ramos might be on a group of ships headed to meet the fleet. Or he's going to intercept it and stop Houston."

"So the CNA is infighting. Who cares? It's better for us the more disorganized mess they become."

"Dani is the wild card. She's the unknown in this equation, Yura. You have not seen the havoc she can wreak in a short amount of time. I have. Oliver was on the ship with Ramos and Dani for three years. Houston must have taken him as leverage."

"Why?"

"Because he's the perfect pawn to use against Dani." *Until it backfires*, he thought.

"How do you know?"

"It's how I got her to Boston. I had that useless kid taken from Maine and brought to Boston to lure Dani in." He resumed pacing. "She just happened to bring the whole goddamn CNA, complete with Ancient jet technology, in her wake."

"So you're saying that because we don't know where Dani is, we could have more CNA troops headed this way than we're expecting?"

He stopped and turned. "Yes."

Yura nodded. "Okay. Stop pacing and get over here so we can figure out where to best place our troops. Reach out to your people. See if you can get more resources to deploy along the coast. Even if we just set up remote-fired artillery in places, that's better than nothing. Get your head out of your ass, Rowan. They're not going to survive this attack."

She wasn't allowing him time to sulk over Boston. Ana would not have tolerated his sulking either. Rowan appreciated Yura's straightforwardness. He sent a quick note to Ella that he would not make dinner tonight.

There was work to be done.

CHAPTER 40

Dani's gut lurched several times as high winds battered the helo. They still didn't know which ship Houston was on, but they'd decided to land on the lead ship and at least get the fleet halted with Ramos's orders. The pilot never stopped hailing the LHA *Karl*, despite getting no response.

The fleet continued on toward Montreal, so they were at least going to arrive and intercept them before they foolishly tried to secure the locks.

"Would they shoot at us instead of answering back?" Dani asked Miles.

He shrugged.

His response didn't make her feel any better. In her mind, the CNA ship should at least have acknowledged the CNA helo, but the Commonwealth had changed. Catherine had changed. She kidnapped children, had already tried to kill Ramos, and was on a path to slaughter tens of thousands of CNA troops. Dani wouldn't put it past her to shoot down a CNA helo just for giggles. She wondered if having the pilot identify the helo's occupants would help get a response or would just get them shot down quicker. *Hmm. If Catherine is on this ship, we'd definitely be shot down.*

The pilot's voice came through their helmets. "I've got a ping back from the *Karl*, Major."

"What did they say?" Miles asked.

"Nothing, sir. Just a ping."

"That means it's okay to land?" Mary asked.

"I think so," the pilot said.

Dani, Miles, and Mary looked at each other.

"Well," Dani said, and shrugged. "It's a reply with a ping and not a reply with a missile."

Miles frowned but still nodded. "Take us down."

"Yes, sir."

The helicopter began its descent toward the *Karl*'s deck. Dani didn't want to admit how tense she felt. She didn't need to, because Miles took her hand and squeezed it. This relaying of General Ramos's orders could go either really well or horribly wrong. Dani couldn't shake a feeling of dread.

She flinched when the helicopter landed a little hard on the ship's deck. Ship crew secured the helo and let them out. Rain and wind lashed them as they followed a seaman toward the ship's bay. Dani placed her hand on the pistol at her hip. The bay door slid open, and it was clear things were well on their way to going horribly wrong. "Shit."

A dozen armed troops with weapons pointed at them were waiting. Dani removed her hand from her pistol. She noticed additional movement, and another dozen troops on both sides emerged from cover. The crew that had secured the helo escorted the pilot to join them. Forty people to capture four seemed like overkill until Houston emerged from behind the soldiers inside the bay.

"Figured it was you three," she said. She turned to one of the soldiers. "Take their weapons and armor and put them in the brig on charges of treason."

Miles stepped forward, and the soldiers inched closer,

causing him to stop. "Colonel, I have direct orders from General Ramos that this mission be aborted and for you to stand down."

Dani was soaked, and the wind-driven rain stung her face while Catherine remained just inside the bay and out of the weather. God, she hated this woman.

Houston turned to the soldier she'd addressed before. "I gave you an order."

"Yes, Colonel." He gestured to the other troops, and in an instant, Dani was swarmed and shoved to her knees, as were Mary, Miles, and the pilot. Dani rocked as they tore her armor off and stripped her of her weapons.

Miles struggled back to his feet. "Release my son!"

One of the soldiers struck him in the middle with his rifle, and without his protective armor, he coughed and sank to the deck. When they were escorted past Catherine, Dani looked for Oliver but didn't see him.

Dani stopped. "Santi's alive."

"Then where is he?" Catherine stalked closer to Dani and grinned. "Your so-called orders are forged. I will accept orders only from the general himself." Without taking her glare off Dani, Houston barked at the solider. "Take them to the brig."

"Dad!"

Oliver's voice woke something in Dani she didn't expect. Her relief at hearing his voice made her desperate to see him and to kill Catherine. Miles and Mary thrashed against their captors, too.

"Ollie!"

"Dad. Dad!"

Their renewed struggle to free themselves was crushed when the volume of soldiers fought back, easily overwhelming them. Dani fell to the deck, curled into a ball, and tried to weather kicks and strikes to her body.

"That's enough," one soldier said.

Dani allowed herself a moment to relax once the beating had stopped. Miles rolled up to his knees and was hauled to his feet by a soldier. Mary was on her hands and knees, blood dripping from her mouth. Dani remained on her side until the pilot helped her up. She was dazed from the punishment she'd received, but she managed a bloodied smile when she spotted Oliver. Javi held him back from the mayhem as the soldiers dragged her and the others away. Houston followed.

They were taken through hatches and passageways into the interior of the brig. It was one large compartment with several smaller compartments that had barred gates.

"Put them in their own special quarters cells," the master-at-arms said to a pair of his officers.

"No," Houston said. "Keep them together."

"Colonel, if they present a risk to themselves or my brig officers, they must be in their own cells for at least twenty-four hours for observation."

"I want them kept together. I'll have your CO confirm those orders once I'm back on the bridge."

The master-at-arms nodded.

The pilot and Mary were led in first. Dani was due to go in next, except a commotion behind her caught her attention.

Oliver darted through the narrow passageways toward them. "Dad!"

Miles maneuvered around his guard to go to his son and embrace him. The soldier raised his weapon at Miles, and Dani leapt onto the soldier's back. She jerked his aim away so the pistol discharged into a bulkhead instead of into Miles.

Dani wasn't sure what happened next, because when she opened her eyes, she was lying on her back on the floor in a cell. Miles lay on his side next to her with dried blood in his hair and on the side of his face. His cheek was swollen and bruised.

"Hey," Mary said.

Dani turned her head and blinked a few times to clear her vision. Mary loomed above her and had her hand on her shoulder.

"What happened?" Dani asked.

"You made the hornets angry."

"It's becoming a habit."

Mary laughed and helped her sit up. Every part of Dani's body ached. She touched Miles's cheek. He stirred but didn't wake.

Dani shifted to lean her back against one of the bunks. "Oliver?"

"Catherine took him with her."

Dani buried her face in her palms and sighed.

"Why don't you lie on a bunk and rest, darling?"

Rest sounded like a good option because she sure as hell wasn't going anywhere. But Dani wanted a way out of this mess more than she wanted to sleep. She lowered her hands. "Did they take Santi's panel off Miles?"

Mary nodded.

"Think it'll do any good?"

"Catherine took it. She'll never let those orders be seen by anyone."

"Fuck."

"Yeah."

Dani ran her fingers through her hair. "Why do I feel so hungover?"

"You took a tranq dart in the back, but it wasn't one of the ramped-up ones for Echoes. So you've been out for only a couple of hours. Miles," Mary said and sighed. "He wouldn't stop fighting, so they beat the crap out of him, and it still took four darts to put him down."

Dani looked up and realized their helo pilot sat cross-legged on one of the top bunks, watching her and Mary. "What's your name?"

"Dylan."

"I'm sorry you got caught up in this mess, Dylan."

She shrugged. "I don't mind. Mary gave me the short version of what has been going on. When you fuck something up, Dani, you go big."

Dani scowled at Mary when she chuckled.

"She's not wrong," Mary said.

Dani's gaze fell on Miles, and her chest ached with a sense of failure. They'd reached their goal of making it to the fleet and on the lead ship. They'd also landed themselves in the brig. It terrified her to know how close Miles had come to being shot in the back by the soldier, and she wished she could make everything right. She saw only one thing she could make right in this moment. "Get your asses over here and help me get him off the floor and onto a bunk."

CHAPTER

41

They had to be getting close to Montreal. Dani figured she'd know as soon as they started taking and returning fire. Even deep inside the ship, those kinds of explosions couldn't be muted. Would they take a massive hit and her life, along with everyone else's, be gone in an instant? Would she even hear a hit like that? Would they take a lesser hit and sink so she could die underwater, drown again during regen, then permanently die?

There was no miracle coming. Oliver was still in the CNA. He was still a soldier. He'd have a rifle thrown into his arms and be tossed into the shredder of war. He'd be chewed up and forever scarred, assuming he survived at all. Or he'd end up with a hole through his chest and buried in dust and ash just like in her dream. She shuddered.

"Dani?" Miles said.

She continued pacing, her arms folded and pressed against her chest. She heard his voice, but her thoughts were elsewhere. The drugs had worn off on him, which was great, but the dread in his eyes upon waking inside the brig and realizing Oliver was nowhere around had broken her. That's when the pacing had gotten worse. He and Mary both had pleaded with the master-at-arms to hear them out, but that got them nowhere. And the pilot, Dylan, stayed on her bunk, silent and observing everything.

Dani had persuaded Miles that Catherine could be swayed. The colonel would follow the general's orders and stand down. She *had* to. That was how the CNA operated.

Except Catherine always did things her own way. Dani knew this, yet she had still believed *this* time would be different.

How could you be so fucking stupid?

Dani turned to pace back the other way and stopped. Mary stood in front of her.

"What?" Dani snapped.

"Sit down, please."

Dani scowled and moved around her friend.

She should have done things differently where it concerned Oliver. She should have seen Catherine's kidnapping of him coming. *But how?* Dani didn't know how she could've known the colonel would go to such extremes, but still, she *should* have suspected Catherine was up to something. She'd tried to kill Santi. Sure, Dani didn't know it at the time, when he went off the grid, but still … kidnapping shouldn't have come as a surprise.

Dani had promised Oliver the war would end before he was enlisted. She'd thought she had another year, but everything with this war took too goddamn long to make progress. *It's all been a waste of time and lives.*

If the Commonwealth gave up, the Wardens would still slaughter all humans, Oliver among them. Their only choice was to fight. *No. Our only choice is to die.*

That was it.

The answer was simple: Die.

The Warden solution was to kill. Everyone opposing them had to die, including Oliver.

Her pacing stopped and she closed her eyes. Tears slipped out when she squeezed them shut. Dani placed her palm against the bulkhead and sighed. Her head dipped lower as the weight of the war crashed around her. *Everyone will die. Today. Tomorrow. It doesn't fucking matter.* The CNA had the lunatic Colonel Houston running the show, and she'd lose the entire war for them.

Dani sniffled and dragged the back of her other hand across her nose.

"Hey," Mary said, touching her shoulder.

Dani finally opened her eyes, but kept her head down.

"Please, take just a few minutes to rest, Dani."

She shook her head.

Mary left, but Miles was at her side next. She wanted to be left alone.

He didn't say anything, but he didn't need to. His hand touched her shoulder, then slid down her back to her waist. She felt his light tug when he pulled her closer, and she didn't resist.

The steady rumble of the engines through the ship's bulkhead changed; she felt it through her palm. Her first few days of living on *Splendor*, Dani hadn't slept. The never-ending engine vibration through the ship was annoying until she'd gotten used to it. Now her head snapped up.

"Something's happening," she said. "The vibration has decreased."

Miles put his hand on the wall next to hers.

"Are we stopping?" Mary asked.

Miles shook his head. "I think we're slowing down."

They waited in silence for a few minutes.

"We've stopped, I think," Miles said. "It's hard to tell since the engines never shut down completely, but if we're moving at all, it isn't with much propulsion."

The minutes dragged on, and Dani wished she knew what

the hell was happening. The *Karl* hadn't started shooting, and the ship wasn't taking fire … yet.

As expected, the *Karl* had moved into the lead position of the fleet. According to usual CNA tactics, the two amphibious assault commanders would be on the same ship. Houston was on that ship; Rowan knew it. Boseman was the likely naval officer working with Houston on this suicide mission to Toronto that wouldn't make it past Montreal.

Except Rowan's plan to sink the fleet hit a snag.

Montreal island was just under two hundred square miles in size, but Montreal and the smaller islands around it created an archipelago. The islands dotting the river meant the ships couldn't stay in formation. The CNA would have to split the fleet to send ships around one side of the landmass while other ships went to the other side. The other option was to string out the fleet into a long procession of ships. The CNA had done as Rowan had expected—they split the fleet.

He'd prepared for this and had placed artillery units on these islands and along the mainland riverbanks to catch the fleet in crossfires when they tried to go around the islands. He hadn't planned for the fleet to stop prematurely.

As soon as they stopped, he'd taken Yura, Curtis, and his best techs on a helo to fly closer to where he could better monitor the CNA. The Wardens had the technology to monitor the fleet from their bunkers, but Rowan could gain a more accurate assessment—so he told himself and others—by watching the CNA himself. The helicopter landed on the deck of the observatory overlooking the river, and Rowan was the first one out.

He watched the fleet through his optics between moments of pacing. He told Curtis what information to relay back to Vice Regent Keran, but he'd been a little vague on his reports thus far.

He peered at the CNA fleet again through his optics, growled, then resumed pacing. The fleet had stopped near Montreal East and well before nearing the first lock. An incoming helicopter landed on the ship he knew to be the *Karl*. The vessel was too far away for him to see anything other than its landing on the deck.

Most of his troops were at the locks, and without the CNA ships going into them, his ground troops couldn't do much. He had artillery and other ground missiles that could reach the fleet, but it wasn't an ideal situation to attack them that way.

"Fuck! What the hell are they doing?" he roared to no one in particular.

His techs stood by in silence, but Rowan knew Yura and Curtis were watching him.

"Curtis," Rowan said, and held out his hand. Curtis gave him the panel, and Rowan studied the screen. He adjusted the map and frowned.

"Sir?" Yura said.

Rowan's head came up, and he glanced at her before gazing back at the enemy fleet.

"There is no reason for them to stop here, so the mission may be aborted," Rowan said.

Yura grumbled under her breath. Curtis seemed unaffected; Rowan thought Curtis should be just as angry as he and Yura were about this.

"Most of their ships will need time to turn around, especially in these narrower areas," Rowan said. "We need to hit them now."

"Sir," Curtis said. "We have missile range to strike them where they are, but we will not be able to hit the fleet with our full force unless they are closer."

"I'm aware. They need to be forced into making more mistakes. We may not be able to sink the entire fleet, but we can put the *Karl* and all its CNA royalty at the bottom of the fucking river. Dani is somewhere on one of those ships too. Relay word to the VR, Curtis. Get me the order to attack."

Curtis hesitated, and Rowan glared at him.

CHAPTER

42

Dani's renewed pacing stopped when one of the hatches leading to the brig opened. Javi entered with a naval officer.

"Master-at-Arms, release them," the officer said with a wave of her hand toward Dani and the others.

There weren't any armed escorts. No soldiers. No I-cuffs at the ready or tranq pistols pointed at them. It was just Javi and this officer. Maybe someone had convinced Houston that the orders were real. *No. No, that wouldn't work. A mutiny?* Dani didn't figure Javi and Anton for being mutineers. There was only one answer.

"Is Santi here?" Dani asked Javi.

He replied with the hint of a smile. "I have orders from General Ramos to escort you to the bridge."

Dani was part of the collective sigh of relief from within the cell. The cell door opened, and they filed out.

Miles grabbed Javi's arm. "Where's my son?"

"Follow me," Javi said, then turned to lead them out. "Preparations are underway to fly him off the ship."

"How close are we to Montreal?" Dani asked. She appreciated Javi's quick pace as she followed him up the ladders and through the passageways.

"Too close."

"But Santi is here? He's on the ship?"

"He's here. Arrived by helo like you. Houston is detained, but—"

Miles interrupted. "Not arrested?"

"General Ramos wanted you on the bridge for the next phase," Javi said.

"Phase?" Mary asked. "What the fuck are you talking about?"

Javi glanced back at them with a frown. "Please just come with me and hold your questions."

Dani had several more questions for him, but she pressed her lips closed and continued to follow.

When they arrived on the bridge, Dani was elated to see Oliver next to Santi, but the general didn't look well. Cameron stood off to the side, and there were two other CNA officers, a man and a woman, with the general whom she didn't recognize. Her gaze fell on Houston. The colonel was flanked by two soldiers, and her pistol had been taken. Catherine bore a scowl that conveyed pure hatred, and Dani was pleased to finally see the colonel dethroned.

Oliver looked up at Ramos, and the general nodded. Oliver rushed to his father and embraced him. Miles pulled his son close, and Dani felt a glimmer of hope that Oliver might finally be safe.

Dani shook Santi's hand. "I'm really glad to see you, but you look like shit."

"Feel like it, too."

Miles moved Oliver behind him and stepped forward, his hands tightened into fists while he glared at Catherine. "You sent General Ramos into the field with doctored intel, and when he didn't die, you sent us after him to die too. You lied about me falsifying Ollie's birth record. He's only sixteen, and you stole him as leverage to make me do your bidding. Except you didn't plan for us to survive your pointless mission."

Houston stared back at him and didn't speak.

Dani wanted to beat the smug look off her face. The mental image of doing so brought her a moment of pleasure, and then she flinched. Dani blinked a few times, surprised by how quickly the rage had built up within her and almost exploded into physical action. One hand began to tremble, and Dani clenched it into a fist to make it stop. She noticed Mary watching her, but Dani didn't dare make eye contact. Mary knew something was wrong with her. Dani knew it too, but she wanted to try to control the rage herself.

Miles continued. "Your shit plan for going after Toronto is for what? Pride? You're willing to kill thousands of CNA troops for no reason. You lied about the plan and falsified the simulations. You're a fucking monster, Catherine."

Dani's attention was diverted from her own anger. She'd never heard Miles call Houston by anything other than her rank.

Miles stepped back to be with his son. Dani smiled, proud of him for confronting Catherine for being the wretched person she'd turned into.

"Anton," Ramos said.

Anton hopped up from his station in front of three different screens. "Yes, sir?"

"You've finished the file transmissions?"

"Yes, sir."

Ramos turned to Houston. "Catherine, you are relieved of duty and will remain confined in the brig on the *Karl* until we return to Boston, where you will await your court-martial. All documentation of your actions has been submitted for processing. Gentlemen," he said to the soldiers at her side, "escort her to the brig. She is not to be released unless you hear the words directly from my mouth." He turned to the ranking naval officer. "Admiral Asllani, Vice Admiral Boseman, I'm taking command of the landing force for this mission."

"There is no mission, General," Asllani said. "Toronto has been aborted."

"We're in the middle of hostile waters this close to Montreal. It is the new target, so I need you to quickly review the modified assault plan. Break radio silence and notify all ships to come to a full stop and to stay away from the locks. We will not deploy an amphibious attack at those locations. Activate your people to start mine countermeasures operations now."

"We shouldn't attempt an assault, General," Boseman said.

"Out here in the middle of this river, we can't easily turn around. We can't rearrange our troops on the vessels for a different type of deployment, so the plan doesn't change too much except for the operational area. We must act soon. The Wardens will be ready to launch an attack on us from land. We can still put our troops on their shore while they're out of position and busy guarding locks that we don't care about."

Curtis's brow furrowed. "Sir, your request is beyond your rank. They will not grant it."

"They won't grant it, or you won't ask?" Rowan stalked closer to him. He'd had enough of Curtis and his delays. Now he was just flat refusing to follow Rowan's command.

"I cannot make that request, sir. It has to come from someone above you. I can contact the chancellors who are best aligned with your objective and—"

"Enough! I'll give the order myself as VR."

"Sir, you can't!"

Rowan turned his attention to his panel, and Curtis grabbed his arm. Rowan had his pistol out in an instant and fired a shot into Curtis's middle. His armor didn't stop the advanced energy weapon.

Curtis clutched at his bleeding wound and sank to the observation deck.

Rowan reholstered his pistol. He turned to the techs. "Alert our artillery stations to be ready to receive orders to attack."

"Yes, sir," they said as a collective.

"Bring him with us," Rowan said.

Yura and one of the techs dragged Curtis back to the helo with them.

"Load him in," Rowan said. "Pilot, take us out over the river on our way back. Yura, toss him out. He can regen underwater and drown."

She nodded without hesitation. Curtis had committed treason against the Wardens as far as Rowan was concerned. It was indeed a crime punishable by permanent death, and Rowan didn't mind passing that sentence and making it happen.

They boarded the helo, and the pilot guided it low and over the river. Yura rolled Curtis, still somewhat alive, out of the aircraft, and then the pilot swung back inland.

Rowan used the panel to send his orders to the artillery bunkers with falsified credentials that the orders were coming from the vice regent. The VR could sort out the mess after they'd sunk at least part of the CNA fleet.

Warden missiles leapt up from the ground and arced toward the CNA fleet.

Rowan grinned.

Dani wanted to insert her agreement with Santi, but the general didn't need her input. He'd already seen the altered plan that Miles and Mary had put together, and he obviously agreed with it. Her gaze left Santi when the soldiers moved with Houston to take her off the bridge. She would have smiled except an explosion rocked the ship and threw Dani and others to the floor.

Alarms sounded throughout the ship. "General quarters. General quarters. All hands man your battle stations."

Asllani had somehow remained upright. "Report!"

"Short-range torpedo …"

Dani stopped listening. Catherine had taken a knife off one of her guards when he had fallen with the blast. The colonel headed for Santi as he struggled to stand. Dani scrambled to her feet. She wrapped her arms around the general to protect him from the incoming attack. The knife sliced through the back of her shirt, cutting her across the shoulder blade. Dani cried out but still glanced behind her. Catherine wouldn't stop her attempt to kill Santi now.

Miles slammed into Catherine, and Dani kept her hold on Santi. She didn't see what had happened, but Miles's pained scream made her shudder. She released the general and turned, hoping he'd just broken a bone or something more minor. The guards tried to separate them, but Miles was in a tangle with Catherine, who now had a pistol.

"Shit." Dani dove for Catherine and the pistol. Catherine rolled away from her to bring the weapon up. Dani collided with a guard and went down again.

Mary shielded Oliver from the scuffle.

Miles had the knife, and he lunged at Catherine, deflecting the hand with the pistol as he crashed into her. Dani feared the gun would go off and kill someone by accident. She knew first-hand what it felt like to be the recipient of a misfire, so she untangled herself from the guard to try to help Miles.

Dani gasped; the look of hatred on his face startled her even though his glare was directed at Catherine. There was blood on him and Catherine, but Dani couldn't see where he'd been wounded.

He slammed the knife down into the center of the colonel's chest, burying it up to the hilt. Catherine crumpled, then collapsed back, her eyes staring upward at Miles. She moved her mouth, but no sound came out.

He snarled at his former commanding officer. "Fuck your lies and fuck you for stealing my son."

Her body relaxed with the onset of death, and Dani felt no remorse for a woman she had once considered a friend. Houston couldn't go after Oliver again, but Dani feared what the colonel had done to Miles. He pushed himself up, and blood spilled from his middle, dripping down onto Catherine's corpse. He placed his hand over the wound and groaned.

Everyone, including Dani, was stunned and staring. The altercation had started and ended quickly, but it also had seemed to last forever, and no one had been able to move fast enough to intervene.

Dani rushed to him. She pulled him into her arms and pressed one hand over his.

Oliver's voice trembled as he neared. "Dad?"

Miles kept one blood-covered hand against his wound and patted Oliver's shoulder with his other. "Hey, Bud. I'm okay."

Mary put her arm around Oliver but didn't try to remove him from his father's side.

Miles was very far from okay; he would die without treatment.

"Cam can fix this," Dani said, and tried to smile at Miles. "You'll be fine."

Naval staff on the bridge started shouting about defensive counterair systems, contacts, and bearings. Dani wasn't sure what was happening but knew it was bad news.

More shouts erupted, but the one that terrified her most was "Incoming! Brace for impact."

Dani and Mary pulled Oliver and Miles closer to them. There was nowhere to go or to run to. There was no hiding. Dani lowered her head next to Miles and closed her eyes. Apparently, *this* was how they would all die in this war.

CHAPTER

43

ani's ears rang, and her shoulder and hip ached from slamming into a wall, but she still had Miles in her arms. She glanced up, relieved to see Oliver with Mary. Cameron was at Ramos's side and trying to talk to him. Other wounded were being dragged off the bridge. There were words exchanged between the admirals and the general, but she couldn't hear them. They pointed at maps and appeared to be arguing.

Dani knew they were in trouble, but Miles was in the worst shape. Blood continued to seep out of his wound. Dani felt the shuddering of the ship through her contact with the floor, and was gripped with fear. Alarms, shouts, and screams terrified her. They weren't dead yet, but she didn't know how long they had until the next impact.

Various screens and monitors on the bridge flashed what Dani figured were more alerts, warnings, and basic "holy fucking shit" alarms. Sailors screamed reports of fires on the different decks and which levels were flooded or actively flooding. Dani couldn't keep up with the damage reports. She just knew their situation was horrible. The vice admiral barked orders at the crew and pointed toward something. Other crew remained at their stations, and Dani was amazed to see the flurry of missiles and other shots fired from the ship.

Some shots destroyed incoming missiles, and others arced high into the air. The navy was returning fire at the Wardens while shooting down most of the missiles the Wardens fired at them.

Santi grabbed Anton and thrust him back into the chair at his station to focus on the computers.

Dani worked her jaw, but her ears continued to ring.

A missile flew past the windows at the front of the bridge and landed in the water, but somewhere else on the ship, something exploded.

The power on the bridge flickered, but Santi remained over Anton's shoulder. Anton was focused on the screen in front of him while his fingers flew over the keys.

The ship began to list, and that's when Dani realized they were sinking. "Oh, fuck. No. No!" She adjusted her grip on Miles. His eyes were closed, so she shook him. "Wake up."

His eyelids fluttered open.

"You have to get up, Miles."

"Okay."

Dani's insides twisted. He was pale, and his words slurred. She couldn't lose him. Not like this. In Boston, Miles had almost died when Rowan had shot him with an armor-piercing round that had gone through his side, but this knife wound seemed worse. She tried to lift him to his feet and failed. The tilting ship wasn't helping.

"Cam!" Dani said. "I need you."

Cameron arrived and hoisted Miles to his feet.

"What do we do?" Dani asked Cameron, refusing to look at the blood on Miles, herself, and the deck. "We can't stay on this ship."

"No, we can't," Cam said.

Mary and Oliver joined them. It pained Dani to see Oliver's expression of horror when he saw his father's condition. She glanced at Mary. Mary understood the same as Dani: Miles would die without surgery.

The ship groaned and listed a bit more to the side.

Cameron started walking while half dragging Miles.

"What were Santi and the admirals talking about?" Dani asked Cameron.

"Non-naval crew are to leave the ship. Boseman is trying to beach the *Karl*. If we sink out here in the river, more people will die. They're going to put us as close to land as they can and ideally on a sand bar, but we'll still be swimming."

"Miles won't be able to swim," Dani said. They'd done abandon-ship drills with the *Splendor* crew. The purpose was to not shit yourself when the real thing happened. But those drill scenarios never included a homicidal colonel stabbing Miles. Those drills also didn't include abandoning ship while under Warden fire. Dani slowed and grabbed Mary's shirt. "Make sure Oliver and Miles get off this ship."

"Fuck off. You're not staying."

"I'm getting off this thing, same as you, Mary. I promise."

Mary frowned in response.

Dani leaned close to Mary's ear and kept her voice so only she could hear her. "Help Cam with Miles. I need to make sure Santi gets off the ship too, because when the troops on this ship reach land, we'll need him there to organize us." Leaving the ship was the first step. The second was to survive long enough to get their feet on land. But once they reached dry ground, they would be met by Warden troops coming to kill anyone who hadn't drowned. And the CNA and Brigands who abandoned the *Karl* would be ill-equipped to meet hostile forces. Dani and Mary wouldn't have armor *or* weapons when they touched land.

Mary finally nodded.

Dani raced back to Ramos. He was talking to Asllani while Boseman handled operations across the fleet. Dani caught snippets of barked orders but still wasn't sure what they were doing. She just knew Miles was bleeding and the *Karl* was sinking.

"Continue to provide air support and take out the shore targets," Ramos said. He pointed at the coastline. "We'll take that beachhead. It's concave and gives us the best place to land under the circumstances. *That's* our landing zone. *That's* our operational area now."

"We can't execute an assault now, Santi," Asllani said.

Dani's eyes widened. Asllani had just gone first-name basis with the general. This was good. They knew each other well enough and had dropped the military formalities. This was now two friends trying to keep everyone else alive. Dani knew that feeling.

"We don't have a choice, Kay," Ramos said. "The amphibious assault starts now. Have Boseman resume his role as CATF and mobilize all air support to help cover the landing force going ashore. I'm going with them. Follow the new plan."

The admiral paused. "This is highly unconventional, but the Wardens will be out of position to counter us initially."

"Yes," Ramos said. "We can still land without a critical reduction in combat power, but only if we go now. Send the drones out for mine countermeasures to allow the ships to come in closer. Start the airlift of troops off all ships, and deploy assault vehicles per the original plan. That deployment schedule isn't changing."

Dani sighed, relieved that they had reached a consensus. She didn't think Catherine would've been able to handle this situation the way Santi had.

"Good luck, Santi."

"Good luck to you too, Kay."

Asllani nodded. She got Boseman's attention and gave him his new orders. He frowned, then glanced at Ramos. They nodded at each other, and Boseman went into action. He gestured to one of his officers, who then started barking orders about deploying air and sea drones throughout the fleet.

Dani turned to make sure Mary had herded Miles and Oliver off the bridge. Her eyes fell on Houston's corpse. Her body lay on the floor against the wall. A wide swath of blood ran the length of the deck from where Miles had stabbed her to where she had been thrown during the missile impact. A seaman dragged the body to clear the bridge, leaving another long smear. Houston was dead. Really dead. Unless … Dani wondered if Houston had taken part in her own experiment. She just wanted the colonel to stay dead and out of her life. Dani startled when Ramos touched her shoulder.

"Helos are already evacuating off the deck and taking soldiers to the new landing zone," he said. "We're going with them."

Javi led, Dani trotted beside the general, and Anton followed. Sixteen hundred ground troops and one thousand sailors were on the *Karl*. The aircraft couldn't all be prepped in time on an increasingly listing ship. The helos could take off, but only while the angle of the ship wasn't too steep.

It would be hard to move the troops, and she hoped the *Karl*'s commanding officer could put the ship on a sand bar soon so fewer troops and sailors would be lost. Another thought struck her: She'd just become part of the assault echelon, the first wave of troops to begin the attack with Santi. She would feel better about that if she at least had a gun in her hand and some armor.

They moved through a smoke-filled passageway, following others who filed into it from compartments and hatches until they finally reached a port to the outside. Some of the sailors and troops were injured. One man had burns covering half his face, and his friend dragged him along. This was all Catherine's fault. Any life lost today was on her, and Dani knew there had to already be some dead and dying on the ship from the initial explosions.

She stumbled out of the port after Santi. Blasts of gunfire from the ship and the anti-missile systems targeting the Wardens were deafening. Wind from the helicopters lashed her with stinging rain.

She spotted Cameron and Mary loading Miles into the back of a tilt-rotor aircraft, a VTOL. She didn't see Oliver and assumed he was already inside. Dani urged Santi in their direction. Javi and Ramos climbed in, and Dani shoved a wide-eyed Anton in behind him.

Dani's mouth hung open when she looked out over the river.

The water's surface was dotted with numerous amphibious assault vehicles and landing craft headed toward the beach. Drones and various types of helos swarmed the air. Smaller, quicker ships like the littoral combat ships provided sea-to-shore fire to protect the inbound troops. A few of the larger ships smoldered after taking hits from Warden missiles, but the CNA doled out a more violent attack against multiple points on both sides of the river. She'd never seen anything so spectacular—or horrifying.

The ship shuddered with another explosion in the lower decks. Dani fell and slid off the VTOL's ramp when the ship rocked.

Hands grasped her wrists, and Dani's slide stopped. She looked up and was stunned to see both Mary and Hattie holding her.

"Can't trust you to do anything without trying to die in the process," Hattie said.

Dani remained too shocked to respond and allowed them to help her up and into the aircraft. "Thanks," she said, then pushed her way through the others on board to reach Miles. Cameron worked on him with a med kit he'd obtained at some point. Miles's face remained pale. Oliver put his arms around her, and she held him close.

She touched Miles's cheek, and he opened his eyes.

"I love you both very much," Miles said.

"Don't start," Dani said. "Not now."

He smiled.

Dani leaned down and kissed him, then moved aside for Oliver to hug his father as best he could in the cramped helo. Cameron snapped more vials of medicine to the patch on the back of Miles's hand.

Dani lost track of time during the flight and startled when the VTOL rocked as it landed.

Ramos was issuing orders, and people shifted to start unloading.

"Help me up," Miles said. "And give me a gun."

Cameron immediately pulled his pistol and put it in Miles's hand. He and Dani helped Miles to his feet and toward the VTOLs deck to unload.

Catherine's eyes flew open, and she gasped. She lay among a few other bodies that had been moved aside to be dealt with later. She removed her blood-soaked uniform top. Most of the blood on it had belonged to Miles. He had to be dead by now. She tossed it aside and pulled a plasma pistol off one of the other corpses. Her undershirt remained bloodied from Miles stabbing her, but physically she was fine. She was in a younger body now, and felt great.

The *Karl* listed hard to starboard, and Catherine realized she'd been a bit slow to regen. She resisted the urge to laugh. The experiment had worked, and she was an Echo now. Echoes in the CNA weren't as noteworthy as they were a few years ago, so she wasn't worried if anyone questioned her about the blood. Plus, she was an excellent liar.

Shouts, alarms, and people darting through the ship passageways made her invisible, so she left the corpse holding area without being noticed. Catherine didn't think anyone would recognize her in the much younger body, but she still kept her head down, following others into one of the helos loading the remaining soldiers to bring them to land. Dani would die today. Catherine would see to it herself.

CHAPTER
44

Weapons fire erupted around them, and Dani tried to shield Oliver. Miles returned fire while she and Cameron maneuvered him away from the VTOL. Oliver tripped, and Dani tackled him to the ground, covering him with her body.

CNA soldiers fired back at the Wardens. Explosions blew chunks of the beach into the air, and then sand rained down on them. Hands pulled at her clothing, and Dani got up, following their tugs. She dragged Oliver along with her.

Mary shoved them down again, but this time they had more cover and sheltered behind a destroyed, smoldering Amtrack, an amphibious assault vehicle with tank tracks. A pair of dead soldiers lay on the ground outside the vehicle. AAVs were great for combat power and mobility for the landing force until they were destroyed. Dani didn't mind having the wreck there for them to use as cover.

She tried to regroup her thoughts, but the chaos threatened to overwhelm her. Miles continued to shoot at the Wardens, but he was too exposed. A round clipped Cameron's lower leg, and he stumbled. Another round tore through the upper part of Miles's chest, and he collapsed.

Oliver tried to go to him.

Dani shoved Oliver against the Amtrack. "Stay here."

She and Mary scrambled away from their cover and dragged Miles back while Cameron crawled beside them.

Miles tried to speak but couldn't. Blood filled his mouth. Dani put her hands over the wound in his chest and didn't know what else to do. Oliver was beside her, talking to his father. Mary and Cameron were shouting at each other while Cam dug into his medical pack.

"I love you," was all Dani could manage to say to Miles when his eyes met hers. His face blurred through her tears. He would've had a hard time surviving the stab wound in the middle of this situation. Because he had no chance of a regen, the bullet that had ripped through his lung was a death sentence.

He put his hand on hers and gripped Oliver's hand with his other.

Dani and Oliver stayed with him even after he'd stopped breathing. Cameron snapped more vials into the patch on Miles's hand, but Dani knew it wouldn't change anything.

Miles was dead, and the war didn't stop for one dead man. She hated the war more than ever.

Oliver moaned, a low and agonizing sound, and Dani understood his misery. She'd never felt so helpless in her life. She groaned and hung her head. She tried to tell herself that he at least hadn't died alone, but what about the pain she and Oliver felt now? What about the pain Miles's friends would feel? All because Catherine was determined to start a battle she couldn't win. Why? Why Miles? Dani wished she could take his place. Oliver didn't deserve this. Grief consumed her thoughts.

Mary had arrived at her side at some point and kept her arm around her. She, too, wept with Dani and Oliver.

Dani wanted to crawl into a hole and die too, but she couldn't. Oliver was still alive, and she needed to keep him that way. Mary was with her, but Hattie wasn't. She wiped her face and drew in a deep, shuddering breath. She forced her head up and her gaze away from Miles. She spotted Hattie with Ramos and a few other people behind cover on the beach.

Dani shifted a few feet away from Oliver to one of the dead soldiers from the assault vehicle and began stripping the chest armor off the least mangled man. The other soldier's armor was of no use anymore. She tried but failed to ignore Miles's blood all over her hands. They trembled while she worked to remove the soldier's armor.

Helicopters swarmed the air, and Dani recognized the one they'd flown in to reach the *Karl* when it swooped low over the beach and strafed the Wardens daring to press their attack on the CNA.

"Is that Dylan?" she asked.

Mary looked up at Dani, then gazed toward the sky. She nodded. "Yeah. When we took that initial hit, she got off the bridge first and put her helo in the air to help protect the ship."

Dani tossed the armor to Oliver. "Put that on."

He stared at the chest piece for a second before Dani took it from his hands to put it on him. He was in shock, and she couldn't blame him. She was operating on survival instincts.

Cameron patched the wound to his leg and then took his gun back from Miles.

Various ships with troops, armored vehicles, aircraft, and other equipment were either unloading on the beach or nearing land to deploy. More help was coming, and once they had the beachhead, the battle would move inland. Maybe it was time to let the CNA have the fight and leave the Brigands out of their mess. Dani could stay on the beach with Oliver and keep him safe.

She watched Dylan's helo as it made another pass. Dani turned her gaze to the Warden line and frowned. "Fuck." Dylan couldn't keep making passes like that without getting shot down, and Dani and the others on this beach couldn't stick around much longer without getting overrun. The CNA had to make a move to force the Wardens back *soon* and give the additional incoming troops a chance to land without being shredded.

She returned her attention to Oliver and finished strapping him into the armor. He kept his head low until she lifted his chin. "I know you're crushed right now, but you have to pay attention. You're not safe here, so you're going with us and you'll stay with Anton."

Oliver gazed down at his father's body, then nodded.

Dani was relieved she didn't need to tell him that they had to leave Miles's body behind for now. She half wished her body was lying next to his.

She glanced around the Amtrack. The Wardens were still trying to press their way toward the beach and shooting everything they had at the CNA. Ramos, Javi, Anton, and Hattie were about fifty yards away, tucked behind a twisted and smoking Amtrack on its side. Dani spotted Brody among them and smiled. The damn dog was perfect and exactly what Oliver needed right now. Hell, she wanted to give the dog a hug too. She hadn't even noticed him before on the VTOL, but he had to have come along with Hattie.

She shifted to a crouch and moved Oliver to her left while she kept the Wardens on her right. Mary and Cameron slid in behind them, and they darted from behind their doomed Amtrack. Sand sprayed up where shots fired struck the ground instead of them, but they never slowed.

They slid to the ground when they reached the others, and Brody pounced on Oliver. The teen's mouth was open, and he didn't speak with the dog on him and licking his face. Oliver recovered and buried his face in the dog's fur, and Dani's chest hurt. She'd done the same thing with Brody after Jace died. She wanted to do it again now. Yes, staying here on the beach with Oliver and Brody was a good idea.

Hattie thrust armor into her hands. "I'm tired of seeing you unprotected and getting shot at, honey. We don't have time for one of your weird-ass regens."

Dani scowled, then started pulling the armored trousers on. "Things wouldn't be this way if Catherine hadn't lost her goddamn mind," she said, her voice sharp and full of bitterness.

"How's your shoulder?" Mary asked.

"Huh?"

Mary reached around her and jabbed two fingers into the back of Dani's shoulder.

Dani's vision filled with spots. She groaned and leaned forward, dizzied by the sudden wave of nausea and renewed throbbing.

"You're wounded."

Dani grunted and tried to straighten a little. "It's not bad as long as you keep your fucking fingers out of it." She wanted to stand and stretch her back and arm, but the continued incoming fire kept her low.

"Cam," Hattie said, "fix Dani's shoulder."

Dani finished pulling her trousers on, then turned to let Cameron access her shoulder.

He talked while he worked. "I'm really sorry—"

"Yep. I get it. Thanks," Dani said, assuming he referred to Miles. He fell silent, and she felt the familiar tingle of the healing pen as it repaired her damaged skin. The Wardens increased their assault, and Dani and the others had to crouch lower behind their cover of the destroyed Amtrack when the Warden shots got closer.

Cameron finished. "I've done what I can. I can't properly clean the wound out here, so I have only partially sealed it. I'll have to work on this a bit more later."

She moved her arm and shoulder. It remained stiff and sore but usable. "It's good for now. Thanks."

Oliver stared at Hattie, and she knelt next to him and Brody.

"Do you recognize me?" she asked.

"Aunt Hattie?" he said.

She nodded and wiped tears from his cheeks. "I saw what happened. I'm really sorry about your dad, kid. We'll get you and him home once we sort things out here. Elise, Jeanette, and Andy are there waiting for you."

"You're an Echo. You were always an Echo," Oliver said.

Hattie shrugged. "I told everyone I was human."

"Dani too?" Oliver asked.

"Especially Dani," Hattie said, and winked at him. "We," she said, gesturing to Dani and Mary, "have to deal with the Wardens coming to kill us, so you will finish armoring up and stay here with Brody."

"I can—"

Hattie's stern expression silenced him. Dani knew how that felt, too. It didn't matter that Hattie looked sixty years younger because of her regen. The presence the woman carried was plenty enough for others to know not to mess with her.

As much as Dani wanted to stay with Oliver, she couldn't. The Wardens had to be pushed back if there was any chance of keeping Oliver alive. She watched him as he sniffled and stroked Brody's fur.

Mary touched her arm.

Dani flinched, then nodded. She fastened her armored jacket closed, grabbed a helmet, then picked through weapons as Hattie pulled them from a pack and placed them with other plasma pistols and older plasma rifles.

"No fancy rifles, Mary," Dani said, lifting an old CNA MP belt with a holster and immobilization cuff attached. She slid her chosen pistol into the holster, then started looking for a knife.

Mary filled her pockets with grenades and then grabbed two pistols. "I'll pick one up along the way." She shoved one pistol into the rear waistband of her armor and one into the front.

Dani wished there was something with more explosive power among the weapons, but she had only standard CNA grenades. She shoved several into her pockets while Hattie spoke with the general.

She paused when she spotted the incoming wave of littoral combat ships. They had a shallow draft and rode above waves like a speedboat. The ships approached the beach ahead of the next group of inbound troop crafts and unleashed a rain of missiles and rounds. The guns on their decks could hit targets five miles away, and they ripped through the Warden line. She had always marveled at their maneuverability when *Splendor* did war games with them. They were also faster than any naval destroyer. She was glad she'd advised Santi to bring them when he came. She was even more glad that he had.

"Dani," Ramos said. "Come here."

She and Mary joined him, and he used his finger to trace over the map on his panel. "This is where we are. This is where we need to go. We have more troops coming in from here and here, but we need to stall the Wardens." He explained the rest of his plan, and Dani nodded. "Ready?" he asked.

"Almost." Dani returned to the array of weapons and picked out a knife. She preferred to carry three blades, but her special belt for carrying and concealing extra blades was still on the *Karl*. She slipped her single knife into the sheath on the belt. "Ready."

Mary pulled her into what would look like an embrace to anyone else. "You're understandably distracted, darling," Mary whispered into her ear. "You can stay with Oliver. You don't have to go."

Dani's anger flared. She frowned and backed away from her. She'd made her decision. She wasn't sitting this one out.

"Okay," Mary said. "Just making sure. But you're not going up that beach with one fucking gun." She took Dani's hand and placed a pistol in it. "Now you're ready," she said, then picked up an older plasma rifle.

Dani's anger at her friend subsided as quickly as it started. Mary was testing her, as she should. Dani turned her attention to Oliver. "I'll be back as soon as I can."

He nodded and continued to cling to Brody.

She wanted to hug him, kiss his forehead, and tell him everything would be okay. Instead, she took a deep breath and gathered with the others. On Ramos's order, they would move parallel to the coastline to join with other troops transported in off the *Karl* and coming in from other amphibious craft before moving inland, all while under fire from the Wardens. This wasn't exactly how the battle was supposed to go, but then most things Dani had planned went sideways early into the process. This was no different. She found it a little strange that this thought comforted her more than she expected.

The CNA's battle plans had pretty much gone to shit with the attack on the *Karl*, but it was also clear that the Wardens were out of position. Santi was smart enough to capitalize on that and change their operational area. They didn't need to attack Montreal head-on. This would work—perhaps even better. If the enemy had planned their initial attack, then Dani and the others would've been decimated before they ever stepped foot on land. The Wardens were winging it too. At least the CNA wasn't the only side trying to figure their shit out on the fly.

Ramos would press the attack instead of taking cover and waiting for help. This aggressive move would keep the Wardens guessing and on their heels; being the aggressor wasn't the CNA's usual tactic.

Hattie was saying something to the group, but Dani wasn't listening. She glanced back at Ramos. He was pale, sweaty, and too ill to be on the battlefield, but he continued to bark orders and send messages to other platoon leaders. His job was to organize the landing force and adjust ground attack plans as needed. He would be in communication with Boseman and Asllani since they would still be sending subsequent waves of troops and assault craft to the landing zone.

When the general gave the signal for Hattie to move out with her group, Dani didn't hesitate to go with her.

CHAPTER
45

No one involved in this war escaped losing a loved one. Mary knew this, but it didn't lessen the impact of losing Miles. When Cameron had worked on Dani's shoulder, Aunt Hattie had leaned in close to Mary and handed her a tranq pistol.

"We both know what it's like to lose someone close to us," Aunt Hattie said. "Put her out if she becomes a hazard."

"To herself?" Mary asked.

"To anyone."

Mary took a deep, shaky breath and nodded. *She'll be okay for now,* she thought. *I think.* She tucked the small pistol away into one of her trousers pockets and hoped she wouldn't need it, at least not for Dani. She had a bit more confidence in her friend's ability to keep going when Dani had refused the option of staying with Oliver.

Now, hunkered behind their cover, Mary shifted her rifle and pretended to clear sand from the mechanism. She stole a glance at Dani, who was positioned behind her.

"Don't bunch up when we move out," Aunt Hattie barked at the group. "You'll make easy targets if you're together."

Dani's head was turned like she was watching Ramos, and

Mary wondered what was going through her friend's mind as she half listened to Aunt Hattie. When Mary focused back on Aunt Hattie, she wondered how many wars the Ancient Echo had been through already. Aunt Hattie was no stranger to battle, that was clear. She was calm and in control. Mary wondered if her own insides would cause her to shit herself or if she could hold it together long enough to survive the next few minutes.

Ramos's signal came, and the group left their cover.

Sand sprayed up everywhere as Warden shots struck all around them.

"Spread out! Spread out!" Aunt Hattie said without slowing.

One well-placed shot and Mary could be ended forever. An intentional head shot from a distance was unlikely, though. A lucky shot to her head was still possible. That was what went through Mary's mind as she darted up the beach. She spotted Dani a few paces behind her. They had several more yards to go before they reached some semblance of cover, and Mary thought they might just make it until the Wardens unleashed their quake grenades.

The first blast obliterated the soldier to her left and took her off her feet. She crashed into the sand but kept her wits. Mary rolled and scrambled back to her feet again with the aid of someone else. She looked at her helper and brightened. "Dres!"

"Hey, Mary," he said.

He began to say something else, but another grenade struck, separating them. Mary was facedown in the sand, and dazed. She started to move, but a wave of sand crashed down on top of her, covering her.

The weight pressed on her back, and she couldn't take a breath. She struggled to move and couldn't. There was too much sand on her. She still couldn't breathe, and panic set in. She would have thrashed and screamed had she been able to.

She was going to die, suffocated by fucking sand. She'd eventually regen and suffocate again, and that time would end her life forever.

Her lungs burned worse, and her mind began to darken. She wasn't ready to die. Something touched her hand, and she wrapped her fingers around it. Someone was digging her out! Mary tried to recover from her panic, but she was desperate to escape being buried alive.

Hands pulled her free, and Mary drew in a deep, noisy breath, then coughed. She was hauled to her feet.

"C'mon. No time for lounging around."

Mary's hearing was off. She thought she recognized the voice, but wasn't sure. Her eyes were full of sand, so she couldn't open them. She clung to her rescuer, forced her legs to move, and blindly followed the person leading her.

A minute or so later she slammed into the ground again, but this time she was seated, her side leaning against sand.

"I can't see. I can't hear," Mary said, panic once again rising within her.

"Water!" the person with her said.

Some of the sand fell from her ears. She tried to wipe it from her eyes, and the person pushed her hands away.

"Wait a second, Mary. You'll make it worse."

Finally, she recognized the voice. "Dani?"

"Yeah?"

"Oh, God, Dani." Mary reached for her, but Dani pushed her away.

"Stop. Give me a sec."

Mary wasn't sure what was happening, but Dani tilted her face up and then water splashed over her face and eyes.

"Open your eyes when you can to wash the sand out," Dani said.

Mary did as instructed and sighed when she could finally

see again. She threw her arms around Dani, and this time she let her. "Thank you," Mary said.

"Are you hurt?"

"No. I don't think so. I thought, I …" Mary eased her grip on Dani. She'd been so afraid she was going to die. "Thank you, Dani. Where's Dres? He was right by me."

"Dead."

Mary released her and wiped the excess sand from her face and dug more out of her ears. Her helmet was gone, as was her rifle. Mary was sitting in a crater created by a quake grenade, and she was leaning against the side of the hole. Dani was crouched next to her and passed the canteen back to someone Mary didn't know. Others were in there with them, and even more scrambled into the crater for cover. Warden shots sailed over them. Some soldiers were shot before they made it in, and their corpses tumbled down into the hole. The screams of the wounded still lying on the beach made Mary shudder.

"Where's Aunt Hattie?" Mary asked.

"She made it up to the rally point."

Mary and Dani were not where they were supposed to be. Aunt Hattie probably didn't know where they were. Dani had stopped to dig Mary out of her sand grave, and Aunt Hattie would be livid with them. But then, Aunt Hattie being pissed off at them was such a common thing lately. Mary snorted a laugh.

Dani pawed through Mary's hair. "Are you sure you're okay? Head injury or anything?"

"No, I'm fine," Mary said, pushing Dani's hands away.

"You laughed. No one should be laughing right now."

"I know. Just a random, weird thought. I'm okay."

Dani nodded and turned to the others. "We're getting out of this hole. One lucky shot with a quake grenade and we leave this beach in pieces. Get your gear and gather extra weapons off the dead." She rolled one of the deceased soldiers over and unfastened his helmet. Dani tossed it to Mary, then grabbed a pair of rifles out of the sand. The others in the crater scavenged off the bodies while Mary checked her helmet. It was free of gore on the inside, so she put it on.

"Don't get buried again," Dani said, and gave her one of the rifles.

Mary frowned. "You don't usually carry a rifle. Where's the pistol I gave you?"

"Tossed it. I needed both hands to dig you out."

"Oh."

She watched Dani as she checked her rifle. Mary had never thought it was possible for her to love Dani more than she already did. She had been wrong.

"Anyone here know explosives?" one of the soldiers asked, pulling a pack off one of the bodies. "This pack is full of things that explode."

Mary's spirit leapt. "*Me!* Give it to me."

Dani grinned. "You do love a good bit of destruction."

"Always." Mary placed her rifle aside and quickly dug through the pack. "Oh, this is fucking gorgeous." She fastened the pack closed and slipped her arms through the straps. "I can do a lot of damage with this." Mary picked up her rifle.

"Good. Let's get you somewhere where you can blow shit up," Dani said. "C'mon."

Mary rolled to her feet and followed Dani out of the crater. She didn't turn to see if the others came with them. That didn't matter. She refused to let Dani out of her sight.

CHAPTER

46

Rowan wasn't surprised to see the CNA returning fire on the Warden missile installations. The Wardens had their own counterair measures in use that destroyed many of the incoming Commonwealth missiles. The *Karl* had taken major damage, and Rowan enjoyed watching smoke and flames billow up from the vessel.

The pilot kept their helo out of the line of fire but positioned where Rowan had a great view of the fighting.

"Sir," the pilot said, "you're being hailed by the vice regent."

"Ignore it," Rowan said. He brought his optics to his eyes and scanned the Commonwealth fleet.

The ship movements were not what he had expected. Instead of trying to turn around, they moved closer to the island of Montreal. "What is this?" he muttered.

Amphibious landing craft and both fixed and tilt-rotor aircraft began launching from the ships. He hadn't been surprised to see helos leaving the listing *Karl*, but he had never expected the CNA to proceed with an attack. It could be a demonstration—a tactical move to make a show of force with the intent to affect enemy decisions. Rowan wouldn't shift troops or make some other error because of some half-assed CNA trickery.

Houston was known to use feints and decoys, so Rowan didn't make adjustments.

The CNA deployed drones for mine countermeasures, and the smaller, faster LCSs maneuvered around the islands. When numerous assault vehicles launched, Rowan knew he'd misjudged the Commonwealth. This wasn't a demonstration. It was a full assault, and the Wardens were way out of position to thwart it.

"Yura, get on your panel. Route any available aircraft to the locks. Send orders to forces at the locks to halve their numbers and relocate the airlifted troops to that beachhead," Rowan said, pointing. "That's where the CNA will land."

He unfastened his straps and moved to the front of the helo. "Put us on the ground there," he told the pilot, pointing at a bunker.

"Yes, sir. The VR is—"

"Fuck the VR. Put us on the ground *now!*"

"Yes, sir."

Rowan returned to his seat and glared at the CNA through his optics. The pilot didn't land the helo nearly as fast as he'd wanted, but once it touched the ground, Rowan leapt out. Yura was right behind him.

He began barking orders at the troops already stationed at the bunker and took command. Yura transmitted other comms to additional ground troops to regroup and converge on their location. The techs unloaded their gear from the helo and set up operations inside the bunker. They had enough weaponry with them to hold the CNA back for a time, but Rowan wasn't sure it would last long enough for the reinforcements to arrive.

Rowan *had* to speak to the VR. He needed more troops that he didn't have under his command. He slipped a comm unit into his ear and hailed the VR on his panel. Keran's acceptance of the hail was instantaneous.

"Rowan, what the fuck do you think you're doing?"

"Sir, I had to order the attack on the fleet using your credentials. The CNA was making fleet movements to suggest an assault, and I couldn't wait for the chain of command slowness and risk losing the advantage." The lies were always so easy, and the leadership tended to be so gullible.

Keran growled in his ear. "I've trusted you, Rowan. But this ..."

"I know, sir. Sentence me to death later. But I was right. The Commonwealth is landing troops in Montreal East, sector thirty-eight. I have forces here but not enough."

"Goddammit. All you had to do was take my first hail. I have naval forces deployed, but now you have aircraft in motion to move troops across the river, and that delays my ability for airstrikes."

Rowan winced. He had command of only a few helos. His haste to move troops meant the helos would be in the way and the inbound jets couldn't easily bombard the fleet from above. He'd been outmaneuvered by the CNA *and* made a tactical error as a result. This looked bad for him. He refused to apologize for his actions, though.

"There are mine webs on the beaches and some mines in the water, but it won't be enough to prevent the CNA landing with the volume of forces coming in, sir," Rowan said. Yura was close enough to hear his side of the conversation. He gestured for her to send the numbers to the chancellors and VR. He returned his attention to Keran. "I need more troops at this location."

"You're there now?"

"Yes, sir."

There was a pause that almost made Rowan insane with anger. It should not take this long to make decisions, especially by the leadership. They should move swiftly and violently. *Always!*

The cost to Warden lives would be high, but they could not lose Montreal.

"I'm sending troops your way, Rowan," Keran said. "Use them wisely and hold that beachhead. Don't fuck this up."

Rowan snarled at the panel, though his comm was audio only. Keran's warning infuriated him. "Yes, sir," he said, then ended the link.

He resumed barking orders at the troops around him and laid out the plan of attack for the techs. CNA troops began landing on Warden soil.

Rowan gave his next order: "Fire!"

The noise was deafening, and Rowan returned to the helo for a moment. He removed all weapons left on board, including a plasma rifle that had belonged to Curtis. Rowan didn't give his former aide another thought as he left the helo. "Put this thing in the air and fire everything you have at the CNA on the ground. Hit those assault vehicles hard."

"Yes, sir," the pilot said.

Rowan sprinted back to the bunker and joined the other soldiers firing at the enemy. He gazed through the scope and expertly shot and killed CNA troops with armor-piercing rounds.

The helo lifted high into the air, avoiding incoming fire from the Commonwealth, then swooped low, releasing its barrage of fire. A few Amtracks were hit, and one made a spectacular flip into the air before landing back on the sand in a heap of flames. Rowan was pleased with the pilot's efforts and amount of destruction unleashed—until the helo burst into a ball of fire from a shot that came from one of the VTOLs. Rowan had never seen that kind of firepower on a VTOL. *Fuck. Ancients.*

The same VTOL could have clobbered the bunker he was in, but it instead turned and headed back to sea to pick up more troops. *Shit.* The CNA was going to trample the Wardens with their volume of troops. Rowan just needed to keep the CNA occupied until reinforcements arrived.

He swept his scope across the beach, hoping to glimpse Houston or Ramos, but he didn't see them. He froze when he spotted a woman with a length of blond hair extending from the base of her helmet. Sure, not every female Commonwealth solider with blond hair could be Mary Smith, but there was an excellent chance she was here. And if she was here, so was Dani.

Yura took her position next to him with her rifle. "You need to be shooting," she said.

He glanced at her and noticed the smirk on her face.

"You mind your rifle, and I'll mind mine," he said with a hint of a grin. She loved killing the CNA as much as he did. "Pick off the officers if you can."

"Not my first battle, Rowan."

He nodded. It wouldn't be her last either. Like him, she was born for war and wiping humans off the planet.

Rowan scanned the CNA troops, but didn't locate Dani. She had to be there. Too many troops made it impossible to find her. He put his scope back on the woman he thought was Smith and watched her. She turned her head enough that he could see her face. It was indeed her.

He kept his aim on her head and started to squeeze the trigger. A mortar round exploded near her, taking her off her feet and sending a spray of sand into the air. He lost his visual of her and figured she was dead. He still didn't see Dani anywhere.

He couldn't stop killing enemy troops to search for her, so he resumed picking off any CNA soldier unlucky enough to get in his crosshairs.

CHAPTER
47

Oliver cowered behind the destroyed Amtrack. He put his hands over his ears every time something exploded, regardless of whether the blast was distant or close by. *This* was the life his father didn't want for him. It wasn't normal to be around this much noise and screaming and death. He understood now why his father sometimes had nightmares. Dani also suffered from disrupted sleep at times. Oliver briefly wondered how anyone could ever function in life after being in this kind of situation for even a few minutes.

Someone grabbed his wrist, and Oliver flinched, not aware that he'd closed his eyes. Anton crouched near him.

"Things aren't as bad here now," Anton said, nodding toward the sea. "We have more troops coming in, and the Wardens are retreating inland. We'll get you out of here soon. Okay?"

Oliver nodded. Anton patted his shoulder, then returned to his station with his computer while other techs set up more equipment near him. Oliver didn't see Santi anywhere, and he hopped up. Brody stayed with him while Oliver crept closer to where Anton worked, his eyes sweeping over the CNA troops for signs of the general.

Anton's screens showed terrain maps with overlays of

buildings and other structures. Blue dots blurred into lines and blobs when grouped together. Oliver looked skyward. Most of the aircraft moved constantly overhead and inland while firing at targets on the ground. A few aircraft remained almost stationary, and he realized that those were the helos tracking the ground troops. He'd done only one practice run during training in New Brunswick with the sensors, but it was enough for him to know the basics of how they worked.

Anton glanced back and spotted him. "See that boat," Anton said, pointing to one of the cushioned landing crafts unloading troops and supplies on the beach. "Get on it. That's the one that will take you to *Splendor*. Go."

Oliver nodded and started down the beach with Brody. His mind wasn't working right, and he couldn't think straight. His feet kept moving, though, until he stood a few yards from the amphibious boat. He turned and gazed back toward where he'd left Anton. His eyes then turned to where they'd left his father's body. Dani, Mary, and Aunt Hattie were somewhere inland, and he was leaving them all.

"Hey, kid. You getting on or what?" one of the soldiers asked.

Oliver stared at him for a moment, then turned and sprinted back toward Anton. He slowed before arriving and ducked behind other soldiers and equipment so Anton wouldn't see him. Oliver glanced back at the shoreline. His ride had left, and he didn't mind not being on it.

He inched closer to Anton's work area and listened in. He resisted the urge to go to Javi and Santi. Anton gave the general updates, pointing to his screens and talking about communications from both Asllani and Boseman. Troop and equipment movements blended with CNA troops' locations, making it hard for Oliver to keep up. But he'd overheard Aunt Hattie's sector location and where she was headed next. Oliver remembered the map markings on Anton's computer and knew where to go.

More troops moved up the beach to support the inland forces. He knelt and removed a cable from around one of the equipment stacks. Oliver used it to tie Brody to the stack. He used the hand signals he'd seen Dani and Mary use when working with Brody. He gave him the commands for "easy," which was for him to be slow and quiet, and then the command for "stay." Oliver hoped Brody would obey.

He slid around to the side of the equipment and slipped in with a passing group of soldiers. Once they joined with the larger group headed inland, Oliver disappeared among them.

He couldn't blend in, though. He wore a CNA uniform and a chest piece of bloodied armor, but he had no weapon or gear. Oliver's hopes of no one noticing this were dashed.

"Where's your weapon, son?" a captain asked him.

"I, uh, came in off the *Karl*. I didn't have time to grab anything before they loaded us on a VTOL to make the landing," Oliver said.

The officer pulled him out of formation. "It's gruesome work, but find you some gear among the dead and get back in line."

"Yes, sir." Oliver left the group and opted to avoid getting too close to the bodies. He picked up a pistol from the sand and cleaned it off. He didn't want to deal with a rifle, so he kept the plasma pistol and slid back into formation.

As the troops proceeded off the beach to go inland, Oliver disappeared into shrubs along the coastline. He moved quickly until reaching the tree line, which gave him better cover.

Oliver recalled the map from Anton's screen. He could still go back to the beach, get Brody, and leave this place and the dead, or he could stay. His dad was gone. His dad always helped keep Dani safe. Mary helped too, but Oliver's dad was always there for Dani. He couldn't do that anymore. Tears stung his eyes at the memory of his father. Oliver didn't want to break down now. If Dani needed help, *he* wanted to be there for her like his dad had been.

Oliver cut through the woodlands and paused before emerging into the more open area of the destroyed portions of the city. Wardens could be anywhere, but there wasn't any fierce fighting in his immediate vicinity. He heard the sounds of the war grinding people to corpses to his left and his right. Aunt Hattie's reported location was ahead of him.

He glanced around one more time to make sure he was alone, then headed for the once-urban area. He kept his pistol ready, though he didn't intend to use it unless he had no other choice. Of course, once he met up with Dani, if he was going to fight alongside her, he'd have to pull the trigger at some point. He'd sort that part out when he had to. He needed to find her first.

CHAPTER
48

Curtis struggled to remain conscious. He'd managed to make it to shore, and he lay in the mud, desperate for sleep and a break from the pain. His betrayal by Rowan hurt more than the abdominal wound.

Their armor had been designed to withstand CNA plasma rounds, but less so for Warden rounds. Curtis considered himself somewhat fortunate, though. Rowan could have just removed his head with his plasma pistol. Curtis wasn't sure why he hadn't, other than Rowan preferred to make things personal.

Rowan's treason by falsifying the launch order would get him executed, assuming he survived this madness with the CNA—no, this madness with Dani.

Curtis was loyal to a fault. He knew this as much as he knew he needed to kill Dani to save Rowan from himself. He struggled to his feet and held his hand against his wound. He'd shed his armor in the river so it wouldn't drown him. His lack of armor was a benefit, given his proximity to a part of the beach where CNA troops were coming ashore. Had he still been in his Warden armor, they would've easily spotted him as the enemy.

Curtis stripped out of his uniform top and threw it into the brush. His undershirt was coated with blood, but he was in generic black trousers and a dark gray shirt now. It made it easier for him to blend in.

He headed toward the fighting, realizing the irony if he was shot and killed by the Wardens attacking the CNA. He might even have laughed at the thought if he hadn't felt like shit.

Curtis stumbled toward the first few dead CNA soldiers and scavenged their armor and a rifle. He could blend in with the CNA now and kill a lot of them, sacrificing himself for the greater good, but he needed to end Dani first.

He merged with the troops moving up the beach and realized that Rowan's attempt to provoke the CNA into making a mistake and trapping the ships in the river had gone awry. Instead of retreating, the CNA had deployed its amphibious assault.

Warden forces were out of position for this kind of move from the CNA. He had to give the Commonwealth some credit for making Rowan's attack plan go sideways. It had been a stroke of brilliance—or dumb luck—on the CNA's part. Either way, the Wardens were fucked until they could regain the attack advantage. Curtis was certain Rowan was frantically moving troops to join them with forces on this beachhead.

He couldn't worry about Rowan's plans and subsequent moves. Curtis had to keep himself alive. He needed to force a regen, but he was among the CNA now. It was too risky, so he resolved to keep his legs moving. He fired a few shots at times at the Wardens but didn't try aiming at anyone in particular. Curtis was surprised how little fighting there actually was until he realized he'd merged in with one of the subsequent waves of Commonwealth troops, not the front line.

The main force had already driven most of the Wardens back or killed them. He slowed and looked at the Warden dead. There were *so many*.

Curtis groaned and wished that the day had gone differently.

The Warden army was made up of only regenerating Echoes. They were practically invincible, but when a Warden died a permanent death, there weren't any replacements—or not enough replacements. They used to be able to keep their numbers up by stealing souls from Brigands and captured CNA and reconditioning those Echoes into the ranks. But the numbers had steadily declined in the last few years after the Brigands and Commonwealths banded together to create larger forces.

A CNA officer barked at him for not moving, so Curtis marched on with the others. His mind was elsewhere.

The Wardens would ultimately lose the war. They would run out of troops even if they kept their tech more advanced than the CNA. Except they were losing that race, too. The Commonwealths had Ancients helping them now.

Curtis didn't think Rowan's betrayal of him could hurt more, but it did. Rowan's actions had started this nightmare, this slaughter of Wardens in Montreal. Rowan's actions by meddling with Oliver Jackman and the CNA in Maine had caused the debacle in Boston that also got Ana killed.

He shook his head and groaned.

"You all right, soldier?" a CNA soldier next to him asked. "You're wounded."

"It's not as bad as it looks, sir."

The lie worked, and Curtis was allowed to continue on.

His wound was deep and bleeding, and he was running out of time. He tried to ignore the discomfort when he bent to pick up a grenade that had been dropped. He slipped it into his pocket. A grenade might be useful.

He wasn't sure how to find Rowan. Curtis listened in on the chatter around him and moved closer to the officers as they marched inland. He wasn't hearing anything useful, though.

He wanted to sit and rest for a while, but he couldn't. His team had stopped on the edge between the trees and the city.

He wiped at the sweat on his brow and noticed blood on his hand.

When he lifted his head, he spotted Oliver. Curtis blinked a few times to make sure his vision was clear. He was certain it was the boy, but he couldn't just walk away now.

He approached an officer. "Sir. Permission to seek a medic?" Curtis lifted the lower edge of his CNA chest armor to show the amount of blood on his clothing beneath it.

"Yes, go," the officer said, waving him away.

"Thank you, sir." Curtis made his way to the rear, then turned to head back inland but using cover to conceal his way.

He could only walk at a brisk pace. When he tried jogging to catch up to the young Jackman, it almost made him pass out.

He finally caught a glimpse of Oliver and renewed his pursuit. Curtis would never be able to overtake him in his condition, but Oliver was operating solo. He had to be seeking out his father or Dani. Curtis continued to follow as best he could, though his weakness worsened.

Again, he considered forcing a regen. But he'd definitely lose Oliver in the time it took for him to heal. He couldn't regen now.

CHAPTER
49

Dani glanced back a few times, and Mary was still with her. Of the other soldiers who emerged from the crater, some made it out to follow them, and others were cut down by Warden fire. She didn't stop and neither did Mary until they stumbled to a halt at the base of a hill with Hattie and other troops rotating return fire at the Wardens. Hattie was thrown back when a round struck her chest armor. Mary was up first to go to her, but Dani snagged her by her pack.

"You take a round in that pack full of explosives, we all die," Dani said. "I'll get her."

Mary relented, and Dani scampered around her. As soon as the bodies of any Echoes killed by the Wardens glowed for regen, they would become instant targets to try to permanently kill. Hattie was too busy swearing to be dead, so that made Dani feel a little better about their situation.

She grabbed Hattie's armor and dragged her back behind the base of the hill to safety. Hattie grumbled and struggled with her armor. Dani helped her get the chest piece open, and Hattie slipped her hand inside.

Dani examined the damaged vest and pulled the spent round from a hole. Hattie *should* be dead and pending a regen right now. "That was an armor-piercing round. We don't have the armor to stop those kinds of rounds, but you do."

Hattie frowned and removed her hand from the inside of the chest piece. There was no blood on her fingers.

"Usman made some upgrades," Hattie said.

"Who is Usman?" Mary asked.

"Live long enough and you'll get to meet him."

"Eh," Dani said, shrugging. "Maybe not. Takes her forever to regen."

Hattie stared at Dani for a moment, then looked at Mary. "It worked?" she asked.

Mary nodded. "But it's messed up. Takes a while before I start glowing."

"Hours, Mary. It's fucking *hours*."

Mary frowned at her. "You still forget everything when you die, so don't act like—"

"Children!" Hattie barked, and they fell silent. "So you both died in the field recently?"

"Yeah," Dani said.

Hattie sighed and shook her head. "Tell me about it later. Mary, what do you have in that pack?"

Mary grinned.

"Good," Hattie said. "Make something that we can throw. Grenades aren't enough for the Wardens up in that bunker."

Mary was already sliding out of her pack. "On it."

Dani checked her rifle to make sure it was clear of sand, and then she and Hattie alternated firing at the Wardens and throwing a few more grenades. Hattie was right. The grenades did some damage against the enemy, but not enough.

During one of Dani's turns at shooting at the Wardens, she tried to pick one off as he darted across an open area. She missed every time, cursing under her breath. Mary wouldn't have missed.

When she took an extra second to put him in the crosshairs, she paused. A hand jerked her back behind their cover.

"What the fuck are you doing?" Mary asked. "Don't stick yourself up there to shoot and then not shoot."

"It was Rowan. I saw Rowan up there."

"Even more reason to pull the damn trigger, Dani!"

Dani yanked her sleeve from Mary's grip. "I didn't know it was him until I got my scope on him. I didn't have time to shoot him before you interrupted me. So fuck off." Dani shifted to return to her spot to fire at the Wardens, and Mary grabbed her again. "Goddammit, Mary. *What?*"

"Just take a break." Mary lifted the two smaller packs she held in her other hand. "It's my turn. I'll take the asshole out."

Dani wasn't sure why her anger kept flaring at her friend. Being shot at by the Wardens probably had something to do with it. She nodded and switched places with Mary.

"Cover fire, now!" Hattie said.

Dani and other soldiers sprayed the Wardens with multiple shots, and then Mary stood and launched one of her packs into the air. Everyone ducked back down.

The first explosion went off.

"Wait!" Mary said to the group. "Just wait."

A second then third blast shook the ground. Mary grinned. "Not yet." She popped up and threw her second pack.

The fourth blast struck a few seconds later, and the ground trembled. The final blast ruptured the Warden bunker into pieces, and everyone cowered a bit lower.

Once the debris stopped falling, all weapons fire from the bunker had ceased. Mary laughed.

"What the hell did you hit them with?" Dani asked.

"My own special version of mixing and matching explosives. There were some higher-end Warden quake grenades in there too."

"You're a little scary with those things."

"Why, thank you."

Dani hadn't meant it as a compliment, but Mary seemed quite proud of herself.

Hattie organized the troops around her, and they left their area to swarm the remnants of the bunker and clear the way for other CNA soldiers to move off the beach and inland. Dani and Mary went with her.

Dani tried to keep her thoughts focused, but she wondered how Oliver was doing. He *should* be safe, but there wasn't any way to know for sure without seeing for herself.

"Go," Mary said, giving her a shove.

Dani blinked and realized Hattie had given them instructions, and she'd been lost in her thoughts. She snapped her mind back to the present and circled around the former bunker with Mary.

They found several dead Wardens, but none were Rowan. Sure, he could've been obliterated with one of Mary's explosives, but Dani couldn't assume that he was dead. If she'd spotted him, there was a chance that he'd spotted her. If he had, he'd hunt her.

A shout caught everyone's attention. One of the CNA soldiers pointed, and Dani spotted Wardens moving through the trees. Some were retreating. Many others were advancing.

"Shit. They have reinforcements," Mary said.

Dani nodded, but there was something odd about the movements of the incoming Wardens. The way they advanced toward them—the patterns were unusual.

Hattie was already barking orders, and Dani interrupted her.

"Look at their approach, Hattie. They're avoiding the clearer areas when they should be charging right through them to come at us."

Hattie observed the Wardens for a moment. In another minute or so gunfire would erupt as they got closer.

Dani continued. "Bet you a pint that when we start shooting, they'll retreat again to lure us in. They have land mines."

Hattie shook her head. "I'm not taking that bet." She turned to two of the soldiers near her. "Run word to our left and right that when the Wardens start to retreat, do *not* pursue them. They have mines planted, and we'll need to locate and disable them. Go."

The soldiers left, and Hattie turned to Dani. "How did you know?"

"I may have had a recent run-in with a Warden mine web."

"That's how you died?"

"Technically … yes."

"Jesus, Dani." Hattie sighed, and waved her off. "I don't even want to know what that means. Mary, you have stuff in that pack to disable mines?"

"Yep. I can assess where the web goes and either disable the network or detonate it," Mary said.

"You and Dani will take that job once we get near the tree line."

Dani glanced at Mary and nodded. She ducked when the Wardens started their second wave of the attack.

Hattie readied her rifle and was the first to emerge from their cover to return fire. Dani and Mary followed.

The CNA and Brigand forces were matched in numbers with the Wardens, but as always, the Wardens had the better firepower. Still, the Wardens made the show of retreat Dani had expected.

Some of the CNA troops either forgot or didn't heed the word to avoid following the Wardens. Explosions ended their lives in an instant.

Hattie screamed more orders at the troops, and they ceased their pursuit. Once Hattie had soldiers guarding the saboteurs as they prepped to disarm the mines, Mary and Dani went to work. Other sabs worked other areas of the island's woodlands, and soon the CNA troops were back to marching inland.

Dani had lost track of Hattie but still rejoined the advancing lines. They had caught up with the Wardens again and begun pursuing them. It was nice to have the Wardens on the run even if the first couple of Warden retreats were more of a feint. This time the Warden retreat was disorganized and they had no reinforcements.

When she and Mary arrived on the outskirts of the city, Dani slowed. Numerous buildings were mostly destroyed, but a few remained standing or somewhat standing with lots of places for Wardens to hide.

She continued forward and moved around one of the crumbled structures. Dani lost her footing and tumbled to the base of a mound of broken concrete, gaining several bruises along the way.

The shooting started again, and Mary pulled her behind a chunk of concrete the size of a small car.

"Well, that's one way to get down a hill," Mary said.

Dani grunted and moved her sore shoulder. It still worked, but it hurt like hell. "I don't recommend it."

Mary laughed and dug through her pack. She created another bomb with the last of her explosives, then placed it back inside the pack. She passed Dani the detonator.

Mary popped up, tossed the pack, then ducked back down. She nodded, and Dani activated the detonator. The subsequent explosion blew debris in all directions and covered them in a plume of smoke and dust.

CHAPTER

50

ani coughed a few times. There was a lull in the shooting after the bombs went off. She risked poking her head around the block of concrete she and Mary hid behind. The dust cleared, and Dani spotted him again.

Rowan's helmet was gone, and she got enough of a look at him during his retreat to know she'd finally gotten the upper hand on him. *Finally.* His face was bloodied, and he was limping. A female Warden was helping him, and Dani recognized her from Santi's files. Yura. They were both armed, which was an issue. The other problem was that he was fifty yards ahead of them, and Dani needed time to catch him without getting shot in the process. She wasn't sure what she'd do when she caught him. In her prior lives, she'd had chances to kill him and hadn't. She decided she'd figure it out later.

Dani slipped back behind her cover.

"What do you see?" Mary asked.

"Rowan."

"Really? Let's get that fucker!"

"Wait a sec. He's got Yura with him. I didn't see Curtis anywhere, so he might be close. Rowan is injured and heading toward a building with four levels to it." Dani tried to clear the jam on her rifle, thinking it was dirt clogging the mechanism, but one of the pieces was damaged and bent. She guessed that had happened during her fall down the mound of concrete. She tossed it aside and pulled her pistol from her holster.

"How many grenades you got left?" Mary asked.

"I'm out."

"Shit. I'm out too. Here." Mary gave her one of her extra pistols. "We're going after him, right?"

"Yep."

"Good."

Dani chuckled. "Ready when you are."

"I'm ready."

Dani held both pistols up when she left her cover and sprayed several shots in the direction of the remaining Wardens who were in full retreat. CNA troops started spreading out to pursue the Wardens as they dispersed into the interior of the island and among the rubble of what was once part of Montreal. Dani still didn't see Hattie anywhere.

Dani and Mary picked their way toward the building she'd seen Rowan heading toward and assumed he'd entered it. There wasn't a doorway, but a hole large enough to drive a tank through existed where a door had probably been at some point. They paused before entering.

Mary frowned. "There are going to be a lot of rooms and corridors to check in here. He can slip out and we'd never know it."

Dani had considered this already and nodded.

"You said he was injured. He's had time to force a regen."

Again, something Dani had thought about already. She nodded again.

"We need a full team to do this the right way."

Pebbles trickled down the side of the building somewhere above them. Dani looked up. She shoved Mary into the building and stumbled in after her. A chunk of concrete slammed into the ground where they'd been standing and split in half.

"What the hell was that?" Mary asked.

"Rowan. Third floor. Still want to wait for a team?"

Mary glared at her, and Dani chuckled. Mary was out for blood now. Dani was glad Rowan would be on the receiving end of Mary's wrath and not her.

They remained cautious in case other Wardens were lurking inside the building, but they found the nearest stairs and started up. They reached the second level, and Dani made the turn to go up to the third floor.

"Hey," Mary whispered.

When Dani turned, Mary nodded in the direction of the entry.

Instead of checking the entry from the second floor to the stairs, Dani had continued up. *Shit.* It was a dangerous mistake, and Dani wasn't thinking clearly. She had been cautious, but not cautious enough. She nodded and shifted to go back down the few steps she'd climbed, but correcting her mistake had come too late. Rowan and Yura had come down one level after trying to drop a block of concrete on them.

Yura was a blur bursting through the door and tackling Mary. Dani leapt back down to the landing, and Rowan had her wrist, twisting it and dislodging her pistol before she could get a shot off at Yura.

Dani rammed her shoulder into Rowan, and they tumbled out of the stairwell and into the corridor. He brought his pistol up toward her head, and Dani slammed her helmet into his face. The blow stunned him long enough for her to knock the weapon from his grasp. He dislodged her other pistol, then gripped her sleeve with one hand and lifted her with his other. She would've cursed out loud had she had time to utter a word before he flipped her and smashed her into the rubble on the floor.

She cried out from the impact and felt warm blood soaking her shirt beneath her armor. Her shoulder wound was reopened, bleeding, and throbbing again. She had trouble moving her arm.

She heard shouts from within the stairwell as Yura and Mary continued their struggle. Dani couldn't help Mary with Rowan trying to kill her. She rolled to stand, and Rowan pounced.

His movements were swift, with no signs of any prior injury other than remnant blood on his black Warden armor. She realized he'd baited her. He could've shot her and Mary from the third floor. Instead, he'd rolled a block of concrete off a ledge at them. He hadn't wanted to crush them. He wanted them inside the building, on his terms. Dani cursed herself for her foolishness.

Rowan was cunning, and she'd fallen for every trick he'd thrown at her, including rushing into the building and up to the wrong level. Her mistakes had left Mary exposed, and now both of them were fighting for their lives.

Dani wasn't giving up. Miles had fought back until he no longer drew breath. Dani would do the same. She tried to roll away from Rowan, but he still landed on top of her. She wrapped her leg around him and put her left arm up to block his strikes. Dani got her right arm moving enough to get her hand on her pistol on the ground. Her grip was weak, and she fumbled with the pistol until she finally got a hold on it.

He pulled her up by her jacket, then slammed her back into the ground. The additional blow to her shoulder almost made her drop the weapon. She fired a shot into the side of Rowan's chest armor. It didn't go through the armor, but it was enough of a blow to make him release her jacket. He attacked her arm until the pistol left her hand to slide across the floor and stop several feet away.

Dani rammed her helmet into his face again. He retaliated by wrapping his arms around her head and wrenching her helmet off. He used it as a weapon and brought it down at her face. Dani rolled and escaped what would have been a crushing blow. She struck him in the face with her fist, stunning him briefly, but it was enough for her to move away from him and closer to Mary, who battled with Yura in the stairwell.

Rowan stood and grinned, blood covering his teeth. "You're not getting out of here alive."

"Neither are you." Dani kept her eyes on him and continued to inch back toward the stairs. Her shoulder ached, but she tried to move in a fluid manner that wouldn't betray how she really felt—battered to hell, sore, and tired. The adrenaline kept her mind sharp, though, and she pulled her knife.

"Where's Jackman?" Rowan asked as he stalked her.

That unnerved her, and Rowan grinned. Dani didn't know what she'd done to signal that his mentioning of Miles had rattled her, but she'd blinked or shuddered or something. Mary's scream brought Dani's mind back into focus. When Rowan lunged, she advanced on him instead of backing away. She arced her blade at his head and took pleasure when he cried out as the blade cut across his skin.

CHAPTER
51

Mary's glimpse of Yura just before she burst through the doorway gave her enough time to turn her body a little before they collided. Mary's side slammed into the wall, and they separated. Mary swung the rifle up, striking Yura's upper arm with the stock. Mary had hoped for a bit more separation to turn the rifle and fire, but Yura was too quick. The Warden countered by lunging at her and using one hand to shove the rifle into the stair railing. Pieces of the rifle broke off, and Mary let it fall from her hands. They traded blows, and Mary stumbled over debris.

Yura shoved her down.

Yura's pistol was still in her holster. She could have shot Mary in the head instead of tackling her, but she hadn't. This was personal. Rowan and Yura weren't out to just kill Dani and Mary. They intended to make the women suffer. *Oh, God. This whole thing was a setup to get us in the building.*

Dani screamed in the corridor. Mary was desperate to reach her, but Yura wasn't about to let her just walk away. Mary rolled and kicked Yura off her.

The Warden attacked again as Mary got her pistol up. Mary's back collided with the wall, which she used to brace her foot and shove Yura back. The woman dropped to the floor and used her leg to flip Mary into the air. Mary landed on her back, and the pistol bounced out of her hand.

Yura reached for her own pistol, and Mary grabbed a handful of dirt and dust off the floor and flung it at her. Mary knew what sand in the eyes felt like, and it was enough of a distraction for Yura's shots to miss. Mary grinned as she slammed her shoulder into Yura's middle, sending the Warden's back into the wall. They wrestled to gain control of Yura's pistol, but they lost it when it fell from the Warden's grasp.

Yura drove her fist into Mary's jaw. Mary stumbled but still managed to pull her knife. She kept the spine of the knife against her forearm, edge out, as she eyed her enemy. Yura appeared unarmed, but Mary knew not to assume she'd bested the Warden.

She heard the sounds of Rowan and Dani's continuing fight, but Mary still couldn't go to Dani's aid. Yura was too deadly to leave alive.

Mary went after her. Yura crouched and clipped Mary's legs with her own. Mary landed hard on her side but managed to swing her knee up and catch Yura in the ribs before the Warden could get a tight grip on her neck. Mary sliced Yura's arm with the blade, then turned her wrist to make another cut going back the other way.

Yura was ready for the second strike with the knife. She trapped Mary's wrist between her hand and gave it a violent twist. Mary yelped, and the blade flew out of her fingers and clattered down a few steps and well out of her reach.

They rolled within their confined area, punching, elbowing, and kneeing each other. Mary's helmet provided a good deal of protection until Yura climbed on her back and tore the helmet off. Yura's arm slipped around her neck, cutting off Mary's air. She struggled to her feet and threw her body toward the wall, slamming Yura between her and the wall.

Her vision began to darken, but Mary repeated the motion with the intent of crushing Yura. Her knees began to buckle, and she made one last lunge. The impact of smashing Yura between herself and the wall caused the Warden to loosen her grip.

Mary suffered a few blows to her head before she flipped Yura off her back. Mary used the wall for support while she tried to catch her breath.

Yura slowly stood and smiled despite a split in her lip.

"No need to grin, Yura," Mary said. "Today you die."

"No, Mary. It's not my day."

Mary narrowed her gaze. This woman *knew* her, and Mary couldn't deny that this fact rattled her a little. The CNA and Wardens had intel on each other's soldiers, but Mary wasn't CNA. She didn't know how Yura would know her, but then she realized the source. Rowan had been hunting Dani for years and would know who her friends were.

Mary glanced around. Her rifle was in pieces. Her pistol was lost among the rubble, and her knife was out of reach. She only had the tranq pistol that Hattie had given her. That was assuming it hadn't been damaged or fallen out of her pocket during her scuffle with Yura.

Dani cried out in pain, and Mary risked glancing in her direction. Yura made her move. *Goddamn, she's fast*, Mary thought just before Yura rushed her, this time with her own knife.

Mary stepped aside and caught Yura's jacket. She threw the woman into the wall, but Yura's hand arced back toward Mary. Mary tried to avoid the blade, but it still sliced through the side of her armored trousers and cut her leg.

The tranq pistol slid out of the damaged pocket, and Mary dove for it. She got one shot off, but missed the Warden.

"Fuck!"

Frustration was making Mary lose focus, and now she was

limping. Yura's arm bled, but it didn't seem to bother her. Mary hated this woman even more.

The two women went at each other again. Mary caught Yura's knife hand between her hands. She brought her knee up and dislodged the weapon. The blade flipped as it fell down the stairs. Yura twisted Mary's arm into a vicious elbow lock. She screamed and couldn't hold the tranq pistol with her arm so contorted. It became clear to Mary that she and Yura would just beat the shit out of each other until one of them died. Mary was determined that the first one to be a corpse would be Yura.

They were in a tangle of limbs, with neither woman ready to give up. Mary grabbed a handful of Yura's hair and used it as leverage to ram the Warden's head into the wall. Yura gave Mary's arm another cruel twist, and Mary screamed. Yura then struck Mary in the ribs with her knee, and Mary lost her balance. Mary tried to tuck herself into a ball as she tumbled down the stairs.

She used her already battered arms to protect her head, but still landed at the base of the stairs in a crumpled heap, in pain, out of breath, and close to passing out. Dani couldn't fight both Rowan and Yura on her own, and Mary struggled to get back up.

CHAPTER

52

Dani kept her knife ready. She stole a glance into the stairwell. Mary and Yura exchanged blows, fell, rolled on the ground while pummeling each other, then somehow were back on their feet, continuing to beat on each other. Dani would have celebrated Mary's success in damaging the female Warden, but Rowan's fist caught her cheek during her moment of distraction.

Dani stumbled back and refocused on him. They parried each other's strikes. Gavin had trained her well for many years, but Rowan had several decades of training.

"Where's Curtis?" Dani asked, hoping to distract Rowan. She truly did want to know where Curtis was and waited for the man to show up and thus outnumber her and Mary against Rowan and Yura.

"Not here."

Dani tried another tactic. "He hanging out with your headless wife?"

Rowan attacked again. The attack, she expected. The ferocity and rage, she did not. She briefly wondered what exactly she should have expected by bringing up Rowan's dead wife. She'd managed to rattle him, but not in a way she'd wanted. He came at her with a flurry of strikes. She cut him a few more times, but he got the blade out of her hand.

Mary's scream woke Dani's own rage. She growled and swung back at Rowan. They exchanged blows, and Dani forced him toward the stairs.

Yura planted a kick into Mary's side that sent her backward. Dani made a grab for Mary but missed her. Mary disappeared down the stairwell.

Dani, enraged, yelled as she slammed Rowan into Yura. Yura fell back against the stairs, and with the impact of both Rowan and Dani landing on top of her, she was pinned. Rowan shoved Dani off of him, but she tripped over debris when she stepped back, landing on her rump. He got up, but Yura didn't. Something was broken inside her or she'd been impaled on something, Dani didn't know. Blood erupted from Yura's mouth when she coughed.

Rowan stalked toward Dani, and she scrambled to her feet. She landed a kick in Rowan's middle. He stumbled back, but so did she. Her boot slipped on the step, and she tumbled down the stairs. She crashed into Mary, and they both lay on the ground, groaning. Dani coughed and immediately wished she hadn't. She wanted a few seconds to lie there and rest. The sound of footsteps coming down the stairs told her Rowan wasn't resting.

Her body protested with bolts of sharp pain when she moved. She shook Mary's shoulder. "You have to get up."

"Working on it," Mary said, then groaned. "Oh, I hate that bitch."

Dani glanced over her shoulder and spotted Rowan. *Fuck. He's pissed.* His descent was labored and slow. *Good. He's injured too.* But he wasn't injured enough to give up or retreat. She tried to move more quickly and didn't want to still be lying on the floor when he arrived.

"Back off!"

Dani turned her head, shocked to hear Oliver's voice. Her mouth dropped open. He held a plasma pistol between two trembling hands, aiming it at Rowan. He wore chest armor and a helmet that were both too big for him. "Christ," she muttered. Dani struggled to her feet and leaned back against the wall for extra stability. She kept her palm pressed against her sore ribs. Rowan stood frozen on the stairs, his hands slightly raised. Dani wasn't buying Rowan's act. He'd make a move and kill them all if he could.

Even if Yura died from her injuries or from Rowan expediting the process before he'd started down the stairs, Yura could regen while Rowan stalled them.

Dani extended her hand toward the teen. "Oliver, give me the gun."

He glanced at her and sidled away a few inches, the weapon still pointed at Rowan.

Where the hell did he get the gun? Not that it mattered, but the last thing she wanted was for Oliver to have a weapon.

"Give me the pistol," she said.

Oliver's eyes flicked to her for an instant. "I can end him. He won't be able to hurt you or Mary again."

"Don't pull that trigger."

"I'll kill him. Make him go away."

Dani inched closer. "Please give me the gun."

"But, he—"

"No, Oliver."

He sniffled and backed away from Dani so she couldn't take the weapon from him. "He won't leave us alone unless he's dead."

She couldn't argue with that point; it was true. Dani left the support of her wall to put herself between Oliver and Rowan.

"*Move*, Dani."

"No. He is not yours to kill."

Oliver adjusted his grip on the weapon.

She tried a different tactic. "Oliver! Give me that goddamn gun!"

He flinched and watched her for a few seconds.

She kept her tone sharp. "You are not allowed to fire that weapon. You are *not* in the CNA."

Rowan bolted back up the stairs. Oliver shifted his aim and Dani stepped in. She stripped the pistol from Oliver's hands. Tears spilled from his eyes, and she pulled him close.

"I could've killed him. I could've protected you," he said.

"All your dad and I have ever wanted was to keep you out of this war. I don't want you to touch a gun again. You're not a soldier, and you will never become one. Not today. Not ever."

"Dad…"

"I know." She hugged him tighter, knowing she couldn't grieve for Miles yet. "I know." After a moment she released him. "Go back to Anton and Javi."

"But Rowan is still here. He won't stop."

"I'll deal with Rowan."

"He's … What if you … Dani," he said, begging.

She gave him a final hug. "Go back, Oliver. I'll find you as soon as I can."

He sniffled and nodded. "Be careful."

"I will."

Oliver turned his gaze to Mary.

"I'll look after Dani, Oliver. I'll keep her safe," Mary said.

Dani resisted the urge to snort. Mary looked like shit, and Dani was quite sure they both felt like it. Footsteps approached, crunching on gravel. Dani shifted Oliver behind her and raised the pistol. Javi rounded the side of the building and paused. They both lowered their weapons.

"You were supposed to keep him with you," Dani barked at the older man.

"Yeah, well, he slipped away," Javi said.

"Take him back behind the lines, *way* the fuck back, Javi."

"You'll come back?" Oliver asked her.

"I'll do my best to be with you soon," Dani said, avoiding the promise she wished she could give him. "Javi, send some troops forward to support us and bring us replacement weapons."

He nodded, then guided Oliver through a blown-out wall.

Dani turned to Mary. "How are you?" she asked.

Mary wiped blood off her chin. "Annoyed."

Dani offered her the weapon. "Want this?"

"I want my rifle." Mary straightened and stretched her back. "Is that the only weapon you have?"

She nodded and wiped blood from her cheek though more blood trickled down from the cut under her eye. "You?"

"Pistols, knives, everything is up there with them."

"Yura was in bad shape right before I fell down here with you. If we can get to her and end her regen—"

"Her knife should be on one of the stairs as we head up. If it's not, I'll just snap her fucking neck mid-glow."

Dani appreciated Mary's determination to end Yura, but Rowan and Yura were clever and devious. Being armed with a pistol against them, even assuming the Warden pair were still unarmed, didn't guarantee success. Dani needed to be careful.

"Ready?" Dani asked, gazing back up the stairs.

"Yeah."

Dani raised her voice. "Rowan, you shit-head. I'm not done with you!"

"Think that pistol will save you now?" he shouted back at her from somewhere inside.

"Nah, but it'll be nice to ram it up your ass when I find you."

"That's your first mistake, thinking you're the predator here."

Fuck. Rowan was just too damn creepy sometimes. "Just keep talking, asshole. We'll see who is the prey." She started back up the stairs with the pistol ready. Mary followed.

CHAPTER

53

ani's frustration grew with each room she and Mary cleared on the second level. There was a pool of blood where Dani had last seen Yura, but Yura was gone. Mary had picked up a knife and pistol from the rubble as they moved through the building, but Dani still didn't like their situation.

"They must have gone up," Mary said.

Dani nodded, and they left the second-level corridor to reenter the stairwell. Yura had had plenty of time for a regen by now.

They worked their way up to the third floor, cautious and watchful for any movement. They began clearing rooms, and Dani was ready to quit. Hunting for Rowan like this was absurd. He was too sly to be caught hiding in a room in a half-destroyed building. Dani was about to signal to Mary that they were done. They'd find Rowan another way, and with reinforcements, but Mary turned and gestured for Dani to come to her.

Dani joined her at the doorway, and Mary pointed at the floor. It was the first time they'd found any amount of blood. It didn't make sense that they hadn't found any in the stairwell on the way up unless Yura's injury had been mostly internal damage. But how had Rowan managed to conceal that much blood based on what they found on the floor until now? Dani guessed he'd covered her injury somehow and maybe carried Yura to this level for her to regen. Maybe Yura had died downstairs, and Rowan had carried her once her body had closed the wound at the start of regen, which would mean little for a blood trail. Dani wasn't sure; it had to be another Warden trap either way.

She and Mary used hand signals to communicate who was going in first and how they would sweep the room. The far exterior wall was broken and had exposed the former offices to the elements for many years. Brush grew in one corner of the area. It reminded her of the building she and Mary had used in Boston when trying to locate Oliver.

Mary went first, and Dani followed. They didn't find any more blood or signs of Rowan or Yura. Still, they moved around the rubble of broken ceiling, partially collapsed walls, and remnants of office equipment until they neared the battered exterior wall.

"There!" Mary said, pointing with her chin.

Dani spotted Yura scrambling down bits of wall and building that had created a mound as high as the third floor. The debris slope was steep near the top, then tapered off to a more gradual grade. Yura was at least sixty yards away. Mary fired two shots but missed. When she moved to pursue the Warden, Dani grabbed her arm.

"What?" Mary asked. "She's getting away."

Dani scanned everything around them again. Rowan would be close. This wouldn't be as simple as just chasing Yura down to kill her. Mary growled with frustration, but Dani didn't release her. Dani spotted the trip line and pointed to it.

"Fucking hell," Mary said, and sighed. "I almost did it again." She knelt near the rupture in the wall that would have taken her out onto and down the rubble pile. A thin string, ankle height, spanned the length of the opening. Dani remained watchful with her pistol ready while Mary inspected the line.

Mary followed the line a few feet to her right. "It's attached to a grenade here in the debris."

"Can you disarm it and take the grenade?"

"Not easily."

"Leave it and let's get out of here."

Mary stood and returned to the opening in the wall. Dani glanced around her shoulder. Yura was still making her descent and was almost to the bottom.

"Rowan doesn't do anything simple," Dani said. "It's always a trap with him. Yura is bait."

Mary turned to face her. "So where is he?"

"I don't know. We don't have the gear to disarm this thing. We'll back up and then throw something to trip the line so no one else gets caught in it. Then we go down the stairs and leave. We'll find some help to finish hunting Rowan."

Mary nodded.

Dani turned to leave. *Where the fuck is Rowan?* Mary's gasp made her spin around. Dani had her pistol up, but Rowan already had one hand gripping Mary's throat and his pistol pressed into the base of her skull. The only thing that separated them was the line touching the back of Mary's boots. Her friend was stiff with fear.

If they had tripped the grenade, he had to have been far enough away to escape the carnage but close enough to finish them off if they weren't killed in the blast. If they hadn't set off the explosive and started after Yura, he would've flanked them from behind. Their current situation sucked, but Dani realized it was possible to be worse. She still couldn't get a shot on Rowan without hitting Mary.

"Ah. Mary Smith," Rowan purred into Mary's ear. "Kindly toss your pistol behind us."

Mary kept her eyes on Dani as she threw her pistol out of the building. Dani's mind raced, but there was nothing she could do.

"Knife too," Rowan said.

Mary sighed but complied.

"Dani, come a little closer and rid yourself of your gun and knife too."

Shit. Shit! She hesitated, and Rowan responded by pressing the end of his pistol harder into Mary's head, causing her to wince. "I am! Stop."

Once she tossed her pistol, Rowan could shoot them both, ending them forever. He didn't know Mary could regen, but that wouldn't stop him from taking her head off. He'd remove her head just because he could. But Rowan liked to play with his prey; he would take his time killing Dani.

She had an awful idea.

Dani inched toward him and removed her knife from her belt. She lobbed it out into the debris pile outside the building. "She's a human and of no use to you, Rowan," Dani said, earning her a glare from Mary. Her friend wasn't insulted, but Dani figured Mary assumed what she was up to. Mary would've been partially correct.

"Going to offer yourself to try to save your friend?" Rowan asked. "So predictable."

He had no idea how wrong he was.

"Toss the gun, Dani."

She crept closer. "Let her go first."

He grinned. "Gun. Now."

"Fuck off."

Rowan stared at her, and Dani didn't waver. Her hand didn't shake as she kept her weapon aimed at Rowan's head, even though he was tucked tightly behind Mary.

She was an arm's length from Mary and close enough now

to make her move if needed. She wouldn't do anything as stupid as trying to disarm Rowan. That would just get Mary shot.

Mary looked at her questioningly, but Dani wouldn't meet her gaze.

Without breaking eye contact with him, Dani lowered her weapon, but before Rowan could smile, she pointed it at the grenade. "This war is shit," she said. "How about we all quit together? I can make that happen. I'd like this to all just end. What about you, Rowan? You must be sick of this shit too."

Mary's eyes widened. "Jesus, Dani. Don't."

"I'm so sick of this goddamn war and him," Dani said. "You'll be collateral damage. Hell, we're all collateral damage at this point. I don't care anymore. I'm ready to die and take this asshole with me."

"Dani, think about this," Mary said.

"You won't do it," Rowan said. "You can't kill her."

"Watch me." She shifted her head like she was going to look down, and Rowan took her bait.

He moved his pistol from Mary's head to point it at Dani. Killing her was the only way to save himself before she set the grenade off so close to their feet. She lunged, swatted his gun aside, and slammed into Mary. When they spilled out of the building, clipping the trip line on their way, Dani heard the grenade activate.

The two women were on top of Rowan when they crashed into the rubble. Rowan cried out from the impact, and Dani knew it had to hurt with their weight on him when they hit the rocks. That's exactly what she'd hoped would happen. He'd also lost his pistol in the fall, and that was something else she had wanted.

Dani rolled away from Rowan and took Mary with her. They wobbled to their feet but managed only a few steps down the pile before the grenade exploded. They cowered together, trying to protect each other when the portion of the building ruptured above them.

Their armor protected them to a degree, but larger pieces of the building began to crumble and fall. They tumbled down the debris pile in their haste to avoid being crushed. Once the worst of the dust began settling, Dani wiped her eyes.

"You okay?" she asked, her voice raspy to her own ears.

Mary coughed a few times and grimaced. "What the fuck was that?"

"A shitty escape plan." Dani twisted to assess a sore spot on her side and groaned. She had to ignore it for now. She didn't see Yura, but knew the woman was also close. Rowan was still somewhere nearby too.

"Can you warn me the next time you plan to throw me out of a building?"

"I'll try. Where is that asshole?" Dani scanned for movement where she thought Rowan might be. It was possible he'd been able to move to a different place, but she doubted it. He had been, at minimum, significantly wounded in the fall with their added weight smashing him into the rubble.

Mary sighed and stood. "Can you see him?"

Dani started to shake her head, then stopped. Rowan staggered to his feet and didn't have a pistol. Dani raised her weapon.

A plasma shot struck her in the ribs and she fell. Dani couldn't take a deep breath, and refused to cough.

"Shit!" Mary dragged her behind a chunk of concrete while Dani kept her pistol.

Dani finally coughed and groaned. The armor had protected her from being killed, but taking plasma pistol shots still hurt.

"Here." Dani pressed the pistol into Mary's hand. "Take out Yura." She didn't mind Mary's assistance when she sat up.

"Gladly," Mary said. "Rest here. I'll get her."

"No. I've got Rowan." Dani rolled to her hands and knees.

"You sure?"

Dani nodded.

"Ready?" Mary asked.

"Yeah."

Mary stood and immediately fired shots in Yura's direction. Dani moved away from the concrete block and started back up the rubble pile to meet Rowan, who was on his way down to rejoin Yura.

He had one hand pressed against his side, and his descent was marred by a significant limp. She loved seeing him in pain.

Dani glanced back at Mary. Her friend was absorbed in her firefight with Yura. Mary moved ever closer to Yura as the two women tried to end each other.

Rowan managed a smile. "Dani. Our lives seem to be forever entwined."

Dani stalked toward him. "Fuck off, Rowan. Yours ends today."

CHAPTER
54

Mary darted between areas of cover while she made her way toward Yura. She had a good charge on her pistol, so she wasn't at risk of draining the weapon anytime soon. Mary fired repeated shots at the Warden to force her to remain stationary. It also prevented Yura from shooting Dani again. The shot that had struck Dani's armor only damaged it. The newer Warden plasma pistols would've burned through it. This meant Yura was using one of the older CNA models that Dani or Mary had lost during their scuffle with the Wardens. She didn't know where Oliver had picked up the pistol Dani had taken from him, but Mary sent him a silent "thank you," because the weapon in her hand was better than Yura's.

Mary dared a glance back. Dani and Rowan were busy exchanging blows, and Dani was holding her own. For all of Gavin's faults and his borderline mistreatment of Dani, he'd taught her well. Not that Mary would ever want to fight her, but she doubted she could best Dani in a ring.

She returned her attention to her target. Mary hadn't received any return fire from Yura, but she didn't think she'd killed or wounded the Warden. She wondered if Yura's weapon had no charge. That would explain why Yura hadn't fired at her.

She rounded the final mound of concrete between her and the Warden with her pistol ready to blast Yura's head off—except Yura was gone.

"Fuck." Unsure when she'd lost Yura's position, Mary turned to find her. Her head snapped to the side when the Warden struck her with her pistol. She was dizzied by the blow and stumbled, but she managed to fire a shot into Yura's chest armor. Her pistol should have done more damage, but Yura's balance was reestablished in an instant while Mary wished her feet would cooperate. Yura should have shot her, but she hadn't. Mary knew when Yura tossed her pistol aside that the weapon was useless. She would have grinned, but her balance was still off.

Yura slammed her to the ground and tried to wrestle the pistol from Mary's grasp. They rolled, and Mary's wrist struck a stone, causing her to lose the pistol. To prevent Yura from grabbing it, Mary remained attached to the Warden and used her feet to send them tumbling to the base of the mound.

They separated long enough for Mary to grab an eight-inch glass shard from one of the many blown-out windows from a nearby building. She was back on her feet and turned to face Yura.

The Warden laughed and pulled her knife from its sheath. Yura sneered at her. "Pity you won't be alive long enough to see Dani and Miles slaughtered."

Mary charged. Tearing this woman apart was something she very much wanted to do. She had her glass ready, and Yura had her knife as they rushed each other. Mary crouched slightly to slice the woman's thigh as she moved past her, but instead, Yura spun the other way and used her forearm to clip Mary's chin. Mary twisted to try to recover her balance, but she still struck the ground hard. The glass shard cut her hand with the impact, and she couldn't hold on to it anymore.

She rolled away from Yura's blade as it came down toward

her. Mary swung her leg up and caught Yura in the head with her boot. The Warden fell to her side but was up in an instant. Mary scrambled back to her feet. The glass was too far away for her to reach it even if she could grip it or use it with her other hand. She scanned the ground and picked up a two-foot-long piece of a tree limb.

"Leave it to a human to fight with a stick," Yura said.

Mary grinned. "You'll have a better respect for humans after I kill you with it."

Yura laughed. "Doubtful."

"Ready to finish this, or you just gonna talk me to death?"

Yura rushed her, and Mary was ready. She shifted away from the Warden's knife and brought the limb up to strike the underside of Yura's wrist. The blade flipped out of Yura's hand, and Mary swung for Yura's head next.

The Warden leaned back to avoid the blow, then wrapped her arms around Mary's upper body. They crashed to the ground. They were too close for Mary's weapon to be of any use now. She dropped the length of wood and slammed her fist into Yura's cheek.

With Yura slightly stunned, Mary pushed the woman away a few inches and swung again. Yura withstood the blow but released Mary.

They were on their feet immediately and charging each other. Mary brought her arms up as they neared, readying to grab the woman and tackle her, except Yura dropped her body, spun, and tossed Mary into the air. Mary wasn't sure how it had happened, she just knew she was flipping in the air, and it hurt when she crashed to the ground facedown.

She coughed and rolled to her side to find her enemy, but Yura was already attacking. Mary tried to curl into a defensive ball, but the woman's boot still collided with her ribs. After the second strike to her side, Mary caught Yura's boot and swung her own leg up, clipping the woman in the back of her knees and toppling her. Mary tried to clamber on top of Yura to pin her, but her bruised side slowed her movement and Yura slipped away. *Fuck!*

Mary envied the woman's speed and agility. Yura was a Warden soldier who could have had anything from decades to a hundred years of training, where Mary had only a few years as a Brigand volunteer. Another thought occurred to her. As a human she would not have been able to endure this kind of a beating from the fight inside the building, falling down stairs, and now fighting outside with this woman. It made her wonder whether Echoes had increased stamina and she'd gotten some of that boost with Dani's DNA. She didn't have time to ponder the idea, but it gave her a bit more hope that she could take Yura down.

Mary stood, and she and Yura circled each other. Yura grinned, and Mary was desperate to figure out a way to survive this encounter. Dani was also up against an opponent who likely had more years of training than Dani had of being alive. Mary knew she'd lose if she stayed in this hand-to-hand battle with Yura for much longer. She needed an advantage. She spotted a piece of jagged metal among the debris around them. It was about three feet long, with one foot of it having a sharp edge.

It would cut a Warden, and Mary wanted to cut Yura. She just needed to reach it, except Yura was in the way. She would take a beating in the process, but Mary didn't have any other ideas. She rushed toward the Warden, and Yura countered with her own charge.

Yura dropped and swung her leg out. Mary fell forward, and Yura pounced on her back. Mary endured several strikes from Yura's fists before she was able to slam her elbow into Yura's jaw and shove the woman off. Mary's vision blurred, but she still had a general idea how far she was from the piece of metal.

Yura staggered to her feet while Mary crawled toward the weapon. She glanced back in time to see Yura retrieve her knife. Mary's fingers curled around one end of the metal rod. She turned it in her hand until she had it positioned the way she wanted.

When Yura lunged for her, Mary rolled, gripped the rod with both hands, and swung it like a bat. The sharp edge sliced into Yura's neck. The woman's mouth opened with surprise, and she dropped her blade to place her hands over the gaping wound pouring blood.

Mary stood while Yura dropped to her knees. She took a second to breathe before swinging her weapon again. Yura's head separated from her shoulders and toppled to the ground. Her headless body slumped to the side. Mary tossed the rod and leaned forward, resting her hands on her knees. She righted and blinked a few times to make sure she could see straight again.

"Let's see you regen from that."

Other Wardens and CNA battled in the area. Mary had been too absorbed in her fight with the Warden to notice them. She still had to see to Dani, so Mary stepped over Yura's body, then jogged to the nearest corpse. She took the pistol from the CNA soldier's lifeless hand and rushed back to where she'd last seen Dani as quickly as her injuries allowed.

CHAPTER

55

owan's smile turned to a sneer, and he limped toward Dani to close the gap quicker. Dani knew what was coming next. They'd beat the shit out of each other until one of them lost. She was okay with that plan.

She ignored every ache, bruise, and scrape and charged him. He tried to sidestep, but he couldn't avoid the collision. Dani tackled him, and they rolled a few yards down the slope, gaining more scrapes along the way.

Rowan struck first, his fist slamming into the charred area of her armor. She cried out with a fresh wave of pain from her ribs, but Dani recovered enough to smash her fist into his jaw. His head snapped to the side with the impact, and his grasp on her loosened. She hit him again.

He regained his grip and flung her off him. She rolled a few yards more down the slope and was back on her feet, ready to rush him again.

Rowan stood and spat blood from his mouth. "Gavin taught you well."

Dani almost flinched at the mention of Gavin's name. Her friend, former lover, then ex had been captured by Rowan and turned into a Warden. Gavin's death had been permanent when Miles had ended him.

"Where is Major Jackman, Dani? He normally isn't too far from you." He paused. "Unless some mishap has befallen him."

She refused to answer him. He was taunting her

"Where's Curtis? Replace him with the woman?" she asked.

"Oh, the woman who's killing Mary Smith as we speak?"

Dani tensed but knew she couldn't take her eyes off him to locate Mary. He may have been lying, but she could only hope that he was. She couldn't do anything to help Mary.

"Yes," he said. "Yura replaced him. How's my friend Colonel Houston?"

He was stalling for something. Dani figured he was waiting for her to make a mistake and look for Mary or get caught by some other distraction. She was done with his bullshit and stalked closer to him. If he was stalling for whatever reason, she wasn't going to let him. "You ever actually shut the fuck up?"

He grinned.

She circled him, and then they crashed together again, mixing kicks and punches as they rolled down the debris mound. Dani was dizzied, but refused to give up, though fatigue was becoming an issue.

They couldn't keep fighting each other like this without becoming exhausted. Dani remembered his taunts about Gavin, Miles, and Mary, and it renewed her desire to end the Warden.

She attacked the side she'd seen him holding earlier with repeated punches. At first it didn't seem to bother him, but when he winced, she wanted to cause him more pain. Dani landed a few more strikes, but he managed to push her far enough away to drive his fist into her middle. The armor protected her to a degree, but it still doubled her over.

He followed up by dropping his elbow into her back with

his weight behind it. He could not have known of her injury to her shoulder, but he knew now. She screamed and collapsed. Spots danced in her field of vision, and Dani couldn't move her right arm.

He was on his knees and rolled her to her back and grinned. "Well, that was interesting."

Being on her back made everything hurt more. She tried to move and groaned. Her fingers tingled while her shoulder throbbed. She couldn't stop him from opening her jacket. She screamed again when he dug his fingers into her wound.

He removed his hand and observed her blood covering his fingers and palm. "Very interesting."

Dani swallowed, suppressing the urge to vomit. She managed to move her right elbow and wrist a little.

"Ready to die?" he asked.

"Fuck you."

Rowan laughed. He put his hands around her throat but didn't attempt to strangle her … yet.

She brought her left fist up, but he turned, and the strike glanced off his shoulder. She almost had her right arm working again, but her fingers still felt like they had pins and needles in them.

He threw his leg across her, trapping her hips under him. She twisted beneath him but couldn't get him off her. He squeezed tighter, and she managed a strangled cough.

Dani's attempts to claw and pry his hands loose failed. She tried punching and kneeing him. Flailing got her nowhere. Rowan had her and would never let her go.

Her vision began to darken when he squeezed her throat closed. He was bloodied and in pain, but nothing would stop him from killing her now. Blood smeared his teeth, and he snarled at her, trying to crush her airway. She'd die very soon, and Dani didn't mind that thought as much as she probably should have … until she thought of Oliver. She had to see him again.

She groped the ground for anything to help her. Her palm landed on something hard and small enough for her to grip. She swung it upward, striking Rowan in the side of the head with it. His eyes fluttered, and as he slumped, Dani rolled him to his back and was on top of him. Finally. She had *him*.

Dani raised her arm to deliver the lethal blow.

She *wanted* Rowan dead. He, like other Wardens, had killed so many of her friends and family. He *deserved* to die.

The stone in her hand remained poised over his head. She wondered why she couldn't slam it down to smash his skull. Her chest heaved as she drew in deep breaths, and her arm began to tremble.

She blinked when her surroundings darkened. Dani was back on a hill in a forest with a dead Warden beneath her, his skull partially intact, with the rest of it smashed open and reeking with the musty odor of blood. She flinched, and the dead Warden turned back into Rowan. He groaned and opened his eyes, still stunned.

His grogginess faded, and his eyes focused on the stone in her hand. His gaze turned to her, and he growled. "Do it."

He wanted to die. She wanted him dead. Dani had the ability to kill Rowan but hesitated. Killing him now would be murder. The act would make her no different from him.

The Wardens had lost this battle, and they would lose Montreal and eventually Toronto and Quebec City. They would lose North America and the rest of the world. Dani knew this. Rowan knew this. Death was too easy, too compassionate for him.

Dani released the stone, and it thudded into the dirt next to his head.

He reached for her, still willing to fight, but she batted his arms aside. She'd concussed the shit out of him, so his movements were clumsy and easy to thwart. Dani pulled the I-cuff from her belt, clipped it to his waist, and activated it. He was instantly paralyzed.

"You're weak. Just like the humans," he said.

"Thank you. I'll take that compliment."

"It wasn't—"

His words stopped when Dani gripped him by the front of his armor. She leaned close to his face. "*You* are done. The Wardens are done. You fucking lost, asshole. Earth will never be yours, and your precious plans for a new Ekkoh are over. Earth will always belong to humans, and *you* will be wiped off the planet." She released him.

"There will always be Wardens to take my place and continue the fight."

"Not from the newer generations, Rowan. We'll make sure the children, *your* children, are placed with good human families to be raised without your horseshit ideologies."

His face reddened, and veins bulged on his neck and forehead. Dani adjusted the I-cuff settings so he couldn't speak again.

Dani moved away from him, exhausted and wanting to lie down. She lowered her head and wiped at blood running down her cheek. She heard footsteps approaching and assumed they were Mary's. The boots that stopped in front of her weren't hers, though. Dani lifted her gaze and sighed upon seeing a plasma rifle pointed at her forehead. One shot and she'd be gone.

But Curtis didn't shoot.

"Stand up," he said.

"Just get this over with, man." Dani was mildly surprised at the words coming out of her mouth, but she was tired and didn't give a shit anymore.

"Stand up."

Dani grunted as she stood. She was unarmed and oddly

unafraid. Rowan's eyes widened and remained on Curtis. Dani figured he was mentally screaming at Curtis to pull the trigger and then deactivate the immobilizer on his body.

"Dani! Get down," Mary shouted from behind her.

Shit. Now she was standing between two people with guns pointed in her direction. If she managed to avoid Curtis's shot, he'd shoot Mary. Mary would happily blow Curtis's head off but couldn't with Dani in the way.

Something was odd about Curtis, though. Dani hadn't interacted with him before, but she knew he had a long history of being Rowan's right hand for many decades and numerous regens. Curtis wasn't recently regenned. His balance was off, and he swayed a little while he remained still. He was bleeding from somewhere under his chest armor. Blood stained the piece of his shirt untucked from beneath the armor and his trousers. Blood had soaked the waist of his trousers and seeped down the side of his left leg. The wound, though hidden, was probably going to kill him. That's when she realized Curtis wore a CNA uniform.

Dani wondered if this was his final effort to save Rowan, to pretend to be CNA and sacrifice himself to get Rowan out. But if that was his goal, why hadn't he just taken her head off when she wasn't looking? His finger twitched on the trigger. Maybe Curtis was twisted like Rowan and wanted to watch her suffer. *No. This is wrong. Something is wrong about this.*

"Curtis," Dani said, knowing him only through CNA intel files on Rowan and his crew.

"Dani," he replied with a flat tone.

He blinked slowly, and Dani knew that feeling. He was fading, losing strength, and would collapse soon. She wondered if she could stall him long enough for him to keel over. Except she, too, was at risk of keeling over, although maybe not as quickly as Curtis.

"Jesus, Dani, move," Mary said.

Dani eased her hand up and turned her palm toward Mary. She didn't want her friend stalking any closer and getting killed by wild shots from Curtis.

"What now?" she asked him.

"You're a traitor to your ancestors and to Ekkoh. We're here to create a new world for our people, yet you fight against us."

"Earth isn't your birthright. It was never your planet and never will be."

"Back up," he said.

Her brow creased. He wouldn't let her go.

Curtis growled. "Back up and take that human vermin with you," he said with a nod toward Mary. He gestured with the gun while he reached into his pocket with his other hand.

Dani didn't understand what he was doing, but she took a tentative step back. He waved at her again with the gun, and she took another step.

He kept his rifle on her and removed a grenade from his pocket. Curtis knelt, never taking his aim off Dani, and placed the grenade next to Rowan.

Dani could only watch the situation unfold. Was he going to blow them all up? Maybe she should consider an evasive move to give Mary a clear shot. Why would he tell her to back up if he was going set off a grenade? Wouldn't he want her closer?

Curtis reached for the I-cuff on Rowan, and Dani frowned. *Fuck.* Her fight with Rowan wouldn't be over once he was released.

But Curtis didn't free Rowan. He deactivated part of the paralyzing effect of the I-cuff, then picked up his grenade.

"Stand up," Curtis said to Rowan.

Rowan glared at him and rolled to his feet, though the rest of his body was immobile, including his mouth. Once Rowan was up, Curtis manipulated the I-cuff again. Rowan was frozen where he stood.

Dani was dumbstruck. *I think Curtis is going to kill him*. But that didn't make any sense.

"You did this," Curtis said. He kept his gun on Dani, but he'd glanced at Rowan when he spoke. "*You* killed Ana."

Dani didn't move. Curtis spoke while looking at her, but she was certain his remarks were directed at Rowan even though she was the one who had accidentally beheaded Ana. She considered responding until Curtis turned to gaze at Rowan.

"The Boston VR was indeed an idiot, Rowan. But not everyone else was as inept as her. All you had to do was listen to me, but you wouldn't listen to anyone after Ana died. I have only ever had your best interests as my priorities in *everything* I did, but you have managed to single-handedly fuck it all up. You have taken the decades of what we built together to create a new Ekkoh and shattered it with your goddamn pride. Your arrogance has lost this battle and Montreal." Curtis shook his head. "Dani is nothing, but your obsession with her is what killed Ana. *You* killed her the same way you have killed so many Wardens. I'll save us both the trouble of a formal trial and execution for numerous counts of treason, and our remaining Wardens won't have to die because you are unfit to lead. Who knows, maybe they can still win the war without us."

Curtis activated the grenade in his hand and dropped his rifle. He grabbed Rowan and pulled him close, staring into his eyes. "But we'll never know."

Dani scrambled back and turned to flee. Mary had been a few paces behind her, so Dani grabbed her and spun her around to get her away from the coming destruction too. They stumbled in their haste, managed a few more clumsy steps, then crashed to the ground together. Dani glanced back. Rowan glared at Curtis, and Curtis looked almost peaceful as he held Rowan. Dani tucked her head next to Mary's and wrapped her arms around her a second before the grenade exploded.

CHAPTER
56

Consciousness returned. Dani remained on the ground and didn't move. She was tired and not sure how or why she was lying in the dust. She groaned when she moved, but the sound wasn't right. Her ears were ringing again. Mary was beside her and stirred when Dani rolled to her back. She remembered the grenade and realized she and Mary had survived.

Dani staggered to her feet. Rowan and Curtis had been ripped apart in the blast. She'd seen bodies torn by explosions, but this was different. She was sad.

Why? *How* could she be sad that those two were dead?

She realized it wasn't their deaths that saddened her. Something had happened to their relationship that had caused Curtis to want—need?—to kill Rowan. Tears spilled from her eyes. What would she have to do to cause Mary or Miles to need to kill her?

Miles. He was gone. He was one of many dead humans who couldn't self-heal and come back. Oliver was an orphan after all. Dani hung her head and let the tears continue to fall.

When she lifted her gaze, she saw nothing at first. A breeze cleared some of the smoke. Buildings were still mostly destroyed and piles of rubble. Bodies were everywhere. She'd been so consumed by her battle with Rowan that she'd failed to notice how the CNA and Warden forces had clashed all around them, leaving the CNA with the most troops still standing.

Some wounded cried out. Others shouted for aid to help the ones still alive. The Wardens had retreated, but the carnage from fighting them remained with the injured CNA and Brigand troops.

Mary stood next to her and said something, but Dani couldn't hear her words.

Dani turned her gaze back to their surroundings. She took a few steps away from Mary. *This isn't real. It's another nightmare like before.*

Mary stayed with her and waved her arms, apparently screaming for someone else to come to her. Dani's hearing was still messed up.

She shuffled her feet and stumbled. Her boots were white and black with a mix of dust and soot. Her hands were covered in blood. Some dark, some bright red, and some that looked grayish where dust had stuck to it.

She stumbled again and stopped. Next to her boot, a dirty, child-sized glove lay on the ground.

Dani stared at it for a moment, ignoring Mary's attempts to get her attention. She wobbled a little when she leaned down and picked up the glove. Dani could hear Mary speaking to her now, but she was mesmerized by the glove.

She passed her thumb over it to reveal green fabric. "Oliver's favorite color," she said—or she thought she'd said it.

Mary shook her by the arm, and Dani looked at her.

"*Please*, Dani, talk to me."

Dani wasn't sure what to say.

Cameron arrived and took Dani's head in his hands. He stared into her eyes.

"She's not answering me," Mary said. "I don't know if it's shock or what."

Cameron turned Dani's head and wiped his fingers at something on her face.

"She's done. Probable concussion. Maybe hearing damage from the blast—"

Dani swatted him away upon realizing what he was saying. "Leave me alone."

He countered her attempts to bat him away. "Mary, take her to the rear. A medic will be able to better assess her injuries."

"No!" Dani shoved him away. "Fuck off."

"Oh," Mary said, eyebrows raised. She glanced at Cameron. "That sounds more like her."

"I'm fine." She wasn't fine. She knew she was the furthest thing from fine, but that was the only thing she could think of to say to make Cameron leave her alone.

"Or, maybe not," Mary said. "Cam?"

Dani started to lower her head into her hands but froze when she spotted the glove still in her grasp. *Oliver.* As much as she wanted to quit the war, she couldn't. It was still going on, and Oliver would always be at risk of being made a soldier until the war was over. There were plenty of Wardens like Rowan and Curtis still alive and determined to wipe out the humans. She couldn't stop fighting now.

Cam shook his head. "Take her to the rear, Mary. I can't stick around. She's walking wounded at this point. I have others out here bleeding to death who need me," he said, then left.

Mary took her hand.

Dani looked at her.

"Come with me," Mary said.

"No."

"You can't stay here. You need—"

"We have to keep going."

"No, darling. We—"

"Mary," Dani said, hearing a resolve in her voice even she didn't expect. "We keep going."

"We don't have to anymore. We've lost too much already."

Dani forced herself to gaze at the dead around them. Miles was back on the beach and would go home in a bag. There had been too much loss to stop now. She rubbed the battered glove with her fingers. She could almost feel every fiber, and realized the glove was made of wool.

"We keep going," Dani said.

"*Why*? What's the point? Miles is—" Tears spilled from Mary's eyes.

"I know." Dani allowed her own tears to come. "This," she said, and waved her arm at the gruesome scene around them. "Oliver can never be a part of this."

Mary's brow furrowed.

"The war has to end. It's the only thing Miles wants." She realized she had referred to him in the present tense and refused to correct herself. "Oliver is to never see this kind of destruction. I won't allow it. I will see the end of this goddamn war if it's the last thing I do, Mary. You can stop if you want. I'll never think less of y—"

"Shut the fuck up," Mary said.

Dani did.

Hattie's voice came from behind them. "Well, you both look like shit." A man was with her that Dani didn't recognize. He didn't look as confident as Hattie did, sauntering through the destruction. His gaze darted around like he expected another Warden to pop up at any moment, but they were all dead in this area.

"The good news is we've made it this far and backup is arriving on the beach as we speak," Hattie said. "We'll move beyond the fire support that the ships can provide, but the extra troops will give us the volume we need to keep pushing the Wardens back."

Dani nodded, but she wasn't following everything Hattie said. Her mind was still fogged.

"Santi is running the show for us now. He had to make some last-minute adjustments to the ground troops organization, but we'll have new orders soon."

Dani nodded again. Santi was in charge, which meant he was still alive. She wiped at the tears still clinging to her chin with the back of her hand.

"Is she okay?" Hattie asked Mary.

"I'm standing right here, Hattie," Dani said, glaring at her. "Don't ask her how I'm doing. Ask *me*."

Hattie stepped closer and locked eyes with her. "Are you okay?"

So much rage swelled within her that Dani's breaths deepened, and she struggled to remain in control. She spoke through clenched teeth. "No, Hattie. I'm not." She took another breath and relaxed her jaw. "Who the fuck is okay in any of this goddamn mess? I'm standing in the middle of a graveyard with bodies everywhere. Miles is ..." She swallowed hard. "Miles is dead. Oliver is an orphan. *No*, I am not okay."

Hattie's gaze never wavered, and her voice remained calm. "Are you done?"

"Yes." Dani then realized that Hattie might be asking if she was done with the fighting and not with her rant. "No. I'm not quitting, if that's what you mean." Dani frowned. "What *did* you mean? You're screwing with my head, Hattie. Stop it."

Hattie shrugged. "I was just asking if you were okay."

Mary sniffled and managed a grin.

"You're staying too?" Hattie asked Mary, who nodded. "Do I want to know how you've both become weaponless and beaten to a pulp?"

Dani pointed to the grenade-mangled bodies. "Rowan's dead."

"So is his bitch girlfriend," Mary said.

"Good," Hattie said. "Get both your asses to a medic now. You're not coming with me looking like that. I'll meet you with more gear. Go!"

Dani was too tired to argue and left with Mary.

"Who is that man with Hattie?" Mary asked.

"I don't know."

CHAPTER
57

Dani stripped out of her armor and sat in the chair before the medic. He looked over her wounds and whistled.

"You're made of tough stuff," he said, handing her a canteen of water.

She grunted in response and drank the water. Her shoulder had stopped hurting the moment he snapped a vial into the patch on her hand. She continued to sip water while he cleaned and repaired the worst of her wounds. Minor cuts and scrapes were left to heal on their own.

Mary arrived at the entrance to the treatment pod.

"That was fast," Dani said.

Mary shrugged. "I wasn't as banged up as you are. Got a nice new scar, though." She raised her hand, showed Dani the long pink line across her palm, then took the canteen. She handed Dani food wafers as a replacement. "Eat."

"I'm not hungry."

"Eat anyway."

"You really should eat something," the medic said.

Now they were ganging up on her. Dani shoved a wafer into her mouth and slowly chewed while the medic resumed working on her shoulder. She didn't know how much time had passed. Everything felt numb. Maybe it was something the medic had given her. Maybe it was just her mind trying to shut down and wall off emotions she wasn't ready to confront. She was thankful that neither the medic nor Mary tried to engage her with small talk.

He snapped another vial into the patch, and Dani's hand tingled as the medication flowed into her system. He removed the patch.

"You're good to go," he said. "That last one was an antibiotic."

"Thanks," Dani said, and stood.

"Ah. There you are," Hattie said. "Perfect timing. Come with me."

Dani followed Mary and Hattie outside.

CNA troops were everywhere. Aircraft swarmed the skies.

"Meet Usman," Hattie said. "Another Ancient and a maker of really cool shit."

"Hi," Dani said, though her attention was on an incoming VTOL and helicopter preparing to land nearby. The helicopter had a lot of damage and probably would not take off again. The swirls of dust were mesmerizing, but Dani managed to pull her gaze back to Hattie.

Hattie continued, "Usman, get your toys off that VTOL and gear them up with all the good stuff. Both are saboteurs, so give them the extras too, including the new armor like mine. Mary will want one of your sniper rifles."

"Oh, no," Usman said. "I don't hand those things out like candy. Those have to be earned."

"Usman," Hattie said, her voice laced with warning.

He sighed, then relented. As he left, Dylan arrived. She dropped Dani's pack at her feet.

"Good to see you. Get your shit off my helo," Dylan said with a hint of a smile. "I have wounded to airlift out of here and need the room."

Dylan glanced around, and Dani knew who she was looking for. The pilot would figure it out soon enough that Miles wasn't there and wouldn't be arriving, ever.

"I'll get the rest of our stuff," Mary said, then left with Dylan. "Can you get that thing back in the air?"

"Oh, yeah," Dylan said as they walked. "She's tough and can take a bit more."

Dani wasn't sure what she should be doing, and no one was giving her new orders yet. She was lost.

"Ah!" Hattie said. "Finally."

Dani followed her gaze. Hundreds of Brigands poured into the area like ants. Dani recognized some of the new arrivals as Bangor residents.

"How?" she asked.

Hattie laughed. "Usman and I rounded up some extra help. All Brigands from across New England. The war will end, Dani."

"At what cost?" Dani's shoulders slumped. Could she keep her sanity intact long enough to keep fighting? She wasn't sure. Curtis had killed Rowan for losing his way. Dani felt she was on the same path as Rowan. She'd been obsessed with ending the war. So had he. *Who am I? What am I? Am I any better than a Warden?*

"Dani," Hattie said, lifting her chin with her finger.

Dani hadn't realized she'd cast her gaze downward until she looked up at Hattie.

"The war will end," Hattie said. "And Oliver will never be a CNA soldier."

Dani nodded. She realized she still held the glove and put it in her pocket. "This isn't your first war."

"No."

Dani sniffled, nodding. She had several more questions for Hattie but went with the most pressing. "What's next?"

"We need to finish taking Montreal. We'll regroup and I'll

take a platoon from the Brigands to be part of the continued attack on the city. You and Mary are my most experienced sabs."

"Just tell us what you need us to do."

Mary arrived with her pack. "We get to blow stuff up, yes?"

Hattie chuckled and nodded.

Catherine had spotted Dani with Mary and Hattie. Her fingers itched to pull her pistol now, but she couldn't be seen walking around, weapon drawn, and ready to shoot someone. She moved in closer, but when the latest wave of civilian troops arrived with several Bangor residents among them, she had to change course to keep from being recognized.

Soldiers nearby moved gear totes, so Catherine fell in with them, picked up a tote, then headed in Dani's direction with it.

Dani knelt, opened the pack Dylan had brought her, and began removing gear from it. Dani froze when Hattie put her hand on the top of her head. It was there for only a moment before Hattie removed it and started walking away. Hattie had never done that before, but the gesture comforted Dani more than she could ever express. Tears stung her eyes.

Hattie glanced back at Dani before speaking. "Take only what you need for food and water. Usman will have much better armor and weapons." She stopped, pulled the pistol from the back of her waistband, and tossed the weapon to Dani.

She caught the pistol and looked it over. It wasn't CNA or Warden tech. She looked up, mouth agape.

Hattie grinned. "Thought you might like that."

"Yeah. Thanks," Dani said. "Hattie, can you arrange to get Oliver back to Maine as soon as possible?"

"It's already in motion, honey. Brody is going with him." Hattie continued on her way, pausing to say something to Usman as he neared before she continued on.

Dani resumed digging through her pack. She pulled out the book she'd begun reading in Vermont while Miles had slept. It wasn't food or water, but Dani didn't want to part with the book. It was a link to Miles, in a way. She opted to keep it.

Usman handed Mary the rifle he'd brought.

Mary looked over the weapon. She got that mischievous grin that she got only with weapons or explosives, and Dani half smiled. So much death around them, and Mary still managed to find a speck of happiness. Granted, it was that bit of happy insanity that only Mary could harness without being a complete psychopath, but Dani still admired her resilience.

Mary caressed the rifle. "Well, fuck me. This is beautiful."

"You like?" Usman said.

"This is pure art."

Usman smiled and puffed out his chest. "Finally, someone who appreciates the beauty in destruction."

"Oh, hell yes," Mary said.

He opened one of the packs he'd brought and started handing them additional gear. Dani's mind glazed over as she exchanged her armor, helmet, and supplies. She was careful to keep the glove with her. It was so small, but it brought her focus back to Oliver. She needed to use it and Oliver to stay sane right now. She had the battered book, too, and transferred that into her new pack.

Once they were re-equipped, Dani and Mary rejoined Hattie, who stood at a table fashioned out of gear totes.

"Here's one more," a young woman carrying a tote said, placing it on the ground.

Dani glanced at the woman, then returned her attention to Hattie. Recognition of who she was registered in her mind, but before Dani could react, Houston slid in behind her and pressed her pistol against Dani's neck. *Shit.*

Hattie and Mary both had their weapons drawn and on Houston in an instant while Dani remained trapped. All CNA and Warden armor had a weak spot, leaving the neck between the chest piece and helmet exposed. Usman's armor didn't have that flaw. Dani was protected, but she didn't know how well his armor would protect her from a point-blank shot.

Dani eased her hand toward her own pistol.

"Don't be stupid," Houston hissed, and Dani froze.

Other soldiers neared with their weapons also pointed at Houston—and Dani. Mary shifted her position in an attempt to flank Houston, but the colonel stayed tucked behind Dani, keeping her close with one hand on Dani's shoulder.

"Catherine," Hattie said, "in what universe do you think you can get out of this alive?"

Houston snarled. "I don't care what happens to me. I—"

"Good." Hattie fired one shot, striking Houston's hand holding the pistol.

The impact threw Dani back, and she landed on top of Houston. Dani rolled away from the colonel and drew her weapon. The colonel screamed and clutched the stump of what was left of her wrist with her other hand. Her pistol lay twisted and smoldering on the ground, but Dani kicked it aside and out of reach anyway. Dani coughed several times, wincing each time. Mary grabbed Dani's arm and pulled her farther away from the colonel.

"Jesus. She was a lab rat like me," Mary said.

Dani tried to nod, but her neck was too sore.

Hattie stood over Houston. "What happened to you, Catherine?"

"Fuck you!" Houston pulled her knife, and Hattie placed her boot on Houston's wrist, pinning it to the ground.

Hattie fired a shot into the colonel's side, just above her belt. Houston screamed and thrashed under Hattie's boot to free herself.

"Hurts, doesn't it?" Hattie said. "In case you don't recall, that's where one of your goons shot me."

Houston writhed while her blood soaked into the ground. Dani felt like she should tell Hattie to back off, that Houston should be taken into custody as a traitor, but she didn't.

Hattie crouched next to Houston. "Remember the second place he shot me?"

"Go to hell," Houston said.

"One day, sure. But not today." Hattie leaned in closer. "You have no legacy, Catherine. Your supposed brilliant military career will always be marred by your treachery. No parades, no statues, and not even a goddamn plaque. You were a good leader once. It's a pity that you began to believe whatever delusions you had concocted in your head. You're no better than a Warden, and you will *not* regen again." She fired a shot into the center of Houston's chest.

Houston tried to speak, but her mouth filled with blood. She choked on the blood, then became still, eyes staring upward. Hattie straightened and kept her pistol in her hand.

"Dani?" Hattie said. "Are you okay?"

Dani holstered her pistol and continued to rub the aching spot beneath the armor on her neck and her upper chest where Hattie's shot had obliterated Houston's hand and hit Dani too.

"Fucking hell, Hattie," Dani said. "You could've warned me."

"Nah," Mary said. "This is the equivalent of you tackling me out of a building to get at Rowan."

Dani started to defend her actions but closed her mouth. Mary was right.

"Yeah," Dani said. "I'll be okay." She should still be lying on the ground, maybe even dead, but she wasn't. "This armor is incredible."

"Don't tell Usman that," Hattie said. "His head gets all big. Hey!" she said to the troops still there with their weapons raised. "This situation is resolved. Go back to your duties, but you," she said, pointing at one soldier, "stick around."

"Yes, ma'am," the soldier said.

Dani marveled at the exchange. A Brigand shouldn't be giving orders to CNA troops, but Hattie's command presence was impressive. The solider stayed while the others dispersed. Dani's hands trembled as she removed her helmet. She touched her neck and winced.

Hattie moved Dani's hand out of the way, pulled back the armor, and inspected the wound she'd given Dani. "The bruise will be nasty, but you'll live."

"Thanks," Dani said, rolling her eyes.

"Aunt Hattie," Mary said. "That was a hell of a shot."

Hattie shrugged.

"Not her first war," Dani said.

Mary shook her head. "Also, not her first time with a plasma pistol. You've gotta tell us—"

Houston's corpse began to glow, and Hattie brightened. "That's my cue!" She returned to the colonel's body and fired a single shot into Catherine's chest. Hattie holstered her pistol and waved the soldier over. "Take the body and put it with the other Warden dead."

"Yes, ma'am." The man lifted Houston's body, wrapped his arms around her, and clasped his hands together over her bloodied and charred chest. He walked backward, taking Houston with him and leaving two ruts where Houston's boots dragged the ground.

Hattie returned her attention to Dani and Mary. "Well, that was fun."

Mary grinned at Hattie. "You enjoyed that, didn't you?"

"Probably a little too much," Hattie said. "Payback felt great, though. Okay, enough screwing around. Back to work!" She gestured to the map before her on the top of the totes. "The CNA is going to struggle with the city at a few key areas. Let me show you what we need to do."

Dani stared at Hattie, impressed with her ability to shift her attention so quickly, but Dani also knew she needed to do the same. She put her helmet back on, and she and Mary moved in closer. Both were ready to get back to work. For Dani, it was the distraction she required.

CHAPTER

58

Twelve Weeks Later

Dani had already messaged Oliver that she and Mary were returning to Bangor, but she was still surprised when he sprinted to her and hugged her as soon as she came off the plane. She held him for a moment and cried, happy to see him again. She'd been gone much longer than she'd wanted, but once they'd had the advantage over the Wardens, they'd had to keep it.

Ramos had sent her and Mary back once Toronto was secured, and Hattie would return in another week after she finished negotiating technological agreements between the Ancients and the CNA.

Oliver finally released Dani and went to Mary next. Brody waited for his turn, and Dani smiled and rubbed the top of his head. She wiped her face with her free hand and was glad to be home. She'd dreaded this moment, too. Leaving the war meant coming back to deal with Miles's absence, and she wasn't ready for that. She didn't have a choice, though. Oliver had been in Maine with Brody and no one else from his family while he waited to see if they would come back alive or in a bag like his father.

Losing Miles had been a catastrophic blow, but ultimately

Dani was glad to be home. Ramos said he'd use her from there to evaluate terrain and sims for any additional targets, but she also knew it was best if she left the front line. The Wardens were close to collapse, and she figured the data analysis slant was just an excuse Santi used to send her home.

Dani hadn't slept or eaten much in the weeks following Miles's death. She performed as she'd needed to during battle, but her body couldn't take the added strain much longer. Dani just didn't feel like eating or sleeping. Battle kept her mind occupied. She knew this was a terrible way to cope with Miles's death, but it was the only thing she knew how to do without unraveling. There would be time for that later. At least, that's what she always told herself when the grief tried to come.

When Oliver released Mary, he returned to Dani's side. She put her arm around his shoulders and smiled.

"I'm so glad you're back," he said.

"Me too."

When they left the base to head to the brothel, Oliver spoke again.

"I heard back from the art community in Portland. They still want me."

"Of course they do," Dani said. "They'd be stupid to refuse you."

"They want me to go down at the end of next week."

Dani's mind froze, though her legs kept moving. That meant a service for Miles before he left. Oliver had insisted on waiting until she was back. She wasn't ready to deal with that now. Her mouth went dry, and her heart felt like it was beating out of control. She stumbled.

Oliver held her. "Dani?"

She blinked. "I'm okay. Just tired." The lies seemed to come so easily, and she hated herself for it. "You're going to Portland. It's where you belong."

"I can put it off."

"No. No, you're going, and so is Brody."

Oliver winced. "I didn't ask if I could bring my dog."

Dani's shoulders relaxed with the topic change. "He's going. We'll figure it out. C'mon. I need food," she said, and smiled, though her gut was in a knot. Another lie.

They reached the pub and ordered food, and Dani picked at her meal while they talked. Mary would disappear for a while, then return and leave again. Dani wanted to ask her what she was doing, but Oliver was busy chatting about everything and everyone in Bangor. He'd been staying in a room in the back of the brothel instead of at their home on the river. Dani couldn't blame him. His friends were here.

Oliver avoided bringing up his father.

Dani knew the topic would change to that eventually, and she tried to ignore the building dread.

Mary returned once more but didn't sit.

"Huh," Dani said. "That's usually the look I get from Hattie when I've done something wrong."

Mary managed a small smile. "I'm kicking you both out on her behalf."

Dani nodded and stood. She followed Oliver and Brody to his room and said good night. Oliver closed the door, and she remained in the hallway. Mary folded her arms and leaned against the wall.

"What?" Dani asked. She was tired, hungry-but-not-hungry, and headed into a foul mood.

"For both of your sakes, talk to him."

"We've been in the pub for the last four hours talking and catching up. I'm tired."

Mary scowled at her.

Dani winced; she knew what Mary meant even before her silly attempt at an excuse. She closed her eyes for a moment and took a deep breath. She opened her eyes and knocked on Oliver's door.

Maybe he fell asleep in the last thirty seconds and we don't have to do this now. Maybe he didn't hear me knock. Maybe—

The door opened.

Shit. "Uh, hey, um." Dani glanced at Mary, then back to Oliver. "I need to talk to you."

He opened the door more. Before Dani entered, she paused. Mary nodded and turned to leave. Dani entered his room and resisted the urge to flinch when he closed the door behind her.

She wasn't sure what to say now. She had never rehearsed what she thought she might say to him in this moment. Her mouth went dry again.

"You look like shit," he said.

She stared at him for a moment. "I know."

"No, Dani. You *really* look like shit. I'm not going to Portland. I'll stay with you."

"No, you can't stay, Oliver. You can't." She sat in the chair by his desk and smiled, glad he was drawing again.

Oliver sat on his bed next to Brody. "I miss Dad."

Her smile disappeared. His eyes brimmed with tears, and she left the chair to sit next to him. They hugged each other for a while without speaking and mourned together. Dani sniffled a few times and wiped her face with her sleeve. Oliver raked the back of his hand across his eyes and then his nose. He'd never before looked so much like the little kid she'd first met at the Standpipe in Bangor when a trio of Brigand assholes tried to kidnap him.

"I miss him too," Dani said. "I'm sorry—"

"Stop." Oliver shook his head. "Never apologize to me for Dad's death, Dani. He died protecting us to the very end. That is who he was. I know you well enough to know you're blaming yourself for everything that went wrong that day."

Dani remained silent. Guilty as charged.

"Please don't do that. I don't blame you and never will. Colonel Houston was …" He shrugged. "I don't know what happened to her. I don't know why she did all those things and created that awful battle plan. I don't care, either. I can't worry about her and all the things I'll never have answers to."

Dani listened, amazed by such wisdom from someone so young. He'd also had a hard life, losing his mother as a child and living among the CNA, never knowing when he'd lose his father. He'd grown up too quickly because he hadn't had a choice.

"I wish so many of these things hadn't happened," he said. "But they did. I couldn't control them, and neither could you. You can't blame yourself, Dani."

She nodded. "I'll try not to."

"I can stay."

"Please go to Portland. I'm not in the war, Oliver. You don't have to protect me anymore. Miles loved the thought of you creating your art and having artist friends. He never wanted you anywhere near the war. I want you to go. It will make me happy for you to live your life."

"What will you do?"

"Santi wants me in sims for their next targets. I'll be busy with that."

"Good. Not to rush you, but when you're ready, everything is planned for Dad. It'll be just the family for us to spread his ashes."

Dani winced but nodded. She wasn't ready to say goodbye to Miles. "The family?"

"You, me, Mary, and Aunt Hattie."

"Okay."

Oliver scrunched his brow. "Do I still have to call her Aunt Hattie now? She's no older than you or Mary. She's not that much older than me."

Dani laughed. "She is far older than any of us. Best to call her Aunt Hattie unless she tells you otherwise."

"All right. How's Mary?"

"Fine."

"She's an Echo too."

Dani stared at him for a moment.

"The scars on her face from the transport truck accident, they're gone now. She's an Echo, isn't she?"

"A hybrid who can regen." She was curious. "If you could become an Echo, would you?"

He sighed and shook his head. "I like being a human. I'll stay this way."

Dani smiled and hugged him. "You're perfect, Oliver. Absolutely perfect."

CHAPTER
59

Dani leaned her shoulder against the tree, her arms crossed, and looked out over the river. She and Oliver had poured Miles's ashes into the water three weeks ago, but she continued to come out every night to the same spot. She didn't much notice the rain falling on her tonight. She didn't care about a lot of things now; her life had been shattered with his death.

Oliver had changed his plans to stay with her a bit longer, refusing to go to Portland until Dani insisted that he go. She knew she couldn't keep herself together much longer and didn't want him to see her fall apart. He'd finally left with Brody two weeks after the service to join his artist friends in Portland, and Dani was happy for him—as happy as she could be.

All Miles had wanted was for Oliver to be spared the war and the horrors of so much death. He and Dani had managed to mostly spare Oliver from becoming a soldier, but they couldn't shield him from the death part. Under General Ramos's advising, the Commonwealth abolished the law for mandatory enlistment when someone turned seventeen, so Oliver was safe from being forced into the CNA. Yet so many had died, and the war had still made Oliver an orphan after all.

She'd shed so many tears over the last several days that she didn't bother wiping them away now. The rain had already soaked her hair and ran down her face in tiny streams, mixing with the tears.

The war hadn't been declared over yet, but that was due to happen any day now. Again, Dani didn't care. The fighting was over. North America's northeast region was in Commonwealth hands. Santi had secretly coordinated with other leaders across all continents. Most battles had gone well for the CNA. Some had not, but the Wardens were losing in a way that they could never recover from now.

When facing capture, most Wardens opted to blow themselves up, but the ones who had surrendered—something no one had ever expected a Warden to do—were found to be Echoes who had been subjected to reconditioning. The CNA, with help from the Ancients, were close to finding a way to reverse the process so they could reenter society as free people. The rest who weren't reconditions or had refused reversal expedited their paths to execution by pleading guilty to war crimes. She'd never know what Gavin would have chosen had he lived.

All Commonwealths would continue to press the Wardens until every territory they had taken was back in Commonwealth hands. At least, that's what she'd been told several days ago. She didn't know the current state of the global war and didn't care. Santi had known, and it was obvious now that he'd shipped her and Mary back to Bangor because they were no longer needed. Using her in sims had been his cover story to send her home a little early. Again, Dani didn't care.

Despite the rain, she heard someone approaching, so she turned her head.

Mary arrived next to her and pulled her hood lower over her head. "Hey."

Dani pressed her lips together. She didn't want company, nor did she want to talk. Mary had been through hell with her, though. "Hey."

Mary slipped her arm around Dani's waist.

Dani glanced at her. "I hope you're not here to try to cheer me up."

"Me? Hell no. That's Hattie's job."

She couldn't stop the tiny smile that formed at the corners of her mouth.

They remained silent for a while, and Dani appreciated having her friend with her. She had been avoiding everyone, wallowing in her grief and crying every night alone in her bed and wishing Miles was still with her. But she also knew Oliver was heartbroken over the loss of his father, and Mary had suffered too, losing the friendship she'd had with Miles. Even Hattie—hard-ass Hattie—had loved Miles.

So much suffering. Dani closed her eyes and let the tears fall. A sob escaped, and Mary's arm tightened around her.

"I can't do this," Dani said.

Mary pulled her into her arms. "You can't do it alone."

Dani rested her head against Mary's shoulder. "I miss him so much, I can't breathe, Mary. I don't want to live."

"I know."

Dani gave in when the sobs overtook her body. She hadn't allowed herself to truly grieve before, and now she couldn't stop. The crushing weight of Miles's loss threatened what was left of her sanity. Mary never wavered as she held Dani and let her weep.

Once the worst had passed, Dani stepped away and wiped her palms over her face. The rain continued to fall, and she realized she was cold and shivering. She could stay outside, die of hypothermia, regen, and wake back up to the misery that Miles was still gone. Sure, she'd forget the pain of his loss for a time—and as tempting as it was to make that happen just to make the grief go away for a little while, she decided to head home instead.

Once indoors, Mary pulled her raincoat off and shook the excess water from it. "Tea or coffee?"

"No, but help yourself." Dani headed for her room to change into dry clothes.

"Hungry?"

"No." Dani closed her bedroom door. A harsh shiver coursed through her, so she stripped out of her wet clothes and pulled on a dry shirt and jeans. Dani found a mostly clean flannel shirt and put it on, too. She paused to look at the clothes on the floor, realizing she'd been in them for the last five or six days, possibly longer. Her gaze fell on her body, and she noticed how her jeans hung off her frame. Dani lifted her shirt and poked the top of her hip bone with her finger. "Huh." Miles's death had caused her to lose her shit and then some. She couldn't remember the last time she'd taken a bath, so she stripped and washed in the cold water sitting in the basin in her room.

After dressing again, she couldn't deny that she felt a little better. When she emerged from the room, Mary was frowning at her.

"I'm glad you took the time to clean up and pull yourself together, but when was the last time you ate?"

Dani shrugged.

"You have nothing edible in this house. Nothing, Dani. What little food you had is rotten."

"Sorry."

"Put your rain gear on. We're going back out."

"I don't want to go into town."

"If you can tell me not only *when* you ate last but *what* you ate, you get to stay home tonight."

Dani stared at the ceiling for a moment, thinking hard. She

came up with no answers and sighed. With slumped shoulders, she retrieved her rain gear.

Their walk to town was quiet except for the pattering of raindrops on their coats, and again Dani found herself glad to have Mary with her. The rain stopped by the time they arrived at Hattie's and entered through the back to the kitchen.

"Sit," Mary said, and Dani obliged, feeling a bit like Brody.

She sat with her hands in her lap, fingers laced, and waited in silence. Mary worked, and Dani didn't move; she knew better. A few minutes later, Mary arrived at the table with two mugs of tea. She placed one before Dani and the other mug to the side.

"I already added a dash of sugar to it the way you like," Mary said, and was gone again.

"Thank you." Dani sipped the tea and was surprised when her middle rumbled at the scent of food. She truly couldn't recall the last meal she'd had. The warm tea felt good on the inside, so she drank more. Mary reappeared and swapped Dani's empty mug with the other one she'd left on the table earlier.

"Thank you."

"You're welcome," Mary stepped away and then returned to place a plate in front of Dani, utensils on the side.

Dani reached for the fork, knowing if she didn't, she would catch hell from her friend. Mary retrieved her plate and mug from the counter and sat at the table with her. Dani's first bite of the scrambled eggs was tentative. She took a bite of toast next and then another. The slice was gone in seconds.

Mary ate at a slower pace and brought Dani more food as the eggs, toast, and fruit disappeared from Dani's plate. When Mary started to rise for a third time, Dani stopped her.

"I'm good, Mary. Thank you. I don't need more."

"You're sure?"

She nodded.

They sat together for a while, Dani clutching her tea like it was a lifeline. The music and noise in the pub area filtered through to the back of Hattie's establishment.

"You're staying here tonight," Mary said.

Dani didn't have the energy to argue. "Okay."

Mary placed her hand on Dani's forearm. "You'll get through this. I know it doesn't feel like it, and hell, you don't even *want* to get through it right now, but you will."

Dani stared at her tea.

"If you do anything stupid to end your life, I swear I will make your world a living hell when you regen."

Dani finally looked up. She'd made a promise to Oliver before to not harm herself. She figured Mary deserved to hear the same words now.

Mary frowned with apparent frustration. "Are you listening?"

"Yes. Because when sympathy doesn't work, you resort to threats and violence." She offered her a small smile. "You've been spending too much time with Hattie."

Mary moved from her chair and leaned down to wrap her arms around Dani. She kissed the top of her head. "I love you, Dani. You know that, right?"

She placed her hand on one of Mary's arms. "I do. I promise I won't do anything to try to end my life."

"Thank you." Mary squeezed her tighter. "Thank you!"

CHAPTER
60

A sharp pain hit Dani's shoulder while she lay sprawled on the bed. The pain came again and she grunted. "Get up!" Hattie said.

Dani responded by turning her face into the pillow, but she snapped up when icy water splashed over her back and head. "Ah! What the fuck, Hattie?" She gasped for air and wiped at the water dripping off her head and face as she tumbled out of the bed. Her soaked tank top clung to her back.

Hattie dropped the empty bucket on the floor, where it bounced with a clatter. The noise made Dani wince.

"Pull yourself together," Hattie said. "You have work to do."

Water dripped off Dani and spattered on the floor. "What work?"

"For starters, you need to clean up this mess, then get your ass in the kitchen. Lunch is ready."

Dani squinted at the window. "Lunch?" She hadn't meant to sleep so late, but her schedule had been erratic with Miles gone.

"It's early fall, and you don't have nearly enough wood for the winter. You'll be moving some of my seasoned wood to your place over the next two weeks so you don't freeze in the hovel you call a home. As payment, you will split and stack my fresh-cut wood to start drying for next winter."

"Oh."

Hattie was right; Dani hadn't done anything to prep for the coming winter. Her life had unraveled, and she hadn't given a shit about anything until she had managed to emerge from her grief for a little while last night. "Where's Mary?"

"Waiting for your sorry carcass. She's doing all the work while you sleep."

Dani winced, guilt-stricken that Mary was stuck with extra tasks. She grabbed her jeans off the back of the chair and started pulling them on.

"Lots of other stuff to do today," Hattie said. "It's official. The war is over. Though you slept through that announcement."

"Oh, that's good. The announcement, I mean." Dani put her socks on and grabbed her boots.

"There will be parades and formal whatevers and other bullshit things we must attend in Maine and some big event in Boston with the CNA."

"What? *We?* No, Hattie. I'm not doing any of that crap."

Hattie laughed with a dismissive wave. "It's so hilarious when you think you have a choice. Clean this shit up and get your ass to the kitchen." Hattie swept out of the room, and Dani was alone.

She passed her hand through her wet hair, then slung the excess water from her fingers. She found a towel in a cabinet and used it to clean up the water while cursing Hattie the entire time. Once she was done, she grabbed her jacket and headed for the kitchen.

Hattie was waiting for her. She pointed at a plate of food on the counter. "Eat that, then go out back."

Dani stared open-mouthed, but Hattie didn't say anything else before leaving. The sound of wood being split filtered in through a cracked-open window. Dani shoveled the food into her mouth, barely noting what she was actually eating. Potatoes, something green, maybe a tomato in there too, and some kind of fish. She drank the glass of water to force everything down. Dani refilled her glass and found another to fill before heading out.

Mary was out of breath and smiled when she took the glass from Dani. She drank deeply from it before speaking. "Why is your hair wet?"

"Oh. Uh. Took a bath—of sorts."

Mary snickered. "Aunt Hattie got you with the bucket of water."

Dani took the ax from Mary's hand. "Have a rest. Sorry you had to pick up my slack."

Mary sat on a log and sipped her water while Dani stacked split pieces in silence. She felt like she should say something to Mary, but she wasn't sure what. Once all the wood Mary had split was stacked, Dani readied the next log and picked up the ax. A few more seconds ticked by.

"Thank you for being with me last night," she said.

Mary gave her a small smile. "You're welcome."

Dani watched her for a moment. Apparently, that was all that needed to be said. She nodded, lifted the ax, and went to work.

A few days later, General Ramos and Hattie dragged Dani to a couple of smaller events in Portland, but tonight, back in Hattie's kitchen, they revealed the much larger gathering happening in Boston in two weeks. Dani balked.

"I'm not going! This is bullshit." She folded her arms across her chest.

"Dani—" Santi began, but Hattie held her hand up to stop him.

Hattie glared at her. "I don't care if you accidentally behead yourself when splitting wood. I'll glue that fucking lump back on your neck and drag you to Boston anyway."

Mary erupted with laughter to the point of tears while Dani sank lower into her chair.

Hattie resumed stirring her tea and winked at Santi. "She'll be there."

In Boston, Dani was there, just as Hattie had said. She sat in one of many chairs lined on a stage and tugged at the collar of her uniform. Mary nudged her with her elbow. She lowered her hand and sighed. The only good thing about this Commonwealth-Brigand event was that she'd gotten to see Oliver before the formalities started. He even made the trip with them from Portland to Boston. He was happy with his friends and had remarked that she looked better. She had to admit she was doing better. For that, she was relieved.

She spotted Oliver at the front of the crowd, smiling at her, and she smiled back while some CNA higher-up blabbed on at the podium before the thousands of people gathered there. Dani tugged at her collar again.

"Stop doing that," Mary whispered.

Dani grumbled and dropped her hand to her lap. She glanced down at her uniform, its decorative crap and a name badge declaring her Ambassador Ireland. "I thought I was done with this stupid thing."

"You look great in that uniform."

"I feel like a clown."

"Just a few more days of this, then you can go back to hiding in your shed by the river."

That thought didn't appeal to Dani at all, and she frowned.

Mary leaned closer. "Shit. I'm sorry. I was only joking about your house. It's better than a shed, and—"

"I know. It's not that." Dani noticed Santi's glare at her. She returned her attention to Mary. "There are a lot of good memories in that house with Jace, Miles, and Oliver, but …"

Mary patted her arm. "I get it. Stay in town as long as you want. You'll always have a room there."

"Thanks."

Mary turned her attention forward, but Dani's gaze lingered on her for a moment. Jace had taught Dani how to survive, but surviving wasn't living. She knew that now and took Mary's hand. "You were right."

"I was? When?"

"I can't do this alone, and …" Dani shifted in her seat, suddenly nervous. "I don't want to do life alone. I need some time, though. We both need some time, I think."

Mary's mouth opened, but no words came out. Her eyes glistened with the threat of tears. Dani feared she'd made a mistake, bringing this up now. Dani knew she wasn't ready to enter a relationship, but in time she would be, and she wanted it to be with Mary. The lingering silence made Dani squirm. She shifted to release Mary's hand, but Mary didn't let her go.

Mary smiled. "Take as much time as you need. I'm not going anywhere." She gave Dani's hand a final squeeze before releasing it.

Dani nodded and smiled. "Thank you." A warmth spread through her that she hadn't felt since hugging Oliver after her return from the fighting in Canada. Peace? Contentment? She wasn't sure which it was. Maybe it was both. She'd figure it out later, after this ceremonial horseshit was over.

Her mind wandered, the speakers changed out, and Santi went to the podium next. Dani sighed and didn't bother trying to look attentive while he spoke. Mary nudged her again.

Dani scowled at her. "What? I didn't touch the damn collar."

Mary nodded toward the general. "You're up."

"*What?*" Horrified, Dani looked at Santi, who gestured for her to join him. "Nuh uh."

"Go." Mary pushed on her arm.

Dani jerked her arm away. "Fuck off."

"Jesus, Dani, it's not a firing squad," Mary said, half laughing. "Just go."

"Goddammit." She continued to mutter as she stood. She leaned closer to Mary. "You're an asshole."

Mary grinned. "I know. Get up there."

Dani walked forward, her gaze darting around. Hattie stood just offstage, grinning ear to ear. Oliver remained in the crowd and smiled at her. *Why me?*

Santi placed his hand on her shoulder, and Dani refused to mirror his smile. "These good people of New England have heard enough speeches from the Commonwealth. I think they'd like to hear from one of the Brigands."

Dani kept her voice low. "I hate you."

He continued to smile, making her want to punch him. When she turned to face the crowd, her mouth went dry. She fiddled with her uniform collar, which was now unbearably itchy. The crowd remained silent, waiting for her to speak. *Her.*

She closed her eyes for a moment and took a deep breath. *Fuck me.* The crowd had cheered some of the earlier speakers. She didn't feel like cheering. She sure as hell didn't feel like celebrating—at least not how the Commonwealth had planned. Jace was dead. Miles was dead. The prior speakers had talked about winning the war, but had they really won? Could one side ever actually win, or did they just lose less? Dani opened her eyes. The crowd hadn't gone anywhere; they were still waiting for her.

"The war is over," she said. "They say we won. Big fucking deal. This shit has chewed all of us up and spat us out."

Santi cleared his throat, and she ignored him.

"There's no trophy for the win. We only have headstones for the billions who have died over decades of fighting. Medals for those of us still alive? No one cares." Dani shook her head and began removing her uniform top. She shrugged out of the jacket and dropped it on the stage at her feet. She stood before the crowd in a plain gray tee with outstretched arms.

"This is what's left. Us. The people who have lost loved ones. No one here has escaped the loss of a friend or family member. No one."

She lowered her arms. "You didn't have to be on a front line to feel the Wardens' threat. It was everywhere, all the time. We fought back because of a sliver of hope that if anyone did manage to survive, they'd have a better future." Tears burned her eyes to think of Miles and his sacrifice.

"We're all still hurting from seeing so much death and suffering. We want to celebrate the end of the war, but we *need* to heal together and remember the people we have lost. The emotional and mental injuries last longer than physical wounds." She sniffled and wiped at the tears on her face. "But the people we lost deserve to be remembered. They fought and died for each of us. It's our duty to maintain this new peace."

Dani swallowed hard. "We must remember people like Miles Jackman."

"And Jace," Hattie said.

Dani turned to find the woman standing next to her. Oliver scrambled up to the front of the stage and put his arms around Dani when he arrived.

"Emily Jackman," he said.

Mary dropped her uniform jacket on the stage floor with Dani's and embraced Oliver and Dani. "Kels."

Dani smiled despite the tears on her face. "Corey."

"Jamie," Mary said.

People within the crowd shouted a few names. Others

began to speak the names of their fallen friends and family, adding to the growing murmur as countless names were spoken.

"Dres," Hattie said.

"Yeah," Dani said, nodding. "Gavin."

Some from the crowd threw their uniform tops up on the stage as names continued to be called out.

Oliver finally released Dani, and she watched him for a moment. "The past was ours, Oliver. Sadly, we fucked up our part. But the future is all yours."

"We'll get through this, Dani," he said.

"We will." And she believed it too. With her family to help her through the grief, she'd be okay.

ACKNOWLEDGMENTS

As always, these writing adventures would not be possible without the support from my friends and family. This novel was, to date, the most complex to write in the trilogy. During my research of military tactics for this novel, I once again worked with my friend and military adviser, Major Mike Henderson, USMC, retired. For additional details on naval strategies, I'm thankful for the advice and information provided by my brother, 2nd Class Petty Officer Rich Campbell, USN, honorable discharge. Any tactical errors in the story are mine.

Jennifer Elmore, Rebecca Hardman, Juan Blanch, Helen Clements, and Mike Krug provided valuable feedback as test readers. I'm forever grateful for their patience and friendship while digging for plot holes and picking apart the story. The final version of this novel is, of course, an improved version of the first draft because of their efforts.

Special thanks to Ray Rhamey and his editing magic. I'm honored to be a repeat client and recipient of his talent.

Thank you, reader, for your time and for going on this adventure with me!

ABOUT THE AUTHOR

Cheryl Campbell was born in Louisiana and lived there and in Mississippi before moving to Maine. Her varied background includes art, herpetology, emergency department and critical care nursing, and computer systems. When not traveling as a nomadic wanderer with her laptop and dog, she lives in Maine.

To follow her blog, visit cherylscreativesoup.com or facebook.com/cherylscreativesoup. She is also on Instagram @cherylscreativesoup.